CLEAH'S BEQUEST

a novel
by Mari Matthias

Unsolicited Press
Portland, Oregon
www.unsolicitedpress.com
info@unsolicitedpress.com
619–354–8005

CLEAH'S BEQUEST

Printed in the United States of America.
First Edition.
ISBN: 978-1-963115-87-1

Distributed by Asterism Books
https://asterismbooks.com/

For wholesale orders:
Asterism Books
568 1st Avenue South, Ste 120
Seattle, WA 98104
(206) 485-4829
info@asterismbooks.com

Editor: Summer Stewart
Cover Design: Kathryn Gerhardt

for my parents, Phil and Kathe
(who are nothing like Cleah)

Once the receptionist had closed the door behind her, Cleah set the ceramic pot on the lawyer's cluttered desk.

He regarded it, saying, "Hmm, yes, that is lovely. It will do nicely."

She perched on the edge of the golden leather chair facing him. The smallness of the office presumed an intimacy that was not really there. From her purse she extracted a single crisp page, handwritten. This, too, she laid on the desk.

"Current contact information?" he said, picking it up. "Ah, yes. Good, good. Elise, Tanna, Kevin: physical addresses, emails, phone numbers, names of family. All here." He nodded approval. "Good. Thank you."

"So that's it." It was not a question.

"Yes, that was the last of it. Documents are signed, witnessed, notarized. All set." He hesitated. "I have to ask, are you sure about this? It's, well... unusual."

"I'm sure."

"And, uh, are you sure you don't want to discuss it with them yourself?"

"No." The brevity of her answers invited no discussion on the matter.

The lawyer smiled, stroking his mustache. "Fine, then. I'll see to it, when the time comes. Not too soon, I'd wager." He chuckled.

Holding his gaze across the urn, Cleah Lucky said nothing.

1

The metal walls offered a dull reflection, like a cheap mirror. Kevin lifted his gaze to a corner of the elevator, an act of avoidance. He clutched the zipper pull of his open fleece jacket, dragging it up and down, itself a miniature elevator climbing the metal teeth, uselessly without its other half. The sudden forced stillness bothered him. All day at work he'd been moving, moving, moving—a welcome distraction. He dropped the pull and crossed his arms.

They were the only two in the tiny space, he and his wife. The word *tomblike* came to mind, which he immediately pushed from his head. He was fairly good at clearing his thoughts, something he'd been practicing since childhood. It usually required less effort.

"Sure hope this doesn't take long," said Mirabelle, shifting from one black leather heel to the other.

Kevin's jaw clenched. "You didn't have to come. Dramatic reading-of-the-will stuff only happens in movies, you know."

"You said the lawyer was clear that we all had to be there." With practiced swiftness, she pulled her cell phone from her purse and started scrolling. "I'm here to help, babe. United front."

He stuffed his hands into the pockets of his slacks.

"Your mom was loaded, right?" she asked.

Kevin bristled. He didn't answer because he didn't know. She had lived modestly, but certainly comfortably. He'd never considered his mother's finances before. All he knew was that his own finances were paycheck-to-paycheck tight.

She went on, "Either way, I wanna hear this for myself." With a *ding,* the doors slid open. She dropped her phone back into her purse and stepped onto the taupe carpet of a well-lit hallway. "I'll bet we're the last ones to arrive."

He could hear the blame in her voice. "Just—" he hesitated, searching for a better phrase than *shut up*. He lowered his voice as he followed her. "Let's just not talk right now." Her quick exhale told him these were the wrong words.

They found the door, which looked like all the other brown, painted doors lining the corridor, unique only in that a sign on the wall beside it read *Kantola and White, Attorneys at Law*. With a barely perceptible pause, Mirabelle looked at him, then huffed, and pushed through into the office. Too late to meet her expectations of chivalry, he swallowed a sigh and followed. Add it to her list of things he does wrong. Mirabelle was gorgeous and driven. Even though they'd been married only three years he was already getting that proverbial seven-year itch.

"Good morning," the receptionist said brightly, her hair a neat orange beehive. "How can I help?"

"We're here about the Cleah Lucky estate," Mirabelle said.

"Kevin and Mirabelle Lucky," he added, wanting to speak for himself.

"Ah yes!" She beamed under the hive with an enthusiasm that verged on inappropriate, Kevin thought, given the nature of their appointment. "I'm Dawn. I'll let Mr. Kantola know that you're here." Dawn was already through an interior door, her nylons scraping audibly past thick thighs with each step.

Mirabelle eased onto a chair and started shuffling through her purse. Kevin shrugged off his jacket and settled onto the chair beside her, leaning his head back against the wall. When she pulled out a lipstick and proceeded to dab, he closed his eyes.

He did not want to be here. He resented Mirabelle for being here, insisting on coming and then acting like it was an imposition. It shouldn't bother him, but it did. His mother's death had surprised him. And it brought up old painful memories. Conflicting emotions best avoided. Especially now—now that she was gone.

Perhaps all mothers are tedious. Perhaps they all lie and cheat.

Again, he forced his thoughts from his head.

The entrance door opened, drawing his attention. In walked a tall woman wearing a long grey cardigan over pink nurses' scrubs. He sat up straighter and swallowed, feeling the dagger of his sister's green eyes as she swept the room and landed her gaze on the empty receptionist's desk. She paused and tucked her chin-length blonde hair behind an ear, which immediately loosed and fell forward. He thought she might leave, the way she sulked just inside the door with fidgety indecision. The silence of the office gaped like a chasm of awkwardness. Why was there no canned music? All at once he felt sad, that this was the way it was: not even a hello. Kevin inhaled deeply and exhaled slowly. Perhaps this time everyone would get along.

Not likely.

Not that it mattered, he supposed.

Dawn burst back into the room, smiling. "All right, Kevin and Mirabelle, this way."

"Excuse me, am I to come also? I'm Tanna, Cleah's middle kid."

"Yes!" Dawn sounded thrilled. Her arm hung suspended in a follow-me gesture. "Hello, Tanna! I'm Dawn. The Rodgers are already inside. This way."

Mirabelle was right behind Dawn, but Tanna shook her head when Kevin motioned her to go ahead of him. Of course. He'd forgotten how she liked to demur and then savor an imagined injustice. He was being polite, nothing else, but she had a way of reading way too much into things, not to mention holding grudges. He shrugged and went through the door in front of his sanctimonious sister.

▼ ▲ ▼

Weary, Tanna tried to relax her brow as she followed the others down the lawyer's narrow hallway. She'd been having trouble sorting through her feelings since learning of her mother's death two days prior, so she focused on being frustrated with how insistent the lawyer had been that they meet right away. She'd had to get someone to cover the end of her shift. And that third reminder text an hour before the appointment felt entirely too pestering.

She'd been dreading this meeting for more reasons than just inconvenience. The last time they were all in the same room together was years ago. Disaster. Regardless of the fact that her marriage didn't last, launching into a very public shouting match at her wedding reception was unforgivable. But she didn't want to fight now, or even engage, for that matter. She'd have been fine to never see any of them again.

They were certainly walking quickly, rushed along by that quirky, young receptionist. Oh well, quick was good, Tanna decided as she checked her watch. She would have to pick up the kids in just over an hour. She didn't want to be late for the new daycare. And she had to remember to get gas on the way home. Tanna's mind spun through its lists as Dawn ushered them into a back meeting room and announced them.

A thin man with a greying manicured mustache sat at the head of a massive oak table. Elise and Jeff were already seated to his left. Jeff raised his hand, presumably in greeting. His hairline had inched back a bit. Elise's brown curls had grown to her shoulders and her face looked thinner. She wore that familiar grating expression of condescension.

The mustachioed man stood. "Welcome, hello, hello. You're all here, that's good; you've met the first Requirement! Please, come sit down. I'm Mr. Kantola, Mrs. Lucky's lawyer."

Mirabelle strode over to shake his hand and took the chair to his right, Kevin following behind. Everything about her brother she found irritating, from the sullen way he walked, to his trendy high-peaked haircut. Tanna took the seat across from Mr. Kantola. With her things clutched in her lap, she concentrated on keeping her face, and her feelings, neutral.

"All right, now that we're all here," the lawyer began. He paused as though waiting for someone to speak, even as they were all waiting for him. Tanna stole glances from her periphery. Elise shifted to cross her legs, her lips pressed into a line. Kevin seemed to stare out an imaginary window. The size of the table made them all look like children. In that moment Tanna felt like a child.

"Well, let me say first, I am very sorry for your loss, so very sorry," Mr. Kantola continued, finally, setting entwined fingers on the table and focusing on his left thumb resting on top of the pile.

Elise murmured, "Thank you," echoed a little louder by Mirabelle.

"It's never an easy time, no, no, never easy."

"Can you tell us any more about what happened?" Elise asked. "You said she had called you the day before yesterday?"

"Sunday. Certainly, yes. As I told each of you on the phone, your mother called me very early that morning saying she wasn't feeling well and directed me to solicit an ambulance, which I immediately did. Apparently, she then had a massive stroke and, well, she succumbed before the ambulance arrived." It was almost verbatim what he'd said on the phone Sunday morning, Tanna noted. And still a shock.

Kevin cut in, "But why would she call you and not just dial 9-1-1?"

Mr. Kantola was nodding. "Ah yes, Kevin, but you know that was her way, it was her way. She liked to have people do those kinds of things *for* her. She called me in June, don't you know, with similar concerns and it turned out she had had a minor stroke then."

"Well, she did smoke all her life," Elise stated. "Virginia Slims."

Disconcerted that she hadn't known about her mother's earlier stroke, Tanna concentrated on a deep scratch in the dark wood of the tabletop. She wondered how it had gotten there. She wondered if Elise or Kevin had known about the stroke. If they did, they weren't saying.

"Again, my sincere condolences to you, each one of you." Tanna looked at her watch as the lawyer yammered on, thick with sympathetic nods and smiles. "Yes, it can be quite unsettling when one isn't expecting it. And why would you, of course, why, with one in such healthy shape otherwise, you know, hmm."

"Yes," Elise said into an opportune pause, "Mr. Kantola says he is going to read the Will to us and then we'll all receive a copy. I think we're ready, Mr. Kantola." Trust Elise to try to keep things moving, bless her for that.

"Oh yes, well, that is correct." He started shuffling carefully through the papers in front of him. "Lots of papers, hey? Hmm, yes, yes, looking for the Testament . . ."

Tanna had mixed feelings about inheriting anything from her mother. Part of her wanted nothing to do with it. Except a cash infusion would help support her kids—damn ex. The potential of inheritance had been enough to get her here, in any case. She again checked her watch, not really seeing it.

"Ah yes, here we are, right here. The Last Will and Testament of Cleah Margaret Lucky dated the 15th of July of this year. And here we go."

Tanna was surprised it was so recently updated. Perhaps that first stroke.

"I, Cleah Margaret Lucky, being of sound mind, hereby declare that this is my Last Will and Testament and revoke all prior Wills and Codicils. I further declare that none of my estate shall be inherited by any of my kin." Here Mr. Kantola drew a slow breath, and Tanna's heart skipped a beat.

"Wait, what?" Kevin interjected.

"Unless," the lawyer continued, "all of my Executory Bequest Requirements are met."

"Oh my god," Kevin mumbled, dropping his head into his hands, and Elise exhaled audibly. But Tanna almost laughed. So typical of Mother, never one to let an opportunity to lecture or punish pass by. She braced herself for some tongue-lashing.

He read on, "For the year following the reading of my Will, my three children (Elise Bethany Lucky Rodgers, Tanna Claire Lucky Hopkins, and Kevin William Lucky) must share custody of my urn, and its contents of my cremated remains, in turn. It must be kept in an open and prominent place in the home, and not left alone for more than 48 hours at a time. If the family with custody will be gone for more than two days consecutively, they must respectfully take the urn along or arrange for one of the siblings to assume custody of the urn in their absence.

"Each of my children and their families must gather at Easter, Labor Day, and Christmas all together, to pass the urn on to the next guardian. They may decide together who hosts which date. At these family gatherings, the whole group must eat a meal together, take an extended family photo as well as general photos during the event, and participate in holiday activities as outlined in the addendum. Elise, Tanna, and Kevin must also meet for a meal together on each of their birthdays, taking a group photo at the birthday event. In addition, each of my children shall compose a letter to me for my birthday, Mother's Day, and Thanksgiving. These letters shall be delivered to the guardian of my urn, to be opened and read aloud by that guardian to my ashes on said day."

Tanna's head was spinning, trying to process this curveball. Their mother was essentially giving them a year-long to-do list, full of sibling interactions. She realized she was holding her breath.

And the lawyer continued, "The entire estate has been transferred to a Trust with additional terms, which are to remain secret and will be divulged by the Trustee in a timeframe as outlined therein. The letters and the date-stamped photographs shall be provided to the lawyer's firm as proof of compliance.

"My three children—Elise, Tanna, and Kevin—must arrange for a Celebration of Life on or soon after the first anniversary of my death and meet again with my lawyer and Trustee, Mr. Kantola, having faithfully complied with all of these maxims of both Will and Trust, at which time the inheritance will be administered through the Trust, and the urn interred in the mausoleum." He lifted his eyebrows, scanning the family members with a smile. "And it goes on with some details, hmm."

He set the papers on the table in the stunned silence that followed. All Tanna felt was a resigned dread.

▼ ▲ ▼

"This is ridiculous," Elise finally managed, annoyed with herself for being caught off guard by the absurd 'Conditions.' She'd been feeling sad about her mother's passing and regretful of their complicated, and now irreparable, rift. But this! Now she was livid. Even dead, that woman was a control freak. This was the ultimate power-play. "I mean, we can't be expected to do some circus act to please someone who's, well, deceased, can we? I mean, she's . . . de—"

"What happens if we don't comply?" Kevin interrupted.

Elise sighed with irritation even though she was wondering the same thing. "Yes, what would happen?" she pressed.

Mr. Kantola was nodding, that faint, ever-present smile on his infuriating face. Slow to respond, he seemed oblivious to the impatient tension in the room.

"Well, uh, that would simply nullify any eligibility of inheritance for you."

"Do you mean only those who didn't comply?" asked Elise, drumming her fingers on the tabletop. "Or everyone—even if some of us are trying to . . . comply?" Elise didn't want to use the word *obey*. God! Leave it to Mom, forcing postmortem obedience!

"Everyone." Mr. Kantola paused to nod like a bobblehead drama queen. "Even those who *did* comply with all Requirements."

"What? That can't be right." Elise insisted. "That's not fair at all."

"Well, in fact, there is a contingency in place for just such a situation as, uh, failure to execute Mrs. Lucky's conditions."

"Can we hear that part please?" Tanna finally spoke up.

The lawyer slowly read, "In the event of any one person's noncompliance, the entire estate will be donated to a qualified nonprofit organization, chosen at my Trustee's sole and absolute discretion."

"How much are we even talking here?" Kevin asked, ever graceless.

Mr. Kantola let the anticipation build as he flipped pages.

"All right, yes, yes, here we go," the lawyer said. "Right here. Well, there's the house, of course, and its contents, and a portfolio, holdings, et cetera."

"Okay. And that's all worth what?" Elise asked. Up until now, she had refrained from dreaming of what she'd do with a pile of windfall money. There was no question: she would use it to launch some kind of career plan, like to start a business. Tutoring. Or interior decorating. Or a coffee shop. Or maybe go back to school. Her heart yearned, in spite of herself.

He said, "Hmm. Not insignificant. But other than that, I really couldn't say."

This incensed Elise further. "What? Why?"

"A provision of the Trust."

"Such bullshit!" Kevin's face was red, his thick eyebrows becoming evil-scientist wild.

Tanna started chuckling, a grating sound. "It's a joke, right?"

"I'm afraid not," smiled Mr. Kantola with exasperating empathy.

"She thinks we won't do it." Elise exhaled sharply. Just like the time Mom agreed to let her take ballet and then forbade it, blaming Elise's bad attitude and 'lack of commitment.' Just like the time Mom had promised Elise could have a sleepover birthday party if she kept up on her chores and grades, then canceled last minute because of a B on a spelling test. There was example after example of her mother's petty, reverse-psychology, scheming mind games.

Kevin scoffed. "I bet she thinks we *can't* do it."

Elise wasn't so sure Kevin could do it. Or if Tanna would care enough.

She had had enough. "Look, can we be finished here? How about giving us each our copy of the Will and we will work out how to *comply* with Mom's wishes. If we have questions, we can call you, right? But I need to leave. I . . . have another appointment." There was no other appointment, but Elise was done with pretentious oak tables and beige walls and her mother's outrageous postmortem demands. She just wanted out of there.

Mr. Kantola stood up slowly. "Certainly, of course. I will have Dawn give you the copies and you may be on your way. Also, the reminder you were all sent prior to this meeting was a group text, so you all have each other's phone numbers. Please save those contacts, if you didn't already have them. Okay then, be right back."

Once the door closed behind the lawyer, Elise couldn't contain herself. "But it is crazy, right? We don't really have to do these *Requirements,* do we?" In her exasperation, she tossed in air quotes liberally. "And secret Trust *terms,* what?"

"I'm eager to read the whole document, but it sounds pretty clear," Tanna said blandly. "I'm sure we are capable of having three meals together over a year's time."

"Well, six for the three of you," interjected Mirabelle. "The birthdays."

"Oh my god, lunches with my sisters," moaned Kevin like a petulant child, elbows on the table and forehead in his hands.

"I'm not hosting Christmas," said Elise. "We're way too busy that time of year. Kevin, you should do that one."

"Oh, I don't know . . ." Kevin hedged, as usual.

"I thought we were going to my parents' house this year," Jeff whined into Elise's ear.

"Whatever. I'll host Christmas," Tanna said, checking her watch for the hundredth time.

"What were the other two?" Kevin asked.

"Easter and Labor Day," Elise and Mirabelle said simultaneously, then glared at each other. Who did she think she was?

"Then I don't want Easter," said Kevin. "All the kids will be expecting an egg hunt. That's a lot of extra work."

"But that's right during my busy season," Elise growled. Kevin was still a selfish lazy ass.

"Substitute teaching is busier during Easter?" retorted Tanna as she pulled her phone from her purse.

"Tax season!" Elise thundered back. This was hopeless. How would they possibly manage six civil meals together if they couldn't even manage a conversation to plan them?

"Tax season is over by Easter." Tanna seemed hell-bent on an argument.

"Not always." They all had their phones out now and were looking at schedules. "See, Easter is early in April next year. I'll be too busy with clients." Elise felt vindicated.

"Fine, I've got Easter," barked Kevin, "but no egg hunt."

"Fine!" Elise shot back.

"That means you're Labor Day, Elise," Mirabelle said.

"I *know*," Elise shouted as she rose and pulled her coat on, having decided to tell the receptionist to mail her the papers. "Jeff, let's go."

"What about the birthdays?" Mirabelle tapped her painted nails on the table.

Elise paused. "We're doing this, right? One year. Is everybody in?"

She looked at Tanna, whose brow was knit.

"Yeah, I'm in," said Tanna. "Money's money."

All eyes turned to Kevin.

He crossed his arms. "Yeah."

"Okay," Elise said evenly, which took effort. "Okay, then don't screw it up. Kevin, your birthday is first. Just let us know what you want to do."

As she reached for the door, it opened, and Dawn appeared. "Here we are, one copy for each of you," she trilled. While she passed the packets out, Mr. Kantola came in carrying a white, ceramic urn painted with blue curvy lines, almost floral but not quite.

Mother had entered the room, and they all hushed.

"State law requires a 24-hour wait period and all necessary documentation before a cremation can proceed. Arrangements for her cremation had been outlined, and as her Trustee and Designated Agent, I contacted the necessary parties to complete the task." He beamed at them, apparently proud of a job well done. "As you can see, Mrs. Lucky had planned quite thoroughly for the eventuality of her death."

"Mom was nothing if not thorough," Tanna said dryly. Elise suppressed a snort.

"Yes, yes, that she was!" the lawyer agreed. "I will also be notifying the appropriate entities of her death: social security, financial institutions, and etcetera. Consider it all taken care of! *And* as per Mrs. Lucky's directions, one of you must take the urn with you today," he said, setting it gently on the table and again taking his seat. Elise did *not* want that honor.

"The nearest gathering time is Christmas," Mr. Kantola went on, "then Easter, then Labor Day . . . so, the person who hosts Labor Day will take initial guardianship of Mrs. Lucky's ashes."

That meant Elise. Shit. "And how does that make sense?"

"At Christmas, it will be passed into the guardianship of the host of Christmas; at Easter, it will be put into the guardianship of *that* host. Then on Labor Day, the urn is returned to the initial sibling guardian again, the host of the Labor Day gathering."

Still standing, Elise handed the paperwork to Jeff and gingerly took the urn, conscious of its malevolent content. Her mother was dead. *Dead.* And yet she had weaseled her way into Elise's home. It didn't seem real. "Do I sign for it or something?"

"Not necessary, my dear," Mr. Kantola replied. "But on your way out, do let Dawn know which holiday you will host."

With a nod, Elise left the room, holding her mother's ashes out in front of her like a baby with a soiled diaper.

2

The urn was smooth and cool but felt precariously slippery as Elise stepped out and pushed the car door shut with her butt. She had a sudden urge to drop it on the front step. Instead she sighed as she watched Jeff speed away in the 4Runner, heading back to the office, regretting having argued all the way home. Was it arguing? It certainly felt like that, although she couldn't remember Jeff saying more than *But we've already got plane tickets* and *What will my mother say?* Swallowing emotions, she struggled to balance the urn and her purse and grasp the doorknob.

The door swung open. Beth and Daphne stood there, full of thirteen-year-old attitude, one with arms crossed, the other with fists on hips. Once she was certain nothing was toppling out of her grasp, she feigned cheeriness to her twin daughters.

"Hello, girls."

"Are you *serious*?" said Daphne with one eyebrow raised and a swish of blonde hair.

"Grandma Cleah's dead?" asked Beth, looking stricken.

How did they know?

"Okay, what's going on here?" Stalling, Elise managed to maneuver into the house and get the door closed behind them all. She flopped her purse down and carried the urn into the living room.

"We know everything, Mom. And we're furious!" started Daphne.

"Yeah! How could she do it?"

Elise pushed an empty metal vase aside to make room on the mantelpiece and set the urn there with resignation. Prominent place in the house.

"Do what, kiddos? Who?" She turned brightly to the girls. "What's up? Where's Caleb, by the way?"

"In his room of course."

"Did he clean out Fred's cage?"

"Don't change the subject," Daphne retorted. Elise's eyebrows raised.

"We saw Mirabelle's tweet," said Beth with her eyes to the ground.

Oh my god! Tweeting? About this? Elise caught her breath but was decidedly not surprised. Could this day get any worse?

"Let me see it." How was it her daughters followed Mirabelle's tweets, anyway? They hardly knew each other.

The girls pulled out their cell phones in unison and started tapping their screens. Daphne finished first and handed it to Elise. The message read: *Only the very wicked can wield such power in death. Why am I not surprised? #MIL #monsterinlaw*

Well, she wasn't wrong. "M I L?" Elise played dumb.

"Mother-in-law, duh." Daphne took back her phone.

"Mom, how did Grandma die?"

"Why would Aunt Mirabelle write something so awful?" asked Daphne. "What does that even mean?"

Elise put her arms around her daughters and pulled them into a hug. "Grandma had a stroke, but she didn't suffer. These things happen. I don't know what Mirabelle is talking about, probably nothing. A misunderstanding. Don't worry, babies," Elise let the girls go and waved her hand over her head. "Okay, is your homework done? Dad has a meeting tonight. I'll get dinner started." Striding toward the kitchen, Elise hid her fury behind tightly set lips. She would deal with Mirabelle later.

▼ ▲ ▼

"So, give me a call back, Kevin. Thanks." Elise ended the connection with a hard poke to the phone's red dot, wanting to poke Mirabelle in the eye. She tossed the phone onto the couch beside her.

"Of course he's not answering my calls," she complained to Jeff as she tucked her feet under her, wanting to curl into a ball. "How many people do you suppose follow her posts? I can't deal with this right now." She could feel her mother judging her from the mantel.

"You're blowing the tweets all out of proportion, Elise," said her annoyingly calm husband, a magazine in his lap.

"See, now it's like I'm not even allowed to tell you how I feel. God! Can't you just talk with me about this?"

"Of course, honey. We are talking." He was staring at the page.

"Yeah, right," she huffed. "Just, what am I supposed to tell the kids?"

"Well Beth and Daphne already know—"

"Not really," Elise interjected.

"—and we can have a family meeting. Talk it all out."

"Right. Okay. Family meeting, good idea." Elise was nodding. "I just don't want them worrying about it or feeling weird about having Mom's urn around. God, it's just—it's all so weird! And she's dead. And these Rules and—"

"I'm more interested in what we tell my parents. I mean, they won't be too patient with anything that keeps them from getting their Christmas visit." Jeff turned his full attention to Elise and put on a now-let's-get-serious tone.

"We tell them the truth, at least enough of it to explain: death and family obligation—not our fault. We'll go stay with them next year for Christmas. They aren't the ones with the nonrefundable tickets, not the smartest choice, by the way."

"Yes, I realize," Jeff sighed. "So, the truth, huh."

"They knew my mom was . . . difficult. They'll probably sympathize. Just do me a favor and keep the Cleah-bashing to a minimum in front of them, though?" Funny how Elise could have her low opinion of her mother but felt defensive if anyone else were to disparage her.

Jeff looked contemplative; she knew he was considering his parents' reaction. That, or wondering if the inheritance was worth the sacrifice of five round-trip tickets to Arizona. At least there was lots of advance notice—ease the disappointment that their only grandchildren will be spending Christmas with their other grandmother. Albeit a dead grandmother.

"Yeah." He grabbed the stereo remote and turned on the radio. A woman was crooning *How wonderful life is when you're in the world.* He clicked it off. "So, family meeting tomorrow night? Remember I leave for that conference on Thursday."

"Conference? What?" Elise asked in alarm.

"I'm sure I told you. Crap! Didn't I tell you? Sorry. It's that hospitality management conference. I'll be back Sunday night. It's not that much time." Jeff grabbed the television remote and clicked it on: a house fire in the news.

"Goddammit Jeff. Halloween, hello? I'm gonna have to do Caleb's costume all by myself?"

"Why are you getting so upset? It's already made. It'll be fine."

She was silent, sure that in another minute her fuming eyes would have burned a hole in the pillow she was holding. She glanced at the ceramic urn before she could stop herself.

"C'mon, all you have to do is help him put it on," Jeff continued. "You're the one who encouraged the shower costume. I think it turned out pretty cool." A pretty brunette on scene was speaking passionately into her microphone. It was dark, and there was nothing happening behind her, but earlier that day there had been an important meeting in that building.

Elise sucked in a breath, with all the positive powers it could afford her. Working hard on her attitude, she said, "Right. I'm sure it'll be fine. It's just too bad you'll miss it."

"Take pictures."

"Not the same and you know it." She didn't even try to keep the edge out of her voice. She was overreacting but couldn't seem to help it.

A car commercial was suddenly shouting at them. He clicked off the TV.

He set the remote down and put his hand on hers. "Yeah, I know." Then he added, "We can carve pumpkins tomorrow all together, 'kay? It'll be good."

Yawning, he got up and tugged his sweatpants from his butt crack. "Going to bed. 'Night, honey." He leaned to kiss her cheek and was gone.

Elise sat for a while, feeling the solitude. She glanced up at the urn, at her mother, her space invaded.

She had a sudden memory of carving pumpkins. She must have been eight or nine because Kevin had watched from a playpen in a corner. Young Elise sat on newspapers spread over the laminate kitchen floor, hugging the pumpkin with an arm and both legs, spooning its guts out with her free hand. She closed her eyes and remembered the wet stringy texture of the cold innards and the feeling of sheer joy in hard work. She had hurried to get it cleaned out with the wide spoon, anticipating the knife her mother had promised her—the first year she would get to carve it herself! Her little sister was only allowed to draw a face on her pumpkin, too young for anything else. Elise had held the pumpkin out for inspection and her mother knelt down and declared it ready. Tanna burst into tears, crying "I want the knife too!" and her mother had paused, and then instead of placing the carving knife in Elise's palm, as she had promised, Cleah had taken Elise's pumpkin to the table, saying "On second thought, you'd hurt yourself. I'll carve it for you, Elise." Elise could still feel the weight of the disappointment, the utter robbery of her right! Her earned and long-promised right to do it herself.

She snapped the light off and fled the room.

▼ ▲ ▼

The warning bell rang; that meant three minutes before class started. Elise sat at the teacher's desk as noisy students arrived. She'd spent the previous half-hour reviewing the day's lesson plans. This teacher always left good directions for the sub. Now she searched the pile to find the other papers for first period: the seating chart, the roll sheet. *Eighth-grade pre-algebra, here we go.* The room rushed to sit down as the final bell rang.

She stood. "Good morning class, I'm Mrs. Rodgers." She had to raise her voice. She knew some of these kids, but not all that well. Not by name. She turned on the ancient overhead projector. "Quiet down please, the bell has rung. Mr. Brown is in meetings today but will be back tomorrow. Get started on these warm-ups while I come around to check your—" The all-school morning announcements interrupted her, "—homework," she finished in a mumble. She grabbed a red pen and tried to get around as quickly as she could, but what probably took the teacher ten minutes was taking her twenty. Then she realized she'd forgotten to take attendance, so she did that. She couldn't figure out why she was so off her game.

Finally, to the lesson for that day, Elise reached the fun part of the job: teaching. When she finished explaining and walking them through a graphing example on the overhead, she told the kids to get started on their assignment.

The room had settled into a moderate hum of pencils scratching, pages shuffling, the occasional whispering, when the classroom phone on the wall by the teacher's desk rang.

"Mr. Brown's room, this is Mrs. Rodgers," she said into the receiver.

"Hi, Elise. I have a call for you from Judith Rodgers. She says it's a family emergency."

Elise's heart skipped as her mother-in-law's voice was patched through. "Elise? This is Judith. What's this I hear you aren't coming for Christmas this year?"

"Judith, is everything all right? I was told it was an emergency."

"Exactly, that's why I'm calling. You're canceling our Christmas?"

She took a deep breath. "We're disappointed, too. I'm sorry, Judith, but I really can't talk right now. I've got a class." How dare Judith call her here declaring a family emergency!

"But you're just substituting, aren't you?"

The classroom was quiet for once and Elise was cornered.

"Yes. So, I'll call you later." She hung up, freshly aware of how talking to her mother-in-law was even more stressful than substitute teaching.

▼ ▲ ▼

The home phone was ringing as she walked in the door. Gotta be Kevin. Quick to the kitchen, she dropped the grocery bag, purse, and keys onto the counter and grabbed the phone before it went to voicemail.

"Hello?" said Elise.

"Hello, Elise. I didn't know why you weren't calling me back. Jeff said you would explain things to me." *Shit.* It was Judith again. Elise berated herself for not noticing the caller ID before answering the phone.

"Hi, Judith! I just got in, literally just this second. Wow, what a day—"

"Of course, dear. So, what's going on with Christmas? Didn't you buy plane tickets?"

"Well, I'm sure Jeff told you that, uh, my sister and brother are, well, having a hard time with my mom's death and were both hoping, well, needing, to have Christmas all together this year." Elise's cell phone started ringing.

"Oh, come now, I don't believe that for a minute."

"Uh," Elise looked at her phone. Kevin! "Actually, Judith, my cell is ringing, and I really need to take this call."

"You've had me waiting all day, honey. I really need to talk with you right now."

"I know, I'm sorry. This is important, though."

"So is this!"

"Yes, of course it is." She was gonna miss his call! "I'll call you right back, I swear."

"I only need a few minutes. I'm sure we can just talk now, dear."

"No, but—" Elise glanced at her cell phone. Missed call. "Shit!"

"What?!"

"No, nothing. I'm sorry. Umm, yeah, let's just talk for a couple minutes right now." She swallowed hard. "Well, the situation is, my mother put some conditions into her Will." God, how to not say too much? "It's complicated. But one of them is to spend Christmas together this year—all of us, my brother and sister and families."

There was a pause. "That is ridiculous. Never heard anything like it."

Elise forced a laugh. "No, me neither. I'm really sorry. We were all counting on coming. We love to spend Christmas there, you know. But I'm sure you understand." She was laying it on thick.

"I'll have to speak to Scott about this. I'll call you later." And Judith hung up.

Elise grabbed her cell phone and dialed voicemail, wondering what her in-laws would have to discuss. She was *telling* Judith they weren't coming, not asking her permission.

"I got your message, Elise. You don't have to worry about Mirabelle. Okay. Bye."

Sigh.

3

The pumpkins were in surgery. Caleb had his orange giant in the very middle of the floor. A wide toothless grin was emerging. There were newspapers spread all over the kitchen, splattered with slimy seeds and chunks of pumpkin flesh; Fred plodded around slowly, though quick for a tortoise, tearing the odd mouthful of newspaper with his beak. The girls were tidier and needed only some table space. Beth's little pumpkin was getting cute features cut in with precision and detail. Daphne had chosen an odd-shaped subject and was creating a shark-like mouth below half-moon eyes. A bowl of pumpkin seeds sat between them, to be washed and roasted later, something Elise had seen in a magazine.

All the kids used their knives with calm expertise.

Elise exchanged a look with Jeff: time for the family meeting. Hard to believe the Will reading at the lawyer's office had been only yesterday. Jeff cleared his throat and got up from the table.

"Those are looking great, kids," he began, as he folded his arms across his chest. He scrunched up his lips like he did when he was thinking, then glanced again at Elise and nodded.

"So, we wanted to talk to you guys about Grandma Cleah. Maybe you've been wondering why there's no funeral planned and why people are upset," he began.

"You mean like Aunt Mirabelle?" Daphne put in, still tackling the pumpkin teeth, shaping them into pointy daggers.

"Yes, for one."

"I mean, didn't she just die on Sunday?" Beth asked.

Elise interrupted, "There's not much to it, really. Some cultures, Native Americans I think, or maybe Eskimos, wait a year before having a funeral and that is what Grandma Cleah wanted as well. So, we *will* have a funeral, a Celebration of Life, just not until a year from now."

"Why?" asked Caleb, paused in his work. Elise looked at Jeff.

He said, "Okay, well you know how Grandma Cleah always did things her own way? She must've thought it would be interesting to do things this way. It's really great, actually, that she put so much thought into it and let us know what she wanted."

Except she hadn't let anyone know besides the lawyer.

"The other part is that we're gonna have Christmas at Aunt Tanna's this year," said Elise.

"What? But aren't we going to Arizona?" Daphne blurted.

A wet newspaper had stuck to Fred's tortoise foot; he stepped noisily toward the wall.

"Yes, that was the plan, but it's okay to change plans sometimes," Elise tried to soothe.

"We'll go there next year," Jeff added.

"Or else we'll start a whole new Christmas tradition." Elise looked at him.

The kids protested in clumsy chorus. Ah, family meetings.

"Look, sometimes things just aren't the way we're used to, or what we want it to be."

"But what does it have to do with Grandma Cleah's funeral being in a year?" Beth asked, getting up to wash the pumpkin off her hands.

"Oh, it doesn't, I guess. Totally different subject." Elise really didn't want to go into the Will Requirements, so she left it at that. "Back to Christmas, we thought it'd be fun to get gifts for the cousins. Also, you should know that the porcelain pot on the mantel holds Grandma Cleah's ashes. We're gonna have it here until Christmas and then it will stay at Aunt Tanna's house for a while."

"Ashes? From Grandma Cleah? All burned up?" Caleb sounded scared.

"Hey, it's okay, sweetie. It's called cremation and it's very common. Also, it's environmentally friendly," Elise blabbered on, playing towards Caleb's earth-conscious temperament.

"Mom, does this have anything to do with Aunt Mirabelle's tweets? 'Cause I still don't understand that," Beth said. Elise looked at Jeff again.

"Tweets—plural? Was there another one?" Elise couldn't keep the sharpness out of her voice. She tried harder. "What did she say?"

"Something creepy about babysitting the dead. Is she talking about Grandma?" Beth's face was ashen.

"I think Aunt Mirabelle is just having a rough time with Grandma Cleah dying. Maybe it's just her way of grieving," Jeff said. Such bullshit.

Caleb looked up from his happy pumpkin. "It's okay with me. It'd be fun to see the cousins. Have I met them? And I really like the presents idea. Maybe Grandma Judith and Grandpa Scott could come too."

"Hmm, maybe," Elise said vaguely, inwardly cringing. She might have to consult the lawyer about that one. Or maybe she would just forget about his little suggestion.

"Well, it sounds fun," said Caleb with a shrug.

"I don't think it sounds fun. We don't really know any of those guys," Daphne said.

Elise turned to Jeff, who checked his watch. "It will be fun, honey, I'm sure," she said, not at all sure it would be fun.

"I'm done with my jack-o-lantern," Daphne muttered, setting her knife down and pushing away from the table. "Stupid to do this only a few days before Halloween anyway."

"Ouch!" cried Caleb, dropping his knife to the floor and holding his thumb that was starting to run red. Jeff knelt down as Elise went for a paper towel.

"Oh, did you cut yourself, buddy? Gotta be careful with those knives," Jeff said, keeping Caleb's hand raised as Elise came back to catch the blood and look at the cut. A clean slice but not too deep. She could just see Cleah's urn from where she was at the table, cool and blue, and could almost hear the *I told you so* that her mother would say about those carving knives. She angrily pushed the thought from her mind and turned her back to the living room.

"I'll get a Band-Aid," offered Beth, bolting from the room. She did not like loose blood.

"Uh, I've got homework," said Daphne, leaving as well.

And that was that. Family meeting over.

▼ ▲ ▼

When she arrived at Caleb's school the holiday chaos factor was already off the chart, so carrying a mini shower down the hall didn't seem too out of place. She had blocked her schedule from subbing so she could help with his Halloween parade. She'd helped with the girls' parades when they were in grade school. This was probably her tenth year. The camera was in her pocket. Jeff would have missed the parade anyway, even if he hadn't been out of town, since it was right before school got out, right in the middle of the workday. It was not unusual for him to go on these work trips, some kind of tourism networking something, but this time she was feeling particularly anxious about him going. She couldn't identify a reason. Nothing was different. No matter how she told herself to knock off the weird, baseless jealousy thoughts, she couldn't shake those feelings.

"Hi Caleb!" she said, waving to the teacher who was wearing a tin foil hat. Most of the kids were already in costume.

"You're so late!" Caleb started hefting up the backpack that the shower was rigged to—a pole running up his back to hold the PVC pipe bent in a circle around his head that served as a curtain rod. A shower head sprouted off the vertical brace and had silver wrapping ribbon taped to it for water.

"I'm sorry, babe. This won't take long," Elise muttered as she helped him balance the structure and snap together the backpack straps. "There. Nothing to it." She stepped back and beamed at him. Other kids were exclaiming and giggling over Caleb's unusual get-up. Elise took some photos of her showering son, with classmates peeking around the sides.

"Okay, I'm gonna get out on the parade route. I'll see you out there, sweetie." Elise kissed him, awkwardly ducking under the rod and through the curtain, and hustled outside to find a place to stand on the street that all the school kids would file down one side three blocks and back on the other.

The day was cool and sunny and smelled of turning leaves. She loved this time of year.

"I'm so sorry to hear about your mother, Elise," a short blonde woman said, touching Elise's shoulder.

"Oh, hi April. Thanks." Awkward. She wondered how April even knew. She was just 'Brad's mom' to Elise, and Brad and Caleb weren't really that close.

"She was so young yet. That's so hard," April went on. Elise smiled and nodded, having nothing to say to this woman. The kindergarten classes started coming by, to the cheers of the parents. Elise started clapping.

"Oh, look at all the princesses!" April crooned.

"Yes, aren't they adorable." Elise had only subbed for one of the kindergarten classes so far this year and therefore wasn't familiar with many of these kids, so small and full of excitement. They were cute, but it was not her favorite place to sub, a group of twenty-eight wiggly kids all new to school routines.

"How is it for the family, the whole ashes business? It seems like such a lovely idea, the sharing," April pressed. This stopped Elise short. She turned and looked at April fully.

"What? What do you mean?" Elise tried to mask her face with a pleasantly blank expression. She forced herself to clap for the costumed kids marching past while her mind raced. How would she know? Does she know? Why would she say that?

April glanced at her. "I read in the paper that she had died. I suppose it's funny that I like to read the obituaries. I just find them interesting, people's lives and all, summed up."

"What paper? What did it say?" Elise could tell she was sounding too frantic, almost aggressive.

"*The Pioneer.*" April took a small step back. "Yesterday's, I think. I recognized your name, is all, and it was interesting how it talked about your mother's gift of community and cooperation and all. Didn't you see that in the paper?" Her voice was getting progressively smaller. The first graders were marching down the sidewalk, Darth Vaders and ninjas, the occasional Harry Potter.

"Oh, sure," Elise lied, wanting the conversation to be over. She tried to peer past the line of Scream characters, vaguely hoping these kids hadn't seen the movie those costumes were based on. Pirates, penguins, mummies. Clap, clap, clap. Here were the second graders. Several waved at Elise, recognizing the substitute teacher. She took some pictures to try to look occupied. April must have found someone else to chat up and moved further down the street.

One kid was dressed as a blue crayon. Spiderman walked in front of a beaming Incredible Hulk. These were third graders now. Elise searched for Caleb's teacher. More mummies, Power Rangers, the Cat in the Hat, finally there was the tin foil hat on Mrs. Whistler. Elise smiled and hefted her camera. Where was Caleb? There was no way to miss him, and yet . . .

The next class started filing by. Elise hurried into the school.

She caught up to him stomping back down the hallway. He was sobbing and trying to rip the plastic shower curtain down. The showerhead sagged to the left.

"Caleb, what happened?" Elise tried to stop his destructive mayhem, feeling a little resentful after all that hard work making the elaborate costume. "Hey, it's okay," she soothed, taking him by the hand and leading him to the classroom.

"I just wanna go home!"

"Okay, come on, babe. Let's just get the costume off for now, okay? Tell me what happened."

It took a few minutes for him to calm down enough. Elise worried that the other kids would get back and Caleb would be embarrassed by his tears.

"I couldn't get through the door very well, and—" he hiccupped, "I broke it or something. I don't want to wear it. It's a stupid costume!"

"It's a great costume, honey! It was your idea," Elise couldn't help adding that last bit, but regretted it immediately.

"They laughed at me." Caleb was barely audible.

"No, it's just a funny costume. It's fun! People really like it!"

"Can we go home?"

She winced at the whine in his voice. "Okay, stop. You can come home if you want, but you'll miss out on the class party. Up to you."

The little boy, now free of his heavy pipes and curtain, breathed hard and thought it over.

"Yeah, I'll stay. I'm *not* wearing the costume tonight, though."

Elise felt a fresh surge of irritation. All that work! "So you're not going trick-or-treating?"

His eyes started watering again and his mouth pouted in stubborn anger.

She sighed. "Okay, Caleb, we'll talk about it later. Right now just—just enjoy the Halloween party, okay?"

The class was returning. Caleb turned away from her and sat down at his desk. She picked up the big, awkward shower contraption and made her way out of the classroom, giving Mrs. Whistler a stiff smile and shrug on the way out. Elise left feeling haggard and like a failure. And needing to find this week's edition of *The Pioneer*.

▼ ▲ ▼

Elise left the living room dark as she sank onto the couch, purposely not glancing toward the urn. She felt like she was sneaking. All she could think of was her mother's default stance: hands on hips, pursed lips, disapproving glower. The kids were finally in bed after the madness of trick-or-treating, and she didn't want to wake them. She hadn't been able to find a *Pioneer,* and she was dying to know what the obituary said. She'd even sent Tanna a text about it, who still hadn't gotten back to her. How was it possible the grocery store was sold out? How was there an obit printed so quickly anyway? Cleah had died on Sunday, lawyer meeting on Tuesday, paper came out Thursday. It had to be just a brief death notice. Those never said very much, probably nothing to worry about.

So how had Brad's mom known about the urn?

Caleb had refused to wear the shower outfit again, instead finding his ghost costume from last year in the box of dress-up clothes. It was an old sheet with only eyeholes that Elise couldn't stand and had meant to throw away because it was stained all around the mouth area. Disgusting thing, but not worth a fight.

Right now all she wanted was to go to bed, but the dirty dishes were haunting her. The thought of waking up to a full sink made her neck hurt. She was pissed off that Jeff hadn't called, not that she should expect him to, but still. Elise passed the dinner table in the dark kitchen, turning on only the light above the sink. Going back to the table, she rifled through today's mail—she hadn't had time to look at it yet. Mostly junk mail, and bills of course. Her chest tightened at something from the county addressed to Elise Rodgers. Opening it confirmed her fears: a jury summons for next month. Oh, this day! Trick-or-fucking-treat.

Leaving the mail in a pile, Elise cleared the sink and turned on the water, letting it run to heat up. Her impatience growing, she plugged the sink and squirted in some soap. As it filled, she shoved dishes into the dishwasher, then she started handwashing the knives, cutting boards, and the big pot. If there was anything Elise hated, it was the never-ending drudgery of washing dishes. The recessed light overhead blinked, or maybe she did. She paused, trying to clear her head. It had been such a long day.

When the light flickered again she looked up, catching a glimpse of a moth. No, it was too big. She squealed as a bat swooped beneath the light, throwing its shadow across her. Splashing and staggering backwards, Elise tried to keep her eyes on the fluttering black bat. In a panic she glanced around the room and back to the bat, trying to devise a plan. A broom! A tennis racquet? Working to control her breathing, she backed toward the pantry.

"Mom?" Beth appeared in the doorway.

"Don't turn on the light!" Elise barked hoarsely.

"Oh my god! Is that a bat?" Beth shrieked. "Mom! A bat!"

"Shh, Beth! You have to help me! Go get a tennis racquet."

"Mom, no!" Beth sounded terrified, shrinking back.

"Okay, uh, get a big bedsheet then! Maybe we can corral it out a window."

Beth disappeared and the bat rested, clinging to the wall. It was cute and little when its wings weren't madly pumping. Elise eased into the pantry and got out a mop, carefully shutting the pantry door again. She could hear Beth's light footsteps running back.

"Okay baby, be slow. Stand on a chair and hold the sheet up in front of the doorway—no, stay on the living room side. Oh my god!" Elise gasped as the bat started flying erratically again, swooping in frantic circles, as if it sensed its enclosure and didn't like it. Damn Jeff for not being here!

In a crouch, Elise got a headlamp out of the drawer and clicked it to a red LED setting. Swallowing back fear, she strapped it onto her head, needing to see—to be sure if the bat flew out. The sheet was shaking.

"No, hold it higher, Beth, or it may fly over your head!" Elise had to work to keep from screeching. She sure didn't want to wake anyone else up.

Beth yelped and tried to steady the sheet, lifting it as high as she could, a few inches shy of the ceiling. God, if the bat got into the rest of the house they might never find it.

Trying to stay low and not panic, Elise went to a window near the sink, opened it and pulled off the screen. She practically crawled to the light switch and snapped it off. Stifling tiny screams, she held the mop high and tried to steer the bat toward the open window.

"You can do this, Mom," Beth said weakly through the sheet. "You're doing great." But the bat couldn't seem to find the window. Shit! The mop felt clumsy in her tense grip.

Beth's sheet was drooping. The bat circled and flew right over the sheet into the living room. Beth screamed and fell off the chair.

"Shit, shit, *shit*!" Elise hissed as she dashed over Beth. But she lost sight of the bat in the dark living room. She raced to the front door, flung it open and turned on the porch light. Bats were attracted to light, right? Or was that just moths? *Shit*!

Beth stayed on the floor where she fell, peeking out from under the sheet, crying softly. Elise scanned the room with her red headlamp. Don't let it have gone upstairs! She could feel her adrenaline starting to short out on her when she caught sight of the bat, hugging the wall just above the mantel where her mother's urn sat. It felt like her blood had turned to ice water and drained from her head.

"Beth, take the mop and stand on the stairs. Do not let it fly up the goddam stairs!" She glanced at her daughter and added, "Please."

"Okay," Beth whispered and crawled in her sheet to the stairs. Elise scooted the mop over to her, but the bat swooped again, flying right out the front door. Elise heard herself yell as she dashed to slam the door behind it. She crumpled to the floor as Beth came to collapse in her lap.

"Did it touch you, honey?"

She shook her head and whispered, "Mom, I was so scared." Elise hugged her close.

"Me too, baby." She forced a squeaky laugh, pulling the headlamp off her head. "Although I don't think we needed to be." Right—never mind that it's Halloween night. What's to be scared about, she thought, glancing up at her mother's remains in spite of herself. In the bat-filled darkness of Halloween night, she was starting to believe in ghosts.

Screw the dishes, Elise decided. She put her arm around her daughter's waist, and they started upstairs.

"Oh, I better close the kitchen window." Elise started to turn, but Beth clasped her hand and followed her back down. "You wanna sleep in my bed with me tonight, honey?"

Beth nodded. In the dimness, her eyes were the shape of the urn.

▼ ▲ ▼

"How was your trip?" Elise asked Jeff as he set his empty beer bottle on the counter by the sink where she was finishing up the dishes. She knew he was cheating on her. She *knew* it. When he got home last night she was already in bed, and he just crawled in, without so much as a whispered "good night." The morning had been its normal kid chaos, and tonight he had come home late and then avoided her, going out of his way to help Daphne with her math and listen to Caleb read his silly book and Beth retell the funny-but-annoying stories her teacher had told the class. No one could be that patient and definitely not that interested.

He hadn't shown any interest in Elise.

Her sub job today had been ridiculous, with several sophomore boys who seemed to be competing for Most Obnoxious Award. She'd had to rush Caleb to his Kung Fu class after school, wait there for his class to end, then pick up the girls from volleyball practice before heading home. And then dinner! The rice got burned a little and the chicken was dry, but the asparagus was perfect. Jeff loved asparagus, but he didn't even seem to notice.

"Oh, you know. It was dull, same stuff every year. Thanks for taking those pictures of the kids in costume. They were great." He dried the finished dishes and put them away, then opened the freezer and pulled out the chocolate chip mint ice cream, while Elise tried to breathe. Such a liar!

She splashed a serving spoon a little too energetically into the sudsy water. Jeff whistled while he scooped a mug full. Why was she so sure? It's not like there had been any proof, no phone messages or silent calls or lipstick on the collar. She glanced at Jeff's collar. Yeah, no lipstick. No damning red flag, just a feeling. She was trying to think of something else to say to him, make him talk to her, when he grabbed a spoon from the drawer and sauntered back into the living room. He even preferred the company of his mother-in-law's ashes to hers. Elise scanned the room for any more dishes, drained the sink, and wiped down the counters.

When she joined him, he had a cop show on, turned low; she avoided looking toward the mantel at her mother, knowing she wouldn't approve of his choice.

"Are the kids in bed?" Elise looked at the mantelpiece clock, to the left of Cleah's urn. 9:40, way past bedtime.

Jeff's focus stayed solid on the TV while he smacked his mouth on the ice cream. "Yeah. I'm going to bed soon, too."

She sat down, angry, wanting to scream at him. *I'm having a terrible day*, she told him in her head. If he loved her, he would hear her telepathically, right?

A commercial came on. Jeff looked over at Elise next to him on the couch and set his ice cream mug on the coffee table. "Hey, come over here." He tried to pull her into a hug, but it was clumsy, and she wasn't gonna fall for it. "What's up with you?"

What's up with me*? Really?!* Elise could feel her face turn to stone as she wondered what the other woman's name was. "Did you know there was a bat in the house the other night?" she said. "While you were gone? Not only did I have to do Halloween by myself, I had to deal with a bat!"

"What? How did that happen?"

"God, I don't know."

"Well, did you get it out?"

She looked at him witheringly. "Of course I did!" She clenched her jaw and didn't go into the less-than-flattering details. He stared at her, expecting more, perhaps, while the television made its sales pitches. Then he sighed as he picked up the remote and clicked it off.

"How are you doing, with," he glanced at Cleah's urn and back at Elise, "with this whole thing? About your mother. Are you okay?"

She felt exasperated. "It's ridiculous, of course. At the Halloween parade, one woman asked about it. There was something in the paper! Can you believe that? Like it's anyone's business!" His glance up had drawn her eyes to the urn. She couldn't look away. Doomed staring contest with her mother.

"You seem so mad."

"She's dead and she's driving me crazy!"

"That's exactly what I mean. You've not been yourself lately. And you don't seem to be . . ." Jeff put his arm over the back of the sofa and faced her, ". . . grieving."

"Are you kidding me?"

"Well . . . no."

"Oh my god. You are unbelievable. You haven't even been around! Do you know what I'm dealing with?" She could feel herself losing control.

"Elise, your mother died. Only a week ago."

"Uh, yes, I know!"

"It was unexpected. And the urn thing and Will Requirements—it's been strange. You hadn't talked to her in a while, right?"

She crossed her arms. "What, Jeff? What do you expect me to say?"

"I just haven't seen you cry at all."

"Cry over the woman who always made us take an extra family photo without you in it, 'just in case,' even on our wedding day?"

"She was something else." Jeff's laugh was rueful. "It's still a loss. It's okay to feel sad."

Elise didn't want to talk about grieving for her damn mother, not when she was so good and mad at Jeff for fooling around on her. He just wanted to distract her from the real issue. She ground her teeth.

"Okay, well," Jeff faltered.

"Yeah, okay, thanks." Elise went upstairs and shut herself into the bathroom, not turning on the light. A tear slid down her cheek as she leaned against the door. How could he turn things around on her like that? Like he was blaming her for *his* wandering eye. Wasn't he cheating? He certainly was! Was he? And what was this stupid argument about, anyway? She tried to remember what exactly they'd just said to each other but couldn't reconstruct it. She only knew that he didn't understand. Alone and lonely, she whispered, "I'm having a terrible day."

▼ ▲ ▼

The public library didn't open until 10:00 a.m. so she allowed herself a long late shower. She had snapped at the kids this morning, in her angst about blocking her availability on her work schedule for that day; it meant a loss of income. But she had to find that obituary.

She sensed she was becoming irrational about it, obsessive. But Halloween was three days ago, and she hadn't had time to track that newspaper down yet. She'd even considered putting a plea on her Facebook page asking for a copy. Elise couldn't stand Facebook. She had set up her page before her twentieth class reunion, and it had been interesting for a while. But now she checked it so rarely that she hardly remembered how. And she would certainly not want to talk about her mother's death on a superficial social-networking site with a bunch of 'friends' she didn't truly know.

The librarian was unlocking the heavy glass door when Elise arrived. Her wet hair chilled her in the cool air. Once inside, it was simple to find the most recent edition of *The Pioneer*. Elise scanned the weekly paper for its obituary section and found it easily, and there it was. Not a death notice, but a full-length obituary! With a photograph! Elise had never seen this photo of her mother. It was a glamour shot that Cleah must've had done years ago. She looked pretty, a bit gaudy and made up, but pretty.

"Cleah Margaret Lucky passed away on October 26th.

"Cleah was born on February 7th, 1948, to Jasper and Elizabeth Nicholson in Douglas, Wyoming. She was a precocious child, a valued member of the debate team, the homecoming committee, and the girls' chorus. She graduated valedictorian from Converse County High School in 1965. Cleah received her certificate in Office Administration from Everett Community College in Seattle in 1968. She moved to Camas, Washington to work for the paper mill, where she met and married Howard Lucky in 1971. She continued working until 1974, at which time she devoted herself fully to raising her children and to improving

education in the schools. In 1999, after her husband passed, she resumed working for the mill.

"Cleah was preceded in death by her husband, her parents, and her sister Betty Nicholson. She is survived by her aunt: Audrey Nicholson, her three children: Elise Lucky Rodgers, Tanna Lucky Hopkins, and Kevin Lucky, and her grandchildren: Beth, Daphne, Caleb, Cassidy, and Susan. Cleah's cremated remains will be cared for by her children in turn, in an attempt to foster cooperation and warm community amongst them and their offspring. Together, they will host a Celebration of Life one year after her death.

"Cleah's astute and benevolent advice will be greatly missed but never forgotten."

With effort, Elise squelched her guffaws. She slapped the paper down, then picked it up, only to drop it again as if it were a nudie picture.

"Wow." Livid, Elise pulled apart her purse searching for her library card, sat down at a computer and wrote an email to Kevin and Tanna: *I read the obituary today, finally. Which of you put that together? And WHAT THE HELL?!?!*

That was all she could manage, feeling rattled and unable to pull her thoughts together. Elise hit 'send' and picked up the newspaper again. Glancing around and seeing no one nearby, she took the entire section and folded it into her purse before putting the rest of the newspaper away. She fake-smiled warmly at the librarian as she pushed through the glass doors. Once in the parking lot, she hurried to her car, thinking, *I didn't know Mom was valedictorian.*

4

"Happy birthday, Kevin," Elise huffed as she slid into the booth next to Tanna, feeling spent from the traffic obstacle course that was Portland. She set her red plastic order-number tent in front of her, to join the two already there. Since it was his birthday, Kevin had chosen the place: the Burgerville in downtown Portland closest to his work, which meant it was inconvenient for everyone else.

"Thanks," Kevin muttered while Tanna smiled faintly, her hands wrapped around a tall plastic cup of water. Kevin was halfway through a vanilla soft serve with chocolate drizzle.

Elise picked up the order number in front of Kevin and waved it at him. "Really?"

"What?"

"Dessert first?"

"I'm a grown-ass man. So what if I eat my ice cream while I wait for my burger? What do you care? Happy birthday to me."

What a total man-child. At least Mirabelle wasn't here to snark at everyone.

A worker delivered Tanna's chicken sandwich and side salad, picking up one of the order numbers.

"I can't do this last-minute crap. Next time, more notice. It's a really far drive for me, you know," Elise said. It was always hard to gauge how long the drive into Portland would take and today the traffic on Highway 84 was terrible, even before noon.

Kevin rolled his eyes, "Not really last-minute. You know my birthday is November 7th."

Elise ignored his retort as she pulled out her phone. "Look, let's just use this birthday lunch time to get organized. Yours is in March, Tanna. The 19th is a Thursday. Do you want breakfast, lunch, or dinner?"

"I don't care. Whatever you guys want."

"Just decide!"

"Wha— dinner? I don't know!" Tanna looked pained.

"Okay, dinner. Is seven okay?" Not waiting for a reply, Elise typed *sibling dinner 7:00* into her phone's calendar. "Mine's on a Thursday. I want to go somewhere closer to my house, and let's do breakfast since it's in summer."

"'Since it's in summer'?" Kevin snipped, as she typed in the breakfast appointment, 8:00 a.m. "How does that make sense?"

"Just, it's lighter earlier in the summer," she snapped back, not wanting to explain the nuances of needing to prepare nightly dinners for a family of five.

"Fine. Whatever. God, that's gonna be so early if we have to go all the way out to Stevenson," Kevin complained. "I have to be at work by 9."

"I came all the way here for yours. It's only fair," Elise countered. "Plan for 7:30 then." She changed the appointment time in her phone's calendar.

"Geez, I'll have to take off half a day from work," Tanna grumbled. Elise ignored her.

"Wait, June what?" Kevin was looking at his phone.

"18th! You're pathetic." Elise was already ready to be done with this birthday lunch.

"He *is* a lot younger than you," Tanna put in.

"Yeah, thanks for that," Elise huffed. How annoying that the little that Tanna did speak was to defend Kevin's ineptitude.

"I just meant that to not remember our birthdays is understandable for a kid."

"Thanks for *that*," snapped Kevin.

"I mean the youngest," Tanna whined.

"You're only a year older than me!" he said.

Ignoring them both, Elise pulled her bag onto her lap, opened it, and fished out the Will packet. It was coffee-stained but intact. She had forgotten it in Jeff's car when he dropped her off after the meeting with the lawyer and she'd been so distracted by everything since, she'd not gotten around to tracking it down. Jeff had finally cleaned out the car last night after spilling coffee everywhere. There was something off about him lately, more so than usual, which only confirmed her suspicions that he was cheating.

Kevin's bacon burger and fries were delivered with a smile. He dug in immediately.

Elise leaned forward as she set the Will on the table in front of her. "Just to catch you up, after I found the obituary the other day and neither of you responded to my email, I called Mr. Kantola and, get this: he says that Mom wrote the obit herself. And she had pre-directed that it be printed in all the area papers, plus in Douglas, Wyoming."

Tanna nodded slowly, eyebrows high, while Kevin shook his head. "Good old Mom," he said, swallowing his bite, ketchup on his cheek. He reached for a napkin.

"Oh, go ahead and eat, Tanna. Or it'll just get cold. It's fine," Elise said. That bacon smelled delicious. Her fish and chips finally came, and she swooped the Will back into the bag. Not worth cold French fries.

▼▲▼

Tanna avoided eye contact, not wanting to talk—not that there was danger of much pause in conversation with Elise around. All this 'organizing' was stressing Tanna out, reminding her of how Elise tended to have that effect on her.

It was weird to be here together after years of no interaction.

Tanna had to rush to get to lunch after picking up her daughter and a friend from preschool, dropping the two kids at the friend's house for a convenient playdate. She didn't want to be gone long. Elise carefully splashed vinegar on her fish before dipping it in tartar sauce. As her sister ate, Tanna started relaxing into the silence.

"So, how's the *babysitting* going?" Kevin smirked at Elise between bites.

"Oh yeah! Good god, I saw Mirabelle's rude comments about 'babysitting the dead' on Twitter! You had better get her to cool it, Kevin. This subject is off limits to her social media shitshow!"

"Whoa, language!" he snorted. "Settle down there, missy!"

"I mean it!"

"She's right, Kevin. Please?" Tanna added, trying to keep the peace.

"All right. Relax." They lunched in silence for a while. Tanna peeked at the others, who were chewing fast, as though to quicken the end of this birthday meal. That's certainly what Tanna was doing.

Elise finished one of her fish pieces and wiped her fingers on a napkin. "Okay, let's go through the Will a little, make sure we don't miss any of Mom's tricks. Have you guys looked at it?" She pushed her dishes across to Kevin's side. Kevin shrugged as Tanna nodded. Elise didn't seem to register their responses. "I haven't," Elise admitted as she wiped the table with her napkin and set the Will in front of her. "Is there much more than what Kantola read to us?"

"Oh yeah, you could say that," said Tanna as Elise found the page and started reading silently. Had she really not looked at all those nitpicky Requirements? That didn't sound like Elise. Tanna braced for the overreaction.

"What?!" Elise's blue eyes sparked. "Each holiday has its own list of required activities?! This is—ugh! She just had to make it as difficult as she could, didn't she!" She read aloud, "'*Light the Cleah Candle to burn during the entire gathering and at least 24 hours*?' '*Toast to Cleah with Old Fashioneds for the adults and lemonade for the children*?' Every detail, even a menu! And recipes! Mom was off her rocker!" She looked frantic.

Tanna concentrated on her sandwich, suppressing a laugh. Kevin had finally stopped eating and seemed surprised. He must not have read through the Will either.

"It's like my graduation! Mom micromanaged the heck out of my party: where and when, the decorations and snacks," Elise complained. "And my wedding. I didn't want a big sit-down meal. Or a veil. Those ridiculous party favors! You know it was her idea for you to wear that dress, Tanna; I didn't really care. You know that, right? I didn't even know you didn't like it until you wouldn't stop whining about it after."

"Aren't bridesmaid dresses supposed to be ugly?" Kevin sounded bored.

"Are you really going to bring up weddings, Elise?" Tanna challenged, thinking of her own reception. If Elise wanted to gripe about her wedding, Tanna could go there.

"Oh my *god*, never *mind*," Elise said quickly. Returning her gaze to the Will, Elise sighed—a cross between a shriek and a moan. After an awkward silence, she continued, "Okay, so Tanna, are you set with all the activities for the Christmas gathering? Can you be sure to follow all the instructions correctly?"

"It's fine," said Tanna, annoyed. "I've looked through it all and it's fine. Mr. Kantola sent me the Cleah Candle already. I still need to get the movie, *It's a Wonderful Life,* though. Do either of you happen to have it?"

Kevin shook his head. He'd finished his meal and crossed his arms, staring at Elise's copy of the Will upside-down across from his empty plastic meal basket.

"I do," Elise said. "I'll bring it along on Christmas. Kevin, do you have *The Farming Game*? You'll need that for Easter."

▼ ▲ ▼

"What game? Farming? What? No!" Kevin suddenly felt exhausted and pouty. A person should get to do what they want on their birthday. This sucked ass.

"I remember that game," Tanna said.

"Right," Elise broke in. "It's a pretty obscure board game; I doubt you'll find anyone to borrow it from. You should buy it online, Kevin. You have plenty time."

"This is really insane, you guys," Kevin pushed his meal basket aside and leaned forward, eyes glued to the Will in front of Elise. "'*Dye eggs with flowers wrapped in nylons with purple cabbage and onions*?' Mirabelle's gonna flip! What does that even mean? Come on! There must be a way around this. I wonder if we could use the Will to prove she was unstable and get a judge to bypass all these crazy Rules and just let us inherit."

They looked at each other; it was actually a good idea, and he hoped his sisters would see that. They tended to spin each other up and not pay attention to anything he said at all.

"We could ask Mr. Kantola," Tanna suggested with a shrug. She checked her watch.

"No way, not him. Let's ask someone *not* on Mom's payroll," Elise shot back.

"I have a friend I can check with," Kevin said, thinking of Jason Amos who now practiced law in southern California. They were in touch on social media, although they hadn't hung out since high school.

"Good. Do." Elise leaned back in the booth and closed her eyes. There were fine worry lines there that Kevin had not noticed before. She opened them. "Look, I should get going. Friday traffic you know."

"Yeah, I need to go, too," Tanna said. She hadn't finished her sandwich, but Kevin couldn't remember her ever finishing a meal when they were kids either.

"Um, do you guys have all our addresses for the Mother Letters?" Elise asked as she put the Will into her dumpy purse. "I'm really looking forward to reading *letters* to an *urn* on *Thanksgiving*."

"God, the letters," Kevin groaned. He hated writing letters under normal circumstances, but writing a letter to his mother's ashes? He remembered Mom nagging him for months after every birthday until finally confining him to the dining room table to write his thank you letters. Even as he got older, she still never gave up hounding him to write thank yous. "Can we just say we did?"

"We have to prove it, remember? Just write the damn letter. I'll email you both my mailing address just in case." Elise looked at each of them. "We can do this, you guys. We won't let her win."

Tanna nodded. Kevin closed his eyes to hide the eye rolls. They all scooted out of the booth and walked out of the restaurant: first Elise, followed by Tanna, followed by Kevin. Déjà vu—he felt like he'd been following after his sisters his whole life. Never leading, never beside. Always following. Always being told what to do.

Elise stopped abruptly. Tanna nearly ran into her.

"Oh my god! The photo!" Elise pulled out her phone again. "Okay get over here."

"God, your phone is so old." Kevin grumped. "So, do we have to smile?"

"The Will said nothing about smiling," Tanna said with a shrug.

"Shocking omission, Mom," said Elise, holding out her phone, Tanna and Kevin on either side. "Come on, lean in."

Elise snapped the selfie but there were no smiles.

5

Aware of the ache in her back, Elise hefted the grocery bag out of the trunk. She hadn't really needed anything, but once at the store, she could always find something to buy. She'd gone shopping to have a break from the house—away from Jeff and his lying-cheater face, away from the kids' constant need for food made-to-order, away from her mother's porcelain disapproval. Usually, she would take one or two kids along, but nothing had been usual since Mother had 'moved in' with them. And on top of it all, she wasn't feeling well: a sore throat and a headache. The urn's presence was a poisonous force.

As she came in from the garage she could see Caleb, crouching behind Jeff's recliner in the front room. He was peeking at the fireplace. She shifted the groceries' weight from one hip to the other and strained to see what he was looking at.

"Honey, are you hiding from someone? Is Fred out?"

He startled and turned to face her, straightening up. "No, Mom, no." His round face was serious. He had something clutched behind him. He'd been acting strangely the last few weeks. On edge. She looked again toward the fireplace.

The urn.

"Baby, are you hiding from Grandma's urn?"

A flinch of fear passed through his eyes. Guilty silence.

"I thought you were over at Justin's house, honey." Caleb and the neighbor kid were often riding their bikes around the cul-de-sac or playing at each other's houses. She set the grocery bag down on a side table and walked toward him. "What have you got there?"

She knelt to his height, and he reluctantly put a book into her outstretched hand—*Complete Stories and Poems of Edgar Allan Poe.*

"Looks interesting." Though trying not to overreact, this didn't look like a book for an eight-year-old.

"I, uh, David gave it to me," he said, looking worried. Or scared. David was not always the *best* best friend. He sometimes was apt to lead Caleb into trouble.

"What's it about?" Elise turned it over in her hands and let the book open to where it was creased. A story called *The Premature Burial.* She immediately regretted her question.

"A lady. They thought she was dead."

Her eyes paused on an underlined passage: *The boundaries which divide Life from Death are at best shadowy and vague. Who shall say where the one ends, and where the other begins?*

He whispered, "Maybe Grandma got cremated so she wouldn't be buried alive."

Jeff burst in from upstairs, "I've got a surprise!"

Caleb grabbed the book and ran out the front door, yelling, "I'm going to Justin's!"

With a sigh, Elise straightened up. Massaging her temple, she turned to face Jeff.

"I was canceling our plane tickets for Christmas, and it occurred to me: Thanksgiving! And to change instead of canceling them meant we didn't lose the full value of the tickets. Isn't that great?! I don't know why we didn't think of that before. We'll just go visit my folks for Thanksgiving instead of Christmas!" Jeff was clearly pleased with himself. At a loss, Elise just stared. Thanksgiving in Arizona?

"Oh . . . kay," she managed, crossing her arms, "I'm sure the Shepherds won't mind." It was a stall, but still valid. Every year since they moved to Stevenson they'd had Thanksgiving dinner with Bob and Dina Shepherd, taking turns hosting. Bob worked at Skamania Lodge with Jeff, and he and his wife were the first friends they'd made in town. It helped that the couples were about the same age and had started families about the same time. "But, god, Jeff, it *is* our turn to host."

"They'll understand. It's the perfect solution! Everyone will be happy, you'll see," he continued, picking up the bag of groceries and walking into the kitchen.

Arms still crossed, Elise and her headache followed after him with growing irritation. "But it's just a couple of weeks away, Jeff." She wasn't sure why she was so reluctant about this plan. It wasn't a bad compromise, really. It was sure to please Judith. And it was already done, tickets bought. Oh, this scratchy throat!

"Oh, Jesus," she gasped as he set the bag on the counter and started unloading it. "Jeff, we'd have to take my mother *with* us. On the plane! Can we even do that?"

Jeff set down a bag of spaghetti noodles and paused as he thought that over. He ran his hand over his balding head, then shrugged. "Yeah, probably." He pulled a jar of butterscotch topping and tofu from the bag. He eyed them, clearly concerned. "Pretty random stuff here, Elise. How about I make dinner?"

▼ ▲ ▼

Elise knew she was being compulsive, checking her phone constantly. She knew she should be pacing between the rows of desks, shushing and redirecting kids to read the assigned pages in their U.S. History book, but Kevin had still not responded to her text. When Tanna's Mother Letter showed up in the mailbox yesterday, it occurred to Elise that she would need those letters to arrive before they flew to Arizona on the 22nd, meaning that Kevin would have to get his letter sent even earlier for her to get it in time. She had texted him right away. Procrastination was a family trait, well, all of them except Mother. Kevin especially was terrible about deadlines, so Elise was worrying.

A student coughed and someone else giggled, starting a small eruption of whispers. Elise set her phone down and looked around the room, then up at the clock. She rechecked the sub notes: ten minutes to go before turning in the assignment. Oops, should've given that bit of info to the kids when she assigned the reading. *What is wrong with me lately!?* She hopped up and started passing out the response questions. Not for the first time she wondered where this job was taking her. She'd started subbing several years ago to have the same schedule as the kids. Though sometimes very rewarding, substitute teaching felt transient, not an end-goal type of job. She was forever trying to find her footing, hopping classrooms and subjects, never in one place long enough to get truly good at it. Always starting over.

"Okay, I hope you got that all read. You need to respond to these questions, both sides. I'll collect them before the end of the period. Work independently—no talking."

Make this day end.

She returned to the teacher's desk to check her cell phone. Still nothing. She sat down and scrolled through the photos absently, smiling at the series of Caleb and his tortoise crawling in the grass. Swiping quickly, she paused when the birthday photo with Kevin and Tanna appeared. The top of Kevin's head was out of frame while hers was barely in frame, cut off at the nose. Kevin's thick eyebrows anchored his blue eyes, Tanna's green ones, such a piercing gaze—both were the same as when they were kids. She liked Tanna's hair styled in a pageboy bob. They all looked so unhappy.

When the bell rang she jumped, startled. The students sniggered as they stuffed books into backpacks and rushed out. Blushing but relieved, Elise wrote an inexcusably short note for the teacher, realizing too late that she hadn't collected the question sheets, oh well. She started gathering her things. She picked up her too-silent, too-dormant phone and punched out another text to Kevin: *Let me know that you got my text and that you're putting your letter in the mail to me tomorrow!*

"Mom."

Elise jumped again when Daphne showed up breathless at the door, then she laughed at herself. "Hey, fast girl, you must've rushed over here from the middle school. Do you want a ride home?"

Daphne shifted her backpack from one shoulder to the other. "No, I have volleyball practice, duh. I just wanted to tell you . . ." She trailed off, biting at her lip.

Elise looked at her phone again, sending the text to Kevin before shoving it into her bag. She walked toward her daughter. Daphne was not normally at a loss for words. "What's up?"

"It's Caleb," Daphne said, blocking the door. "He's being weird. I heard him crying in his room last night, so I went in to see if he was okay. He tried to shrug it off and then said that he didn't like how Grandma's been wandering around our house since she died. I couldn't tell if he was trying to be tough or trying to freak me out." Daphne's concern appeared to go beyond her normal irritation with her little brother.

Weird was the right word for it. Elise remembered catching Caleb staring at the urn. The creepy Poe book. But Grandma wandering around the house? "Okay. Yeah, he does seem agitated lately."

"Like someone else I know," Daphne scoffed.

"What's that?" She felt her hackles rise.

"Yeah, he's *agitated.* Does Grandma's urn really have to stay with us in our house, Mom? Can't she be put in a cemetery or something, headstone and all that? Isn't that how it normally works?"

Flustered, Elise stared at her daughter. What can you say when the dead is in control?

"Whatever. I gotta go, Mom. I just thought you should know." Daphne disappeared out the door again. Elise exhaled heavily, piling worry onto worry and feeling like she was going crazy.

▼ ▲ ▼

The wine swirled, murky and foreboding, as Elise poured it into a tumbler big enough to hold almost half a bottle. Some drips fell onto the counter, like drops of errant blood. Just a little left, she gulped the rest straight from the bottle and set it empty onto the counter next to the other empty, before upending the porcelain urn into her biggest mixing bowl. Fine, dry powder tumbled down, careful, careful, until the bulk of it dropped into the bowl with a muted thud and a puff of airborne cinder. A little bit poured wide and ended up dusting the counter.

"Oops, there's a finger. An earlobe. Won't miss that, though, will you, Mom." She remembered the big pearls her mother always wore. Did she take them off to sleep? Were they now reduced to ash, mixed with her mother's remains? Elise felt suddenly lightheaded, hyperventilating. Was she dehydrated? Not enough rest lately? She snorted a laugh, choked out like a sob. *I really am going insane.*

But am I insane if I know I'm insane?

It was late, really late, the kids in bed. Jeff was at an 'Important Function' at the Lodge; who knew when he'd be home. He'd left just before dinner with a vexed door slam. They couldn't seem to say a civil word to each other lately. Well, she couldn't seem to say a civil word to him. Elise took another long swallow of cabernet and set the glass down, checked her phone. Nothing.

"Important Function!" she jeered, making air quotes, and laughed again. They were leaving for Phoenix in the morning, and she still hadn't gotten that damn Mother Letter from Kevin. *Fucking Kevin!* She needed that inheritance money. If Jeff was cheating and her marriage was over, well she couldn't support herself on a substitute teacher wage: no benefits, no pay in summer, no security whatsoever!

Elise pulled her hair into a short ponytail using the hairband on her wrist and rolled up her sleeves.

"Shit, shit, shit; can't fool me," she mumbled as she drove her fingers into her mother's ashes, combing through, searching. Little plumes wafted up, tickling her nose. She paused, suddenly aware that she was *digging through her mother's remains*!

But she didn't trust her mother. She was convinced there'd be something in the urn—a knife? pistol?—something that would show up on the x-ray machine at airport security and she'd end up in jail and her mother will have shown her who's boss once again, Important Function! She wasn't going to take any chances.

What was left of her mother was soft. And quiet. Elise listened to the house as she stared at her ash-coated fingers, trying to hear her mom walking around. She hadn't figured out how to talk with Caleb yet. He was having a hard time with this. Since their 'little chat,' Daphne did nothing but glare at her for her inaction.

"Do you see what you're doing to us, Mother?" she hissed at the ceramic vase. "Get out of my house! I should dump you in the backyard!"

She pawed through, continuing to feel around, needing to be thorough, and getting mesmerized by the sifting feel of the powder. She gasped as she bumped into something solid, roundish. A pearl. With thumb and forefinger, she carefully plucked it from the bowl, blew away dust, and examined it. Her wine-slurred brain slowly realized it was not a pearl, but a molar. Revulsed, she let go. The tooth landed silently, making a tiny crater in the charred remains.

Oh my god, what is wrong with me?

Her phone pinged beside her elbow, drawing her attention. A notification appeared showing Kevin's text: *I emailed the letter.*

Elise stared at it, the long-awaited text disappearing as the screen went black. She shook ash from her hands, wiping them on her leggings before seizing her phone and looking for that email. *Yes! Finally!* His Mother Letter was brief, but it was there. Good ol' Kevin! Elise stretched out her arms, palms flat on the counter, as though bracing herself. She took a deep breath, filling her lungs. She surveyed the mess she had made. Salvageable. She wouldn't let her mother beat her, ha! She washed her hands in the sink and found a funnel, which she used to pour her mother back into her porcelain cage. She secured the lid. The ash in the air settled as she picked up her wineglass and toasted the urn.

Bring it on, damn you.

6

Perhaps she shouldn't have felt so confident.

Elise was hungover, not the best start. She was a little appalled at herself for dumping out and digging through her mother's ashes the night before. But she took consolation in the fact that she had the Mother Letters from both her siblings, and she knew there was no hidden weapon inside the urn. She had wrapped it tightly in Saran wrap, nearly an entire roll, to be sure the lid wouldn't come off in transit. She felt adequately prepared to handle a week at her in-laws' even with the Motherly complications.

But she hadn't checked airline regulations so when she couldn't produce the necessary paperwork, the urn was not allowed to board.

"Just figure it out! Catch a flight tomorrow," Jeff said with a shrug, as the long line behind them to get through security grew longer. Elise nodded, exasperated. She watched Jeff and the kids disappear into the airport, her carry-on roller in one hand and the urn dangling in a plastic bag in the other.

"Okay, so what exactly do I need again?" Elise huffed at the TSA worker.

"Death certificate and certificate of cremation. Could you step aside, please?"

Elise was shuffled back, and she turned to retrace her steps out of the airport. She stood for a moment just inside the entrance, staring at the revolving door. Dammit, Jeff had the ticket for the car parked in long-term parking. And the car keys! She pulled out her phone and called him, but it went straight to voicemail. Shit! She looked around for the taxi queue, unsuccessfully. She might have to call a cab. This'll be expensive.

"Hello?" he said.

Elise surprised herself by dialing Kevin instead. And even more surprising, he had answered after only a few rings.

"Uh, hi Kevin, hey. Look, are you busy right now? I am in a bind and I kinda need a favor. And it's Mom-related, so in a way it's kinda your bind, too." God, why did she have to say that? She needed his cooperation right now, not for him to be pissed off at her. Kevin didn't respond right away so she laughed nervously.

His sigh was all impatience. "What? What do you need?"

"A ride." As she explained her predicament, she could feel the tears coming and her voice getting higher and higher. She had to pause to swallow it down.

"So you needed those certificates to travel with?"

"Yeah. I know I'm dumb for not checking. Maybe *you* could hang on to Mom for the week?"

Kevin grunted. "Hold on a minute."

Elise steered her stuff over to a row of chairs, her stomach queasy and her head throbbing. She didn't want to make Kevin drive her all the way home, but what choice did she have? Sounded like a miserable ride, forty-five minutes of fun-Kevin-time. She sat down and held the phone to her ear, waiting. Maybe she would catch a flight on Wednesday. Four days all alone—that would be excellent! The whole house to herself, not even a tortoise to take care of; Fred was at Justin's house for the week. Maybe this idiot mistake was good luck after all!

"Hey. I've got copies of those papers," Kevin said in her ear. "They were in the packet the lawyer gave us. What time is your flight?"

Aw shit. She looked up at an arrival/departure monitor. "Nah, it's already boarding. It leaves in thirty-five minutes."

"Meet me in Departures in twenty. I'll be driving the Wrangler." And he hung up.

▼ ▲ ▼

"Mommy!" Beth and Caleb cried out from the row in front of Jeff and Daphne, raising arms in a hurrah. Daphne had her earbuds in and stared out the window as Elise rushed down the aisle, stumbling in her hurry. She couldn't read Jeff's expression when he saw her. Disappointment? Relief? Exasperation? Definitely surprise. Sweating, she shoved the urn at him and searched for room in the overhead compartments for her suitcase.

Kevin had been curt and quick. She was so perturbed by the whole fiasco, not to mention her hangover headache, that she had grabbed the papers from him without a word of hello or thanks. She supposed she should be grateful. It was definitely an imposition on him; he had to drop whatever his Saturday morning plans were to come to her rescue. Probably he was just glad to bring papers to her instead of having to drive her all the way to Stevenson: a twenty-minute imposition instead of a two-hour one. God, those four days home alone would have been nice.

The plane started rolling backwards.

"Ma'am, please take your seat," the flight attendant called from the back of the plane, which wasn't too far from them.

"Yeah," Elise panted. "Working on it."

"What happened?" Jeff asked, handing Mother back to Elise. "How are you here?"

"God! Just hang on to her until I can buckle myself!" she said as she slid into the seat behind his. She then briefly explained about Kevin's help; Jeff nodded, seemed impressed.

But Elise was too spent to appreciate his approval, if that's what it was. It had been a long-ass day, only just ten o'clock in the morning. She cradled the urn in her lap and leaned her head back, eyes closed, wondering if they would serve alcohol on this two-and-a-half-hour flight. Chasing a hangover away with a breakfast drink sounded like a good plan.

▼ ▲ ▼

"Judith, you've outdone yourself. It's just beautiful," Elise exclaimed, knowing her duty to praise her mother-in-law. They all found their assigned seats according to their personal napkin rings. Elise's was a gaudy copper butterfly, the ugliest one. She was placed between Beth and Daphne on one side, Caleb between Jeff and Scott's bachelor brother Carl across, with Scott and Judith on either end. The table was set with the good china—the ones with pink and blue flowers. Traditional Thanksgiving bounty covered the long table, smelling rich and salty, but the masterpiece was the turkey. It must've been twenty pounds and was roasted to a flawless golden brown, never mind that Beth did not eat meat. After an awkward grace given by Jeff, as requested by his mother, the kids greedily started scooping food onto their plates, to Elise's chagrin. Scott stood and began carving the turkey with the electric knife while Judith poured Burgundy into the adults' wine glasses.

For Elise, the week had been long with tension and whispered quarrels with Jeff, beginning with the placement of her mother's urn on the old wooden dresser beside the bed. Jeff didn't want it there, but she'd argued where else could it go. Every morning the kids were up early to watch Nickelodeon cartoons, something they never got to do at home. The television was on all day, cartoons or news or football, terrifically loud; the house was kept at a parching seventy-nine degrees. But the worst was how Judith wouldn't let Elise help with anything, as well as Scott's habit of clearing away her water glass the minute she set it down when she hadn't been finished with it. She felt very conscious of being both a guest and an imposition, so nothing new after all these years. She found herself retreating to read her paperback in the back bedroom a lot, but that wasn't right either, as Judith started making passive-aggressive comments about her absences—another thing to fight with Jeff about.

Scott finished slicing turkey and proudly presented the platter to Carl to pass around.

"Yeah, that is a beaut! Sliced thick, done right, tha's a man's work," Uncle Carl slurred, on his second glass of wine, having pre-gamed with some whiskey before dinner.

Even before the turkey got to her, Elise's plate was overfilling with the seemingly endless lineup of perfect side dishes: garlic mashed potatoes and gravy, green bean casserole with those crispy onions, homemade potato rolls, bacon Brussels sprouts, cranberry-orange sauce, a mixed green salad, marshmallow yams, and an amazing sausage and fennel stuffing. She tried to take the smallest portion possible of each without offending Judith.

They ate and they ate, while a Nora Jones CD looped in the background. Beth absently hummed along as she concentrated on her vegetarian options, unfazed by Judith's admonishments for not eating her masterful turkey. Damn, but it was delicious. Elise started planning out how she would get away to read the letters to Cleah's ashes. Before pie or after? She realized with a start that she had not written her own Mother Letter.

Scott got up and clicked on the game as the kids asked to be excused. Perfect! She was sure the TV would serve to cover her escape. Elise hurriedly finished the remaining potatoes and salad still on her plate. She put her napkin back into the butterfly ring as she stood up.

"Judith, can I help with cleaning this up?" Elise asked, certain she would be again prohibited.

"Yes, thank you, dear, won't you, though? I sure am tired from cooking all day."

▼ ▲ ▼

Elise sat down heavily on the guest bed, facing the urn. Jeff was still in the great room watching TV, his head lolled back and his mouth slack. Just like his dad. The dishes had taken much longer than she had expected. She'd gotten the girls to help at first, but they quickly disappeared. She was determined to comply with all her mother's Will Requirements, so would have to read those letters to the urn before midnight, which was distressingly near. Finally, Judith had been satisfied with her efforts, and Elise had gotten the kids away from their Gameboys and cell phones and into bed.

Reaching into her suitcase on the floor, she found Tanna's unopened letter and sat again on the bed, tucking her feet beneath her.

"Ready, Mom?" she said, searching through emails on her phone. "Let's start with Kevin. You're gonna love this." She read, "Dear Mom, Happy Thanksgiving."

The door opened. "Hi, honey." Half-asleep, Jeff stripped down to his t-shirt and underwear and turned off the bedside lamp. He mumbled, "Tired," as he crawled into the bed. Elise exhaled into the darkness, gathered her phone, Tanna's letter, and the urn, and she left.

That's how she ended up sitting on the closed toilet lid, whispering to the stupid urn with its pretty blue flowers on the bathroom floor. She suddenly remembered sitting in timeout in her childhood bathroom, countless times, being punished for not completing a task quite to Cleah's specifications. Or else for sassing, or some other equally heinous crime. Little girl Elise would sit on the closed toilet seat hugging her shins, her forehead on her knees. Here she was, being punished again.

"Dear Mom, Happy Thanksgiving. Hope you're well. Best of luck. Kevin."

Elise sighed as she tore open Tanna's blue envelope, trying to think of what she wanted to say to her mother. Truth was, she didn't want to say anything.

She unfolded the matching blue stationery inside. Another short one. "Dear Mom, The kids are so smart and so sweet. You should be proud of them. I am. My life is full. Love, Tanna." Elise sat looking at her sister's handwriting for a while. She refolded the letter and put it back into its envelope. Getting up, she found her toothbrush and proceeded with her nighttime routine: brushing, flossing, washing, moisturizing. Finally she sat again. She picked up her phone and created an email to herself, wanting documentation of her own letter, to prove she met the Requirement. In the subject line, she put 'Thanksgiving Mother Letter' and then she paused. It had been one month since her mother had died.

On impulse, Elise called her mom's number.

"I *know* you're not home; you're right here!" she whispered shrilly as it rang and rang, feeling her heart beat fast in this crazy compulsion. Just as Elise was recovering her sense of reality and moved to disconnect the call, her mother's voice spoke, telling her she was not at home, to leave a message, and she would return the call as soon as possible. Unnerved, Elise cut the connection and stared at her phone, then at the urn. It occurred to her they should clean out her mother's house. The fridge must be atrocious.

She began typing her email. It, like the others, was brief.

When it was finished and sent, Elise read it aloud: "Dear Cleah, You've got me in timeout in the bathroom again. What power you wield—I hope you're satisfied. I hope you're in hell." She dropped her phone onto the bathmat. Elbows on knees, head in hands, she quietly wept.

7

"But really, dear, no need to worry! It's all been taken care of," said Dawn on the phone, her voice syrupy and bright.

"Okay, but what does that mean, exactly?" prodded Elise. Earlier that day she had asked Dawn to have Mr. Kantola return her call, and instead it was this Dawn calling back again, who didn't seem to know many details.

"Mr. Kantola said to say he was following through with all the arrangements that Mrs. Lucky had laid out prior to her death in the event of her death." Elise was sure she could hear Dawn smiling. What a pleasant woman. It was infuriating.

"I'd just like some more specifics. I mean, I called my mom's phone number last week and still got her voicemail—a month after she'd died. Wouldn't disconnecting the phone service be one of those arrangements? Has anyone cleared out the refrigerator? I'd just like to get into the house, check for myself." Elise wasn't sure why she cared. She was exhausted from her day being the music teacher at the grade school. Those little kids, a new group shuffling into her classroom every twenty minutes, with their hopelessly short attention span, and she still had the song "I Am a Pizza" on repeat in her brain, then picking up her own kids and making dinner; it had been a long Friday that wasn't over. They were about to leave for the K–8 PTO's fundraiser craft fair and cake walk. But the fact that she couldn't find out anything about her mother's effects made her want to find out even more. Classic childish reverse psychology—*Wait, was this another of her mother's games from the grave?*

"Look, on second thought Dawn, I don't care and don't want to know." Elise unceremoniously ended the call.

She looked around—no one. They were already running late, before Dawn had called. Elise had finally gotten them to the garage door when the phone rang and then they had all dispersed, absorbed back into the house—husband and kids alike—and now she had to re-gather.

"All right, troops! We're leaving for Santa's Cake Walk! Right now!" she called up the stairs impatiently. Elise turned to see Caleb in the living room. He was carefully dusting the urn, whispering to it. Before she could say anything, the girls were tumbling down the stairs as Jeff appeared and Caleb came running, and all the momentum was again moving toward the garage.

"Why didn't you just take the kids on ahead?" Elise grumbled at Jeff, as everyone pulled on coats, hats, and gloves. Jeff shrugged as they piled into the minivan and the car (they needed to take both because Elise had volunteered to help clean up afterwards), and they backed out into the street in turn.

By the time they arrived at the middle school gymnasium, the cake walk games were over, the student performances had finished, and the craft fair booths were packing up.

"Two coffees and, I guess, three pieces of fruitcake." Jeff paid the volunteer as he looked over the now-sparse dessert table. Fruitcake was the only choice. They took the cakes and coffee, napkins and plastic forks, and sat down. Bing crooned *Let It Snow* from a little boombox in the far corner while people started to take down decorations.

"Dad, why'd you get us only three pieces of cake?" Caleb asked as he picked up a fork.

"Well, I thought we could share. I don't think any of you've had fruitcake before, right?"

Caleb took a big forkful and made a face. Beth took a bite and set her fork down slowly, saying, "You can have mine, Dad." Jeff laughed.

"What's in this?" Daphne scrunched up her nose and ate a bite.

"Fruit, I think," said Elise, reaching for Beth's fork. Daphne chewed slowly and took another I'm-gonna-like-it-just-because-no-one-else-does bite.

"Want some coffee?" Jeff offered generally, as he took a sip.

"Yeah!" Caleb jumped at the chance to try grown-up things. He made another sour face after his gulp. Daphne reached over and took the cup from him, taking a big swig. She considered the bitter black liquid, as though deciding.

"Grandma Cleah always put four tablespoons of sugar in her coffee before breakfast," Elise mused, as she dumped a packet of Sweet'N Low into her not-quite-hot Styrofoam cup.

"Whoa," said Beth. "Grandma Cleah liked the sugar!" Daphne snickered.

Caleb cocked his head pensively and then glanced at the empty tables on all sides.

"I think the Cake Walk is over!" Caleb cried, suddenly noticing the disassembly happening around him. "Did we miss Santa?!"

"Well Santa's pretty busy, sport," Jeff said. He drained his coffee cup.

Caleb sighed. "Oh man!"

"So can we go home?" Daphne said.

Jeff nodded and took another bite of fruitcake. They gathered up the mostly uneaten cake and threw the leftovers in the trash by the door. "See you at home," Jeff said to Elise as they left.

Unsure why she felt so grumpy, Elise watched them go before going to help take laminated Twelve Days of Christmas posters off the cement-block gym wall.

▼ ▲ ▼

It was a chilly Monday afternoon, nearly four o'clock. Elise drove home carefully, not feeling fully functional. A fantasy thought of calling in sick the next day flashed through her head—dismissed immediately with a snort. Getting a sub for the sub; she'd probably never get another substitute request again. Hopefully a good nap would fix it. And takeout was definitely all she'd be able to manage for dinner tonight. Maybe Jeff could bring something home from the Lodge, be useful for once. She dug her phone out of her bag, unmuted it, but decided she couldn't manage more while she drove. She would text him when she got home.

Elise had shown up at the courthouse for jury duty that morning feeling positive, having decided she would be glad to do her civic duty. It was the first time she'd been summoned, somehow. In the nearly twenty years living there, Jeff had been called to jury duty four times. The process was interesting and new to her. There was a lot of waiting and delays, but once the lawyers started vetting jurors, she was quickly vexed with the defense attorney. Every question he asked her made her feel belittled, presuming she had an inevitable bias, just for being a mother. They couldn't be briefed too thoroughly on the case, but it became clear the defendant was being charged with child molestation. She and her fellow prospective jurors were grilled for several hours before breaking for lunch and pounded with more questions afterward. Although indignant to be perceived as unable to give objective due process by that stupid defense lawyer, Elise was relieved to be ultimately dismissed. The experience had given her a migraine. She could only imagine what attending the full trial would have done.

Elise parked the minivan, closed the garage door, and sat for a moment until the garage light turned off. Her knit hat felt too tight; she pulled it off. A bath by candlelight sounded good.

Walking through the door from the garage into the house, Elise heard a clunk and saw a commotion over by the fireplace. At first alarmed, she realized it was Caleb. He was home alone, having taken the bus after school. The girls were at basketball practice.

He swung around to face her, hands hidden behind his back. Elise was often catching him in this position lately, and it was starting to creep her out. She saw that the urn's lid was off, sitting next to it, on the mantel. She hadn't unwrapped the ceramic urn from its Thanksgiving Saran Wrap protection, which was now pulled apart haphazardly.

"Honey, what are you doing?" Elise was tired and didn't really even want to ask. *No more Mother drama!* She just wanted to get through until the Christmas pass-off. She walked over to him and pulled his arm from behind his back. Caleb held an open bag of white sugar. "What—?" She pulled his other arm, revealing a measuring spoon in his other hand.

"Mom, don't get mad," Caleb was starting to cry, then gathered himself. "I'm just trying to make her happy! You said she liked four tablespoons!" He wrenched away from her and headed toward the kitchen with his sugar and spoon. She watched him go, confused.

"What? Caleb, it's okay," she called after him, too late. She heard the back door slam.

Sugar? Finally understanding, she peeked inside the urn. Sure enough: Caleb had spooned sugar into Grandma Cleah's ashes. *Oh god! Should I try to scoop it out?*

With a sheepish smile, Elise replaced the lid and picked up the urn. Holding the lid on tight, she gave the urn a little shake, mixing it in. She pulled the rest of the plastic wrap off, wadding it into a ball. Only another week and a half before she could be rid of the cursed urn! Someone else could take a turn at bearing the burden of Will Compliance.

She eased her purse off her shoulder as she sank onto the couch, sliding down into it. Elise pondered Caleb. At least he didn't seem so scared anymore; the poor kid was trying so hard to make the best of this. *Maybe* I *just need a little sugar.*

It took Elise several rings to register that she was getting a call; she must have started falling asleep. She fumbled her cell out of her bag. The caller ID said Tanna.

"Tanna?"

"It says 'Exchange presents!' In the Will! You have to bring presents!"

"Okay, okay! Geez." She did not have patience for a freakout.

"Christmas is in ten days. I just don't want anything to get screwed up!"

"Sure. I'm sure you've got it covered." Elise tried not to sound flippant, even though she felt annoyed. She didn't want Tanna to screw up the Requirements either.

"Yeah, well, I'm not so sure! Mom always had a way of catching us in mistakes—like she was trying to *make* us mess up. Did you see that list of what foods to prepare? God! I finally looked up a British Christmas Pudding recipe today and it said it should be made six weeks in advance! And I never knew what suet was. Did Mom really go to this much trouble every Christmas? I had no idea!"

"Are you quitting?" Part of Elise hoped she'd say yes.

"Well, no." Tanna's voice was high and small.

"Then calm down. The suet doesn't have to taste good. Don't let her stress you out!" Elise glanced up at the urn and stuck out her tongue. Pain shot through her eyes. "Just review the Christmas Requirements section in the Will. It's all laid out."

Elise could hear Tanna take a deep breath. "Don't tell me to calm down."

Elise snorted. "Sorry." They were both silent. Elise's head throbbed.

"You know what feels weird? Not having had a funeral," Tanna said.

There was another pause.

"Would you have gone?" Elise countered, massaging her temple. More silence.

"Look, I have to, uh . . . make dinner for the girls," Tanna said curtly. "You review the part with the Christmas Requirements, too."

"Yeah. Okay, bye." Nearing tunnel vision from the migraine and forgetting that she forgot about texting Jeff to bring dinner, Elise went upstairs to see about some Advil and that bubble bath.

▼ ▲ ▼

"Who's next? What's on that list of yours?" Jeff said, hands stuffed in his coat pockets, staring down the aisle of kid's toys. When had he become so mean and shifty? Winter break had started and the whole world was at Target that Saturday before Christmas. Beth had just put a purple stuffed dog, for Susan, into the shopping cart Elise was pushing. Caleb had chosen a very soft penguin for Cassidy, and Daphne had picked out two coloring books, one for each girl, and a mega crayon box to share. Even though they didn't know their four- and five-year-old cousins well, it all seemed like safe assumptions. Elise consulted her incomplete-and-vague list self-consciously. They still needed gifts for the adults.

"Let's look at perfume for Tanna and Mirabelle?" Elise shrugged her shoulders. Her list was stupid. Perfume was probably not what Tanna would want. She regretted making everyone come help shop for presents. She had foolishly thought a family trip into Portland would be fun. At least they had found Christmas sweaters to wear to the dinner—another Requirement from her dead mother.

"Okay, kids, let's find the perfume aisle," Jeff directed. The kids surged ahead. To Elise, he laughed and said, "What are the chances Mirabelle will like anything we buy for her?"

"You're not helping," Elise said coldly.

Jeff raised his hands. "Okay, sorry. I'm just trying to have some fun here, Elise." He pouted as she swatted the air and marched ahead of him, pushing the cart earnestly. What was he hiding? How could she trust him? The stress of trying not to fight in front of the kids was unraveling her nerves.

They found the perfume aisle. The kids presented lots of choices, but Elise couldn't decide on anything. They looked at jewelry, bath salts, hand lotion. Why was this so hard? They checked out ties, men's wallets, grilling tongs, toasters. They were walking aimlessly down every crowded aisle. The kids began bickering. Elise was starting to feel desperate and resentful. They found themselves in the office supplies section and Elise picked out two blank journaling books, deciding not to care whether anyone would like them.

The checkout line was long, the world conspiring against her. Jeff gave each of the kids ten dollars and sent them to the food court with instructions to stick together.

The kids were out of earshot. Elise said, "I think you should move out. After New Year's, once the kids are back in school."

She had spoken her angry impulse thought aloud, taking herself by surprise.

Jeff sighed and said nothing.

▼ ▲ ▼

Elise crept down the stairs as quietly as she could. A panic dream had wakened her, and she found herself alone in bed. Again. She peeked into the living room, aware of her mother's judgmental stare from the mantel. She could see the glow of Jeff's cell phone from the couch, where he'd been sleeping each night for the past several weeks.

"Jeff, can we talk?" she whispered into the darkness.

His cell phone light went out as he shifted to sitting. Had he been texting someone?

"You want to talk *now*?"

"Well, yeah. The kids are sleeping. We're both awake."

"True."

"Not here." Elise gestured toward the mantel, even though it was too dark to really see her movements. "Mother."

"Oh, right."

As Jeff stood to follow her, Elise turned toward the side door. They put coats on over their pajamas, went into the garage, and climbed into the minivan—Elise in the driver's seat. Though her mother had chased them here, it hit her that they used to retreat to the garage for stolen moments, to make love in the backseat while the babies napped, later to discuss a teacher's report or the pediatrician's concern out of earshot. Sitting together in the van inside the garage bubbled up tragically wistful nostalgia. Tears started welling.

When the lights clicked off and they were in darkness again, Elise said, "I don't want you to leave." She didn't know what she wanted, couldn't keep her mind straight or make decisions. She wanted him to leave. Except she wanted him to stay. Her mother's derisive laughter rang in her ears.

Jeff stared at the closed garage door in front of them.

Elise went on, "I don't know what's going on with us these past few months, if it's just this crap with the Will or what, but I'd be up to trying couple's counseling." They sat in silence for several minutes. Elise felt breath-holding dread.

"You know, I think you're using your mother as an excuse," Jeff finally said.

Elise considered that, working hard not to jump to defensive anger. "I don't know, maybe." She didn't know what to think anymore, what was real. She was floating, off-balance. She clutched the steering wheel.

Jeff exhaled. "Look, what if I take the kids and give you some space—a few days. I'll take them to stay at the Lodge," Jeff offered, "or maybe see if we can use the Shephards' cabin. Take them skiing."

The idea sparked a tiny hope in Elise. "Okay." She felt like crying. Or laughing. Screaming.

Jeff continued softly, "I mean, I think there's more going on here that we're gonna have to deal with, Elise, but . . ." he hesitated, "I do love you." He waited almost long enough for her to reply, before adding, "Counseling is probably a good idea. But maybe for now we just take a breather, a little time apart, and then," he shrugged, "we'll see."

Elise closed her wet eyes. *Only four and a half more days with the urn!*

8

Eggnog
From the kitchen of: Cleah Lucky
Serves 8

Mix:
6 eggs
4 c. whole milk
1 c. heavy whipping cream
2 t. vanilla extract
½ c. white sugar
½ t. ground cinnamon
pinch of salt

Beat until frothy.
Gently mix in:
1 liter Dark Rum
1 liter Rye Whiskey
2 c. Bourbon
Pass ground nutmeg over serving.

A juniper wreath hung on Tanna's door in the quiet east Portland suburb, with bluish-purple berries that smelled peppery and sharp. No Christmas snow here. Caleb rang the doorbell. When Tanna opened the door, Elise smiled widely and presented her with the urn. Her smile widened further as Tanna took it. She felt immediate, irrational euphoria.

"Come on in." With two little girls peeking around each side of her khaki slacks, Tanna ushered the Rodgers family into the house. It opened straight into the living area, where the decorated spruce tree dominated the room. Tanna set the urn on the coffee table next to a thick red candle, intricately carved into swirls of what looked like wind or fire. It was lit.

"Cute house. How long have you lived here?" Elise said, pulling off her coat while looking around. It was small.

"Just three years. We moved in after Joe . . ." Tanna trailed off.

"Oh. Is that the Cleah Candle?" Elise asked, pointing, eager to steer away from talking about the weddings, the divorces. Tanna nodded. Elise felt awkward, so she said, "Nice sweater." It was green with little brown reindeer flying all over; the green matched Tanna's eyes. It really was pretty. Elise had on a Scandinavian snowflake design in ombre shades of blue.

"Merry Christmas, Tanna," Jeff said, handing her a bottle of wine. His sweater was simply red, which is why it was Christmassy, he'd claimed. "Here's that movie you needed." He set *It's a Wonderful Life* onto the coffee table next to the urn, eased off his coat, and sat down on the blue denim couch.

"Thanks," said Tanna. "Wow, you kids have gotten so big!" She gave them each a quick hug. Elise could tell the kids felt awkward and realized they wouldn't remember her well. A sad realization, really.

Daphne carried the wrapped presents in a Target bag over to the tree, Beth and Caleb close behind. This drew Susan and

Cassidy out from behind their mother. Tanna's girls wore tasteful cardigans, Susan in red with gold stars around the collar, Cassidy in white with candy-cane-striped arms, while her own kids wore colorful and cartoony sweaters with cheerful elves and Santas.

Jeff had taken the kids to stay Sunday night at the Lodge, since he had to work Monday. Apparently, the kids thought it great fun to be spoiled in a suite for a day, mostly unsupervised. Then they had driven to the Shephards' cabin on Mt. Hood where they stayed two nights, having one full day for skiing at Cooper Spur. Meanwhile, the days at home had dragged by for Elise, so aware of the custody countdown. She looked over the Will and, in particular, the Christmas Requirements, complaining and mocking her mother with verbose abandon. She had a staring contest with her mother, which she'd lost, so she read half of Dan Brown's *Angels and Demons* aloud to Fred—tortoises don't make the best of audiences (nor do human ashes). She took a bath, which became two baths a day, she had another staring contest with Mother, she wrapped presents—no thanks to Fred. She put red self-adhesive star bows all over the urn, she made cookies and cinnamon rolls, she ate cookies while binge-watching *Breaking Bad.* She removed the bows from the urn and had to clean off the adhesive, she stared out the kitchen window while alternately drinking mint tea and tequila. With no one else around, Cleah's presence had filled up the void in the house and in Elise's head—even more so than before.

When Jeff and the kids had returned home yesterday on Christmas Eve, Elise had a kielbasa hash ready, a family favorite. Though perhaps not entirely refreshed, Elise was both extremely happy to have them home again and that the urn countdown was down to one day. The kids had put out the Santa cookies and milk and gone to bed early with no arguments, same as every Christmas Eve. In the morning, they'd woken up before 6:30 to open presents, then they ate up the cinnamon rolls smothered in butter, and Elise could not stop smiling. She still couldn't stop. Today Mother was moving out!

"Okay, so we've got the Christmas sweaters and the comfortable shoes." Elise pulled out the list of Cleah's Christmas instructions and activities from her pocket. "Comfortable shoes—weird."

"I double-checked the food list," Tanna said, stony, still holding the wine. "I'm worried the pudding won't light on fire like it's supposed to."

"Mommy, can we decorate the houses now?" Cassidy asked, tugging at Tanna's sleeve.

She turned to her oldest daughter. "I think you could get started, sure. Can you girls take your cousins into the kitchen? You can show them all the stuff we set up. Oh, hey, and put this bottle on the counter." She handed her the wine.

"Okay!" Cassidy breathed, leading the way.

"I put the gingerbread houses together already; they just need decorating. We can do ours later," Tanna said, turning back to Elise, "after Kevin and Mirabelle get here."

"God, I hope they won't be late," Elise grumbled. "The Will is so specific about that."

Tanna lifted her wrist and they both checked her watch; it was 10:58 a.m. now. Yikes, only two minutes to go! The doorbell rang. The sisters looked at each other, relieved.

But it was Dawn at the door, not Kevin, and her arms were full. "Merry Christmas, all!" she exclaimed, her long red peacoat accentuating the bright orange of her beehive.

"Hi," Tanna stammered, clearly as surprised as Elise was wary. "Um, please come in."

"I'm Dawn, if you remember, from Kantola and White. Is everyone here?" Dawn asked, striding into the room. She carried a stack of round boxes, like an unwieldy wedding cake, and had a black satchel strung over her shoulder like a pageant sash.

"All but Kevin and Mirabelle," Elise forced a smile, "but I'm sure they'll be here momentarily."

"Yes, let's hope so," Dawn beamed at her. As she leaned to set down the boxes, they started slipping, and Tanna and Elise jumped to help. "Oopsie, thank you!" Dawn said. Each pressed cardboard box had a different faded print on it, one blue, one yellow, and a smaller one dark brown.

"Wow, working on Christmas Day. I hope you're making triple time!" Jeff grinned.

Dawn laughed as she pulled off gloves. "I'll not be here but a few minutes, don't you worry!"

"Excuse me, I'll be right back." Elise shot Tanna a look of panic as she clutched her phone, stepped out the front door, and called Kevin. She peered up and down the street as it rang. It went to voicemail. Elise cut the connection, texted: *GET HERE NOW!* and phoned again, wishing she'd grabbed a coat. Kevin's car raced into view and parked abruptly on the street in front of the house. They emerged from the car looking like an Old Navy holiday commercial, annoyingly stylish and gorgeous, as Elise motioned them to hurry. As the three burst into the house, Tanna and Jeff were laughing at something Dawn had said.

"Oh good! There you are!" Dawn clapped her hands. "Ooo, nicely done with the sweaters!" Kevin's had thick red-and-green horizontal stripes while Mirabelle wore a red cashmere with silver tinsel woven through. She also wore a tight black miniskirt and shiny black ankle boots.

"Are your shoes comfortable, Mirabelle?" Elise couldn't help herself.

"Yes, Elise. They are," Mirabelle retorted.

"Well let's get started then!" Dawn said. She sat everyone down and pulled three manila envelopes and a sheet of paper from the satchel, setting the envelopes on the coffee table. "One for each of you, they're all the same, you'll probably want to look at those later." She consulted the piece of paper, and handed the blue box to Tanna, yellow to Elise, and brown to Kevin.

"Sorry, just the biological children this time," Dawn said, looking around with an apologetic red smile and tilt of her head. "Go on, open your hat boxes!"

Pulling off the lid, Elise found a fur cap and matching stole inside. She lifted out the stole—so soft! —then gasped to discover little feet and a brown head still attached. Tanna's box held a shaggy silver fur muff and Russian-like hat set, while Kevin received a smart herringbone fedora and a tobacco pipe.

"Oh my! Lovely!" Dawn exclaimed. "And I am to read you an accompanying note from Mrs. Lucky: 'These belonged to my mother and father, Jasper and Elizabeth. Elise has the mink and Tanna has the silver fox. My father loved to surprise my mother with a fine fur. His fedora feather is pheasant. He mostly wore the fedora to church. I have fond memories of him smoking his pipe after dinner. The pipe belonged to his father before him. Treasure all these treasures, as I did.'"

"Thanks?" said Tanna. The siblings exchanged a look, perplexed.

Dawn again referred to the paper. "Have you listened to the song yet?"

"No, but I have a YouTube video queued up on the computer here." Tanna stood. "Do the kids need to come in? They're decorating gingerbread houses in the kitchen."

"No, they can keep working. My, but you're doing so well with the Requirements!" Dawn beamed. Clutching the muff, Tanna went over to a computer on a desk, slid into the chair, and started the song. Elise picked up one of the manila envelopes. As the schmaltzy notes floated over them, she peeked at the stack of papers inside and partially drew out a page. It was a family Christmas letter from 1976. Feeling suddenly nauseated, she replaced it and leaned back on the couch.

Who's sorry now? Who's sorry now? Whose heart is achin' for breakin' each vow. Everyone grew very still as the song played in a slow swing. Dawn drew a line across her sheet.

Who's sad and blue, Who's cryin' too, Just like I cried over you. Elise felt tense and confused. She stared at the porcelain urn, the representation of her mother's force and presence, now so familiar. She concentrated on breathing evenly.

Right to the end, just like a friend, I tried to warn you somehow. They sat there awkwardly, furs and fedoras in laps, waiting out the song. Elise wasn't sure what the purpose was. She'd never heard this song before. Was it sweet or accusatory? Was it supposed to make her feel guilty?

You had your way, now you must pay, I'm glad that you're sorry now.

What the hell?!

After a key change and a solid second time through, the song ended, and Tanna closed the browser. Dawn was straight back to business.

"Hmm. Okay, there's just a few more things. We couldn't know this at the time of the Will reading, because there's a lottery for teams and, anyway, here it is: you are to run in the Hood to Coast next summer! It's a relay, the last weekend in August. The five of you and myself will be half of a team, all together in one van!" Dawn seemed overjoyed. "You will need to train, and each be prepared to run three legs of the relay. You'll be responsible for a total of fifteen to eighteen miles, each, over the two days. The race starts on Friday and ends on Saturday. Okay? Okay!"

Elise was horrified.

Dawn looked at her paper again, not giving them time to process. "And the last thing is that you all are to help out at the food kitchen today with the Christmas meals, and then deliver a few to shut-ins. They're expecting you at noon. I'll leave you the address." She handed the paper to Tanna as she went on, "I'll take your family photo for you before I go, but first, Tanna, can I see the kitchen real quick? Check the food?"

"Oh. My. God," Mirabelle exhaled after Tanna led Dawn to the kitchen. "I hate running."

Elise secured the dead animal around her neck with two little hidden hooks, put on the soft fur cap, and giggled, because what else could she do? Jeff chuckled too. Petting the stole, Elise caught his eye and they laughed together, loud and long and insane.

It was all so insane.

They were still suppressing giggles for the family photo.

▼ ▲ ▼

Kevin glanced in the rearview mirror, checking that the others were still following him. He was peeved at everyone. Especially Elise! What was with the laughing? She really seemed unhinged.

"Take the next exit, then turn left." Mirabelle was good at navigating. Kevin had expected her to bitch and complain all the way there. He was glad to be wrong. He was reeling from all that information Dawn had dumped on them. Relay race? An old hat and pipe? And now they were on their way to a soup kitchen? It felt like a bad dream. He was too tired to think. They had been up late, spending Christmas Eve in Salem with Mirabelle's devoutly Catholic cousin's family: that long midnight mass in English and Latin, all translated into Spanish, and every festive thing leading up to it. They'd reluctantly dropped the girls at doggy daycare that morning; judging from the number of dogs there, spending Christmas Day in the kennel was less rare than he would have guessed.

When all three vehicles had parked at the Salvation Army in Vancouver and they'd found the director inside, they discovered they were to wash dishes. Kevin shot a worried glance toward Mirabelle, but she was rolling with it.

"I guess this is why we had to wear comfortable shoes," Tanna quipped as they hung up their coats, donned red and white checkered aprons and latex gloves, and were shown to their stations—with advice to roll up their sweater sleeves. Even the kids were being put to work bussing dishes. The director made a point of saying this was a special concession, as kids normally aren't allowed to volunteer. Oh, those lucky kiddos.

It was an assembly line: the kids brought in dirty dishes and set them onto the stainless-steel counter (except Susan who didn't want to go into the dining area), Mirabelle scraped food off plates with a giant spatula, Elise did a pre-rinse at one deep sink, then Kevin washed at a double sink of sudsy water and rinse water, Tanna loaded the cleaned dishes onto a tray to roll through the sanitizer, and Jeff and Susan dried and stacked dishes onto massive rolling carts. The work was hard, and they were getting wet from the splashes of the powerful sprayers.

"Hey Kevin, did you ever ask your lawyer friend about getting around these Will Requirements? I mean, now we're running a relay race?" Elise asked, handing Kevin a slippery plate.

Kevin had forgotten to check with Jason and his gut churned in aggravation. "I haven't heard back from him yet," he lied. They fell silent again. Kevin was having flashbacks of his first job as a teenager, washing dishes for a breakfast café. Cleah had gotten him that job, as she was friends with the owner. Backbreaking work. He hadn't lasted three weeks, to his mother's ever-present disappointment.

He was very aware of Mirabelle working too slowly, like the princess she was, not wanting to get dirty or break a nail. He worried what she was thinking, how she was handling this craziness. But she was a tough princess, her apron bearing the spoils of her war on leftovers: cranberry sauce and gravy. He smiled to himself, just a little bit proud.

Their two-hour-long shift felt like forever to Kevin, but it did finally end. Only the kids seemed sorry to be finished. The director showed up again as another crew arrived.

"Thank you for your good, hard work!" she said as the new volunteers took their spots. "We sure will miss having your mother's help with the meal planning and prep. That woman had endless energy and sure liked to take charge! I'm so sorry for your loss." The director led them to a table near the door, ready with plastic bags full of takeout boxes. "Now! Each of you have three homebound folks to deliver meals to. Here are the addresses and it shows how much goes to each place, too." The director handed each sibling a different paper with the vitals. Kevin realized his mother had known this short woman with a grey ponytail and huge hazel eyes.

"How long had our mom been volunteering here?" Kevin asked.

"Oh, let's see, just since June, or so." The director smiled like a cheery elf. "But she was here almost every day, such commitment. She'd become a fixture."

June was when Cleah had her first stroke.

They put on coats, double-checked which bags were whose, exchanged Christmas well-wishes with the director, and loaded up.

"I guess see you back at my house," Tanna said as they all exited into the cold.

The other family units had their kids to help, but Kevin and Mirabelle barely made it to their car in one trip, several bags in each hand. After filling the trunk of their jeep and consulting their address list, they sped away. Mirabelle put the first address into her phone and again navigated.

The first delivery was to a shriveled old man living alone with two agitated Chihuahuas. Second stop was a smiley toothless woman in a trailer park who wouldn't stop talking. The last was an old couple barely able to get up and answer the door. There's an interesting interaction that occurs when housebound people are brought a meal, he noticed, a happy disarming gratitude that Kevin had never known, but it was coupled with an awkwardness, like an underlying shame of their dependence. He felt humbled. Without really meeting these people, such a quick exchange, he felt connected and invested. He almost forgot how his mother had manipulated the moment.

"Well that actually didn't suck," Kevin said as they drove south on the freeway.

Kevin glanced at Mirabelle. "You're very quiet," he said. She seemed contemplative, staring out her window, no longer navigating since they were now returning to Tanna's.

She turned to him, looking intent. "Ya know, I get why your mom would have us do this food kitchen stuff—give to the poor, teach us a lesson in helping thy neighbor—but why the relay thing? Is she just being cruel? I mean, I know she didn't like me, even though she never met me. But running? Really?! That's just torture. What a *bitch*."

There she was: Mirabelle being Mirabelle. Kevin sighed.

"Yeah. I don't know," he said. "Maybe she wants us to get into shape."

She scoffed, "I *am* in shape," and turned to the window again.

▼ ▲ ▼

Tanna had her daughters watch for the others at the door, something Cassidy and Susan were quite happy to do, while she set the dinner table and baked/reheated her mother's intricate Christmas food dishes. She had rushed through the deliveries to the shut-ins, feeling pressure to be the first back. Even in their reluctant hurry, the girls delivered the meals with enthusiasm and had impulsively serenaded the old folks with carols, which inevitably turned into a singalong.

Preparing to host the Required Christmas Gathering had felt like cramming for a final exam. No—more like preparing for battle. She had spent weeks agonizing over every detail. Her friend Denise was invaluable with the massive food prep at the last minute when Tanna had realized she'd misjudged her timing; Tanna could never have done it alone. It didn't help that she'd only managed to get Christmas Day off and had to work the two days prior, twelve hours each. Worse yet was the anticipation of all of them spending real time together! Yet even with the pressure of it, there was something comforting in having all the over-specific Requirements; that way she could make everything be just the way her mother wanted. Then the urn showed up, and she felt sure that she was getting it right.

At least until Dawn brought Cleah's Christmas surprises.

She couldn't fathom what running a relay would entail. She tried to work out in her head whether she or Joe would have the girls that weekend in August, and if it was her weekend with them, how could she get Joe to switch with her? And how would she find time to train? She was already too busy being a single mom with a full-time job. That *Who's Sorry Now* song felt like a face slap—as though her mother was giving her a fat told-you-so regarding her choices in men. She had chosen shitty men—maybe all men are shitty—but she didn't need her mom to tell her that. And the furs! Was that just what it seemed: a gift? At first she thought she was meant to wear it to the food kitchen, but since Elise didn't wear hers, she didn't either. And what about the envelope of letters? She hadn't looked through it yet. Were they old letters? Or recent ones from Cleah? She had felt so in control this morning! And now—

Now she needed to concentrate on making sure the day's activities went as planned.

And that everyone stayed civil and played nice.

"They're here!" chorused Cassidy and Susan from the living room. Tanna hurried to put in a CD of acoustic guitar playing holiday classics on repeat.

Somehow the two families arrived almost simultaneously. It was a slow process coming back in and removing coats, Cassidy and Susan again shuttling armloads to lay on Tanna's bed. The girls clearly loved to play host. The chitchat was superficial and light as they all worked their way to the dining room table, mostly exclaiming over the houses the kids had decorated, lined up in rows on a card table in the corner like festive prison barracks. Finally everyone found their seats per the name on the place cards.

"There wasn't room for the food on the table, so it's just over here on the counter. We can serve ourselves buffet style," Tanna said, picking up Susan's plate. She willed herself not to be flustered. A bar counter separated the open kitchen from the dining room, and it was covered with elaborate dishes. On the table there was so much dishware, to accommodate the soups and salads and all, it was hard to tell which was whose water glass or wine glass or soup bowl. There was barely room in the center for the urn and the Cleah Candle, still lit, which Tanna had placed between two baskets of bread rolls. She had really done her best with everything and was feeling shyly proud of herself. "One soup is leek and the other is pumpkin carrot." The adults let the kids go through the line first, Tanna helping Susan. It took a long time, with the second trips for soup.

Cassidy had designed the seating arrangement; Tanna wished she had overseen that piece of the planning. She was seated at the head of the table, with Susan on her right and Beth on her left. Cassidy had put all the boys on one end around Kevin at the foot. Tightly packed on one side was Beth, Cassidy, Mirabelle, and Jeff—though the sides were really only long enough for three. On the other side was Caleb, Elise, Daphne, and Susan. At least it wasn't Cleah controlling where they sat. The table was largely silent as they ate. Several got up for seconds, Tanna was pleased to note.

"I guess I remember Mom serving these particular dishes at Christmas, but never all in the same year. The food is good, Tanna. Love the roast beef and the butter-sauce parsnips. The potatoes are a little bland," Elise remarked, as folks were slowing down. The kids were clearly done and looked bored, except for Susan who picked at her plate like she always did: slow but interested.

"There's dessert," Tanna offered.

Kevin stretched and moaned, like he'd done as a kid when he was too full. "How about we open presents first."

The group agreed and moved to the living room, with much shuffling and scuffing of chairs. They brought their wine glasses. Tanna was not used to having this much company. She started clearing the table, but Elise stopped her with the admonishment, "Later."

The kids looked pretty excited, sitting close around the tree. Elise said, "It was always the youngest who got to distribute the gifts when we were growing up. Susan? Are you up for it?"

"You have to keep it fair, don't give too many to the same person in a row," Cassidy coached, clearly jealous of her sister's honor. Susan picked up a small bright package and stared at the tag until Daphne leaned in to look, then softly whispered "to Caleb, from Uncle Kevin and Aunt Mirabelle" in her ear.

Daphne pointed discreetly at Caleb. Susan excitedly presented the gift to him. Tanna smiled.

Though the Whole Foods gift card from Kevin and Mirabelle was great—practical, albeit impersonal—Tanna especially liked the journal from Elise. It was pink with a yellow and orange marbling. She had spent her high school years filling up blank books with teenage dreams, ideas, and doodles, although Elise couldn't have known that; she had gone off to college when Tanna was fourteen and never lived at home again, in fact rarely came to visit.

When Kevin opened the pair of personalized "Lucky Brew" beer glasses that Tanna and the girls had ordered special, Tanna held her breath. "Oh yeah! Nice!" he exclaimed and even Mirabelle's smile seemed genuine, making Susan and Cassidy clap and giggle. Then Elise and Jeff unwrapped the wine glasses that read "Cheers Rodgers," they too appeared pleased, to Tanna's quiet satisfaction.

It went on like this, Daphne gently assisting Susan, until all the gifts were received. It was nice. The whole day, in fact, had been surprisingly civil. So civil, it made Tanna worry.

She checked her watch. "So, let me start re-steaming the pudding. And then shall we watch *It's a Wonderful Life*?"

▼ ▲ ▼

Elise had done her best to ignore the urn throughout dinner. The wine helped. Although annoyed that Tanna had put Mirabelle next to Jeff and across from Elise, it turned out bearable, as Jeff talked only to Kevin the whole meal. The food really was tasty; Tanna had outdone herself—inflating expectations, Elise thought with exasperation. But then she remembered that Kevin was to host next, and she figured he would be an easy act to follow.

She relaxed into the gift exchange and was pleasantly surprised at receiving the personalized stemless wine glasses, very classy, and the Whole Foods gift card, although it wasn't where she usually shopped. Kevin didn't seem to like the journal, no surprise there, but Tanna acted happy about hers. And the girls were thrilled with their stuffies. Tanna's living room was a little too cozy for ten people to watch movies in: Elise and Jeff sat on the couch with Tanna, Susan in her lap. Kevin and Mirabelle took the loveseat. Caleb sat in the chair while Cassidy, Beth, and Daphne sprawled on big throw pillows on the floor by the tree, which stayed lit throughout. The three youngest fell asleep.

They finished off two bottles of wine during the movie. When it ended, with James Stewart and Donna Reed smiling at each other while the bell on the tree rang, Tanna rushed out of the room, returning with a bottle of peppermint Schnapps and a grimace.

"I was gonna bring everything for the hot chocolate toast in here, but if we could just do it in the dining room, that would be a lot easier. I think it's the last Requirement that involves the kids, and my girls really ought to get to bed soon," Tanna bossed, rousing her daughters.

"Yeah, sure," said Jeff, getting up to turn off the TV.

Their used dishes were where they'd left them.

"You can stack this stuff in the sink," Tanna ordered.

"I'm having deja vu from the soup kitchen," Mirabelle mumbled under her breath.

Tanna set a crockpot of hot chocolate with a ladle onto the table, without bothering to wipe the table off, and brought out ten blue mugs and a bag of mini marshmallows. The urn was still there, of course. Poor Mom had missed the movie, Elise thought snidely.

It took a bit to assemble, Tanna slow with her torturous perfectionism. Finally, they lifted their mugs and looked around at each other, waiting for someone else to toast.

Eventually, Jeff spoke up, raising his mug to the urn. "Okay, uh, to Cleah Lucky! Because . . . it's a wonderful life!" Elise groaned, but surely it was enough to satisfy that Requirement of toasting the urn, and they got down to drinking. It was overly sweetened.

"I hadn't seen that movie in ages," said Jeff.

"Me either," Elise said, reflecting. She'd always liked the Frank Capra classic, although figured it might be spoiled for her, now that it was all about how meaningful her mother's life had been. Was that the message Mom was trying to give them? Was Cleah supposed to be the George Bailey character, unhappily tied down by kids she hadn't wanted, but saving the town in the end? Wasn't Mom really more of a Mr. Potter, selfish and mean? Such a great movie, albeit mawkish and preachy. Elise kept sipping, now on her second mugful. She couldn't help but feel the contrast between receiving the furs and helping at the soup kitchen. It had been a long and confusing day. Some of it good, surprisingly.

Kevin said quietly, "That movie makes me think of Dad."

"Let's have dessert with our drinks," Tanna said, cutting him off. Rude. Controlling. Passive-aggressive. She set down her mug and brought out a stack of small plates and forks to the table. This she followed with the British Christmas pudding, the strawberry rhubarb pie, and the sweet potato pie. She also put eggnog and wine on the table. Elise was increasingly perturbed by the array of choices, though she couldn't say why.

"I helped make it!" Cassidy said excitedly as Tanna poured brandy over the pudding and Jeff started singing *Now bring us a figgy pudding*, the kids joining in. Tanna took a lighter and, with great concentration and several tries, lit the pudding. There were gapes and aahs.

"There you go, Tanna. And you were so worried," Elise said, feeling resentful and jumpy as she topped off her hot chocolate with more Schnapps. No mini marshmallows this time.

"Hey, it's like the fruitcake we had at Santa's Cake Walk," Daphne said, chewing.

"But that one wasn't on fire," Caleb noted. Elise cringed.

▼ ▲ ▼

Kevin had never liked British pudding much, meaty with nuts and dried fruits, and heavy with spices and gin. But he hadn't had it in probably twenty years and this stuff wasn't as bad as he remembered. The kids mostly stuck with pie. Tanna took her little girls and put them to bed, then asked Elise if her kids would want to watch *Elf* while the adults decorated their gingerbread houses—the last unfinished Will Requirement. Mirabelle switched back to wine as Elise and Jeff put the undecorated houses onto the table and set to work.

To Kevin, Tanna's place bordered on claustrophobic, it was so crowded and tight. It must've been two bedrooms, three if they were small. The refrigerator was covered with kid art and school photos. There were kid things everywhere: crayons on desks, stacks of children's picture books, a dollhouse in the corner. Kevin gulped some wine and could hear the movie start playing in the other room as he picked up a sleeve of icing. He squeezed a white line across the ridge of the roof. A bit wobbly. Maybe he was a little drunk. Maybe more than a little. Going with the flow. As he pressed M&Ms into the line of icing, Tanna returned with the manila envelopes from the lawyer, dropping them on the table with a smack.

"Those're our family Christmas letters, that Dad wrote and sent out every year," Elise said too loudly, pouring more Schnapps into her hot chocolate mug.

"I forgot they sent those out," said Kevin, pulling the stack of papers from one envelope. He skimmed through. They were photocopies, the oldest from 1972 announced Elise's birth; Kevin didn't show up in them until 1977. The earlier years were handwritten, later ones typed, finally laser-printed. They were somewhat superficial, just reporting on activities the kids were involved in and trips they'd taken during that year. They were always so polished and positive; it made their family look idyllic. There wasn't one every year, but each one was signed *Howard and Cleah Lucky* in his dad's handwriting.

"Listen to this: 'This summer the Lucky family took a lucky road trip to the Grand Canyon, camping at the south rim. The weather was perfect, as were the views.' 1984. I remember that trip." KevIn's jaw clenched.

"I remember you two complaining all through every hike," Elise slurred. "And Mom and Dad fighting, especially in the car."

"Mom hated camping," Tanna added. "I'll bet she never went camping again."

The last one was for the year 1997, the year Kevin had dropped out of college. No mention of that, of course. It was the last Christmas letter because his father had died the following spring.

"You know, I'm proud of us, really," Tanna, her voice petulant and judgy. "Today's been so . . . calm."

"You are so passive-aggressive!" Elise shrilled, out of nowhere. "Can you *stop* being so mad about your wedding? I'm sorry if things got out of hand, but it was seven years ago, for god's sake! Get over it! You're not even still married to the guy!"

"Oh my god, I didn't say anything!"

Kevin was confused and irritated. "At least we all came to *your* wedding," he said to Tanna before he could think.

"I wish you hadn't!" Tanna scoffed.

A dam had burst. So Kevin continued, "Only Elise came to ours, although you brought your bad attitude."

"As if you noticed," Elise threw back at him.

Tanna huffed at Kevin. "You know that I was taking care of two little babies on my own when you got married! It's not like I just didn't come, not like Mom! What is your problem?"

"You both were the problem! Dad died just after you got divorced, the *first* time," Elise pointed at Tanna, "and you'd flunked out of college." She pointed at Kevin.

Tanna shook her head. "Well, it didn't help that you kept borrowing money from them, Elise!"

"You were *all* too much for Dad's heart!" Kevin shouted, hopping to his feet. "You two with your backstabbing bickering, and Mom with her cheating!"

They had never acknowledged Mom's affair aloud to each other before. What was he thinking? Everyone seemed shocked into silence—a silence that howled in Kevin's ears with the thrum of his fast-beating heart. He became aware of Beth standing in the hallway, watching them. He had to get out of there.

Jeff stood. "Look, we've all had a lot to drink. Things are getting said that aren't meant," he said, reaching out his hand in an everybody-calm-the-fuck-down gesture.

Everyone's cell phones chimed or vibrated, disjointedly. They glared at each other a little longer, then got out their phones. Dawn had sent a group text of the cheerful family photo she had taken before she'd left that morning. Kevin stared at it. It was a lifetime ago. They'd come so close to making it through the day . . .

"I think the houses are decorated enough," Mirabelle purred. "Shall we call it a night?"

9

"Hey, are you all right? You seem kinda spacey," Georgia observed, holding open the door that she'd just gone through. Tanna, sporting her puffy orange coat over blue nursing scrubs, looked over and smiled as she followed Georgia into the parking garage.

"Spacey? I'm just tired, I guess." Tanna was exhausted. She'd had to work the two days after Christmas and then spent yesterday putting the house back in order (thank god the dialysis center was closed on Sundays), not to mention the twelve-hour shift she just finished.

"When do you work next, Tanna?" asked Georgia, pulling her long brown hair out of its ponytail.

"Saturday." Tanna usually worked Tuesdays, Wednesdays, and Thursdays, but the holidays had temporarily upended that schedule. She resented not having her girls with her, now that she would have a real day off, but maybe it was just as well; she could seriously use the rest. She'd been so distracted and busy before Christmas, with all the laborious preparing. Then Joe had picked up Susan and Cassidy that Friday night for a solid five days of the winter break. At least she didn't need childcare while he had them. Tanna was looking forward to the holidays being over and getting back into the routine of school and work, and of Joe having the girls only every other weekend and on Wednesday nights.

"Nice! You have the whole holiday off! I work again on Thursday, so no being out all night on New Year's Eve for me." Georgia sighed.

"That's a bummer." Tanna had no plans to stay up and ring in the New Year but was not about to suggest swapping shifts. Joe was bringing the girls back on Wednesday.

The women wished each other Happy New Year and climbed into their cars. Tanna maneuvered her Ford Fiesta out of the tight garage, into the dark rainy streets, and headed home. Traffic wasn't bad on this Tuesday evening.

The empty house was so still. With the Pandora app on her phone, Tanna chose a Brandi Carlile mix and Bluetoothed the music loud through a set of speakers in the living room and dining room. She peeked into the bedroom that the girls shared, missing her daughters. Singing along to *Wherever is Your Heart*, she fed the guinea pigs in the girls' playroom and refilled the cat's dish in the kitchen. She filled a little bowl with leftover carrot pumpkin soup for herself and heated it in the microwave. After pouring a glass of water, she turned the music volume to low.

"Hello, Mom. Mind if I join you?" The urn was on the dining room table where it had been since Christmas Day. Not waiting for an answer, she sat down, stirred the soup, dipped out a spoonful, and blew on it. Brandi started singing *Raise Hell*, as Tanna slurped the savory henna-colored liquid, eyeing the urn.

"What? Am I eating too loudly?" Tanna took a drink of her water, set the glass down, and picked up her spoon again. While stealing glances at the porcelain urn, she ate her dinner. The icy rain fell steadily outside.

"Since you're going to be staying with us for a while, I want to lay out the ground rules," she said evenly, pointing her spoon at the urn.

"This is *my* house. There'll be no special treatment—no different from any other pot here. I'll respect your space if you respect mine." She scraped soup from the sides of the bowl, deciding what else she wanted to say. She was aware of how ridiculous this was, but it felt good. Boundaries. Once the soup was finished, she gave the urn her full attention.

"No mind games and no guilt trips, and I'll go along with your Bequest Requirements. I'll do my part, as your daughter." She exhaled sharply and leaned forward, "But absolutely no messing with how I parent my kids. No criticizing, no undermining! I'm not going to treat them the way you treated me!" Tanna glared at the urn for emphasis. She leaned back in her chair, smiled, and said, "Okay. Good talk." Satisfied, she left the table, putting her bowl in the dishwasher before leaving the room.

▼ ▲ ▼

Joe was late dropping off Cassidy and Susan, and the girls were tired and snarly and hungry, like they always were after they stayed with their dad. All they wanted to do was watch TV. It took so much energy to re-establish their routine of dinner and baths and nighttime storybooks. It was way past their 8:30 bedtime before Tanna got them settled. But they fell asleep pretty quickly, being so overtired. Tanna slipped into comfy fleece jammies and curled up on the denim couch with a plate of Christmas leftover dessert and a glass of wine, flipping through channels. It didn't take long before she was pretty much done eating, sick of figgy pudding for the fourth day in a row. Her cell phone rang.

"Hi Denise, welcome back! How was it?"

"Sun Valley was great! Lots of skiing. How about your family deal?"

"Let's just say it was your classic dysfunctional family disaster: bearably tense until the ugly shouting fight after dessert. But I gotta admit, those holiday sweaters did make for a festive photo," Tanna snarked.

"Oh, honey. I'm sorry." Denise had been Tanna's closest friend and confidant since moving to the neighborhood after she and Joe divorced.

"It's just what happens, eventually, when we all get together, I guess. Hey, thanks so much for helping with the food! Not everyone is lucky enough to have a chef for a best friend."

"Of course! So how did the girls handle the fighting?"

"They were already in bed." Tanna clicked off the TV, and the room quieted into the cozy dark of a winter night. She set the plate on the coffee table. "It was really just the last few minutes at the end of the night. I don't think the girls woke up."

"Well that's good."

A little black cat wrapped herself around Tanna's leg, looked up, and meowed dramatically. "There you are, baby!" she cooed, petting her.

"Oh, do you need to go?" Denise's voice said through the phone.

"No, it's just Poppy. I think having so many people in the house, especially with the yelling finale, was super traumatizing for her. She went into hiding. I've hardly seen her since Christmas. Poor honey." Tanna scratched Poppy's chin.

"So what was the fighting about? What happened?"

Tanna sighed. "It was a series of escalating accusations, like who's holding grudges and who was most responsible for my dad's death."

"Oh my god, honey! How'd he die?"

"It was his heart, we think. I was twenty-two. It was just a really stressful time, like life gets. Kevin and Elise will tell you it was my fault because of my divorce, which was pretty ugly I'll admit. But everyone was screwing up their lives—and each other's. Kevin was partying and getting into all kinds of trouble. Elise and her husband, Jeff, were struggling to keep it together. They all went out of their way to dump their problems on Mom and Dad. Mom, of course, wouldn't help anyone with anything, so Dad would sneak help, like money to Elise, and I know it was killing him that Kevin dropped out of college." Tanna fell silent. She didn't want to talk about Cleah's affair. Not yet. Maybe not ever.

Denise said, "That sounds really hard."

"Yeah." She put her feet up on the coffee table. Poppy hopped onto the couch next to her and curled into a ball.

"But them blaming you, that's messed up. I mean, you can't really feel responsible, right?"

Tanna shifted uncomfortably. "Yeah. I know that, but I don't. Know what I mean?"

"Sure. Like your head knows but it forgot to tell your heart," Denise said.

"Something like that. I mean, you don't know my family."

"So if you were twenty-two, that must not have been Joe you'd just divorced, right? I didn't know you were married before him. What's the story there?"

"Yeah. Alex—he was my high school sweetheart. We eloped a few months after we graduated, like idiots. It was nothing but rocky for the nearly two years it lasted. Thank god we didn't have kids. I moved home after we ended things, but I couldn't stand living with my mom again. I mean, god, twenty and divorced! Plus, I didn't want to be a burden. So I moved in with a girlfriend. I was waitressing. That's when I started nursing school."

"Oh, okay," said Denise. "That's cool, Tan; you totally rebuilt your life. Good for you!"

"I mean, my dad died like a year and a half *after* my divorce! It wasn't *me* stressing him out," Tanna said. To the left of her stockinged feet, the blue hat box still sat on the coffee table, where it had been since it arrived days before. She tapped it with her toe.

"Totally! He was probably so relieved when you got rid of that guy," Denise said.

"Exactly! But it's been shitty with my family ever since, like, it's just hard, you know? I started dating Joe pretty soon after Dad died. I knew him from work, and he'd been pursuing me for a while. He was less of a dick then. Even so, it was never quite right—on again, off again. But eventually, we got married. I mean, we'd been dating for eight years! My family shows up—I didn't want them to come, but I figured you have to invite family to your wedding. It goes okay until the reception, and then it turns into a Springer episode. Everyone's drinking and getting loud and then my mom, well, Kevin starts telling her off for flirting with Joe's dad. I mean, I don't even know if she was or not, but then Mom gets mad and calls Kevin's date a hussy and accuses *Elise* of flirting with *Joe*! So Elise starts yelling at Mom while Jeff is trying to calm her down, and then Elise starts telling me how *Joe* is the asshole flirt, and I mean—oh my god, they ruined my wedding, and I guess I had a little tantrum. It was so stupid."

"No way! Wow. I can't fathom."

"Yeah, well. It was pretty unbelievable. I mean, could you blame me for holding a grudge?"

Denise was quiet for a beat, before saying, "You know, Tan, it actually sounds like you all have made progress."

"What?" Tanna was incredulous.

"I mean, at least at Christmas you guys weren't inventing new reasons to be mad at each other, no name-calling or accusations of flirting and whatnot. I mean it almost sounds like you had a pretty frank and honest exchange—going back to the root of the angst, you know? Each of you wanting to blame someone for your dad's death."

Tanna thought about it. "Well hell, D, you have a crazy way of looking at things."

"Well, what do I know." The conversation lulled, and Denise continued, "Hey, I say forget nightmare relatives. Come out with me tonight! It's New Year's Eve! You have to!"

"It's almost 10 p.m.!"

"No problem! We're not leaving until 10:30, and you know New Year's Eve parties don't really get going until 11," Denise coaxed, in her most cajoling voice.

"The girls are already in bed." Tanna held the phone with her shoulder as she pulled the lid off the hat box. She stroked the silver muff inside.

"Just bring them over here! I've got beds. You can share my babysitter."

Tanna didn't want to go out for New Year's Eve, especially not as a third wheel with Denise and her husband, Paul. "Thanks, D, but I'm beat. I just want a quiet night at home; that sounds like heaven to me." She stared into the hat box.

"Okay. I'll come over on Friday then. Jakob misses the girls. They can have a playdate while we drink moderately."

"Sounds good," Tanna laughed. "Oh, but Joe picks them up Friday! It's his weekend. Can you do tomorrow?"

"Oh geez, Tanna, it's New Year's Day tomorrow . . ."

"Oh. Yeah." She pulled out the cylindrical muff with one hand and rubbed it against her cheek. She set it on her lap and put her hand inside. It was lined with satin. The cat roused and smelled at the fur. She leaped off the couch and slunk away.

"Tomorrow is good," Denise compromised. "I'll wake up eventually."

"Great! Hey by the way, I have tons of leftovers still. Everyone left so abruptly, I didn't have a chance to send food with them, though I probably wouldn't have wanted to, I was so mad. You want some pie at least?"

"Sure, I'll help you with leftovers!"

"Any time after 9 tomorrow; give me a ring and come over."

"Yeah, unless you want just Paul and Jakob over, it won't be before noon, honey."

Tanna laughed. "Okay. Have fun tonight." She put the phone down and sat in the quiet dark, running her fingers through the fine sleek fur. Closing her eyes, she tried to recall her mother's parents. Had she ever met them? She thought perhaps not, but she did have a vague memory of a framed photo from a black-and-white era beside her mother's bed, of a young, serious couple that must have been Elizabeth and Jasper. Elizabeth's silver fox fur was so silky, so soft. Sleepy and mesmerized, Tanna's mind drifted.

One summer, she'd returned from band camp to find her mother had culled through her clothes, tossing at least a third. Even things she hadn't outgrown, including her favorite sweater. She'd been heartbroken. After she'd eloped with Alex, Tanna retrieved all her belongings from her parents' house—things she hadn't needed when she'd moved out. Her mother had gotten rid of her letterman jacket, probably sold it. Her band letter was there; her mother had cut it off. Cleah was anything but a pack rat. Yet she'd kept these things of her parents all these years.

Putting the muff back into its box, Tanna noticed the pink-marbled journal Elise had given her. She picked it up, thumbing through the blank lined pages, and decided to write in it daily—a New Year's Resolution. She also resolved to put the hat box with its fur away in the closet tomorrow. Carrying the journal with her, she brought her plate into the kitchen, her footfalls the only sound. The urn sat alone on the dining room table. Yawning, Tanna set her plate on the counter and looked at her watch. She must've dozed; it was past midnight.

"Happy New Year, Mom," she said over her shoulder, heading to bed.

10

"Mommy, push me!" Susan squealed, clutching the swing's chain with mittened hands. It was a sunny-cold January day, the Monday back from winter break, and Tanna had brought Susan and Cassidy to a nearby city park after school, along with several other moms.

"Coming honey!" she called from beside the tree she had walked over to for a private conversation. She glared at her phone in frustration, Joe having abruptly hung up on her. He had called in response to an email she'd sent last night.

"MOMmmuh!" Susan whined, kicking her legs ineffectively.

"You've gotta lean, honey. Watch your sister," Tanna said as she pushed her youngest daughter. After getting her swinging high, Tanna returned to the park benches with the other moms.

"God! Ex-husbands," Tanna moaned, finding a place on the end next to Kim.

"Oh no, what?" Kim said with anticipatory sympathy.

"He . . ." Tanna sighed. "He called to tell me he doesn't like the phrase 'on the same page' and that I'm to avoid saying it. I mean, it's only my whole point! It would be good if we were on the same page about the kids, had some consistency with routines and rules and consequences, you know?"

The women laughed, groaned, and nodded knowingly, watching their kids climb on the red plastic dome.

"Men. They get so easily distracted from the big picture," Angela said.

"He just doesn't like what I'm saying so he's picking a fight. It's intentional. He's a dick." Tanna leaned back on the bench and crossed her arms, legs stretched out. Joyful kid-screams filled the air as a game of chase began.

"Tell him you just want to be in the same ballpark," Denise smirked.

Tanna laughed. "Yeah, I'll just find another way to say it." She thought a minute. "I just want us to be walking the same dog."

"Just trying to be in the same solar system," Helen offered, chuckling.

"Eating the same pizza," Denise said.

"Running in the same race," Kim added.

"Maybe better to be running on the same team," Denise suggested. "Let's not make it a competition!" They all laughed.

"Oh, it's so exhausting. It's like he's my third child," Tanna sighed. She wondered if her parents had been on the same page. No, probably not.

"I don't know. At least he wants to be part of things," Helen mused.

Tanna rolled her eyes.

The kids were red-cheeked and plump in their poofy winter jackets, topped with colorful knit hats. Running on short kid-legs, they puffed out white breaths while Tanna was feeling chilled. She pulled her scarf tighter around her neck and pushed away her irritation with Joe. Tomorrow she would start her grueling three-day work week. It was nice to let the hard-playing kid-laughter and the mom-camaraderie flow over her and just enjoy the moment.

That night, she wrote in her journal:

climbing the same tree, chanting the same mantra, using the same potting soil, ordering off the same menu, drinking the same kind of beer, walking on the same beach, laughing at the same jokes, washing the same car, skating on the same frozen pond, sneezing in the same direction, eating the same beets, having the same mood swings, yodeling from the same mountaintop, cleaning out the same drain, sleeping in the same library, buying the same toothpaste, climbing on the same climbing wall, running with the same scissors, burning the same bridges, talking to the same urn

She crossed the last one out.

▼ ▲ ▼

Tanna stepped briskly into the elementary school office and asked to see Principal Stone. She swallowed, trying to settle the fluttering moths in her chest; Cassidy had never been in trouble at school before.

The kids had been back in school after winter break for almost two weeks. Tanna had gotten Principal Stone's voicemail after work on Wednesday, when the girls were at Joe's house, asking for her to come in. On Thursday during a break at work, she'd called the school back, arranging to come in on Friday at 10:00 a.m. That Thursday night, after reading *Sleepy Bears* to the girls, Tanna asked Cassidy what the principal might want to have a meeting about, but the five-year-old insisted she didn't have a clue. Now Tanna was in that tired-so-therefore-alert mental space after a night of waking every few hours to worry.

"You can go in now." Alice, the front office receptionist, led her to the principal's door.

"Thanks," she said as she walked into the room. He was sitting behind his wide messy desk. "Hi, Mr. Stone." Tanna extended a handshake.

"Thanks for coming in, Mrs. Hopkins." He rose and leaned forward, holding his tie against his chest with his left hand while shaking her hand with his right.

"Oh, call me Tanna."

"Sure, Tanna." He gestured toward the chair in front of his desk. "Do you know why I asked you to come in today?" Mr. Stone said as they both sat down.

"No idea. Neither did Cassidy," she smiled nervously. "Is there something wrong?"

"Well, it's common to be in touch with kindergarten parents. Those little guys are settling into school rules and appropriate school behavior, and we try to make sure to stay on top of anything, at the front end. But it is less common to call a parent in."

"Okay." This was not comforting. As Tanna waited for Mr. Stone to elaborate, the door opened and in came Ms. Holloway, the quintessential picture of a kindergarten teacher, with her chubby smiley face and her short stature. She gave a little wave, which Tanna returned. She only knew Cassidy's teacher a bit, since most days Cassidy rode the bus to and from school, home, and daycare. Tanna would drop off on the occasional Monday morning, but Cassidy liked to ride the big-kid school bus.

"Hi, Tanna! I just have a few minutes, the kids are at recess, so I'll be brief. Cassidy has been having an excellent year: no problems, beyond spilling water that she pours into her cup at snack time." Ms. Holloway laughed. "However, recently I've noticed a trend that, frankly, is concerning."

"Why? What trend?"

"Cassidy is not eating lunch."

Tanna was confused. "But her lunch box comes home empty every day." She wondered in dismay about the early Tuesdays and Wednesdays when she would drop the kids at

Denise's house at 5:15 on her way to work, and the Thursday mornings that Joe was responsible for packing the girls' lunches.

"Yes, she does bring food. Cassidy actually seems to be bringing in more than normal, lately. But she gives it away, to the other kids. All of it."

"She doesn't eat any of it?"

"No," Ms. Holloway said. "It's the same at snack time. I asked her about it, and she agreed to eat some, but then she gave her snack to the kid beside her. I had her talk to Mr. Stone, but I don't know. I'm worried she's on track to developing an eating disorder."

Principal Stone broke in. "Cassidy was quite jovial when I talked with her. She said it was her grandma's idea."

"Oh." Tanna was taken off guard and suppressed a chortle. "Interesting. Okay. She does eat just fine at home." Sharing food seemed a trivial thing to have to speak in-person with the principal about. Tanna couldn't help feeling a little sour about her morning being disrupted. She was always so tired after her brutally long workdays, so badly needing to recover. And not to minimize eating disorders, but she really didn't think that was the issue with Cassidy.

Still, now she was worrying.

She checked her watch; Susan would be out of preschool at 11:30.

"We were hoping you could get Cassidy's grandma to talk with her. Make sure she isn't encouraging an unhealthy view of food," Mr. Stone said. "We don't want to see things go down a path of poor body image and low self-esteem. It's such a problem for young girls." Mr. Stone set folded hands on his desk and smiled patronizingly.

Tanna smiled faintly. "Yeah. I'll do that. Thanks so much for telling me."

▼ ▲ ▼

The friendly strains of Jack Johnson's *Curious George* songs floated through the house as Tanna finished cleaning up the dishes after dinner, the cat threading a figure eight through her legs. She had the washer and dryer going, clean clothes piled on the living room couch. Susan and Cassidy were noisily playing with the doll house in the corner of the dining room. The dolls were having a birthday party and being very silly.

"Come here, Mommy!" Susan pleaded. "It's time to blow out the candles!" Tanna started the dishwasher and went to help sing *Happy Birthday* to the little doll of honor. The birthday cake was a bottle cap. They all clapped as the doll blew out all the candles in one breath.

"Yay!" Tanna laughed, sitting on the floor. "Hey Cassidy-babe, come here a minute." She pulled Cassidy onto her lap as Susan made the dolls dance around the little doll table. Joe had dropped them off earlier than usual from their weekend with him, which was nice as it gave Tanna more time to get everyone into a night-before-school mode. It had been a lovely afternoon of bad-weather inside-playtime and catching up on laundry.

"I talked to your teacher a couple days ago. She told me how you've been giving away your lunch every day. What's that about, honey?" Tanna had watched Cassidy all through dinner; her daughter hadn't seemed to have an unhealthy relationship with food, no red flags.

Cassidy smiled. "I'm sharing. Like Grandma Cleah had us do with the Christmas meals!"

"Aah, right." Now Tanna understood. "Yeah, that was a fun time, delivering those meals."

"Yeah. It makes Grandma happy, and it makes people happy. So it makes me happy!" Cassidy leaned contentedly against her mother.

"It is really nice to share, honey, but you know Grandma Cleah wants you to have some lunch, too, right?"

Cassidy pondered. "Yeah. She does." She picked up her foot and cradled it in her arms. Tanna never ceased to marvel at how flexible kids are.

"Can Grandma Cleah's urn sleep in our room tonight? Please?" Susan suggested, trying to wiggle into Tanna's lap too.

"Yeah! Please, please, please?" Cassidy begged. Tanna smiled, hugging her girls to her and rocking them, watching the birthday celebration scene in the dollhouse.

"Hmm. You don't think Grandma Cleah is happy here on the table?"

"Sure. But then she's lonely when everyone goes to bed," Cassidy said, craning around to look up at her, Susan doing the same. The cat padded over to join the group on the floor.

Tanna looked at her girls' sincere faces. "Lonely? Why do you think that?"

Susan looked at Cassidy, then explained, "Caleb told us how nice Grandma Cleah is and how we can help her be happy. He said she's special, like a special baby doll."

"Please, Mommy? I won't give *all* of my lunch away. I'll eat some of it, too," Cassidy bargained.

Tanna kept her face neutral as she considered. On the one hand, she was recoiling and wanted to shut this weird friendship-with-the-urn thing down right now. But wouldn't it be worse to make a big deal out of this? The urn guardianship would only be until Easter. And strangely, Tanna could relate to the notion of wanting to see Cleah's final wishes met, the same underlying urge as when she was preparing the Christmas gathering.

"All right. Come on, I'll bet Grandma would like to hear me read *Goodnight Moon*," Tanna said, getting them all to their feet. The girls swayed and danced to Jack's *With My Own Two*

Hands in celebration. "But first, gotta put the clothes into the dryer and you girls are having your baths!" Picking up the urn, Tanna and two dancing girls left the dolls' birthday party to get ready for bed.

11

Tanna double-checked Mr. Kepler's blood pressure levels as he talked about his miniature railroad set. It had been a slowly expanding project that she'd heard about throughout the nine years she'd been overseeing Mr. Kepler's care. It was his favorite subject during the commercials of the afternoon soaps on TV that he always watched when he was in for his four-hour treatment, three days a week. Lately his attention was on a new trestle that he was building from scratch. The photos were amazing.

She looked over his charts. They showed his numbers had been a bit too high on Saturday when he was last in, a little concerning, and he was somewhat short of breath today—not too uncommon, really, but she wanted to keep an eye on him. She wasn't thrilled with the tech that was administering Mr. Kepler's dialysis treatment. Cody was young and new and not quite as careful as Tanna would prefer, but with five techs under her, all with four patients each, it was sometimes a juggle. Tanna had to trust her team.

"How is Dawson? Is he still doing Taekwondo?" she asked, referring to Mr. Kepler's eleven-year-old grandson.

He brightened. "He's testing for his green belt next week!"

She'd come to regard Mr. Kepler as a father-like figure over the years. Mr. Kepler was 73, the same age her dad would've been if he were alive. There were a lot of ways Mr. Kepler reminded her of her dad, too, like the way he winked at her in greeting, and how he would shrug and smile when he didn't know what to say. He gave great dad-advice—such as watching how a man treats his mother, because he will treat his partner the same way. It was something her father would have said.

"Wow, that's awesome! Tell him good luck for me!"

He turned back to his soap as she patted his shoulder and moved on to check another patient's vitals; Vivian appeared to have fallen asleep.

It was only just Tuesday afternoon, the first of her three consecutive days of twelve-hour shifts, but already Tanna was spent. The girls had been extra cranky getting up this morning; 5:00 a.m. is a truly ungodly hour, but they only have to move from bed to car to couch, the short distance to Denise's house. Cassidy would then catch the school bus to the grade school at 7:30 and Denise would drive Susan to preschool, along with her son Jakob. Tanna always sent their backpacks fully ready with school clothes and packed lunches, and on Mondays and Fridays she would take the preschoolers to and from school. Even so, Denise and Paul were absolute saints to take the girls so early two mornings a week. Tanna tried to make it as convenient and low-maintenance as possible for everyone. Oh, what a single mom has to do to make it all work! At least Joe had the kids Wednesday nights, so they were spared the early schedule on Thursdays.

Last Wednesday morning, as Cassidy had climbed into the car to drive over to Denise's house, she was suddenly wide awake and adamant that she bring Grandma Cleah's urn along, to spend the night at Daddy's with them. It was a ferocious 5 a.m. battle that Tanna ultimately won. There was no way she was going to let the urn go into Joe's house where she couldn't be sure it would come out in one piece.

Yesterday Tanna had made a point of picking Cassidy up from school so she could check in with Ms. Holloway about the lunch-eating status. While the kids romped on the grass, Ms. Holloway reported that although Cassidy still shared her food, she did now eat a fair enough portion herself. The teacher had assured Tanna she would continue to monitor closely—oh good, Tanna wanted to roll her eyes, but admittedly it was nice to have someone looking out for her daughter.

She continued her rounds of checking on the dialysis patients. The machines hummed and pumped as the soap stars on TV flirted, pleaded, and accused. The afternoon circled on in the busy routine of filtering people's blood, to live another day.

▼ ▲ ▼

February 7th was a Saturday. The girls had voted for Chinese takeout to celebrate Grandma Cleah's birthday. But now dinner was over, and Tanna was seriously worried. She hadn't received the Mother Letters from Elise or Kevin. She'd kept her eye on the mailbox all day and when the mail was delivered and still no Letters, she'd sent a frantic group text to let them know their Letters hadn't gotten there in time. She'd asked them to either drop something by or email a copy ASAP. Now she was thinking through the logistics of driving to each of their houses . . .

"I'll be right back, kiddos," she said, going to the laptop in the living room. She checked her email again—there was the letter from Elise! Tanna needed to read the Letters to her mother's urn before bedtime, since the girls still insisted on Grandma Cleah sleeping in their bedroom with them at night. Right now, the urn was hanging out on the dining table, where it spent its days. Tanna avoided looking at it as she walked back into the dining room where the girls were cracking open their fortune cookies.

"Want me to read your fortune cookie to you, Suz?" Tanna asked.

"Yes!" Susan thrust the tiny paper toward her mom.

Taking it, Tanna read, "You are a kind and generous person. Well, that's certainly true, although I'm not so sure it's a fortune." She handed it back to Susan.

"A fff-, frr-," Cassidy tried to sound it out. She held it out to her mom. "Now do mine!"

"Yeah, you were on the right track there, honey." She held it out and traced where she was reading with her finger. "It says: A fresh start will put you on your way."

Cassidy took the paper back and stared at it reverently.

"What about yours, Mommy?" Susan asked.

"Mine says: A beautiful, smart, and loving person will come into your life." She looked up and smiled at the girls. "Hmm, those are all good ones! Okay, bath time. Let's go."

"We have to sing the happy birthday song to Grandma Cleah first!" Susan said, clearly appalled at Tanna's oversight. So, the trio sang to the urn before eating the fortune cookies.

Bath time was always a loud and messy affair. It involved bubbles and a fleet of very active yellow ducks between the two girls in the tub. Tanna usually ended up wet up to her elbows and sometimes splashed all over. There were lots of singing and giggling. The kids continued playing in earnest as Tanna sat on the bathroom floor and texted Kevin to please send an email Letter. If she was going to have to drive to his house, at least he was in the same town—little kids fall asleep on long drives. She breathed in and smiled at her frolicsome daughters.

Tanna had finished writing out her own Letter the night before. Although she used the same stationary that she did with the first Letter, it felt different writing this one knowing that her siblings wouldn't be reading it. Even so, it hadn't been an easy thing to do.

After the girls were clean, dry, and in jammies, Tanna said, "How about a little bit of The Wiggles? We can watch fifteen minutes, but then we've got lots of books to read."

"Yaaay!" was the exuberant unison response as they ran to the living room. TV before bedtime was not the usual routine, but she figured she could get the two letters read and then figure out Kevin's. Tanna started up the DVD and checked her laptop again and, thank god! Kevin's email Letter was there! She carried the laptop to the dining room, plugged in, and set up on the table next to the urn.

"Okay, Mom. It's your birthday. You know what that means." She pulled her Letter out of the blue envelope and read, "Dear Mom, Happy Birthday. I'm trying to not let things get to me. I'm also trying to not be mean, but I miss Dad more than I miss you. Honesty is important—I tell my kids that, and I do believe it, too. Love, Tanna." She looked at the urn, almost waiting for a reply, then turned to the laptop. The goofy music on the TV floated down the hall.

"Next one: Dear Cleah Lucky, Happy Birthday, Mom. You would have been 67 years old. Now you'll never age—congrats. Thanks for the good long visit and all the Christmas fun. Please let Tanna know that I'm sorry about how it ended." Here Tanna paused a beat. "I've started going to therapy and I like it. We're doing much better. But enough about me, haha. Take care. —Elise"

She stared at Elise's email, rereading. Clearly Elise meant for her to hear her apology about Christmas. And therapy. If Elise wanted Tanna to be a little less mad at her, it was working.

Tanna clicked on Kevin's email and read, "Dear Mom, I'm mad at you for making us all fight with each other. Happy birthday anyway. Kevin"

Tanna thought about what Denise had said about the Christmas fight—how at least there weren't new personal attacks. It did seem like their anger with each other was borne out of caring, albeit twisted and hurtful. Kevin cared that Tanna had missed his wedding. They all were sad that Dad had died so young. It didn't sound like Elise or Kevin wanted to fight.

Tanna definitely didn't want to fight.

"Mom, we all blame you," Tanna said quietly. She didn't say that they were right to blame Cleah, but she was definitely thinking it. Tanna picked up her phone and called Denise.

"Hello?"

"Hey, D, are you up?"

"Duh." Denise laughed. "What's up, Tanna?"

"I'm worried about the Easter family gathering with my family. I just don't want it to end in a fight again. Do you think you could come with me? My brother's hosting it."

"Oh sorry, Tan, but we always spend Easter with Paul's sister. Can someone else go with you?"

Tanna thought. "I can't think of anyone. I will, though."

"It's a good idea, bringing someone. Nothing like a guest to make everyone behave."

"It's a long shot, I mean it didn't stop them at my wedding, but I'll try anything."

"Do," Denise said. "Hey, I have to go. Bedtime kisses."

"Sure. Thanks, D. Talk later." Tanna set her phone down, picked up an empty glass, and carried it to the sink. She stood there a minute, leaning against the counter and staring out the window into the descending dusk. Who in the world could she bring to Easter?

A bird darted at her, and she reflexively jerked her head back. It swooped back around, hovering, its black wings a blur. She realized it was a bat. They stared at each other through the pane.

"Maybe I bring you." The thought made her smile.

She went to watch the last few allotted minutes of The Wiggles with her girls.

▼ ▲ ▼

Tanna was halfway through a long drudging workday, where all the patients were in foul temperaments, when it finally occurred to her to invite her great aunt Audrey to the Easter gathering! It was a mood-changer; the day got easier. Checking her watch, she couldn't wait to reach out. On her next break she called the lawyer's office to see about contact information. Dawn answered and swiftly found a mailing address in Michigan that Tanna wrote out on a blank nursing-care-plan form, double checking with Dawn for accuracy.

That evening, after a quick stop at the grocery store because you have to fit it all in, she sped home and got out her stationary. It was Wednesday, the kids were staying the night at their dad's, so no distractions. Tanna sat at the dining table eating leftover pizza, staring at the blank blue paper. She was suddenly at a loss for what to say.

"She's your aunt, right Mom? Your father's younger sister? Do you think she'll want to come?" she asked the urn. After tapping on the table with her pen, Tanna wrote out her great-aunt's Michigan address on the envelope. She clicked the pen top, in and out, click, click, click. Sighing, she got up to do a loop around the house. Perhaps the guinea pigs would have a constructive suggestion, or at least provide more pleasant conversation. She put on a Lyle Lovett CD in the living room: Joshua Judges Ruth. Mmm, yeah, that got her shoulders shimmying, bit of gospel-country-ragtime piano. She folded a pile of little shirts that were waiting on the couch and carried them to the girls' bedroom, depositing them in drawers. On to the playroom. The piggies started squeaking the minute she entered. She'd forgotten to feed them when she got home, an error she quickly and contritely corrected.

"Sorry, Merv! Sorry, Anne Shirley!" The guinea pigs ate the timothy hay noisily. Anne Shirley, a rusty orange, tended to nose Merv out of the way. Merv, splotchy white and brown, compensated by drinking extra water. Tanna would need to replenish their bedding soon.

"Hey, guys. Wish you could help me out. I'm looking for the right words . . ." she said. She sat down at the Lego table, thinking, and procrastinating. The girls had been babies when they'd moved in, and she had put them in the same bedroom of the little three-bedroom ranch-style house. Tanna had recently suggested to the girls that they each could have their own room, but they had decided that a shared room dedicated to their toys would be much better. She looked over the pictures on the wall. It was certainly lively and colorful in here, jungle animals and rainbows and roly-poly children playing, whereas the girls' bedroom was more restful, mostly Winnie the Pooh and sleepy farm animals.

Poppy found Tanna at the Lego table doing nothing and she stepped onto Tanna's leg, purring loudly and squinting in anticipation of a petting. Instead, Tanna got to her feet, swept up Poppy, and returned to the dining table and to the unwritten letter. She set the cat down, picked up the pen, and wrote:

Dear Great-Aunt Audrey,

Perhaps you have heard about Cleah (Nicholson) Lucky's death, your niece. Please accept my condolences. I am Cleah's daughter, her middle child. I remember meeting you one summer when I was in grade school, maybe middle school. We stayed with you a few days at your house. I'm sorry to not be in touch much since then, but I wonder if we could make up for it now. Would you please come visit us over Easter weekend? It would really mean a lot.

I could pick you up from the airport and you could stay with us at my house. I'd even be happy to buy you a plane ticket. My two little girls would love to meet you, and I would really like to reconnect. Cassidy is five and Susan is four, and they're as sweet as can be. I hope you can come.

Awaiting your response,

Tanna Lucky Hopkins

She included her phone number and email address, found a stamp, and set the letter ready to go by the front door. Lyle was singing *Since the Last Time.* Easter wouldn't be so bad with a referee in attendance. Leaving her unwashed dishes on the counter by the sink, she went to bed smiling.

12

Turns out that to get anywhere, you have to start somewhere.

It was about a week after Cleah's birthday when Tanna got Dawn's letter, on law firm stationary, explaining the Hood to Coast legs. It was a little confusing and required rereading and study. The whole relay was 198 miles, split into thirty-six legs. So a full team had twelve runners, each doing three legs of the relay. What was confusing was that each runner was identified by the first of the three legs they would run. If you were leg one, you were responsible for legs one, thirteen, and twenty-five.

The runners rotated in and had to stay in the same sequence, Dawn explained. There were two vans with six runners each, that would leap-frog each other. Each of the thirty-six legs showed a distance, four to eight miles long, and were rated from easy to very hard. All the legs looked impossible to Tanna.

Dawn made it clear that Cleah's Bequest Directives did not require them to finish in a set period of time, only that they participate and finish, with limited exception for serious injury. They were to be in Van 2, and she would be the Van 2 captain (more power to her, as far as Tanna was concerned), so Dawn would be assigning each of them one of legs seven through twelve and was happy to consider any preferences. Tanna looked through the breakdown, trying to figure it out. Leg seven had the shortest total distance in Van 2, at 15.1 miles, but it consisted of two moderate legs and one very hard leg. Good god. Tanna needed to start training.

So, she was going for a walk.

"I ran cross country in high school. Well, okay, just my freshman year," Tanna told Denise that Monday, after dropping Susan and Jakob off at preschool. Their breath puffed out in white crystals that trailed behind them as they walked fast through the neighborhood near the preschool, block by block. At least there were sidewalks. It had been a while since Tanna had worn workout clothes. She had on several layers, topped with her orange puffy coat, the fringe of her hair barely poking out under her black fleece hat.

"We should've been doing this all along," Denise huffed, sporting a green hat that she had knitted herself. She'd had a late night at her restaurant and was being such a supportive friend.

"Yeah," Tanna agreed. "Gotta be able to outrun the zombies!"

"Exactly! Or at least be able to outrun someone else who can't outrun the zombies," Denise laughed. "Hey, slow down! Your legs are longer!"

Conversation lulled as they struggled to breathe. A car zoomed past.

"God, we're pathetic," Denise remarked.

Tanna snorted in agreement.

"How's that new kid doing at work? Getting any better?" Denise asked.

"Cody? Yeah, actually. Slow, but progress," Tanna said with shortness-of-breath effort. "At least he doesn't have an attitude. The patients like him."

"That's good."

Another conversation-standstill punctuated with huffing.

"What's the new special this week?" Tanna asked. Her fingers were getting numb.

"Gonna do a hearty lentil soup. Vegan. Coconut milk, curry, cilantro."

"Yum!" Tanna approved.

"So why just your freshman year?" Denise asked, breathing hard.

"What?"

"Cross country. You said you only ran the one year."

"Oh." Tanna panted. "It wasn't fun."

"Yeah, running sucks," Denise agreed. They crossed a street to start a loop back.

"No, the running with the team was fine." Tanna was pensive. She looked down at her feet, stepping quickly. "It was the racing. My mom came to every meet."

"But that's good, isn't it?"

Tanna scoffed. "No, she would harangue me during and after with her little criticisms. Nothing was good enough; she was only ever disappointed. Made it not worth it. Not fun. The coach finally banned her from coming to meets."

"Geez, Tan, I'm sorry," Denise said. "What about your dad?"

She paused, catching her breath. "He didn't come."

It started to mist-rain.

"Okay, that's it," Tanna said, feeling chilled from the damp sweat. "I'm cold. The coffee's on me." They beelined for the car.

▼ ▲ ▼

Tanna took Cassidy and Susan to the high school track that Saturday morning. The track was Mr. Kepler's idea. She didn't talk about the whole Will Requirement situation with him but did mention about the Hood to Coast relay at work. She'd been bemoaning her single-parent dilemma of how to train with the girls underfoot, and he suggested it as a way for her to run while they played on the grass in the middle. Brilliant!

It was March and thankfully not raining or windy, but it was still cold, so she'd dressed all of them in several layers and brought a blanket for the girls to wrap up in if they needed. She also brought a soccer ball and a Frisbee and a bag of stuffies. There were a few other people there at the track, a running pair and a power-walker, not too many. Leaving a water bottle with their pile, Tanna started out with a slow jog. At first the girls jogged with her but quickly lost interest. Tanna ran one embarrassingly slow lap before slowing to a walk and peeling off a layer of sweatshirt, tying it around her waist. She decided she would do intervals, one lap run, one lap walk, and see how long she lasted.

On her phone, she queued an upbeat playlist, using only one earbud so she could still hear, and stayed in the outermost lane, sticking to the intervals. A small group of teenagers showed up, apparently meeting for a workout with their coach. They stayed in the 100 meters next to the bleachers, back and forth, not going all the way around.

The girls were very involved in their play in the center field, with the blanket spread out and stuffies lined up. Tanna had done seven laps at this point. She did the calculation and was dismayed to realize that she'd only done one running-mile and three-quarters of a walking-mile. She was beat and glad to be starting a walking lap. She checked her watch; she hadn't timed her laps, but clearly her pace was slow. Putting her hands on her hips as she walked, Tanna shook her head. She was healthy and active; how was she this out of shape? The girls looked over and waved at her; she waved back, glad they were doing fine. Maybe she'd try to get to three miles total—another five laps, groan!

She was back around to the bleachers side again, where the teens were grouping at the start of their 100 meters. Just as

Tanna started a lap of running, a girl stepped backward into her lane, flinging her head back in a laugh. They collided and were both knocked to the ground.

"Oh," shrieked the girl, hopping to her feet. "I'm so sorry! Geez! I totally didn't see you!"

"It's okay," Tanna chuckled, surprised at finding herself sprawled on the black rubber track; she hadn't been running fast enough for such an impact. She was almost glad at the interruption to her run-lap. The girl helped her to her feet as the coach hurried over.

"Are you guys okay?" he asked, a timer hanging around his neck. He was cute.

"I totally didn't mean to run into her!" the teen girl told him, clearly mortified.

"I'm fine," Tanna said to them both. "It's okay. It was an accident." She glanced over at her daughters, who were engrossed in their game and apparently hadn't seen her fall.

"If you're not injured, go ahead and run your sprints, Shannon," the guy said. As the girl took off, he turned back to Tanna. "Sorry about that. Kids can be pretty unaware."

"No, don't worry. I'm fine," Tanna smiled. "Are you their coach?" An obvious, stupid question.

"Yeah, I'm Leif. I coach the distance kids on the track team here. We're doing some voluntary Saturday workouts, to take advantage of the space while the sprinters aren't here."

"Cool," Tanna nodded. Hmm, maybe she'll be running at the track every Saturday . . . Leif picked up her phone, which had dislodged, somehow, in the spill. The earbuds were a tangle.

"What are you listening to?" he asked, handing it to her.

"Oh, you'll laugh, but I find Dolly Parton quite motivational."

Leif did laugh. "Sure, I can see that; I like Dolly. Beck is good for distance. I also listen to a lot of Florence and the Machine when I run. *Dog Days* kills it."

"Yeah!" Tanna nodded, smiling.

"So, you sure you're not hurt?"

"Yeah, no, I'm fine," Tanna wondered how many times she had said 'fine'—she didn't want to sound too dumb. "Thanks."

"Okay, good." He was smiling, too. "I better get back. Maybe see you again, I hope?"

Heart fluttering, Tanna nodded.

He turned to rejoin his runners, then stopped and called back, "Hey what's your name?"

"I'm Tanna." She could tell she was beaming.

"Nice meeting you, Tanna." He gave a little wave and jogged back to his teens.

Deciding she'd had a good enough start to her training, Tanna returned to her girls to pack them up and take them home. She knew she'd be feeling that bruise on her hip the next morning. Worth it.

▼ ▲ ▼

I saw Leif again yesterday, at the track. After he was done coaching and I was done with my laps, he invited me to grab coffee with him! I was hoping, but didn't really expect it. Leif Turner. He's a draftsman, something with making CAD drawings for builders, so his time is flexible enough for him to coach, which is his real passion. He's never been married but has an 18-year-old daughter. Hmm...Didn't get too deep into that story, but he's helped raise her and sounds like he's friends with her mom. That's good. He's smart and kind and handsome and funny. And he has good taste in music! I like him.

Tanna was in bed, surrounded by blue and purple jewel-tone bedding, writing in her journal. She'd woken up early and made coffee, but didn't want to share this journal entry with her mother on the dining table. She was too happy about it.

She leaned back on her pillow, remembering the way he talked, how his eyes twinkled when he smiled. It was Joe's weekend to have the girls, which was convenient for a kid-less Saturday run at the track—and running into Leif again. (She 'happened' to time it perfectly.) They had talked about music over coffee; she shared an old live audio of Emmylou Harris's *One of These Days*, and he showed her a Foxy Shazam's *Unstoppable* music video on his phone. She told him she was training for the Hood to Coast—That her family had convinced her to be on a team with them. He said he had run the relay before, a couple of times, so offered to help her prepare. He recommended Mumford and Sons for her running playlist.

Up to this point, she'd been carefully trying to not feel one way or the other about having to run the relay, but now she was feeling strangely grateful. Grateful to her mother! What a completely odd, not to mention unwelcome, sensation. She closed the journal and set it on the bedside table. She hadn't kept her New Year's resolution of writing daily, but what the heck. She wrote when she felt like it. Today she had something she wanted to remember.

Her sore muscles groaned as she climbed out of bed: the good kind of sore. She grinned again, thinking of Leif in his running shorts. Just as she grabbed the granola from a kitchen cabinet, her cell phone rang. She glanced at the clock: 7:20 a.m. Who would be calling at this hour? She didn't recognize the number. Her first thought was her kids, an emergency.

"Hello?" Tanna said.

"Hello, darling. Yes, I'll come." The woman sounded old and abrupt.

"Come?" Tanna was confused. "Um, can I ask who's calling?"

"It's Audrey Nicholson, your great-aunt. You invited me for Easter, dear. I usually spend Easter at my daughter's house, but I'm intrigued."

"Oh yes! Hello, Audrey! I'm so glad you can come!"

"My plane arrives Friday, the 3rd, at 4:25 p.m. your time. Can you meet me?"

"Yes, absolutely! Great!" Tanna said.

"Okay then. I'll see you at Arrivals." The line went dead. Tanna set the phone down and clapped her hands. "Yes!" She went over to her mother's urn.

"Mom, your aunt said yes! She's coming with us to Easter lunch!"

Her excitement and relief turned suddenly to dread, and she dropped heavily into a chair. She really didn't know this woman at all; what if her house is too small or not clean enough, what if the kids annoy the woman? Was this a completely crazy plan?

She pushed the anxiety away; crazy might be entertaining. Whatever happens will happen, and it'll all be over eventually.

Tanna got back up and went to the fridge for some yogurt. She grabbed a banana and put together breakfast, bringing her bowl to the table. She queued up a Mumford and Sons playlist on Pandora. As she ate, she kept mulling, re-convincing herself it'd all be okay.

"Yeah, it'll be fine, Mom. I hope it's something you would've wanted, I mean, I don't know why you *wouldn't* want Audrey there." Tanna wondered how well her mother had known Audrey. Aside from that one visit in her childhood, she couldn't think of any other contact there was between them. Oh, but she couldn't stay worried; she was in too good a mood, still in the afterglow of yesterday's coffee date.

After eating breakfast, Tanna launched into some never-ending chores: feed the pets, do the dishes, laundry, clean the bathroom, vacuuming. Audrey wouldn't be there for two and a half weeks, but Tanna knew she'd feel better staying on top of things. She started planning out how to turn the playroom into a temporary guest room. Maybe move one of the twin beds in…

The morning passed quickly. Tanna started thinking out what to make for dinner, and if she'd need to run to the grocery store, when her phone chimed, a text from Denise: *Hey woman! What are we doing for your birthday on Thursday?* Tanna realized she'd not told Denise about having the sibling birthday dinner yet. She texted back: *Can't. Have to eat with E and K* puking-face-emoji. The phone rang.

"What?!" Denise demanded. "Do you mean Elise and Kevin? Is this another Will Requirement?"

"Hi, Denise. Yeah. But we could maybe go out after. Wanna do nightcaps at Vintage? I was gonna get a babysitter anyway that night, for while I'm at dinner."

"Absolutely yes! Hey, should we bring dates?" Denise's tone changed to coy. "I'm sure Paul would wanna party, and maybe Leif . . .?"

"Oh gosh, I don't know," Tanna balked. "I mean, for my birthday? I don't know him that well, I mean, Leif and I have only just gotten coffee. Once! I'm not sure that even counts as a date. A birthday date for a first real date—is that too much?"

Denise laughed. "You only live once. Why not? You were completely bubbling yesterday after seeing him. That's a good thing!"

"Hey, my great-aunt Audrey called me this morning. She's coming for Easter!"

"Excellent, Tan! That's perfect! But you're changing the subject . . ."

"I'll think about a birthday date, geez, I don't know, D." Tanna really wanted to invite Leif. "I have to digest it, get used to the idea. Walk tomorrow morning?" Tanna checked her watch, wondering when Joe would get the kids home; it was usually a little after lunchtime and they were usually starving, so probably soon.

"Heck yeah," Denise said. "I'll drive."

"No way! Mondays are *my* day to drive the kids to preschool!" Tanna said.

"Okay, fine, you drive," Denise laughed. "I gotta go—I'm heading to the restaurant. Love ya." Denise hung up.

13

"How's it going, with the urn?" Elise asked Tanna, looking at her sideways over her menu. Tanna scrunched her eyes, watching her. It seemed like Elise had either forgotten about the Christmas Day argument or was pretending she had. They were sitting at a small round table in the back, classic rock playing above the ambient sound of conversation. Tanna had chosen McMenamins Edgefield for her birthday dinner. She'd decided that if she was going to have to get a babysitter and go out and spend money, she might as well choose a place she'd been wanting to go. She just hoped her siblings wouldn't ruin it for her.

"It's fine," Tanna said, going with Elise's charade, contemplating how much she wanted to elaborate about the food-sharing and the urn-sleepovers. "I try to not think about it; it's just a jar to me. I can't let her invade my headspace. The kids are a little odd about it, though. Said Caleb said something to them at Christmas. Was there something I should know about?"

Kevin looked up from his menu.

"Caleb was afraid of the urn for a long time, but then he became protective, taking special care to make Cleah 'happy'," Elise said, dismissively. "All I know is, for me, having Mom's urn out of our house has been . . ." she paused, "a relief."

A server in a smart black apron set three waters on their table and said, “Can I get some drinks started for ya?” Elise ordered a Manhattan, Kevin an IPA, and Tanna got a nut brown ale. The server left and the conversation lagged.

“By the way, I invited Great-Aunt Audrey to come to Easter,” Tanna announced. She sipped her water, not sure what reaction she’d get. For a moment there was none.

“Wait, is that the old lady we visited on that road trip when we were kids?” Kevin squinted, as though he were trying to remember.

“She’s Grandpa’s sister,” Elise said. “We stayed with her a few days, the summer before I was in tenth grade, I think. She was odd.”

“Yeah,” Kevin recalled, “Didn’t she make big clown dolls? They were everywhere in her house. Holy shit, that was creepy. I remember being too scared to sleep.”

“Yeah, me too,” Elise nodded with a grimace.

“Right, well, I just thought . . .” Tanna bristled, questioning her stupid idea to bring Audrey into this. She’d forgotten about the dolls. “Well, she’s coming.”

“But is that okay with the Will Requirements?”

“She must be so old now! Mirabelle won’t like having extra people coming,” Kevin said.

They seemed to think it was up for discussion. “I think Mirabelle will be fine. She won’t have to change anything; the menu Mom planned out is plenty of food. The Will doesn’t say no guests. Audrey’s staying with me; just think of her as my ‘plus one’.”

“Here we are!” the server announced as she set their drinks in front of them. She stood poised to write. “Are you ready to order?”

▼ ▲ ▼

"Hey, did you guys ever see this?" Elise asked, bringing up a video on her phone while they waited for their food to come. Curious, Kevin leaned in as Elise played a Saturday Night Live spoof of an alternative ending for *It's a Wonderful Life*. While they watched, the audience laughter cued Elise's giggles. Kevin wasn't sure what to think as the SNL George Bailey beat up the SNL Mr. Potter.

"Hmm, that is pretty silly," Tanna said, her voice flat. "I hadn't seen that one before."

"Elise, that's just weird," Kevin had to say.

With a big exhale, Elise put her phone away. "Yeah, I know. I've re-watched that movie probably a dozen times since Christmas. I'm trying to figure Mom out. I know it sounds like obsession, but my therapist said to just go with it, see where it leads. And so: SNL!" Elise snorted and shrugged. It was so asinine that Kevin laughed.

"Oh, don't laugh, Kevin," Tanna admonished in her I'm-older-than-you way.

"No, I'm sorry," Kevin objected, still chuckling. "It's just funny that trying to understand why Mom made us watch that movie would lead to an SNL skit of George kicking the shit out of the crippled old man! I just don't know that that's what Mom was trying to say."

"I don't know, maybe," Elise said. "I could see Mom wanting the bad guy to get his karma in the end. She was always one for putting people in their place and making sure a person got what she thought should be coming."

"By 'people' you mean you," Kevin said to Elise, a little sassy. He stopped laughing and was thinking he could probably be nicer. He didn't want to get into an argument again. To change the subject, he said, "So, Elise, are you getting pretty busy with tax prep stuff yet?"

"Oh yes, this next month is the busiest. I probably won't sub much at all. You know, the line that's been sticking with me about that movie? It's the angel guy, Clarence, talking about how when a person is gone, they leave a hole. Something about each life touching a lot of other lives. He called it strange."

Kevin rolled his eyes; Elise would not be distracted away from the darn movie.

"I liked the part in the movie where the bartender was handing out wings by making his cash register ding over and over," Tanna said with a smile. "They should spoof that."

"Or when Clarence wrote the inscription in the book at the end that a man with friends is a rich man, or not a failure, or something like that," Elise sounded excited.

"I'm surprised you can't quote it. Next time you watch the movie, you should write that bit down," Kevin quipped. He didn't intend his comments to be mean but, once said, it felt barbed. He really did want to change the subject. The food arrived and after that was sorted, Elise with the tuna sliders and tots, Tanna with the burger and salad, and a steak for himself, Kevin said, "So has anyone started running yet? Training for the Hood to Coast?"

"No, god! I really should," Elise said. "Did you guys get Dawn's letter?"

"Yeah," Kevin said. "Mirabelle was not happy." That was putting it mildly. She had whined endlessly about how awful running is and that Cleah shouldn't have required her children's spouses to run. He considered not telling her about Tanna bringing Great-Aunt Mirabelle to Easter, in an effort to avoid a fight. Or would letting her be surprised be worse?

"I've started running," Tanna said. "I mean, just a little. Mostly walking. I'm trying to start getting into a routine."

"Good for you, Tanna!" said Elise, her voice edged with thorny sarcasm.

▼ ▲ ▼

Elise tried not to be annoyed. Of course perfect Tanna would already be training for the relay that wouldn't happen for another five and a half months. She thought about what her therapist advised: one choice at a time, one day at a time. She decided she would choose to be nice, pretend to be nice at the very least. She smiled. "So, what's your routine?"

Tanna shrugged. "So far, I walk on Mondays and Fridays, and I run on Saturdays."

That didn't seem like a very rigorous routine to Elise. She thought again of the kindness in the Christmas movie and dialed back her irritation.

"Anyone care which leg they run?" Kevin asked.

Elise shrugged; she hadn't looked too closely at the options.

Tanna shook her head no. "I'll run whatever," she said.

"Mirabelle wants leg 10."

"Why?" Elise asked. Mirabelle mystified her.

"The last of the three legs of 10 is an easy one; she wants to end with an easy leg."

"Well, it's a reason. She can have 10 as far as I'm concerned. I mean, they all look hard to me," Tanna said, and took a big bite of burger. She looked completely unconcerned.

Elise had to admire Mirabelle's decisiveness. She felt like she should care which leg she ran, but she couldn't figure out the strategy of which leg combination would be best: some in gravel, the hills, running in the dark, hardest leg first, hardest leg last. Jeff had tried to talk through the scenarios with her, but he hadn't settled on the best set of legs either. Maybe she should be the last runner, might be fun to run across the finish line; but then everyone else gets done and you still have a leg to run. Maybe be the first runner in the van so you're done soonest; but then there's the stress of getting to the van exchange site early enough. She sighed, "I don't know how I would decide."

"You just decide," Kevin snarked. He sure was being impatient.

"Or I could let Dawn assign me whichever she thinks," Elise retorted.

"Yeah," Kevin conceded. "It doesn't really matter, does it? As long as we can run that far by then." He gave his steak his full attention. The conversation lulled.

"I'll be right back," Tanna excused herself. "Bathroom."

"So, what about you, Kevin?" Elise asked after Tanna had left. She set one elbow on the table and looked at him. "Are you and Mirabelle running yet?"

"Not running, but Mirabelle does her spin classes and yoga, and I play basketball pick-up games a couple times a week and lift weights. I don't think it'll be much of a leap," he said.

"Yeah. Good." Elise was not surprised. Kevin was always a bit of a jock, and Mirabelle was too much of a power-player to let her figure slip. She sighed and they busied themselves with eating in silence. *Choose to be nice*, she reminded herself.

"Hey, I have an idea," Elise said.

▼ ▲ ▼

Tanna was just outside the door. The sun was setting, and it was a little chilly without her coat, but she couldn't bring that 'to the bathroom' without seeming odd.

"I know it's last minute, but I hadn't really made plans and it's my birthday," Tanna inhaled, "and I wonder if you'd like to go get some drinks tonight with me and a couple of friends." With her phone to her ear, she waited, not wanting to breathe and jinx it. She was suddenly aware of how tired she was, like usual at the end of her third workday. The anxiety and adrenaline of anticipating the sibling birthday dinner was abruptly wearing off.

"Sure!" said Leif. "I'd be up for that."

She exhaled, relieved, feeling just as suddenly revived. "Great! Okay, um, how about meet me at Vintage at," she checked her watch, "9? On Stark." She smiled as he agreed, wanting to cartwheel. She quickly texted Denise before returning to endure the rest of dinner with her siblings.

▼ ▲ ▼

Kevin got back to the table just after Tanna returned, giving Elise a slight nod, intentionally devoid of emotion. A server brought him another beer. The talk settled into the "How's the kids" and "How's work" and they each shared the superficial glossy latest. It was starting to sound like the Christmas letters Dad would write, but at least no one was throwing jabs at anyone else. It was pleasant enough. They lapsed into silent eating for a while. He was mostly done with his steak and Elise still had a few tots but Tanna, in true Tanna-form, was nowhere near finished with her burger.

"I hear there's a birthday over here!" the server announced, appearing from nowhere. She set a big dish of vanilla ice cream topped with chocolate sauce in front of a clearly surprised Tanna. Their server lit the blue candle sitting on top, and they sang "*Happy Birthday*" as Tanna giggled. Elise clapped in rhythm along with the two other servers that showed up to help celebrate. They all applauded as she blew the candle flame out.

"It was Elise's idea," Kevin said after the servers left, feeling pleased at Tanna's reaction.

"Thanks." Tanna smiled and took a big spoonful of ice cream. "Oh, you guys have to help me eat it though!" she laughed. When a server came by again, she asked for extra spoons.

"And can you take our picture for us?" Elise asked, handing up her phone.

It was fun, actually, to share the ice cream. Kevin was surprised to find himself enjoying the rest of the evening, cumbersome small talk and all. Tanna seemed in a great mood and Elise was being completely agreeable. It was nice. When the server came by to see if they needed anything else, on impulse he asked her to bring him the check. Almost immediately he hesitated; would Mirabelle disapprove? But he so rarely was impulsive. Tanna and Elise looked shyly bewildered as he settled the bill with a generous tip.

As they stood and gathered their coats, Tanna paused and spread her arms. "Hey! Do you wanna come get drinks with me and some friends of mine?"

14

"I don't *know* why I didn't decide about drinks sooner. I'm sorry!" Tanna lamented aloud, as she drove a little too fast to the bar. She'd picked Denise up after dinner. The whole evening was a series of alternating highs and lows, anxiety and fun, and now she was entirely stressed.

"But so now we're meeting Leif *and Kevin* at the bar? What were you thinking?" Denise looked straight ahead in the passenger seat, her arm braced on the dash. "And let's please not have a car wreck on the way!"

"Right!" Tanna slowed slightly. "Well at first it was an awkward dinner, so I snuck out and called Leif, you know, like we'd talked about, and then it was a pleasant dinner somehow, and, I don't know why, I just invited them, too! Elise couldn't stay longer, but Kevin said he would come, and . . ." Gasping with panic, Tanna trailed off.

"Maybe dinner became pleasant when you knew you had a date after," Denise smirked.

"Oh my god! Do you think?" Tanna cried. "And I should've known you wouldn't have time to get a babysitter, which means Paul couldn't come! I just forgot to decide about drinks before, but oh my god! I'm so glad *you* are coming, D!"

"Well, I am too. This could be quite a show!" laughed Denise.

"Oh, don't scare me! I don't think I can take it!"

"Look, you know I've been wanting to meet Leif, and I'd love to meet your crazy-ass brother, who maybe will behave; you said he was okay through dinner tonight. Don't worry! You'll just make the best of it," Denise assured her.

"Yeah. Yeah okay, make the best of it." Tanna breathed deeply, clutching the steering wheel. "I just hope this doesn't scare Leif off. Shit." She had this image of herself as the center of a very spindly wagon wheel, and none of the spokes knew each other or spun in harmony.

"A person doesn't make it to age thirty-nine without some baggage, Tan, so own it. Might be a great test. Why waste your time on someone who can't handle a little complexity?"

"Oh god, Denise," Tanna moaned as the bar came into sight. She parked the car and checked her watch. It was a few minutes past nine. They hurried in.

▼ ▲ ▼

Kevin ordered a beer while he waited, totally questioning what he was doing here; this wasn't a Will-Required activity. He didn't have to stay very long, he reminded himself. Elise had looked disappointed to not be able to come, but maybe she was just smarter than him. He considered calling Mirabelle to come meet up, but knew she was having her weekly girlfriend wine night. Keeping an eye on the door, he took another swallow and leaned against the counter. The bar was well-patronized for a Thursday night.

Tanna came in with a striking black woman a few inches shorter. His sister smiled at him and then at the tall guy standing next to him also nursing a beer, apparently another friend of hers. She made introductions, and the four got a booth. Kevin found himself sitting across from Tanna and next to Denise. The women ordered drinks, as the men already had theirs:

Denise a Sprite, and Tanna a lager. They had to talk loudly to hear each other.

"So, how do you all know each other?" Kevin asked.

"Denise is my neighbor, and dearest friend," Tanna smiled at her, then turned to Leif, "and Leif, we met a few weeks ago. He's, uh, helping me train for the Hood to Coast." She crossed her arms, resting her elbows and her gaze on the table.

"Yeah, not quite two weeks ago," Denise added with a grin.

"Oh," said Kevin, surprised. Tanna exuded a vulnerable, nervous happiness. Kevin couldn't guess why she'd invited him along. Not what he expected, this seemed a motley group.

"And you're the brother, huh?" Leif asked Kevin. "Which of you is older?"

"She is."

"By sixteen months," Tanna added. "Only one grade apart."

"Yeah, Tanna was a hard act to follow in school. She's good at everything," said Kevin, managing to state this simple truth without betraying the jealousy and dissatisfaction it had always carried for him, and the perpetual disapproval in him it had inspired in his mother. "Plus, all my friends had crushes on her."

Tanna blushed and took another sip.

"So, you guys are close?" Leif asked. Kevin and Tanna looked at each other and laughed.

"We are . . . not really, no," she said.

"Maybe we were too close in age to be close," Kevin added, "and then our lives have taken pretty different paths."

Tanna shrugged, saying, "Yeah, you know how people get busy with families." It felt strange to Kevin to be coordinating this explanation with her.

The drinks arrived and Leif toasted Tanna's birthday. They all clinked glasses and took a swallow. Conversation flowed comfortably. Leif talked about how busy his daughter's senior year had been: working, volunteering, taking SATs, and applying for colleges and scholarships. Denise talked about how her four-year-old didn't always appreciate being experimented on with menu ideas. Tanna talked about Cassidy's classroom celebration for losing her first tooth, and the very serious letter she had Tanna help her write to the tooth fairy. Kevin told about a glitch in getting concession vendors organized for the basketball game at the Moda Center coming up that weekend.

As Denise and Leif got into a discussion about Portland hipster-hype, Tanna leaned across the table and asked Kevin, "Are you guys doing okay with the Easter prep?"

"I think so. Mirabelle's taking care of most of it."

"I mean, I know how much work it was before Christmas. If you want me to bring one or two of the dishes, just let me know."

"Okay, thanks. I'll check with Mirabelle," Kevin said. Tanna was being so nice. He leaned closer to her ear and said in a less shouting voice, "He likes you. I can tell by how he looks at you. He seems like a good guy."

Tanna nodded. "Okay, cool. Thanks." They both took another drink. Tanna leaned in again. "You know, I really am sorry that I missed your wedding."

"Don't worry about it. I get it," Kevin said, and he meant it. He drained his beer and set the glass on the table. In a louder voice he said, "Hey, I should get going, worknight and all. Nice to meet you!" he directed to Denise and Leif as he stood up and grabbed his fleece coat. "Happy Birthday, Sis." With a grin, he went to the bar to settle his tab.

▼ ▲ ▼

Sunday afternoon at OMSI was crowded, as Tanna had predicted. Denise didn't seem to mind, and the kids certainly didn't. Once through the doors of the science museum, they surged to the earthquake simulator, always a favorite. Denise and Tanna ambled after them.

"When will you see him again?"

Tanna shrugged. Her birthday had only been a few days ago.

"What? You don't seem excited all of a sudden. I thought the drinks went great!"

"Yeah. It went great. I don't know."

They stood before the small shaking room on hydraulics, designed to simulate different intensities of earthquakes. Inside, the kids shrieked and laughed as a magnitude eight jarred them off their feet.

"Talk," Denise demanded.

"I don't know what's wrong with me. I like him." Tanna shrugged again, feeling her friend's disapproving stare.

Denise shook her head and turned back toward the kids, trying to stay upright as the floor swayed and pitched. "You're being a coward. You always do this."

"You're a brat."

"Idiot."

"Bitch."

They giggled. Tanna's laugh ended in a sigh.

Denise crossed her arms. "Love is being vulnerable. Kiss some frogs."

"I *have* kissed frogs," Tanna said ruefully.

"So you know Leif isn't one."

"What if he is?"

"What if he's not?"

Tanna scanned the big room, its soaring ceiling, wanting to trust Leif, wishing for him to truly be a good guy. She didn't need any more loser assholes in her life.

It was also possible that part of her hesitation was because she didn't want to owe her mother for finding happiness. It was because of the Requirements that they'd even met.

The kids leaped from the earthquake room and ran to the engineering station, joining a couple of kids building a chain of gears. The moms followed.

"You deserve happiness, Tan. Chance it."

"Can we do the submarine tour?!" Susan shouted.

▼ ▲ ▼

"Who are we getting from the airport again?" Cassidy asked. Again, Tanna explained they were picking up their great-grandpa's sister, the sister of Cleah's father, but the connection was just too distant for the girls to grasp.

"She's your great-great-aunt because she's my great-aunt," Tanna said.

"That's a lot of 'greats'," Susan said.

"True. Let's just call her Great-Aunt Audrey, okay?" Tanna tried again, "Okay, she's Grandma Cleah's auntie—like your Auntie Elise is to you, only she's Grandma's auntie, not yours." They were silent, thinking that over, until Susan asked the inevitable 'why.'

"Why is she coming, Mommy?"

"Because on Sunday we're going to Uncle Kevin and Aunt Mirabelle's house for a family gathering, like Christmas was, and Great-Aunt Audrey is coming, too. Even Grandma Cleah is coming."

"Really?!" Cassidy said. Susan drew in an awed breath, mirroring her sister's excitement.

"Yes, really," Tanna smiled into the rearview mirror at the girls buckled into their booster seats. "It's Uncle Kevin's turn to have Grandma Cleah visit. Her urn is going to stay at his house for a while."

"What? NO!" gasped Cassidy. Susan began to cry as Tanna turned onto Airport Way.

"Hey now, honeys," Tanna said, "you know it was just going to be temporary. We've had a lovely visit with Grandma Cleah and now we have to share." The girls continued crying and protesting. They were almost to the airport. "Come on, now, let's not scare Great-Aunt Audrey with our tears. Grandma's not leaving yet." She was not too concerned; she'd been floating on a high the past few weeks, feeling good about how her birthday had gone, and her first real dinner date with Leif last weekend. The weather was beautiful, Joe was being tolerable, even the custody timing was perfect: she'd checked the calendar and would have the kids for Easter and Labor Day while Joe had them for the weekend of the relay race. Things were really good. She wasn't even too anxious about Easter, making her almost wish she hadn't invited Audrey.

As Tanna drove in the Arrivals lane, she searched for the tallish woman wearing a pink hooded-trench parka, self-described as a "hunchback flamingo" in her text. She was not hard to spot, standing on the curb outside the row of terminal doors with her purple roller suitcase. Tanna pulled over and popped the trunk. She hopped out to help, the car idling, and was surprised to receive a big hug from Audrey.

"I'm so sorry for your loss, dear," Audrey said before stepping into the passenger seat. She had the same blue eyes as Cleah. Tanna loaded the suitcase in the trunk and pulled back into traffic. Although tired from travel, Audrey seemed especially pleased to meet the girls and asked them questions of all their favorite things: favorite food, favorite color, favorite teacher, favorite book, on and on. The girls were quite taken with this friendly stranger.

Once home, the kids showed Audrey the guest room/playroom and chattered proudly about how they'd helped drag the bed in from the other room and squished their toys together to make space. Audrey was introduced to the pets: Anne Shirley and Merv, and the elusive Poppy.

"Oh dear, I'm afraid I am allergic to cats," Audrey declared. The girls gave a sharp inhale. "But never fear, I always carry medicine. Perhaps Miss Poppy won't be too dander-full, we shall see!" It was a defiant proclamation. Tanna was amused, and nervously hopeful, while the girls were thrilled at the prospect of triumphing over allergies.

Then Cassidy and Susan insisted on playing their favorite Enya CD for Great-Aunt Audrey and, with ultimate reverence, they introduced the ceramic Cleah-urn to her. They made Tanna take a picture of all of them using her camera timer on her phone, after a minor scuffle vying for prime proximity spots closest to the special guests: Audrey and the urn.

They gave her a tour of their art creations on the dining room table, page after page of special paintings and drawings, the string-of-buttons necklace Cassidy had made for Tanna before Christmas, the cardboard picture-frame Susan had brought home from school just that week, orange and red macaroni glued to it. Great-Aunt Audrey gave each masterpiece her full attention. Susan declared she would display the photo they'd just taken in her macaroni frame.

For dinner, they had a vegetable lasagna and garlic bread. Tanna had prepped it earlier that day and popped it in the oven when they got home from the airport. While they ate, they made plans for the next day; Audrey had never been to the west coast before and wanted to see some of the city. The girls wanted to take her to Voodoo Doughnuts and go to the zoo. Tanna momentarily considered bringing Audrey along to the track in the morning, not wanting to break her running routine (or miss seeing Leif!) but decided it would be better to skip this week. It was only awkward momentarily, when Audrey asked quite pointedly where Tanna's husband was. She kept her explanation brief and quickly changed the subject.

She thought about telling Audrey about the Will Requirements, warn her a little, before Easter, but it didn't seem the right time; she wondered if there was a right time.

It took a little prodding, but they got Audrey to tell some stories of her childhood. She talked about the pets on the family Christmas tree farm: the goats and chickens, the dogs and especially the barn cats. She called them "mousers" and said they were very good at their job. The kids were captivated by Great-Aunt Audrey's recounting of how her brother, Jasper, would hypnotize the chickens, and about the rooster that befriended the dog and bunked with him in the doghouse. Tanna wondered how she had never heard stories about her grandfather, Cleah's father, before; she didn't even recall knowing that he'd grown up on a Christmas tree farm.

Over protests from Cassidy and Susan, bedtime arrived. The girls whined and begged, but Audrey announced that she must get to sleep; Michigan was two hours ahead, after all, and her energy and patience had run out.

Sunday came too quickly.

15

Sausage Egg Casserole
From the kitchen of: Mrs. Jasper Lucky

browned ground pork sausage
eggs
sour cream
half & half
milk
grated cheddar
cubed white bread
chopped green onions
salt and pepper

Pour into greased casserole dish
Cover and chill overnight
50 mins at 325°

Although convincing the kids to wear the right colors was contentious, deciding who got the privilege to carry the urn was a battle. To keep the peace Tanna did the carrying, with each girl walking sentinel beside her. During the car ride over,

Audrey held it in her lap. It was a somber affair, ending with a funereal march from the car to Kevin and Mirabelle's front entrance. They arrived just at noon wearing the Required earth tones: Cassidy in a simple ocean-teal dress, Susan wearing blue-and-lime-striped leggings and a long green top, while Tanna had on a grass-green sweater and tan twills. Great-Aunt Audrey was not subject to the dress code of Cleah's Will, nor even aware of it. Clad in a yellow-and-white-chevron fitted skirt-suit beneath that pink trench of hers, and with a white pillbox hat, she was a page out of a 1960s glamour magazine.

Tanna directed the girls to the panel of buttons next to the door, instructing them which one to push. Even after Kevin's disembodied voice said, "I'll come let you in," the girls continued to inspect the panel with great interest. Tanna warned them not to push any other buttons.

"Is Kevin doing landscaping?" Audrey said. "How nice!" Outside the door were sitting three young cedar trees about four feet tall, their roots wrapped in burlap.

"I wouldn't think so," Tanna shrugged. "I don't know how it works in condos. Probably there's a homeowner's association and they hire a landscaper." She looked around; there was a small shared green space between the two matching condo buildings, a good place for an egg hunt.

Kevin opened the door wearing a short-sleeved brown and blue plaid button-up with blue jeans.

"Hi," he said generally to all of them. "You must be Great-Aunt Audrey; I'm Kevin." He extended a handshake. She pulled him into a hug and walked in past him. He accepted the urn from Tanna with a sigh, seeming just as sullen about it as the girls. As he held the door open with his back to let them pass, Elise and her family got there, all in blue: jeans and sweaters in various shades.

"Do you have the candle already lit?" Elise asked Kevin.

"Hi, Elise. Yeah."

He led them up two flights of stairs and down a long hallway. Tanna watched her girls be awed; they'd never been in a condominium before. She felt some trepidation at the prospect of another family event and wondered how today would go. It seemed like a big group now, ten people in the narrow hallway. Elise caught up to Audrey and introduced herself and her family as they walked.

Tanna was hit with a strong vinegar smell as they followed Kevin into his condo entryway; she could see the aroma register on the others' faces. Seemingly oblivious, Kevin pointed out the closet and the bathroom to the left. They walked straight ahead several steps and to the right was the kitchen with an island, where he set the urn of Cleah's ashes beside a large bowl of white eggs in what Tanna assumed was cider vinegar, source of the smell. He bobbled the urn somehow, which nearly toppled. There was a collective sharp inhale, but Kevin managed to save it with an awkward reach. Tanna was surprised to see a flash of a tattoo on his upper arm; Mother would have never approved. She shook her head, annoyed that this thought had even occurred to her.

To the left was the dining area, with a card table set up next to the long rectangular table that displayed a vase of red tulips and a familiar lit red candle—the Cleah Candle. Separated by a wraparound couch to the right of the dining area was the living area, decorated like an Ikea catalog. The whole space was flanked by a wall of windows overlooking a busy street, and the far wall held a huge flat screen. The ceiling extended to a loft, up a staircase to the right. The condo was light and spacious. Definitely not a kids' zone, Tanna assessed, although there was some telltale evidence of dog.

The door between the kitchen and the stairs opened, and Mirabelle emerged wearing a scarlet smile that didn't reach her eyes. Her white summer dress was sexy and cool, perfectly complementing her black hair and caramel tan.

"We should take the group photo first thing," Elise said, ever on task, adding, "Hello Mirabelle. Lovely home."

▼ ▲ ▼

Kevin tried to introduce Mirabelle to Great-Aunt Audrey, but Elise was persistent and so they hung up coats and gathered around the long couch to take the photo. He knew Elise would take control and he knew Mirabelle would not like it. Cassidy ran to get the urn from the kitchen island and settled on the couch with it cradled in her lap. He could see Mirabelle bristle as Elise placed everyone in their family groups, set her camera timer, and rushed back into her spot beside Jeff. Then Audrey picked up Elise's phone and insisted on a few pics without her. She got them relaxed and laughing by making faces and "look here!" and "say spaghetti!" and an oddly infectious cawing laugh.

"Great!" Elise said, taking back her phone as Cassidy carefully replaced the urn on the counter. Elise pulled a paper from her pocket and, consulting it, she said, "Shall we dye eggs first or do the song and the toast?" Kevin worked hard to not roll his eyes.

"Eggs," Mirabelle said firmly. "I've got it all ready. Elise, come help me set up. The rest of you find seats around the table." Clearly not willing to cede her role as host, she directed Elise to transfer the eggs onto a thick towel on the counter and then back into egg cartons while she turned the stove top on under two big pots. Donning an apron, Mirabelle brought a bowl of foliage and flowers to the table, scissors, twine, and a small pile of nylons. Elise ferried the reloaded egg cartons over. Taking one egg, Mirabelle demonstrated how to place leaves and flowers on the egg and then keep them in place with the nylon, tied tightly with twine. She warned them the eggs were still raw, and they all set to work, putting the prepared eggs in a new bowl.

Kevin was the last to sit down, so he was stuck at the card table with Jeff and Caleb. He couldn't help but be annoyed at the self-important children who thought they deserved to be at the adults' table. Kids these days.

The spring sunshine bathed the room. The craft project was a little tedious but not out of reach, even for the youngest. Everyone really got into it. This was not something Kevin ever would have done given a choice, but he wasn't suffering.

"There are fewer Required Activities than there were for Christmas," Elise said at the head of the big table looking at her paper again, which must have been the list. "Probably because *The Farming Game* will take a while to play."

Kevin's stomach plummeted. "Fuuuck." The room hushed. Elise gave him a sharp look of rebuke. He shrugged, not giving a shit. "I forgot to find the game."

▼ ▲ ▼

"Kevin, I *told* you to figure that out *months* ago!" Elise shrilled, feeling a flash of familiar dread in anticipation of failing her mother. She felt the panic rise, but then it tempered into an odd calm. Her mother wasn't there to be disappointed. She forced a deep breath. They had failed Cleah's Will Requirements; a fact is a fact and what's done is done. But money is only money. It was almost a relief to have the struggle and stress over. "Well, I guess that's it." Her statement was met with silence. Elise wondered if they should leave.

"We could check for it at Mom's house. *She* had the game; it's probably still there," said Tanna.

Elise scoffed. "There's no way! Dawn said they took care of all that." Hopeless, she shook her head. "The house is probably sold and everything either gone or in storage."

"Maybe not," Mirabelle said, looking petulant. "Don't just quit. The egg dyeing will take a while, and then I can get the kids started on the egg hunt. You'd have time if you hurried."

"Must be a pretty fantastic game," Great-Aunt Audrey commented, a look of puzzled amusement on her face. But Elise couldn't worry about what Audrey might be thinking.

"Didn't she always have a hide-a-key somewhere?" said Kevin. "What do you bet she's there at home and not dead at all." The egg Caleb was trying to wrap in nylon slipped and splatted on the table, and Elise strained against the urge to curse Kevin for his careless actions and words for what they might do to her son.

Nothing to lose and no time to waste, Elise and Tanna rushed out.

The traffic was thankfully light. There was a bubble of tense focus in the minivan as Elise drove the twentyish minutes to their childhood home.

"I can't believe Kevin screwed this up! This is probably a total waste of time. And what if Dawn shows up unannounced while we're gone?" Elise realized she was verbalizing her stream-of-consciousness. They were off the main streets now. There'd been a lot of development to the area since they were kids, she noticed.

"What was Kevin saying?" Tanna asked, after a while. "About Mom not being dead?"

"That's crazy, I can't believe he said that. He should keep his mouth shut!" Elise said, remembering the presence she had felt while Cleah's urn lived with them, and how Caleb said he saw Cleah and talked with her. She didn't tell Tanna about any of that, though. She was mad at Kevin for messing up the

Requirements by not getting *The Farming Game*, but also for his wild suggestion that Cleah might be alive. The thought of all of this being a joke was even more maddening. Mostly because she felt no choice but to go along.

"You're being pretty hard on him."

"My therapist says I'm hard on other people because I'm so hard on myself," Elise said without thinking, a little more honest than she'd intended. "Something I'm working on." She was embarrassed, and glad when Tanna didn't reply. Elise changed the subject: "God, what are the chances we'll find a house key, let alone find the game! Stupid Kevin." Aside from fuming at Kevin, she found herself wondering about Great-Aunt Audrey, as she had so often since Tanna told them she was coming. It was possible she was here to try to muscle into inheriting. Elise asked her if Audrey was privy to the situation, was assured that she wasn't. *As far as Tanna knows*, Elise thought darkly. She imagined there would have to be some kind of explanation now; what Audrey must be thinking after this weird display over a board game, Elise could only guess.

"Did you see his arm tattoo? Feathers. Some kind of bird thing, I think," Tanna said.

"No! I didn't know Kevin had any tattoos." Elise was a little shocked, but then chalked it up to a drunken peer-pressure frat-boy thing. Stupid Kevin.

"Yeah, me either. Do you have a tattoo?"

"No way!" Elise did not like tattoos. She'd never put too much thought into them but suspected at least part of that was her fear of needles, if she was being honest. "Do you?"

"No, no tattoos," Tanna said. "I'll bet Mirabelle does." Elise wondered if that was a glint of envy or respect in Tanna's voice. *Interesting*, she thought.

As they pulled into the driveway, Elise was startled to see someone sitting in the wicker chair by the door. Staring at it, she realized it was a witch, probably still waiting for Halloween.

"Oh gosh! For a minute I thought that was Mom sitting there," Tanna said.

"Because it's dressed as a witch?" Elise snickered. She turned off the van and got out.

"When's the last time you came here?" asked Tanna, slamming the door shut and following her up the cement walkway.

Elise could not recall offhand and searched her memory. "Uh, just after Caleb was born. Mom insisted on meeting the baby at her house."

"Same."

The one-story ranch-style house had been painted blue since the last time Elise had been there. She didn't want to be here any longer than she had to be. The place didn't look particularly occupied. The grass was mowed but not watered. There were several pots set around either side of the door and the chair, absent the plants and filled only with dirt. Elise knocked, not expecting an answer. There was none. They searched under the mat and under the pots and any rocks, even under the stuffed witch. No key.

"Let's try around back," Tanna said, leading the way. "We can break a window."

"Okay. Let's hurry; the last thing we need is someone calling the police on us." Grateful to the trees and bushes giving some privacy, Elise glanced over her shoulder; an old lady was crossing the street, coming straight at them! She poked Tanna hard in the back and whirled around as the neighbor lady cupped a hand to her mouth.

"Is that you, Elise? And Tanna? Hello-oo!" the woman called out, waving and huffing as she reached the curb. A pom-pom on her brightly crocheted hat bobbed with each step.

"Yes, hi, Mrs. Cushing! How are you?" Elise called out, putting on a cordial air.

"My goodness, you're so grown up! Such a shame about your mother." Mrs. Cushing caught up to them, pulling her cardigan closed around her sturdy belly and drawing a big breath. "So! Are you clearing the house out? I was wondering when someone would get to that. Will you put it on the market?"

"We were just checking on the place today," Tanna said, "but we've forgotten our key."

"Yes," Elise laughed, playing along. "I thought Tanna was bringing it, and she thought I was . . ." Mrs. Cushing joined them in their chuckle.

"Easter's a funny day to do that, isn't it? Well, I still have my spare that Cleah gave me years ago, for emergencies. I should give it back anyway, now . . ."

"Thanks, yes! That would be excellent!" Tanna said. Mrs. Cushing strode back across the street to collect the key.

▼ ▲ ▼

Thanks to Caleb searching for the bathroom, the dogs had been freed. They knocked Caleb to the ground as they escaped the spare bedroom. Great-Aunt Audrey cawed a surprised laugh. Their exuberance scared Susan, who cowered into Audrey's arms. The other kids only made it worse, hopping around, trying to help corral the barking dogs. Annoyed and surly, Kevin grabbed the yellow labradoodle to calm her down, while Mirabelle, still wearing the apron, collared the beagle. She had just deposited the prepared eggs into the two pots of water: one stewed with yellow onion skins and the other with purple cabbage.

"Are the dogs okay with kids?" Jeff asked cautiously.

"Of course they are," Mirabelle snapped. By this time Susan had stopped crying. "That's our labradoodle, Bo. And this is Sally."

"Sally's short for Saliva," Kevin added. Caleb giggled.

"I had a beagle just like this one," Great-Aunt Audrey said, kneeling to pet her. "You're a good girl, aren't you? Yes, you are!" Sally yelped and gave her kisses.

"Sally's just like Snoopy!" exclaimed Cassidy. She and Daphne joined Audrey in fawning over the dog. Caleb and Beth were hovering around Bo. Susan kept her distance, watching closely.

"Was that when you were a kid, when you had a beagle?" asked Jeff. Audrey affirmed with an "uh-huh" as Sally licked her face.

The pots came to a boil, and Mirabelle disengaged from Bo to take them off the heat and set a timer. Now that the chaos had calmed, Kevin straightened up. So did Audrey, prompting Sally to direct her licks to Cassidy and Daphne.

"So, tell me about this game," Audrey said, adjusting her hat. "What's so important? A family tradition or something?"

"Yes," Jeff said quickly. "Family tradition. Something like that." Audrey looked at him, waiting. Jeff just smiled. Thankfully, Audrey didn't pursue it.

Kevin sidled up to Mirabelle. "Should we do the egg hunt in the courtyard or up here?"

"Let's just do it here. Put the kids in the bedroom and we can hide the eggs."

He nodded. What was taking Elise and Tanna so long?

▼ ▲ ▼

Tanna wished they weren't in a rush to get back. Now that she was here, she would have liked to find some photos of her dad, maybe raid her mother's collection of quilts. Most of the furniture and home decor was the same as it'd always been, to her recollection: bulky '70s style in browns and orange. In truth, there was not much she wanted.

It had been a little awkward, getting Mrs. Cushing to leave them alone. Tanna left that task to Elise, who had skillfully ended the interaction with well-wishes at the door as they went in, leaving the nosy neighbor outside. Tanna was still somewhat rattled by Kevin's suggestion that Cleah could be alive and searched for signs of someone living there. The fridge was mostly empty but running. The place wasn't freshly dusted, but she couldn't say for sure it wasn't lived in. She imagined that a tidy woman living alone could go a long time before needing a deep clean, no kids or husband to make messes.

"We should come back sometime, and go through her things," Tanna said, opening a linen closet in the hall. "You know it'll be up to us in the end. If we do it little by little it won't be too daunting." It was so strange to be here without her mother's oppressive supervision.

Elise stayed on task, and Tanna reluctantly joined her, searching cabinet doors and drawers in the living room, a wealth of VHS movies, puzzles, and games. True to form, it didn't take Elise long.

▼▲▼

"Why does Mom keep making us drink?" Tanna whispered to Elise, after the group had toasted to Cleah with the prescribed Old Fashioneds for adults and lemonade for kids.

"Do you mean why does Mom keep driving us to drink?" Elise giggled.

"Cheers to that," Tanna smiled as they clinked glasses again.

They had arrived back at Kevin and Mirabelle's condo just as the others were sitting down to eat; having found and re-hid the Easter eggs three times, and then eating all the candy out of the plastic eggs—to Elise's chagrin—as they'd lost patience with waiting.

"Mirabelle, everything looks just amazing," Elise said louder, as people continued eating the spread that Cleah had planned: egg sausage casserole, roasted carrots, fruit salad, green veggie salad, deviled eggs, French onion soup, and baguettes with butter and jam. She was pretty sure most of it was catered but didn't want to ask, in case that was against the Requirements. Instead of acknowledging the compliment, Mirabelle swatted Kevin on the arm, who immediately got up and messed with the speaker system. The Required song, *Who's Sorry Now,* boomed out and he quickly adjusted the volume.

Listening to the cheesy old tune, Elise was pleased, again confident they would meet all the Requirements to inherit. Ha! She ticked through the list in her head: candle, photo, egg dyeing, egg hunt, toast, meal, song—all done. What else? Just the cake and the game, unless she was forgetting something. She would double-check with the list in her pocket later.

▼ ▲ ▼

There were six game pieces—one for each adult. Kevin read the instructions aloud as Elise set up the board on the table. He had already found a cartoon channel and a deck of cards for the kids to play War or Go Fish or Solitaire. He was a little miffed that neither of his sisters thought to bring something for their kids to do; he and Mirabelle didn't have any kid games. At least the dogs provided some entertainment for them.

"Okay, so we all start at Spring Planting," Elise said after Kevin finished reading. "Here are your 20 grain acres and your $5,000 loan."

Now that it was set up and in front of him, he did remember this game. Cleah had made him play it with her long after no one else was willing to play. It wasn't his idea of fun. He couldn't remember why he would go along with that—just didn't like to complain, he supposed. Or pity? He remembered feeling a little sorry for his mother; her world just seemed so small and insignificant, and his sisters gave her so many teenage-angst battles. The pity and the game-playing stopped after he'd found out about her affair.

"Oh, this is so fun!" Great-Aunt Audrey clucked, that infectious chuckling again. Kevin smiled. He hadn't known what to expect from the ancient broad, but she had turned out to be all right—an easy guest. Maybe it was partly the way she talked to Mirabelle, including her. Audrey seemed to make a point to talk with everyone.

The game was slow to get going, especially with so many players. There was a lot of waiting for turns. Elise took several photos with the time, to prove they played, Kevin assumed. Remembering his old strategy of big risk for big reward, Kevin tried to plant as many crops as he could as quickly as he could, because only in harvesting could you make any money. Cattle was especially profitable. But as in games of chance, a roll of the dice could pay big or lose big. They moved their pieces around the board, each full-circling representing a year on the farm. Elise was having no luck and getting pretty grumpy. Mirabelle and Tanna looked bored. Jeff was calm and hard to read. Audrey seemed to be really enjoying herself. She employed the big risk/big reward theory as well, and she and Kevin were each pulling in money and pulling away from the competition.

"How does this game end? How do you win again?" Mirabelle asked. Kevin handed her the instructions. The game was closing in on two hours. It was Elise's turn. She was agonizing over buying or not buying five acres of cherry trees.

"Just decide," Tanna said. It was her turn next.

"I am! Just a minute!" said Elise.

Tanna huffed, then turned to Audrey. "What happened to the Christmas tree farm? Did your parents want it to stay in the family?" This caught Kevin's attention. He hadn't known about a family Christmas tree farm.

"Ah yes," Great-Aunt Audrey said sadly. "Jasper had planned to take over management, later in life, like a second career, after the kids were grown."

"Now remind me," broke in Jeff. "Jasper is . . .?"

"My older brother, Cleah's father. We grew up on the farm in Michigan. But he wanted to try out a different life first, so he went to Wyoming, married Elizabeth, and raised their girls."

"Girls?" Tanna asked. "I thought Mom was an only child."

"Cleah was the second daughter, but little Betty died of the whooping cough quite young. I think six or so."

"Oh," Elise said, apparently forgetting to finish her turn.

"So, did Jasper and Elizabeth change their mind about working the tree farm?" Kevin prodded.

"Oh honey," Audrey said, straightening her game money for a minute. She stopped fidgeting and looked at Kevin. "They died in that car accident instead. It really was tragic. My folks sold the farm after that." She shook her head. "But no one blamed Cleah. It's just something that happened."

▼ ▲ ▼

Tanna was confused. "Blame Cleah?"

"No, of course not. Look, Jasper and Elizabeth didn't agree with her choices, you know how parents can be. I mean, I was concerned when Cleah joined the convent; she was awfully young for so big a decision, and I really wasn't surprised at how that turned out. Not that I knew much of how things were; I was in Michigan raising my own family, but every time I called Jasper, he seemed fit to be tied. That's why they did what they did. I sometimes think of how different it could've been. But no one can know what will happen tomorrow, don't you know." Audrey nodded, as if this cleared everything up, but Tanna was more puzzled than ever.

"Wait, what?" Mirabelle said. "Cleah joined a convent?"

"Can you tell us the whole story in order, Audrey? Mom never told us any of this," Tanna said.

"Oh. Okay, well let's see. Cleah was seventeen when she graduated high school and right away, she entered a nunnery. I don't know why, but there it is. Well, within six or seven months she ran away with a young man to Seattle, and we can all guess why on that. Jasper and Elizabeth begged her to come home and finally drove out after her, maybe a month or two later, to try to convince her. She was eighteen by this time. She wouldn't leave. She wanted to stay put and she sent them away." Audrey leaned in and whispered, "The car crash happened on their way back home."

No one spoke. Tanna was stunned. SpongeBob and Patrick were laughing on the TV.

"Wow," Elise finally said. "Poor Mom."

"Well, life is a string of countless formative moments, don't you know. Loss is hard; change is hard. Even love can be hard. Things happen and each thing affects us, good or bad." Audrey shrugged. "I lost track of Cleah for a while. It seemed she wanted to disappear. It was so lovely when you all came to visit me. Lucky I didn't move!"

"You didn't hear from her until the summer we took that road trip?" Kevin asked.

"I got your Christmas letters! After she married your father."

"Was he who she ran away from the convent with?" Tanna asked.

"No, no. I believe they broke up soon after Jasper and Elizabeth died. She met Howard a few years later, after she went to college."

"Oh yeah." Tanna remembered the death notice in the paper, saying she had met her husband in Portland and then they'd moved to Camas. She stole a glance at the urn, feeling a little naughty for talking about Cleah behind her back. She was surprised to also feel empathy towards her mother.

"I think you won the game, Audrey," Kevin said, starting to put it away.

"Oh! How nice," Audrey chuckled. They packed the game back into the box. Tanna's mind was still reeling. For some reason, she found herself thinking of Leif.

"We have to eat this cake," Mirabelle said, bringing it to the table. "Please don't leave it all for me and Kevin!" This got the attention of a kid or two, and soon all five kids had rushed over to 'help.' Kevin got the dessert plates and Mirabelle dished up fat wedges of yellow cake with pink frosting.

"Hey, be careful though," Kevin said. "There are surprises in the cake. Don't break a tooth."

"Oh wow, is this the cake with the coins in it?" Tanna asked. She hadn't looked too closely at the Requirements for Easter, since she hadn't needed to. "I love that cake!"

"Yup," Mirabelle smiled. "They're wrapped in tin foil. Anyone want anything to drink?"

"I'll set up the slide projector," Kevin said, getting up.

▼ ▲ ▼

With a pang of worry, Elise pulled out her list again. "What's this? Slide projector? It's not on the list!" She didn't think she could take much more of this Easter family gathering. She was really trying to not snap at everyone, but the day was getting too long and had been too jarring. She took a hurried bite of cake, spitting out another metallic-tasting tin-wrapped coin, which she unwrapped and added to her pile. She now had $1.45 in change.

"Yeah, Dawn brought some things by on Friday," Kevin said as he set up the machine to project onto the wall above the television. While people finished their cake, he turned off the lights and started clicking through slides, the light from outside dimming the pictures somewhat. It was of Cleah and Howard's wedding, a small church ceremony in the early '70s. Cleah's lacy white dress was long-sleeved, high-necked, and down to her knees. A short veil sat atop her bouffant hair. Young and beautiful, there was yet a seriousness to her in the few pictures from the ceremony itself. Then there were a few posed shots of the cake-cutting and several candid reception pictures full of mostly strangers. Elise recognized Howard's parents. Mindful of the story Audrey just told, Cleah's parents were glaringly absent.

Elise leaned toward Audrey. "Do you recognize anyone? Other than Cleah and Howard?"

"Not a soul. My, but they are a lovely couple, aren't they. I wish I'd been invited."

There weren't many slides; they were through them quickly.

Kevin turned off the projector and flicked the lights back on. "Hold on—there's a couple more things from Mom, and a note." Elise's breath caught, bracing for Cleah's next crazy thing. But it would have been a surprise to not have a surprise, Elise supposed. From the bedroom, Kevin retrieved a blue Walmart bag stuffed full of what looked like an assortment of reusable grocery bags. He fished out an envelope, opened it, and read, "I'm giving you each an incense cedar. Plant them in your yard or a special place of your choosing by Earth Day and give the photographic proof to Mr. Kantola. The reusable bags should be used for shopping, because we must love our Earth. I had the DVDs made for you to know where you came from." He finished reading and held up three disks in thin cases. "And these are DVDs of their wedding slides." As he stuffed the letter back into the envelope, he said, "The cedars are outside the front door. You probably saw them on the way in."

As Elise processed this, Jeff calculated, "Okay. Earth Day is the 22nd. We have two and a half weeks."

"What's this about?" asked Audrey.

"It's the other stuff Dawn dropped off on Friday. Did you see the trees by the entrance? One for each family," Kevin said. Elise knew this did not answer Audrey's question.

"Mom arranged for some messages to be delivered to us," Elise explained to Audrey, not giving the whole story. "And some . . . parting gifts."

Great-Aunt Audrey smiled, still looking confused. "Well, isn't that nice."

"Well!" Elise exhaled. "We should really be going. Thanks so much for a . . . lovely day!"

"You have to take some of the eggs," Mirabelle commanded. "There's a dozen for each of you. Did you see them? They turned out really cool." She pulled two egg cartons from the fridge and displayed the eggs in their varying hues of purple-brown and burnt orange, each imprinted with white leaves or flowers, like a negative effect. Involuntarily aahing, Elise could not believe how beautiful they were.

Elise opened a white Fred Meyer shopping bag and put a few of the other random bags in it, along with the wedding DVD and the dozen dyed eggs. As her kids gave effusive goodbyes to the dogs, she wondered how the tree would fit into the back of the minivan. Before she could stress too much, she found herself in a big hug with Great-Aunt Audrey. Elise laughed. "I'm so glad you came." She later realized she forgot to feel animosity toward the urn.

16

"Why can't you take this seriously?" Mirabelle said. She was cleaning up from dinner but now paused to face Kevin, her finger pointing at his nose. "What if Tanna hadn't figured out how to get *The Farming Game*? It would've been over. I did all the food and the activities! The game was the one thing you were supposed to do! God, do you even care?"

Kevin wasn't sure if he did care. He sat pouting on his barstool at the counter between the kitchen and the dining table, not answering, as silent as his mother's ceramic urn in front of him. He slid it to the side, plopped his elbow next to it and, leaning his head on his hand, he put his back toward it. Work had sucked that day; even the train ride home had sucked, some weirdo wouldn't stop talking to him. Mirabelle had made pea soup for dinner and that sucked.

Ever since Easter, life had been more tense than usual and there hadn't been time to talk things out, confront each other. There wasn't time now; Mirabelle's girlfriends would arrive in ten minutes. Kevin wasn't sure if he was frustrated with not having time to talk or if he was relieved.

"You don't care!" Mirabelle declared.

He didn't know what she wanted from him. "I wish *you* didn't care so much about the damn inheritance."

She snorted and threw her arms wide. "Kevin, you hate your job! Wouldn't it be nice to have some breathing room to figure out a new direction? I want this for *you*!"

"Oh, please," he muttered. She was right, though. He hated his job managing concessions for ball games and concerts, so mindless and meaningless.

But a part of it was that his job was lower level in the executive echelons than hers.

The dogs were restless, ready for their walk. Sally was pacing the hallway by the door. Bo nudged Kevin's toe and looked up with those pleading eyes. He stared at the labradoodle while Mirabelle, arms crossed, stared at Kevin.

"Don't be so hopeless," she said. "Do something! Either make sure you comply with all of your mother's Bequest Requirements or call that lawyer guy already, find out if you can get out of them. You've been saying you would call him since your birthday! What are you waiting for?"

Kevin reached down and petted Bo. "Yeah. I should get going."

"What is the inheritance anyway?" Mirabelle went on, crossing her arms and jutting out a hip. "Convenient that we can't know. I just can't help wondering if all this is even worth it!"

Getting up, Kevin sighed. "You know as much as I do." He went to the closet and pulled on his windbreaker, then gathered up the customary dog-owner paraphernalia: leashes, a tennis ball, the little plastic bags for poop. Sally and Bo rushed the door, a few yips escaping their canine efforts at self-restraint.

Mirabelle muttered something and Kevin, wanting to just leave, almost let it go. But he thought that might make things worse. "What's that?" he asked.

"You heard me." She had picked up her phone and was scrolling.

"No, I didn't." He stood with one hand on the doorknob, the dogs at his feet staring intently at the door, him looking back at her.

Mirabelle harrumphed, shook her head, and locked eyes. She looked close to tears, which surprised him. "God, Kevin. Fucking lazy. You don't listen. You don't think. You don't try."

The door buzzer rang. Kevin broke eye contact, buzzed Mirabelle's friends in, and went out the door. He said polite hellos to the two women ready to wine and gossip with his wife as he passed them in the hall on his way out, knowing they would likely get an earful about him.

Walking to the jeep, the dogs were oblivious to Kevin's foul mood. They were wholly happy with anticipation. He smiled at them. "Yeah, all I need is a walk in the park." He clicked his fob and the jeep blinked at them. They piled in.

"I really didn't hear what she said. I wasn't playing dumb," Kevin complained to Sally, who sat attentively drooling in the front passenger seat as they drove to the dog park. Bo lounged in the back. Kevin sighed, shaking his head.

He used to just walk the dogs around the block a few times when it was Mirabelle's turn to host Girls Wine Thursdays. On the other Thursdays, Kevin would walk the dogs only once around the block before settling down in front of the TV. Until one time he took Bo and Sally to a dog park. He'd been going there every Thursday since. He didn't like to admit to himself the real reason—better to not think too hard about it.

The dogs knew the routine and grew more excited the closer they got. After he parked the jeep and opened the door, they leaped out and he laughed. It was a beautiful night, a little before sunset. It didn't take Sally and Bo long to herald their dog buddies, or for Kevin to find himself standing next to Amy.

She greeted him with a warm smile, and he relaxed into the easy and comfortable banter. He was breaking no wedding vow, deceiving no one. His ring was on his ring finger where it belonged. Even so, Kevin was aware—in a carefully avoided corner of his brain—that this friendship was not exactly what it should be. He looked forward to seeing Amy more than he ought. She was danger, and he was flirting with it.

But Mirabelle was right; he had a talent for not thinking.

▼ ▲ ▼

"Hey man! It's Jason! How the hell are you?" his voice boomed into Kevin's cutting-edge wireless earbuds, after a week of phone-tag. In an attempt to smooth things with Mirabelle, not to mention the voicemail Elise had left a few days after Easter asking again what the lawyer had said, Kevin had finally called him.

"Hey! I'm good! I'm good. Thanks for calling back." He'd just gotten to the transit station from work and would walk home from here. The phone call interrupted the podcast he was listening to.

"So, what's up?" said Jason.

"I . . ." He hadn't really thought out what he wanted to say. "I wanted to pick your brain about something. My mom, uh, recently passed away."

"Oh shit, man! I'm sorry!"

"Thanks." Kevin felt awkward. They were friends in a broader friend group in high school. Jason had never come over to Kevin's house, probably never met his parents. But Jason was the only lawyer he remotely knew. "So, it's about her will."

"Is your father still alive?" Jason asked.

"No. He died just a few years after we graduated." Kevin said, crossing a street.

"Aw, I'm so sorry, man. I hadn't heard."

"Thanks, no, that's okay." Kevin was regretting this call. "Yeah, well the thing is, she put some, uh, Requirements into her will."

"Requirements?"

Still walking, Kevin hiked his backpack higher onto his shoulder. "She put a shitload of contingencies on the inheritance. Most of them are outlined in her will, but then she's arranged for surprise Requirements to be sent to us periodically."

"Huh, interesting. Sounds like those would be Trust requirements," Jason said.

Kevin didn't care about the correct legal technical terms. "Either way. It's completely insane, right? So, I'm wondering, can we have her declared insane and just skip to inheriting without having to jump through any more hoops?"

Jason took a minute to answer. "A Will can be contested, but it's not easy to show no capacity. Laws vary from state to state, and some have pretty antiquated laws that make the process, let's just say 'cumbersome.' Wills are pretty formal. They have to be in writing and be witnessed by two non-interested parties, to verify the person's identity and their mental capacity."

"Well, I think it's pretty clear she was crazy if you just look at everything she's making us do." He'd reached his condo now, but didn't want to go in yet in case Mirabelle was home.

"Like what?"

"We're required to have holiday meals together where we watch certain movies, play certain games. Um, we had to work at a food kitchen for Christmas. And plant a tree!" Kevin stood at his door, staring at the lone little tree still waiting to be planted.

"Huh, that is unusual. How many holidays?"

"Three. She's even planned out what we have to eat at these gatherings!"

"Thoughtful of her." Jason chuckled. "She sounds over-the-top controlling, but not insane."

Kevin huffed. "It's driving us bat-shit." He set his backpack on the ground, unzipped it, and pulled out his water bottle, which he emptied over the top of the tree's burlap-wrapped root ball. He dropped the bottle back into his pack.

"I'm sorry, man," Jason laughed. "I mean, you could contest, bring a lawsuit. How much more of these Requirements do you have to go?"

"We have to meet for Elise's birthday and then for Labor Day and then at the anniversary of her death at the end of October. Oh, and run the Hood to Coast relay in August."

"Oh shit! But still, that doesn't seem like too much to me—compared to trying to contest the Will."

Kevin thought about it, leaning against a wall, arms crossed. He and Mirabelle had already hosted their holiday, so he wouldn't have to worry about forgetting to get another game. It wasn't really on his back from here on out; all he had to do was show up for things: not so hard. A lawsuit sounded like a big hassle, and probably expensive.

"Yeah, well that gives me a lot to think about. Thanks, man," Kevin said. "So how are the kids?"

"They're great! Walt is in second grade and won't do anything but read. Tina is in kindergarten and is loving coach-pitch baseball. Fucking cute! And fucking boring; she spends a lot of time picking flowers in the outfield. You got married, right?"

"It'll be four years this summer. Mirabelle is great." Small talk.

"Finally! Seems like you've always had a different honey on your arm since high school. How'd you meet her again?" Jason asked.

"At work. I'm managing concessions now at the event center. Mirabelle basically oversees everything there." With his free hand, Kevin got his key out and fiddled with it.

"Whoa, bedding the big boss!" Jason exclaimed in a congratulatory way that made Kevin cringe. "Hey, you going to the reunion this summer?"

"Oh, I don't know. Maybe." Kevin had not given his 20th high school reunion much thought.

"You should go! I'm going."

"Yeah, well, maybe see you there. Thanks for all the info. Good to talk to you."

"You too! Anytime. Good luck, man."

Kevin pulled one earbud out, shrugged his still-unzipped backpack onto his shoulder, and let himself into the building, thinking out what he would tell Mirabelle.

17

The damn tree. Every time he passed it at the door Kevin was surprised it hadn't been stolen, yet day after day he put off figuring out where to plant it. As the deadline neared, Mirabelle's nagging increased. But he couldn't think of a place. He considered the dog park but didn't want to have to explain his family weirdness to Amy. She was a bubble for him, where he didn't have to deal with his real life, and he wanted to keep it that way.

He looked at his watch. It was after ten o'clock Monday night. Earth Day, the planting deadline, was Wednesday. The dogs looked wary as they paced the cement sidewalk, not normally out for walks so late. But Kevin had needed some air; Mirabelle had resorted to giving him the silent treatment this evening, but her glares were loud, as were her stomping and slamming of doors and drawers. And he thought a place to plant a tree might possibly present itself.

Zipping up his fleece against the spring night chill, he watched Sally and Bo walk in and out of the glare of streetlights, their leashes tethering the three of them. Cars whizzed by. Two women walked past briskly, laughing together. He groaned as he realized he'd stepped squarely in some gum, dragging his left foot with each step to try to scrape it off. Someone was smoking, leaned against the brick wall; the smell of cigarette dwindled as he walked further away. A cyclist blew past him from behind, surprising him almost off his feet. He briefly considered stopping in at the bar down the street, but he glanced again at the dogs and kept walking.

He saw plenty of trees that he'd had no reason to notice before, all strategically placed in pockets of city greenspace, but there was nowhere to plant one random little cedar. Shit.

He had told Mirabelle that there was no way to get out of the Trust Requirements and still inherit, according to the lawyer. He had lied. Well—stretched the truth. It did sound virtually impossible. No, it sounded like a lot of tricky and potentially expensive work that he didn't want to deal with, not to mention a questionable result. But he didn't want to explain all of that. However, the disappointing news only served to fuel Mirabelle's insistence that they meet all the damn Requirements, starting with getting that tree planted in time.

Suddenly inspired, he put his earbuds in and dialed Tanna. It went to voicemail.

"Uh, hey Tanna. This is Kevin. I was wondering if you had space in your yard for a lovely cedar tree, haha. Let me know." He sighed as he disconnected the call.

Avoiding his thoughts, he wandered the nearby city blocks for as long as the dogs would tolerate.

▼ ▲ ▼

He pulled up to the house, a gnawing acid stone sitting hot in his stomach, calculating how many years had passed since he'd been here: nearly seventeen. Kevin remembered the exact date: September 3rd. His father's wake. Any happy memories of growing up here were eclipsed by the blackness of that day. He turned off the ignition and sat for a minute, not thinking, just sitting, until he shook himself and set about his task.

Kevin pulled a shovel from the back of the jeep, then stood scrutinizing the house, watching for movement in the windows. A life-sized stuffed witch sat in the Adirondack by the door; that would be smart of his mother to leave that there, suspiciously out of season, in pretense of the place being unlived-in. He surveyed the yard: the roses were gone, the rhododendron bushes flanking the house had grown massive, and the blue fir tree in the corner of the yard—that had sat a year in its pot in the living room after serving as their Christmas tree—was now at least thirty feet tall. Someone had mowed the grass recently.

Another glance at the windows: no movement. He quickly chose a spot and started to dig.

Tanna had returned his call early the next morning, Tuesday, leaving a message that she didn't have room in her yard for Kevin's cedar. He had then called Jeff, knowing he and Elise had an acre lot, and left him a message with his plea. Kevin hadn't heard back from Jeff by the time he left for work the next morning—this morning: Wednesday, Earth Day—so he'd put the tree in the back of the jeep before heading to work. He would plant it somewhere today. Jeff did finally call back mid-morning, and they'd had a decent chat. Kevin found it easy to talk with Jeff; he had a calm way about him, didn't tend toward agitation or overreaction. And it helped that Jeff already knew all of his shit, from the crazy family history and deceased mother's Requirements, to Kevin's own stupid personal bumblings and failures. But Jeff said it was too last-minute to come out and plant it at his house.

It wasn't until he was leaving work that it occurred to Kevin to plant the tree at his mother's house. He had driven straight there, stopping only to buy a shovel on the way.

The mound of dirt upturned onto the grass grew bigger as he dug. His black leather dress shoes were getting ruined—should've brought boots. It had rained the weekend before and the ground was soft and still moist, exuding the potential of life. The hole was slightly larger than the root ball, and he was wishing he'd bought work gloves as a blister was developing on his thumb, when the neighbor lady showed up.

"Hello there, excuse me. Could you be Kevin, possibly?" she said, grey pigtails bouncing. With a pang of guilt, as though caught in a crime, Kevin paused and leaned on his shovel.

"Yes, I'm Kevin." He hadn't put any thought into whether it was okay to plant the tree here or not; he was just going to do it. Defensively, he decided he had every right.

"My, my! Wonderful to see you! I knew you weren't the regular yard maintenance crew. Not with wearing a tie and all!" She giggled at his office attire, and he had to agree. "I saw Elise and Tanna here a few weeks ago, and now you! How are you, dear?" She continued smiling but he couldn't remember her. He realized he'd been too into his own little childhood (and then teenage) life to notice any neighbors back then, especially adults.

"I'm well, thank you," he said, wanting to just finish the job and get out of there. "The old neighborhood looks great," he added, looking down the street, remembering riding his bike off plywood jumps he had rigged up as a kid, remembering the bus stop where he'd waited in dread of the older boy on the bus who bullied.

"Yes, yes." The old woman followed his gaze down the street, then settled up onto his face. "You look so much like Howard."

This surprised him, but he felt pleased. "Oh. Thank you."

"How old are you, dear?"

"Thirty-seven."

She nodded. "Yes, that's about how old Howard was when your folks moved here with your sisters. Your mother was pregnant with you, I think."

Kevin stood stiff under her appraising gaze.

"Lovely family. It was a pleasure to watch you kids grow up, trick-or-treating every year, snowmen in the yard when enough snow fell. You were particularly busy, had me worried sometimes with your antics on that bike of yours, my, my!" She laughed and he smiled with her, somewhat speechless.

"Well, time rolls the story along. Sad to see the house empty now," she said, looking at it.

"So, it is empty?" he asked before he could stop himself.

She looked at him in surprise. "Well, yes. Isn't it?"

"Oh, yeah, of course." He had no idea why he was so sure his mother was alive. It wasn't very rational, he supposed. Except Cleah would want to witness the headaches and stress she had inflicted; she would want to supervise. Was it really so farfetched that she would have put her elaborate plan into action *before* her death? He dismissed all these thoughts; there was no resolution to them and so were hardly worth the effort of wondering.

She looked down at his freshly dug hole. "What're you up to?"

"Oh. Planting a tree," he shrugged, gesturing with the shovel.

"Oh," she nodded, looking amused. "Funny outfit for it. Are you planning to move in? It's a nice place to raise a family. You got kids?"

"No," he said quickly. Then he smiled, not wanting to elaborate. "Just planting a tree. I better get back to it." He walked to the jeep, with the neighbor following, opened the back and carried the tree over to the hole.

She closed the door for him and followed him. "You need to make the hole bigger, and then give it a good soak." She looked around. "I don't know where her hoses are. Is the water still on?"

He stood there. "I don't know."

She went to a spigot on the side of the house and turned the handle. Water gushed out and she quickly turned it back off. "Yep, water's on. We can use my hose. Be right back."

Kevin hurried to finish the planting before she returned. He enlarged the hole and, after a struggle with the cord, freed the roots of the burlap. He had settled the cedar tree into place and was refilling dirt around the root ball, pressing the dirt with his dress shoes, when the neighbor returned with a hose. She let him screw it onto the spigot and watched as he saturated the tree roots in its new home.

"Cleah was much younger than Howard, wasn't she?" the neighbor asked.

"Yeah." Kevin had to think. "At least six years younger. Maybe seven." For the first time, he realized that this matched the age difference between himself and Mirabelle. It seemed an ominous coincidence. He decided to shove that little fact out of his mind.

"They both died pretty young," she said. "So sad."

He nodded. Cleah was sixty-six. His dad had been fifty-seven.

He repositioned the hose to soak from the other side of the tree. They watched as the water pooled around its base.

"That'll be a nice tree," she said, flourishing her hands like a magician.

"It's an incense cedar, so it's supposed to be pretty drought resistant," he said, going back to the spigot to turn off the hose. "It shouldn't need any extra watering after this." He pulled his phone from his pocket, remembering the Requirement for photographic proof. "Would you mind taking my picture? With the tree?"

"Of course!" She took his phone, held it out, peering through it and stepping back. "Your mother would've loved that tree there," she said, tapping the phone to take his photo. He wasn't so sure, but he smiled anyway.

▼ ▲ ▼

It wasn't his intention. He knew immediately it was big, and probably a mistake, but he pushed that knowledge down deep, stubbornly, selfishly, wanting to enjoy the moment.

It started out like any Thursday: work, a quick workout at the gym, and then home. A letter from Tanna on blue stationary had arrived in the mail, the first unusual thing. Kevin had opened it before making a sandwich for dinner, then realized it was the letter he was to read to his mother's ashes on Mother's Day. He was shoving it back into the envelope when Mirabelle got home from the office. Things had been less stressful between them since the tree was planted, but stayed cold and busy, with neither one putting in much effort. He finished his sandwich and didn't stay long before clearing out with the dogs while Mirabelle went to drink wine with her girlfriends.

It was still light now when he got to the dog park; things looked different in the daylight. Amy had him laughing all evening, starting with recounting an awkward interaction she'd had with a physical therapy client earlier that day. She could always make him laugh.

He was in such a good mood, she was so great, that on impulse he'd gone in for the kiss.

She'd seemed surprised at first, as was he, but quickly showed her approval, wrapping her arms around his neck and kissing him back with a passion that he found startling and amazing. "What took you so long?" she'd whispered in his ear. There was not much talking after that. Just the excited flush of fresh attraction reciprocated. That heart-catching feeling, like when you miss the last step of the stairs. Kevin felt shy. Happy.

The evening melted away in a blink, holding hands, leaning close; he could tell she didn't want him to go when he finally called Bo and Sally over. Amy kissed him sweetly, longingly, as the dogs paced around their legs. Wanting to stay, he smiled and said good night.

The dogs suspected nothing. He drove a few blocks and pulled over, not wanting to go home to real life just yet, wanting to let the warm, heady feeling last a little longer. Not wanting to think, but needing to think. The dogs watched him, waiting expectantly. He called Jeff.

Surprisingly, Jeff answered. "Hello?" he whispered. "What time is it?"

He checked his watch. "10:45. Shit, it's late, sorry."

"No worries." Clearly, Jeff had been sleeping. Kevin could hear him moving around, probably getting out of bed and going somewhere he could talk. "Uh, are you okay?" He was starting to sound more awake.

"Yeah. Sure, I think so." Kevin balked, not sure what he needed, or why he'd called. It started raining.

"Hey, two phone calls in two days! Excellent! Did you get the tree planted? What's going on?"

"I planted it yesterday, but that's not the thing." Kevin paused. Amy was the thing, but he couldn't bring himself to say that. He watched the world beyond the windshield slowly obscure, drop by drop, and said, "Do you ever wonder about what's real in your life? What we assume about other people, what rules really matter and, like, what if everything that we *know* is the way it is, is just in our own head, and the other person is in a whole different reality in their head?" Kevin knew he was babbling. He just couldn't articulate how confused he was feeling.

"Different reality?" Jeff sounded patient, so Kevin took a breath and tried again.

"I'm just . . . I just was thinking." He exhaled. What was he trying to say? "When I was a kid, I could never be sad, or angry. Or scared. I wasn't allowed. It's like my mom wouldn't tolerate any of it. She would argue with me to not be mad—like to almost convince me I wasn't mad. Same if I was afraid, or when I was sad. So I would hide it; I worked very hard to not show any of it. It got easier. But it wasn't . . . real." He leaned back against the headrest of the car and closed his eyes, still wanting to keep hold of the intoxicating feeling Amy gave him. It hadn't been like that with Mirabelle for a long while.

"Damn. That's tough," Jeff said. "I guess, yeah, it feels that way sometimes."

"Yeah. It's crazy because, even so, I thought the world of her. Of Mom. Then." Kevin wasn't entirely sure Jeff understood what he was trying to say. He wasn't altogether sure himself.

"Did you and Mirabelle have a fight?" Jeff asked.

He hesitated. "Kinda. Yeah, I don't know. Just . . . life. Stupid. I shouldn't have called." He shook his head and reached over to place his hand on Sally's back.

"No, it's cool. You can call me; I may not have any answers, but I won't think you're stupid."

"Right, well . . . It's late; I should go. Don't tell Elise I called. I feel dumb enough."

"Forget it," Jeff said. "And, hey, it'll be okay. Your mom's not stopping you from having feelings anymore. Talk it out with Mirabelle." Bo gave a little whine in the backseat.

"Yeah." Kevin rubbed his temple. "Okay thanks, man." He hung up and drove home, his jeep splashing through black puddles.

18

Mirabelle was at the wheel when they finally arrived, the motion light blasting on as they pulled into the driveway of her parents' split-level bungalow. Every time Kevin saw it, he again marveled at how the family of seven had possibly fit in there. Bianca, her mother, burst from the house, long black tresses swinging and arms raised in excitement; her dad, Max, came right behind. It was long past midnight, but of course they had waited up.

Once parked, Mirabelle leaped out to give her short mom a hug. Max, tall and thick, folded the both of them into his embrace, like a vertical dogpile. It was sweet: the parents in their jammies sandwiching their sophisticated adult daughter in her pantsuit and heels. He always liked to watch them having this moment of reunion.

With a smile and a little wave across the car, he climbed out and opened the backseat door, freeing the dogs. After visiting the front yard for a quick pee, Sally and Bo dashed up to greet their 'grandparents.' Kevin went to get the bags from the back. He hesitated over the urn, tucked safely into an empty beer box. The urn was too tall for the box, but it served to keep it upright, with Tanna's letter and some crumpled paper bags stuffed in one side to guard from shifting. They would be gone from home four nights, so Requirements mandated that the urn come along.

Kevin was exhausted. It had been a push to get there; a four-hundred-something-mile drive south gives ample opportunity for unexpected delays. The trip started out as a virtual parking lot, but traffic improved as it got later and commuters made it home. They'd taken turns at the wheel, picking up fast food via drive-through only once. There wasn't much conversation; Mirabelle was on her phone while Kevin drove, and she didn't like to talk when she was driving. It didn't matter; he was tired and had a stomachache, and it rained the whole long way. Every day for two-and-a-half weeks since the night of that first kiss with Amy it had rained, at least a little, Kevin had noticed, which he supposed was good for the freshly planted tree. Not that he cared about the tree.

All he could think about was Amy, and he didn't know what to think. He had taken the dogs to a different park the Thursday after, avoiding the situation like a coward. It was further away, and it had been wet and gloomy; he was pretty sure the dogs liked the old park better. *He* certainly did. As the days went on and Thursday was again approaching, he wasn't sure which park he would take the dogs to. Then Mirabelle had decided at the last minute that they would leave Thursday after work instead of Friday morning, saving him from choosing. His reaction to this unsettled and confused him. He was disappointed to not see Amy; what would she think when he didn't show up for a second week in a row? But he was more relieved to put off making decisions about the whole thing, still not sure what he was doing.

His swirling thoughts went nowhere and were draining.

Bianca stepped toward Kevin as he got to the door, a bag in each hand. Reaching up, she cupped his face in her hands and said, "Hello, my darling."

"Hello," Kevin smiled, uncomfortable with his in-laws' displays of affection, but loving it all the same, every time.

"We were just starting to worry. Anyone hungry?" Bianca put her arm around Mirabelle's waist, ushering her into the house. With a silent bodyguard-like air and a very big grin, Max held the door for the dogs and for Kevin, who wanted nothing more than sleep.

The urn could wait.

▼ ▲ ▼

The air was pungent with chili spice, peppers, and garlic. It was meditative to smear the masa onto the corn husk, then press it out. Kevin was not new to the job, but he had only ever done it here in this house. He was set up on the dining room table where he could see the television, though a bit far for his liking. The stadium of fans cheered and booed behind the sportscasters' narration as the Saturday baseball game progressed. Sally and Bo lounged in front of the game on TV, a little too close, really. A platter of husks was on Kevin's left, a big bowl of masa to his right, and in front of him was the tray he was filling with masa-lined husks—this step in the assembly. On the other side of the table, Max took Kevin's prepared trays and added shredded pork filling. He then expertly wrapped and folded the husks, finishing the tamale. Mirabelle and Bianca went busily between the kitchen and dining room—resupplying the rinsed husks, ferrying back a tray of assembled tamales ready for the steamer, and pitching in on a job that was falling behind—keeping the assembly line moving. Mirabelle took lots of photos, documenting the whole process for her social media feed.

Yesterday, Kevin and Mirabelle had gone grocery shopping, which meant visiting several stores to find the many vital specialty items on the list. It had been a long time since they'd done something as mundane as shop together. Kevin had felt his guard relaxing, enjoying the time with her. They did use his mother's grocery bags, however; Mirabelle had easily incorporated Cleah's reusable bags in her routine, but Kevin usually resisted them. Although Cleah's note had said to use them, he viewed it not as a required-to-inherit Requirement, but as an unenforceable dictate that he could ignore. On the way back from shopping they'd picked up some take-and-bake pizzas and arrived just after Max and Bianca got home from work.

They used to make tamales all in one day, but at some point over the years it was decided the sauce was much improved with an overnight stewing. So over long hours into last night, while a hard-fought soccer game played out on TV, they had prepared the two family-recipe sauces: pork in a green sauce, chicken in red. Mirabelle's younger sister, Risa, who lived nearby, had come to help, although she didn't stay to the end. She was heavily pregnant with her first, but her lively energy matched the group's party attitude—lots of female chatting and laughter while they worked; the men were more reserved.

The seasoned-meat fillings had stewed and slow-cooked to perfection throughout the night, and this morning were ready to be assembled while a different sport played on TV.

"This game is close. It's a good fight," remarked Kevin, just to say something, as he used up the last of the masa. He moved to help with the filling. "This pitcher throws nothing but strikes."

Max focused his attention on the game. "You played baseball, right?" he asked.

Kevin looked over at him. They were the first words Max had spoken in hours. "Yeah, in high school."

Several tamales later Max said, "What position?"

"Catcher." They continued plopping a portion-size of meat sauce onto the masa and wrapping the tamale. Kevin glanced at Max again, then back to the sauce. "Did you play?"

It was a moment before Max responded, his eyes alternating from the television to the tamales. "Yep. Shortstop." Kevin was used to these sparse exchanges with his father-in-law; he was a big, quiet man. At times, he was also surprisingly intuitive. Kevin worried that Max could see the betrayal on his face, the cheat in his heart. He tried to keep his thoughts off Amy to avoid being read.

Bianca breezed in, her face thick with makeup. "Very nice, you're almost done in here!" She cleared the platter of unused husks and the bowl lined with drying masa dregs back to the kitchen. A few minutes later, she returned to pick up two trays of assembled tamales. "All of the chicken ones are out of the steamers and cooling. It's going fast this year!" She disappeared to the kitchen.

The TV crowd roared as a batter landed a hit. Both men paused and watched to see how far the ball would fly and how many bases the hitter would get. As the player settled at second, they returned their attention to their trays: only one and a half to go.

Mirabelle came in and blocked the TV, scrunching to their seated level to take a picture of the two men working. "Smile!" she commanded, holding out the phone toward them. She tapped several times, then her fingers flew to post the photos. Satisfied, she tucked her phone back into her pocket. Picking up a spare spoon, she settled in a chair next to her father to help fill and wrap the masa-lined husks. Sally padded over and stood looking up at her lovingly. "Oo, hi there honey, my pretty girl," Mirabelle cooed at her. "Looks like the sauce will be just enough to fill them all," she observed. Kevin saw she was right. It always worked out that way; he had to marvel at the precision in the planning of the expert cooks, Bianca and Mirabelle.

With all three working, they quickly finished the tray. Sally had grown bored and returned to Bo's side. Mirabelle took the tray to the kitchen while Kevin and Max tackled the final one. It did not take long; they finished before the baseball game did. Max picked up the tray and walked it to the kitchen, Kevin following.

"Good job, papi," Mirabelle said, toweling off her washed hands as Max set the final tray of prepared tamales on the counter. She gave her dad a peck on the cheek and a quick hug. She looked toward Kevin, walked over, and kissed him too. It was not long or passionate, but it was on the lips, and Kevin was unnerved by the way she looked straight into his eyes after it.

"What a fine man this is," swooned Bianca, coming from behind Kevin and ducking under his arm to wrap him in a short-armed squeeze. "You two are so good together!" She reached out and clasped Mirabelle's shoulder, like a conduit connecting them. He was simultaneously pleased and gut-punched with guilt. Bianca was a relentlessly hopeful person, always extolling Kevin's worth, as though saying something enough times made it true.

"Hey, let's play a round of croquet," Mirabelle said with a demure smile. "As I recall, I'm undefeated."

"Challenge accepted!" cried Bianca. "You two boys set up while we finish in here."

As the women loaded tamales into a steamer, Kevin and the dogs followed Max out the sliding glass door from the dining room to the backyard. The croquet storage rack was tucked next to the house. Max handed him the metal wickets and walked to one side of the yard, driving in a stake to mark out this edge of the playing field. Kevin started there, pushing wickets into the soft earth, thinking again of the cedar tree, wondering how well it liked living in his mother's yard. He realized Max was watching him. He stood upright and met his gaze.

"Something bothering you, son?" his father-in-law asked.

Kevin averted his eyes and moved to the next spot. "No." He concentrated on setting up wickets.

"You seem distracted. Unsettled," Max said, walking to the other side of the playing field. He placed the other stake, then surveyed Kevin's progress with the wickets, landing his stare on him. Kevin straightened up, his stomach churning. Max continued talking as he walked toward Kevin. "I know you've had a hard time with Mirabelle being promoted. A man can feel small when his wife is the bigger breadwinner." He reached Kevin and put a hand on his shoulder. "But no one else sees it that way. Who earns more—that doesn't matter, you know."

Kevin stared at him, taken aback. He wasn't sure he'd ever heard Max say so much at one time, and although it wasn't the biggest issue consuming him right now, it was a pretty perceptive assessment. He nodded. "Thanks. I appreciate you saying it."

"She knows that's not what it's about. She loves you," Max said. "A marriage is a partnership." Max took one of the wickets Kevin still held, and they finished setting up as Mirabelle and Bianca joined them, each carrying two beers.

"I call the red mallet!" Mirabelle said, handing a beer to Kevin.

▼ ▲ ▼

The house was chaos. This did not surprise Kevin; Mirabelle had three older brothers, all married with children. But he'd not seen them all since Thanksgiving and the kids were bigger, louder, moved faster, and seemed to have grown in number. Add to that Sally and Bo, and Ruckus, one of Mirabelle's brothers' chihuahuas.

The Mother's Day tamale meal was delicious, celebratory, and somewhat of a blur with the big busy group. Kevin now sat full and dazed with the other men at the dining room table, sipping beers. From here they could keep an eye on the seemingly lawless kid-croquet game outside, while keeping the other eye on a soccer match between Brazil and Spain on TV. Kevin suspected the 'keeping an eye on the kids' part was less earnest; no one appeared all that concerned with keeping track of the semi-feral children. There were a few young sports fanatics lying in front of the TV, some following the dogs around, and the women had cleared the table and were 'doing dishes' in the kitchen, with the littlest on hips and underfoot.

Kevin sat slumpy in his chair. He was glad to be idle, after the two industrious tamale-making days and this morning's mass with its up, down: standing, sitting, kneeling.

Mirabelle's oldest brother, George, was talking about his youngest son. ". . . while I was driving, out of nowhere Isaac says, Dad? Why did the duck poop on the map? And I'm like, What duck? Where did it poop?" George made a wide I-don't-know gesture. "And he says, You're supposed to say Why, so I say Why? And he says Because it's a poop map!" The men roared with laughter. More stories about their kids followed, including Max who prompted his third son, Frank, to tell the story of being caught, just in time, he and his brothers, in the midst of an 'experiment' to test an umbrella's floating-Mirabelle-down-from-the-roof qualities.

Kevin realized that all of them were dads (or an expectant dad), other than himself. Same with the women: all moms (or an expectant mom), except Mirabelle. So he wasn't surprised when Risa's husband, Shane, the father-to-be, turned to him and said, "When are you guys going to have a kid?"

Mirabelle walked in just as Kevin was shrugging and she answered, "Oh, you'd be the first to hear, Shane, don't worry." As the group laughed, she leaned down and whispered in Kevin's ear, "Wasn't there something you needed to do?"

"Huh?"

She exhaled. "Read some letters?"

"Oh crap! I completely forgot!" Kevin got up and followed her to the base of the stairs.

"You didn't leave it at home, did you? It was in the beer box . . ." she sounded anxious.

"No, no, it's just still in the car."

"Okay, well," she smiled, eyebrows raised, "no time like the present. Key's next to the bed." She went back to the kitchen as he took the stairs to the attic bedroom. A few minutes later he walked out the front door, Mirabelle's Outback flashing to life as he zapped it with the fob.

Digging around in the back of the car, Kevin reflected on her reaction to Shane's question. She had been light and dismissive, but he wondered what she really did think about having kids. Somehow they'd never discussed it, which now struck him as odd.

It was dawning on him that he couldn't find the urn. A more panicked search ensued, and it was there, thank god, in its stabilizing beer box hidden beneath coats and his dead mother's reusable grocery bags. He carried it back up to the bedroom quickly, trying to avoid any interactions. He put the box on the floor and slid the urn out, setting it on the bedside table; it barely fit beside the lamp. He fished out Tanna's letter from the beer box and opened it.

"Dear Mom," he read aloud, sitting down on the bed, "Things are really good. That is why you wanted us to write to you, right? What all good mothers want, right? You would hope the best for us? Well, you can rest assured. Love, Tanna." He set the letter beside the urn. He liked the sassy sentiment. Kevin hadn't written his letter yet and considered just plagiarizing Tanna's—only he wasn't sure that things for him were 'really good.'

He got out his phone, realizing he hadn't checked to see if Elise had sent him an email letter for Mom. Shit.

The phone was dead. Shit! He searched his bag for his charger but remembered he had left it downstairs.

So down he went.

The soccer match was getting intense. The chihuahua kept barking excitedly and kept having to be settled by whichever nearby kid. Kevin found the phone charger plugged in beside the couch, right where he'd left it the night before after a late rom-com movie chosen by Bianca.

Back upstairs and into the guest bedroom.

Where he found four-year-old Cindy, lid in one hand, dipping her finger into the urn. She startled and turned as Kevin walked in, simultaneously popping her ash-coated finger into her mouth. "No!" Kevin gasped, as Cindy's face crinkled in displeasure. "What are you doing?"

Tears sprang to her eyes as she said, "I thought it was a candy jar!"

Kevin took the lid from her and replaced it on the urn. Then seeing her consternation, he kneeled to give her a hug, still holding the charger.

"Doesn't taste very good, huh? Not candy."

"I'm sorry Uncle Kevin!" she whimpered, clearly mortified at doing something wrong.

"Oh, hey, it's okay, Cindy." He patted her back, then pulled away to look into her serious little face. "I think there's some goodies downstairs. Why don't you go ask?"

Cindy brushed away her tears, nodded and smiled. She rushed off.

Sighing, Kevin plugged in his phone to be charged in the outlet behind the bedside table, bumping and nearly toppling the urn. He grabbed it with both hands, making it settle. He took a breath, really wondering if all this was worth it, and sat on the edge of the bed. Reading the Required Mother Letters was becoming more of an ordeal than he'd anticipated.

It took a couple of minutes to get the phone going and access the internet, but soon he was tensely searching for Elise's email.

"Ha!" he barked involuntarily when he found it, with a subject line of *Mother Letter for Mother's Day* sent a couple of days ago. He opened it, looked at the urn, feeling silly and annoyed to be reading to a jar. At this point he had no one to blame but himself, having unilaterally chosen to ignore the possibility of contesting the Will. Resolving to just do it, get it over with, he read out loud, "Dear Mom, Mother's Day is coming up, the day we celebrate women who happened to birth a child. Thing is, being a mother doesn't always mean she's worth being celebrated for her motherhood. But, hey, I know it's hard, so I won't curse you posthumously. Stream of consciousness, don't mind me. Love, Elise"

He chuckled; gotta love Elise. Then he sobered: he still needed to write his own letter. He took up his phone again, remembering that Elise had instructed him to send himself an email of the letter, for proof. He hemmed and hawed, feeling pensive and inarticulate, and finally tapped out a few lines. Before hitting 'send' he read out, "Dear Mom, Happy Mother's Day. I wonder how becoming a mother affected you. I wonder if it was something you'd wanted, and if you liked being a parent. I wonder if you ever thought about it. I've not had to deal with that, so I don't know. Maybe the key is to not think. Your son, Kevin."

As he spoke the last words, Bo burst through the door, followed by a kid. Startled, he leapt to his feet, his stomach suddenly constricted into knots.

"Hi, Uncle Kevin." Deann, Frank's seven-year-old daughter, looked around the room. "Who are you talking to?"

"Oh," Kevin feigned laughter, "I was on the phone." He tapped to send the message and looked again at the girl. "Just finished up. Let's go back downstairs."

The two rejoined the mayhem of the family, united in celebrating a goal by the Brazilian team. Mirabelle sidled next to him, with an amused glint in her eye. "Cindy wants to know why we have a candy jar full of dirt in our room." Kevin guffawed and nodded, glad to be done with reading the Mother Letters. He put his hand on Mirabelle's back. She responded by leaning into him. Encouraged, he took a deep breath and slid his arm around her waist, pulling her close.

The worst was over.

Or so he thought.

▼ ▲ ▼

Partway home on Monday, somewhere around Roseburg, Kevin and Mirabelle stopped for dinner. Sitting across from her in a booth, he fondly watched her scrutinize the menu. The waitress had just brought them their drinks and he had ordered a Rueben sandwich.

The mood was good: comfortable and content. He was even having stirrings for her, starting with respect and admiration. There was something about the way she was with her family. Mirabelle usually was rejuvenated by seeing her parents, no exception this time. They went to visit them every Mother's Day, Father's Day, Thanksgiving, and Christmas, as well as whenever else they could manage it, usually big family affairs.

"A house salad with a cup of your chowder. Oh, and I'll need an order of grilled chicken to go, please. No sauce," Mirabelle told the waitress, handing her the menu. "For the kids," she said to Kevin with a grin. She poured her tangerine-flavored sparkling water into the glass with ice and took a drink.

"Yeah, I figured," he smiled, amused that she felt she needed to explain. Sally and Bo would appreciate their to-go order.

"And, oh my god, can you please get that off the table?" Laughing, she pointed at the beer box holding the urn.

"Sorry, I didn't want the unsupervised dogs to accidentally knock it over." He carefully set it on the bench seat, between himself and the wall.

"Why didn't you just put it in the back?"

"Well, it *is* a hatchback . . . I mean, they get back there, too." Perhaps his logic was a bit flawed. He took a drink of his root beer.

Mirabelle changed the subject. "Risa is so huge! Oh my god, she looks so good. I'm gonna have to go back down there when she has the baby."

He smiled at her enthusiasm. "Sure. She's due in a week or two, right?"

"A week from Thursday," she nodded, her eyes sparkling. The waitress breezed over and set down their dinners. They ate quietly for a while. His sandwich was delicious.

Mirabelle set down her spoon. "I keep thinking about Cleah, losing her parents so young. And the circumstances! With the accident, and after being estranged." She shook her head. "Really tragic."

Kevin's eyebrows raised. "That's quite empathetic of you," he observed.

"Maybe I'm just being sappy, having just spent Mother's Day with my mom and our whole family. But it's sad, no matter how mean she was."

"Yeah," he said. "Sad for sure."

They lapsed into silence as they ate. The whole idea of children, a family. He remembered how he and Mirabelle would mock and pity people with children, crying in line at the grocery store, friends having kids and not being able to go out much anymore. He'd not had a strong feeling about starting a family and figured Mirabelle would call the shots. Had they talked about kids? He couldn't remember. Finally, Kevin asked what had been growing in his mind all weekend: "Did you ever think about being a mom? Do you want kids?"

"Why? Do you?" she practically spat at him.

Taken aback by her abruptness, he stumbled through an answer. "I, well, I don't know. Never gave it much thought before." She looked at him keenly. He shrugged and lifted his hands. "What?" he said.

She shook her head, placing her hands in her lap. The good mood had dissipated.

"It's okay," he mumbled. "Forget it."

She looked pained. Kevin tried to think of something else to say. He took a long drink of root beer and set his glass back onto the table.

Mirabelle played with her napkin. Very quietly, she said, "I had an abortion," and exhaled. "It was before we got married, right before." She looked up at him. "It was yours."

He started to speak, and she held up her hand. "No. I know I should've told you at the time. I know."

He waited, dumbfounded. Mirabelle was staring at her salad.

She continued, defensively, "There was so much tension with your family; I was worried you weren't ready for a kid. I don't think I was ready. And . . . I didn't want you thinking I was trapping you." She paused. "I'm sorry."

They sat there.

"I still think it was the right decision." She shrugged. "Thing is, I didn't think it would bother me. I—" She shook her head.

After that they picked at their food. He didn't know what to say.

It wasn't until they were home and unloading the car that Kevin realized he'd left his mother's urn at the restaurant.

19

It wasn't really raining, more like drizzling. Or spitting. It was the kind of rain that made driving really suck because it's not enough to use windshield wipers but it's too much to not use them. The cloud ceiling seemed to have dropped to being level with Kevin's eyebrows. In fact, it was as though his furrowed brow was generating storm clouds. He'd taken a sick day to drive back to the restaurant and recover the urn. Sick day was appropriate; he was in a funk. He'd brought Bo with him, for company.

Kevin kept turning Mirabelle's words over in his mind as he drove. He wasn't mad at her, exactly; he believed in a woman's right to choose, to make their own health care decisions. He even understood her reasoning. Part of him was relieved; he couldn't imagine having a kid right now, this whole time. A little kid, a mix of Mirabelle and himself . . . Even so, he felt somewhat betrayed at being left out of the decision. She'd said it had happened before they were married, but didn't the fact that they were getting married give him maybe at least the right to know?

He knew now. And it was no big deal, except it kind of was. To him. Maybe going to work would've been better. Maybe this road trip was giving him too much time to mull. But of course there were his mother's ashes and those damn Requirements to consider.

After discovering the urn missing last night, he had immediately found the restaurant's number online and called. It was closed. He'd suffered through the night, pretending to be fine, wrestling between Mirabelle's revelation and worrying over the fate of his mother's urn. He called again in the morning; the restaurant was still closed. So he called in sick to work, got in his jeep, and drove south. He was now almost there. He checked the time: just after 10:30 a.m.

"Six hours yesterday; six hours today," he complained to Bo, annoyed with how much time he was spending on the road. He exited the freeway and maneuvered through the streets of the little town to the restaurant, parking in the same spot he had the day before. Few other cars were there.

Leaving Bo in the jeep, he walked to the front door. Still closed. The posted hours said it would open at 11. He checked the time on his phone: ten minutes 'til. He knocked on the door, peering through the window, but no one was in sight and he couldn't tell if the urn was still in the booth. Turning around, he slumped against the door, not feeling patient at all.

He heard a latch turn and jumped back as the door opened.

"We're not quite open yet, but come on in, hon'," said a thickset middle-aged woman, not the waitress who had served them last night.

"Hi," Kevin said. "I was here last night."

"I remember you," the woman interrupted. Your girlfriend is very beautiful."

"Wife. Uh, thanks. Hey, I think I left something here. Did you happen to find a, uh," he decided to not be too specific, "a ceramic jar? It was sitting in a beer box. I left it right over here." He walked toward the booth where they'd eaten their dinner, searching the seat.

"Jar, hmm, no," the woman looked to be thinking hard, tapping her temple with a finger. She dropped her hand and laughed. “Nah, I’m just kidding! I’ve got your urn. Be right back.” She disappeared into the kitchen, leaving Kevin to wonder if she’d opened the jar to know it was an urn. He sighed. Pretty embarrassing. But the relief of finding it made it easy to shrug off the embarrassment. He ordered a club sandwich for the road and the woman chatted him up while he waited, until thankfully another customer came in.

Since Bo preferred the backseat, Kevin set the urn on the floor of the front passenger seat and blasted 80s hard rock for his mother’s benefit; she’d always hated it.

Somewhere during the return trip, with the traffic worsening the closer he got to the city, his thoughts turned to Amy. He realized that he hadn’t thought about her for days. Right now, though, he was yearning for the simplicity of that relationship.

▼ ▲ ▼

The following Thursday he took the dogs to the old dog park again. He hadn’t just ended up there; no, it was intentional. He had decided—he was choosing Amy. Smart, pretty, fun Amy. Not quite as beautiful as Mirabelle, but not as complicated.

Amy smiled shyly when she saw him. “I thought you’d ditched me. Haven’t seen you for three weeks.” The dogs ran past her, tails wagging fiercely as they found their canine friends.

“Hi.” It was all Kevin managed before grabbing her into a passionate kiss and embrace. It was a moment of perfect happiness.

She punched his shoulder playfully when they finally separated.

“So, what happened to you?” she pouted.

“I . . . was out of town,” Kevin said, wondering why he hadn’t anticipated this question. “I’m sorry. I’ve been going through some things. Work, obligations. My mother recently died." He rattled out a list of excuses.

"Oh god! Your mother died? I'm so sorry! I'd be devastated if my mother died." Amy moved to comfort him with a hug. He realized he'd made it sound like his mother had died recently and he debated whether he should correct her assumption, but she started talking again, telling him about when her grandparents died, funny anecdotes getting ready for the funerals, and how the trick was to keep busy and time heals all. They stood next to each other, watching the dogs play on the grassy field in front of them. Kevin suddenly felt anxious.

"So, when's the funeral?" she asked.

"Oh. Not 'til October," he said.

"Oh?"

"Yeah, there's relatives all over the place so it's way out there so people can plan." He didn't know why he was making things up. Thankfully conversation lulled and they concentrated on snuggling and keeping tabs on the dogs.

The night before, while Mirabelle was at a marathon spin class, Kevin had gotten drunk and called Jeff. Things had been tense at home since they'd gotten back from Mirabelle's parents' house. It felt to Kevin like she was waiting for him to make a move, to fix things, as if he'd been the one to drop a bomb on their marriage. But thinking about it and trying to figure things out just didn't feel good. It resulted in a stand-off; they went about their days together, separate.

On the phone last night, drunk Kevin had been all happiness and good times. "Hey Jeff, my old buddy," he'd said. "You're the best. Really, man. You are! Yeah, you're my best friend." Kevin couldn't remember the whole conversation, but Jeff had hung in there with him; who knows what he'd made of it.

Thinking now about that absurd, mushy late-night phone conversation with Jeff, and the cocky confidence he'd been feeling all day, Kevin felt his bullish certainty diminish. It was dusk now, the park dimly lit by a few lampposts. It was a pretty romantic scene and Amy was getting more amorous, but his ear was itching, and his chin, and so was his finger—the ring finger. He was suddenly feeling quite conscious of his wedding ring. He'd always been wearing his wedding band, and now he wondered why it didn't seem to bother or deter Amy.

It was probably time to go, yeah, the dogs looked about ready to leave. Was he suddenly overthinking? He'd been so sure. He was drawn to this wonderful, new, uncluttered thing with Amy, but now he wondered how real it really was.

Still, she gave him a pretty sweet kiss goodnight.

▼ ▲ ▼

Torture. Every day was a repeat of the same inner torture of confusion and indecision for Kevin. When Thursday night inevitably arrived again, he was slow to get home, slow to eat dinner; it was a hopeless attempt at holding back time. As Mirabelle's wine girls started to arrive, she gave him a sideways questioning look.

"Don't the dogs need walking?" she asked as she uncorked a red.

He cleared his throat, "Yeah," put his fleece coat on, and went through the motions of gathering up the dog-walking items, slowly. He was picking up more things than he usually did, more than he needed, stuffing them in pockets: some snacks, his grandfather's pipe, the dogs' toenail clippers, in his effort to put off the next step. Was he going to the dog park? As Kevin left the building with Sally and Bo, he pulled out his phone.

Hey what's up, he texted.

He stared at his phone while walking the sidewalk, letting the dogs lead him.

Not much. You? Jeff texted back a few minutes later.

Walking the dogs

Cool

What an inane exchange. He called, and Jeff answered on the first ring.

"Hey. What's going on?" Jeff said.

"Hey! Wanna meet somewhere? I'm kinda kicked out of the house while Mirabelle has some friends over. Wanna grab a beer?" He could hear an edge of desperation in his voice. Pathetic.

After what felt like a very long pause, Jeff said, "Are you okay?"

Now Kevin was slow to answer. "I just . . . yeah, I'm just feeling, I'm just . . ." If he hadn't been walking he would've been pacing. "Uh, I think I messed up." The dogs, happily exploring, pulled him along the streets past the weekday city nightlife. "There's this woman. Amy. We . . . kissed. I kissed her."

"Huh. Okay. What do you want to do with that?"

Kevin thought the question was stupid. "I don't know. When I'm with her all I want to do is take it further. She's... fun. She makes me feel good."

"But why are you calling me then? Maybe that's *not* what you really want."

"Yeah, what do you know? You and your perfect marriage," Kevin scoffed.

"No, I do get it. Elise and I have been married almost twenty-one years. I am human, you know."

Kevin sighed. "I should be on my way to see her right now..."

"Let's meet somewhere halfway," Jeff said. "Hey, what about Cleah's house?"

"That's where I ended up planting the cedar. Is that about halfway?"

"Yeah, meet me at your mom's old house. You bring the beer."

▼ ▲ ▼

It wasn't a very long wait, sitting in his car in the dark in front of the old house, but long enough for Kevin to feel like a creeper stalking his own old life. He'd parked on the street away from the one streetlamp, an attempt at obscurity. He certainly didn't want a visit from the neighbor lady this time. The cedar tree looked good; it looked the same, so he figured that was good. The small tree did seem out of place, an interloper; that was how Kevin felt. There were no lights on in the house, but Kevin scrutinized the windows for movement. He couldn't help it; part of him still could not believe she was really dead.

When Jeff showed up, they left their cars and walked up the driveway together, not talking. Kevin brought the dogs along off-leash and had a six-pack in tow. Jeff carried a little paper bag and led the way around the side of the house. Screened by trees and overgrown bushes that hid a wooden-slat fence, the backyard was very secluded. It was darker here, without the streetlamp, but the filtered light from the waning moon was enough to see by. They still hadn't spoken as they sat down on the top cement step just outside the back door. Sally and Bo began a systematic investigation of the yard.

"I haven't been here in years," Jeff said, looking around. Kevin offered him a beer, but Jeff waved him off. "First this," he said as he opened the paper bag, pulled out a baggy, and gave it a showy shake.

"Whoa, I forget that it's already legal here," Kevin grinned as Jeff ground the bud in a grinder, then pulled out a little glass pipe. "Wait!" Kevin said as he produced his grandfather's wooden pipe from his coat pocket. "Let's use this!"

Jeff laughed. "You just carry that thing around?" Kevin explained how he'd picked up random items before leaving his apartment, holding up the toenail clippers as proof. They decided it was providential, and Jeff proceeded to pack the bowl of the old wooden pipe. The spark of his lighter illuminated his face as he took a pull. He then held it out to Kevin, who puffed and tried to coolly suppress his cough. They both laughed, the unmistakable skunky smell permeating the air. Cleah never would've approved of smoking weed on her back steps.

"Is that the pipe Dawn brought you at Christmastime? Your grandfather's pipe, right? That's pretty cool," Jeff said.

"Jasper's pipe, and his father's before him," Kevin nodded, having given it no thought until now. He started feeling himself unwind. A memory surfaced. "Mom once said she had a grandfather who would stare at what he wanted on the dinner table until someone passed it to him. At the time I found that impressive." He handed the pipe to Jeff. "I wonder if this was *that* grandfather's pipe."

"Yeah, maybe!" Jeff said as he accepted it from Kevin and took a puff. He waited a beat before exhaling the smoke and passing the pipe back.

Kevin pointed the pipe toward the left edge of the small cement patio. "I chipped my tooth right over there." He laughed. "Tanna and I were playing chase. God, I was a clumsy kid. Yeah, my mom did not appreciate my clumsiness; I think she thought I ran into things on purpose," he said, incredulous. "She was all about behavior and decorum. Rules, rules, rules—that *she* made. And she was always right. According to her." He examined the wooden pipe closer. It was dark walnut, smooth and solid and not ornate.

"What was your dad like when you were growing up? I only met him a few times. He seemed pretty supportive."

"My dad?" Kevin said. "Howard was not around much. He was pretty hands-off, as a parent." He paused, pondering. "I think he tried more when we got older. But even so, if I ever asked him about, well, anything, he would just repeat the question." He shrugged, watching the dogs. Bo squatted and took a dump, but Kevin had no intention of cleaning it up.

"Hey, did you and Elise talk about having kids?"

Jeff gave him a funny look. "We *have* kids."

"I mean when you were getting married, or at least before you had them. Mirabelle and I . . . I don't think we talked about it. Is that weird?"

"Yeah. Probably. Maybe you just don't remember."

"Maybe." Kevin took another hit, accompanied by a bit of coughing. Jeff leaned against the back door. Kevin went on, "Mirabelle had an abortion. My baby. She never told me."

"Wow. When?"

"Just before we got married."

"Geez. Imagine how hard that must've been for her, carrying that secret this whole time."

It was not the response Kevin had expected. It had not occurred to him to wonder about how hard this was for her. He sat with that for a while.

He felt sleepy and mellow. And floaty, like his head had detached and was levitating a foot above his neck.

Done with the weed, they each cracked open a beer and clinked cans in toast.

"Have you ever cheated on Elise?" Kevin found he was almost hoping so, and immediately felt guilty.

"No." Jeff shook his head, staring into his beer can. "It's just not worth it, especially with kids in the picture. Marriage has ups and downs. It's hard; you've got to expect that."

Kevin paused before saying thickly, "Am I like my mother?" He remembered the day in his senior year of high school when he'd found out about her affair. A kid at school had told him, snickering, and he'd defended her. He'd gone home and confronted her. The truth had shattered his world, his trust. He had hated his mother. He reshaped all his memories and blamed her for every bad thing that had ever happened in his life. "I thought Amy was everything that Mirabelle wasn't, but now I can't tell how I feel."

Jeff asked, "How long has this been going on? How far has it gone?"

"We haven't had sex, if that's what you're asking." Kevin looked up at the small hazy patch of night sky between the trees. "It's been a few weeks. I only see her on Thursday nights and just at the dog park. So far."

"Listen, you and Mirabelle are going through a rough patch. This doesn't have to mean the end of your marriage. Unless you want it to." Jeff paused and took a sip, then held up his beer toward Kevin, extending his index finger to point at him, and looked at him squarely. "But if you want my advice, *you* make a decision about it, don't just let things happen. You're not that guy."

Kevin stared back at him, blown away. He took a deep breath, swirling the beer still left in his can. "Yeah okay. Yeah. Fuck me." Mirabelle didn't deserve this. For that matter, neither did Amy. Real life. Shit. "Don't tell Elise."

20

"What paper is this again?" Kevin asked. Mirabelle had responded to the door buzzer and let in some reporter while he had been engrossed in a Counter Strike game online.

"The Oregonian," the overeager young man said, tugging on his tie. "The owner of the restaurant was pretty excited about it and apparently told everyone who's come in since."

"How did you track it to me?"

"This restaurant owner remembered your name. I think it's a great human-interest story."

Great, just what I need. Kevin shrugged. "Not much of a story, really. Accidentally left the urn, went back and got it."

The reporter, who had introduced himself as Gerald Montgomery, was seated at the table facing Kevin, who was in the kitchen facing him, leaning his elbows on the stand-up counter. Mirabelle had left to go to a yoga class. Sally and Bo were quite interested in the visitor, surrounding him and peering up, waiting to be noticed.

"Is that the urn there?" He pointed to the ceramic jar on the counter beside Kevin, who nodded. "So, you were on your way home? From where? Why did you have the urn along?" Gerald had a notebook and pen out.

"I, uh, my wife and I had been visiting her parents for Mother's Day. I brought the urn along because, well, it's my mother, and it was Mother's Day. There's no story here, really. You should probably drop the whole thing."

"Why did you bring the urn into the restaurant?"

Kevin sighed. "Didn't want to leave it in the car with the dogs. It probably wasn't necessary, but that's it."

"Mind if I take your picture?"

"If I say yes, can we end this interview? I'm pretty busy," Kevin said. Lie. It was a lazy Sunday afternoon and the only pressing concern was the firefight on his computer. He smoothed the sides of his hair and straightened his shirt.

Gerald pulled out a camera. "Sure." He snapped several photos, asked a few more questions, made some more notes, and finally shook Kevin's hand and left.

Kevin went back to his game.

▼ ▲ ▼

You're not that guy, Jeff had said. Kevin didn't want to be that guy, although it didn't seem as profound and dramatic now as it had that night, without the high. But he resolved to decide and to act with intention.

On the Thursday following that backyard talk with Jeff, when Mirabelle left for her wine night, Kevin took the dogs and drove the familiar route to the dog park. On impulse, he pulled into a gas station convenience store. "Be right back. Be good," he told Sally and Bo. Several minutes later he returned with a bouquet of flowers.

When they got to the park, the dogs bounded out to run and play. He found Amy quickly and before he could change his mind again, he ended things with her. "I'm married," he'd told her. "I love my wife. I didn't intend to hurt you. I'm sorry." She said little, just nodded. There were no kisses, no final hug, he didn't stay long enough to see if there were tears. Now reflecting as he drove away, it was not pretty or nice but at least he'd shown up and been straight with her. He had considered ghosting her. Almost did. *You're not that guy.*

"We'll find a better park, right guys?" he said to his trusting canine companions as he parked the car back in front of the condo. They'd seemed only slightly confused about the uncharacteristically short playtime.

Once inside, he put the flowers in a glass vase and set it on the counter. His mother's urn was the only other thing there. He examined the blue swirling lines flowing over the jar and sighed. She was a cheater; he was a cheater. He didn't know to what extent was her infidelity. He stopped himself. *I am not my mother,* he thought.

Surveying his heart, he found peace there and knew it was the right decision. It was Mirabelle. It was always her. He was determined to fight for his marriage, to put the work in. He had not decided if he would tell her about Amy.

It was early yet; Mirabelle wouldn't be home until much later. Feeling more settled than he had in a long time, Kevin got out a beer, turned the TV on to a CSI rerun, and opened his laptop. In the search engine he typed 'romantic weekend getaway ideas.'

▼ ▲ ▼

"You dumb fuck."

Kevin flinched at Tom's admonishment, as Tom helped him settle the barbell back onto the rack. "Yeah, you're probably right."

"You know I'm right, and you're an idiot," Tom said as Kevin sat up, sweating, and they traded places, Kevin now spotting him.

It was Monday night and Mirabelle had been gone since Saturday night. Kevin needed to burn some energy and punish his body. And he needed to get out of that condo where his mother sat in silent rebuke in her urn.

Tom had listened to Kevin recount how he and Mirabelle had gone to her cousin's kid's high school graduation party in Salem on Saturday. The closeness, the flirting between them, the playful fun and laughter. Things had been going so well, he had decided to tell Mirabelle everything. He wanted no secrets between them. After they got home that night he told her about Amy, but that he had ended it. So why was he surprised when she slapped him and screamed, "And that's why you got me flowers? You're such a cliché!" She had packed a few things, including Sally, and went to stay with her friend Katie.

"You *never* tell them. It just makes it too hard for them," Tom said between bench presses. "Telling is selfish, really; you want to not feel guilty."

Kevin was not sure he agreed. He had thought he was being brave to be honest, and valuing the honesty in his marriage. But was Tom right?"Shit. So, what do I do?" He stood at his lifting partner's head, hands poised below the bar Tom was pumping, ready to help. He thought of all the voice messages he'd left her, the texts he'd sent, saying he was sorry, asking to talk.

Tom finished his repetitions, reset the barbell, and sat up. "Make a grand gesture. And a million little gestures. You're starting over, man. Digging out of that hole is gonna be a lot harder than it was falling into it."

As they went through the routine of the workout, Kevin ruminated darkly. He wanted to blame someone: Amy, Mirabelle, his mother. But there was no one to blame but himself.

▼▲▼

He set about with those million little gestures, starting with sending a dozen roses to her office every day, each with a different short message: *I miss you. I love you. I'm sorry.*

He tried to space out his texts and not overwhelm her: *Bo misses you and Sally. I know I messed up. What can I do? Please talk to me.*

I'm sorry.

He called her friends—he only had the phone numbers of two—but one didn't answer and the other told him off. It was all so frustrating. He tried to be patient, but he felt desperate. His heart hurt, his stomach in knots.

Finally, on Friday near the end of the day, he went to her office. He'd avoided going there before, out of respect, trying to keep their personal life separate from work. Although they worked for the same corporation, their paths rarely crossed there. It was a very big operation. They were fully into basketball season now. With an arena that seated some 20,000 spectators, there were a lot of concessions for him to coordinate and a ton of overseeing in general for her. But his heart was really not in it lately.

Mirabelle seemed surprised when he knocked at her open door. Sitting behind her wide oak desk, she sighed but didn't say anything. Kevin walked in and closed the door behind him. "Brought you some chocolates." He held out the box.

She groaned. "Jesus, Kevin, don't you see what a typical cheater-douche-man move this is? Do you really expect chocolate to solve anything?"

"Please, just hear me out."

She crossed her arms. He took a couple of steps forward to set the box on her desk, but then backed up again to give her the space of the room. "I'm sorry." His apology sounded so weak. He noticed the bouquet of roses was sitting on her desk and felt a tiny twinge of hope.

"I've gotten your messages," she said coolly.

"Mirabelle, I know I don't deserve a second chance. But I'm asking for one." He paused. She didn't offer to fill the silence, so he went on. "All I want is you. I won't make excuses. I was just plain dumb. But I'm clear-headed now. I want you to know that I see how special you are, and how much you mean to me. I want us to make it through this and be together."

"I, I, I," she mocked, arms still crossed. She sat there; he stood there. The room was full of disappointment. "How do I trust you again?"

"Because you can. Because I'm sorry. I love you. I don't know what else to say," Kevin said. "What can I do?"

"Well stop with the flowers. You're going to go broke."

"Look, I'm so sorry. I want to try. Do you want to try with me? Regain our footing together? Come out on a date with me. Please?"

She made him wait. And squirm. He took it; he knew it couldn't be easy. But he was all in and would work through it, whatever she needed.

"I'll think about it. Now get out."

▼ ▲ ▼

The days went by, agonizingly slow. Kevin modified the flower-sending to about every third day. He started just texting her about his day, trying to put some normalcy into it: *Watched Jeopardy tonight. Bo is starting to get the handshake command. I fixed that squeaky cupboard door. I'm going to grill fish for dinner if you'd like to join me.* Then later: *I'll save you some.*

Mirabelle never responded. He didn't let that deter him. Perhaps it was hopeless, but he would give it a good effort. Her

"I'll think about it" had inspired tunnel-vision optimism and worried patience in him.

It was Sunday morning. He was eating Cheerios and watching cartoons with Bo when his phone chimed. He leaped at it, but it was not Mirabelle. The text was from Tanna: *You left our mother's urn in a restaurant? And then did an interview about it?! You are unbelievable.*

21

What had he been thinking, agreeing to carpool with Tanna to Elise's birthday breakfast? She was badgering him relentlessly, asking the same questions over and over: *Why did you talk to a reporter? Why didn't you put a stop to the story? Why did you bring the urn into a restaurant? What were you thinking?* Why couldn't she get it through her head that he had no good answer, and that wasn't going to change no matter how many times she asked?

The morning sun shone in Kevin's eyes as he drove east, making him squint, which felt like a scowl being branded across his forehead. Tanna had the newspaper along and would periodically read bits of his article aloud to him. That stupid reporter! Maybe he shouldn't have been shocked to see it in print, on the front page of the lifestyle section, making him look like an idiot. This was really not what he needed right now.

"Come on, Kevin, just help me understand," Tanna prodded for the umpteenth time. "How the hell did you forget it there?"

"I got distracted, okay?! Mirabelle told me about the abortion, and I was in shock!" Kevin blurted. Tanna was silent, the first time since climbing into the car. "Look, I shouldn't have said that. This subject is done, all right? I left the urn by mistake, I drove back and got it, no harm, it's over. Just forget the whole thing!"

After a pause, she said, "Abortion?"

He huffed. "It was before we got married."

"But you just said you were in shock. You didn't know?"

"It was before we got married!" he repeated. "And now she's moved out! I'm sorry about the article! Yeah, I wish I'd told that reporter to go to hell. But it's done! At least it's not *your* picture attached to the damn story. Can we just fucking drop it?"

The tires hummed on the pavement of the freeway, a welcome white noise competing with the roaring in his ears.

▼ ▲ ▼

For a minute Tanna thought he was going to cry. "Oh, Kevin, I'm so sorry." He was clearly going through something. She felt guilty for haranguing him about the article. She folded up the paper and tucked it behind her feet on the floor.

Kevin laughed gruffly. "Just forget about it. I didn't mean to bring any of that up. I'd appreciate it if you'd not repeat that stuff. It sounds worse than it is. I'm just throwing a tantrum." He seemed to have recovered himself.

"Sure. It's just a stupid story. People don't remember those things after a day."

They were quiet for a while, the river rolling along on the left and waterfalls flashing by on the right. She wondered if the abortion was connected to Mirabelle's moving out, but wasn't sure how much he'd want to talk about it.

"You know, I would've liked to have had someone to talk things over with back when Alex and I were breaking up." Tanna looked over and shrugged. "So, I'm just offering." She remembered how great Kevin was when they went out for drinks on her birthday, how much fun they all had together.

She changed the subject. "Remember Mr. Wallace, English class? You had him, right? Did the kids in your class give him as hard a time as we did?"

"Oh yeah. He was way too easy a target, with his lisp and those 'inspirational sayings' he would write on the board." With one hand he did half an air quote as she groaned.

"'You have to look through the rain to see the rainbow!'" she said dramatically. "I think of that every time I see a waterfall. I know that doesn't make sense . . ."

"How about: 'You'll miss 100% of the shots you don't take,'" he said.

"Right! And that 'Hang in there!' kitty poster!" They both laughed. "So cheesy! Oh my god, little did I know how blissfully simple those days were," she sighed. It occurred to her to wonder what would happen to the Will Requirements if Mirabelle didn't participate. Tanna dismissed the selfish thought. She didn't know Mirabelle very well, but was she really a good match for Kevin? Maybe he was better off.

They drove in silence the rest of the way.

▼ ▲ ▼

"They're called 'Dead Jocks in a Box'," Elise said. They'd finished ordering their breakfasts and she'd been describing the Hood to Coast documentary that Jeff had discovered. It had increased her anticipation for running in the relay, surprisingly. "It's a team. They've run it every year since the race started in 1982 because it's so fun, they say."

"Do we have a name for our team?" asked Kevin. He was sitting slouched in his chair with his arms crossed and seemed to be distracted by the trinket display beside the cash register.

Elise shrugged. "I don't know but I think we should make one!" The team-spirit-party aspect that the movie had shown was very appealing to her. She'd never been much of a runner and didn't feel very coordinated or graceful but had gotten to where it wasn't drudgery to go for a run; she found herself almost looking forward to it.

Kevin snorted. "Like 'Running for the Urn'?"

"Weird," Elise said.

"I think you have to register with a name, so we must already have one," Tanna said.

"How do you know?" she asked.

"I have a friend who's run in the relay. The one who's helping me train."

"That's Leif, right?" Kevin asked. "Are you still seeing him?"

Tanna blushed. "Yeah."

This was news to Elise. "You've met him?" she said to Kevin.

"Uh-huh," he said. "He came for drinks after Tanna's birthday. He seems cool." At this, Tanna's blush deepened. Elise felt oddly jealous that he'd met the boyfriend.

"So, you've both been running, right? So you'll be ready for the relay?"

"Yeah," said Tanna.

Kevin shrugged. "I'll be ready."

The food arrived. Elise's cream cheese and sprouts bagel didn't look as appetizing as it had sounded, especially next to Tanna's Denver omelet and Kevin's hashbrowns, steak, and eggs. He picked up his knife and fork and started to saw.

"Oh, hold on!" Elise said. "Let's take the picture while we still have food on our plates!" She conscripted a passing server into doing the honors. The three of them raised their orange juice and toasted to Elise's birthday. After she thanked the girl and took her phone back, she said, "Just a reminder, you guys, you should send all the photo verifications from the family gatherings and lunches and the Mother Letters, all that stuff, to Dawn now, so you won't have to find it later. It'll just be done." She proceeded to text her sibling-birthday-lunch photo to Dawn.

Elise dusted her bagel with pepper and took a loud crunchy bite.

▼ ▲ ▼

"So." After an awkward pause in the conversation, during which they'd all concentrated on eating, Tanna thought she'd kick around some small talk. "Are you and the kids glad to be out of school, Elise?"

She nodded, setting down her bagel. "Yeah, the kids are, especially the twins. They're pretty proud to be official high school students now. But I signed them up for a few camps over the summer and they're all taking tennis lessons so I'm looking at a lot of mom-taxi duty. What about you? Any travel plans?"

"Well, not me. But Joe has big plans for the girls. Too big. I'm trying to negotiate him down from a two-week trip to Hawaii to just one. It's always gotta be a battle. What about you, Kevin? Any good concerts coming up at work?"

He looked up. Although distracted, he seemed okay, considering the conversation they'd had on the way out here. "Um, there's a Fleetwood Mac concert coming up next week and Daniel Tosh the week after."

"Cool," Elise sounded impressed. "Do you go to a lot of concerts and events?"

Kevin nodded, finishing off his steak. "I guess. Sometimes."

Tanna picked at her omelet. It was pretty big, and she was full.

Elise asked, "How's Great-Aunt Audrey doing? Did you get her home okay?"

"Yeah. The girls have developed a routine of sending her art they've made. Every time she gets one, she calls and chats with them. She's become their superfan." Tanna loved that Audrey paid that kind of attention to them. "She seems to be doing good."

"That is one spunky lady," commented Elise.

"What made you want to invite her to Easter?" Kevin asked.

Deciding to be honest, Tanna shrugged. "Look, I just thought we would be less likely to fight if someone else was there."

There was a pause before Elise raised her glass and said, "Damn. And we didn't fight at all. Good call, Tanna." They laughed it off, but Tanna reflected on the Easter gathering. She wondered if Elise was just being sassy or if she had blocked the whole Kevin-forgot-to-get-The-Farming-Game crisis.

▼ ▲ ▼

Kevin was struck by Tanna's explanation of not wanting them to fight. It made sense, actually; it was a smart move, but he felt awkward, disappointed even, that it would be deemed needed. A server showed up and asked if he could get them anything else. They all said no, and Elise asked for separate checks. Kevin excused himself and followed the guy to the register. There were earrings for sale there and he wanted to get Mirabelle a pair.

"Can I add a pair of earrings to my tab?" he asked the server, who was calculating their separate checks.

"Sure" he said. "Which ones?" Kevin pointed to the earrings, simple yet elegant silver loops he thought she might like. As the server took them from the display, Kevin remembered that he'd paid for Tanna's birthday dinner. He hesitated and glanced back at his sisters, who were deep in conversation, heads leaned together. Elise must not have seen the article, and he appreciated her not bringing it up.

"Actually, I'll pay the bill for the whole table," he said, pulling out his credit card.

He tucked the earrings into his coat pocket when he returned to the table.

"Well, there could be lots of reasons someone is unfaithful," Tanna was saying, rather tensely. "But none of them good." Kevin bristled, thinking she was ratting him out to Elise, but then remembered that he'd only spilled the bit about the abortion and Mirabelle moving out, not the part about him kissing another woman.

"Some people cheat because they're unhappy," Elise said. She sounded unhappy.

"It's not a stretch to imagine Mom was unhappy, but I don't think we should be feeling too sorry for her," Tanna replied. Kevin agreed but didn't say anything. He was just glad to not be the subject of this debate.

"Oh, I'm not defending her, hell no." Elise knocked on the table. "But if Dad hadn't cheated on her maybe she wouldn't have cheated on him."

This was met with silence. Kevin looked over at Tanna, wondering if she was as shocked as he was, before saying, "What the hell are you talking about?"

Elise sat back and crossed her arms. "You guys were a lot younger, but they couldn't hide it from me. Dad had a thing with a coworker's wife. I don't think it went very far or lasted very long, but Mom was different after that."

"When was this?" Tanna asked. "Why did you never tell us before?"

Elise looked thoughtful, "I was in second grade. You were three and four, just babies still."

"But how do you know?" Kevin asked. He was feeling mixed-up and agitated.

"I heard them talking one night. Well, yelling."

"Yeah, but maybe they were just arguing," he pushed.

"Right, but about a year or two later, Dad flipped out at Mom because she had an affair. I heard the whole thing," Elise said. "I don't think Dad cheated on her again."

"So, when she cheated on him again my senior year, it wasn't the first time," Tanna said darkly. Kevin was a junior and remembered the turmoil well. "I couldn't wait to get out of there. Sometimes I wonder if I would've run off with Alex. If things had been different."

"Yeah, you should never have married that guy," Elise said.

Tanna just shrugged. "Don't I know," she said. Elise had married Jeff that same summer and it now occurred to Kevin that both his sisters may have been making decisions, in part, to escape from home.

"I just wish they'd both given *us* a thought, while they were busy punishing each other," Elise said, shaking her head. Kevin wondered how much they all didn't know about their parents' marriage.

The server came to clear dishes, asking Tanna if she wanted a box. Kevin's phone chimed. A text message from Mirabelle: *Why aren't you home if you called in sick? Where are you?* His heart leaped. She must want to talk!

He got up. "Sorry, I have to make a phone call." Grabbing his coat, he walked outside while dialing.

"Where are you?" she spat. She was livid, which seemed like an overreaction.

"In Stevenson. Elise's birthday breakfast. I forgot to get the morning off, so I just called in sick. I'm sorry."

"Well, Sally's run away."

"Oh shit!"

"Can you get here and help me look?" She sounded desperate.

"Yeah, of course. I mean, it'll be forty-five minutes probably."

"Just get here. I'm at the condo." She cut the connection.

22

"So, this is where you met that woman?" Mirabelle asked, as Kevin pulled up to the park to look for Sally.

"Only ever here." He didn't know if this was helpful to say or if it just made things worse, but he wanted her to be clear that it never moved to a bedroom, or anywhere private. He hoped that they wouldn't run into Amy; it was Thursday after all. Kevin shrugged as he pulled the key from the ignition. "It's a nice park for dogs."

Mirabelle scanned the area as she got out. "I don't care. We have to find Sally before it gets dark." They'd spent hours trolling the streets around Katie's house, where she'd been staying and where Sally had escaped from, but the little beagle was nowhere around and didn't show up at their condo either. The dog park was a long shot, but they had to try everything.

To cover a wider swath, they walked separately but within eyesight of each other through the grassy park, peering around every tree, circling bushes, calling for the lost beagle. Mirabelle had a picture of Sally on her phone and showed it to every person she encountered, but no luck. Kevin started thinking where else the dog might have gone.

They had circled back nearly to the parking lot when Sally found them. She ran up barking and Mirabelle cried, dropping on the ground to hold her. Kevin wanted to envelope them both in his arms, but instead put his hand on her back and squatted to pet the found dog.

"She looks good," he said, relieved.

"Hi, honey! Hi! Are you hungry?" She pulled some dog treats from her pocket and Sally wolfed them down. "I was so worried about you. Where have you been?"

"Today has been quite a day," Kevin said carefully, after a bit. "Would you wanna get takeout and let Sally hang out with Bo for a while?"

With Sally leaning against her chest, Mirabelle had stopped crying and seemed to consider. Looking up, she said, "Why are you fighting for us? How do you know what you really want? Isn't that why you went looking in the first place? Because you're not happy with me?"

Feeling so very sorry, he sat down with them, still focusing on the dog. "I know I've been half-assing our marriage. But I don't want it to be like that anymore. I honestly didn't go looking; I just really screwed up." He didn't want to say Amy's name. "By telling you, I was hoping for a fresh start—no secrets." Sally licked his face, and he smiled ruefully. He turned to Mirabelle. It had been nearly two weeks since she'd left. "You know my mom had an affair. Today I found out that my dad cheated on her, too. It was like a tit-for-tat relationship, and they hurt each other a lot. I think we can do better if we're both intentional, you know? Good communication, and those daily decisions to keep being on the same team." He shrugged. "That's what I want. With you, Mirabelle. I'll do the hard work. I love you."

She stared at her dog, still petting her.

"You were right," Kevin went on. "I am a cliché; I didn't know what I had until it was gone. I wouldn't make the same mistake twice."

She took a deep breath. "You were an idiot to do that interview."

"Yeah. I am an idiot." He nodded slowly. Standing up, he said, "You and Sally should come home, for Sally's sake. I'll move out."

She stood up to face him. After a minute, she said, "You need a haircut. And a shave." They looked at each other. He resisted the urge to pull her to him, but then she leaned into his chest, so he wrapped his arms around her. It was so welcome and so longed for that it was painful. Achingly good.

"We'll move home," she said quietly. "And you can stay. For Sally's sake."

▼ ▲ ▼

She stayed at Katie's that night, but on Friday after work, Mirabelle and Sally moved back home. Kevin had excitedly cleaned up and planned a special dinner, pesto ravioli. But she had her defenses up. He realized it would take more than just being in the same house to regain her trust.

He lit the candles as they were sitting down to eat, and her cell phone rang.

"It's Risa," she said, looking at it.

"Go ahead," he told her. "I'll get the food on the table."

"Yeah, I'll be quick." She hopped up and walked toward the wide living room window, the phone to her ear. "OH MY GOD!" she screamed. Kevin and the dogs looked at her in alarm. "Okay, I'm coming!"

She wheeled around clutching the phone to her chest. "That was Shane. She's finally gone into labor!"

In a whirlwind she packed a new bag, explaining that Risa, on bedrest, was a week overdue and had been calling constantly, bored and anxious.

"Should I come too?"

"No, stay here with the dogs."

"Text me when you get there," he said, knowing it would be after 1 a.m. before she'd arrive.

"Okay," she said, bursting in her excitement for her little sister.

"Drive carefully," he said. "I love you."

She paused. "I love you too."

Kevin managed to get a bite of ravioli into her as she flew out the door.

He stood at the window where he could see her throw her bag into the backseat and jump into the front of her Subaru. After watching her drive off, he turned to the dogs. "Looks like it's just the three of us." He put the still-corked wine away and got out a beer, pouring it into one of the Lucky Brew beer glasses that Tanna had given them for Christmas. Dishing up a hefty plate of ravioli, he sat down. Though he knew it was for a very different reason, he felt the absence of Mirabelle settle over the house again and sighed.

"Cheers, Mom," he toasted and drank, then pulled out his phone for some companionship while he ate. Only then did he see the text from Elise berating him about the newspaper article about him forgetting the urn in the restaurant. Ah, yes, our mistakes never quite go away.

▼ ▲ ▼

Mirabelle sent pretty consistent updates about Risa's progress throughout the next day, although in brief snippets. The stubborn baby was taking forever. Kevin cringed, trying not to think about it. Poor Risa.

Finally, early Sunday morning, a photo flashed onto the screen of his phone with a ding: a baby with a squished purple face in the arms of her proud auntie. Mirabelle's long hair was pulled into a ponytail and she looked gorgeous, he marveled, even under the sleep-deprived circumstances. The text read: *Harper Lilly born 2:28 am June 21*

She's beautiful! Everyone okay? he texted back from their bed.

Risa's exhausted but good.

He paused, wanting to ask her when she was coming back, but not wanting to sound too whiny. *That's great,* he texted. *You must be tired too.* Not usually one to send emojis, he attached a red heart to the message, feeling somewhat sheepish.

I'm gonna stay until Tuesday. Let's go for a run on Wednesday night.

Her text surprised and delighted him. *Sounds excellent!*

I'll call you later, she wrote.

He sent a thumb's-up emoji, then burrowed back into the bed, knowing he was not likely to sleep more. Too happy.

▼ ▲ ▼

"I am," Kevin panted, "so screwed," desperately trying to keep up as Mirabelle and Sally jogged lightly ahead. Turns out she had added running laps to her workouts at the gym, before her spin class or after yoga. Although he still lifted weights a couple days a week, he hadn't been hitting any basketball pick-up games lately. He wasn't sure why, maybe distracted by his marriage being in shambles. Now with the relay race only two months away, he could see he had a lot of work to do.

She had recounted Harper's birth for him as they ran, which was good because then he wasn't expected to contribute to the conversation. Too busy trying to breathe. Mirabelle was animated with the telling and would start running faster in her excitement. But then she'd reel herself in, staying beside the recipient of her words. Now that the story was told, she seemed lost in reverie and started pulling away again.

Bo tugged on the leash, chasing after Sally, trying to catch up, he assumed. It was hopeless. Mirabelle turned to face him and slow-jogged backward, letting him catch up, a wide grin on her face. He knew she probably didn't intend to signal a stop, but he slowed to a walk anyway, nearly doubling over to catch his breath.

"Geez, Kevin, impress me why don't ya," Mirabelle teased. Oh, she was enjoying this, and he had to smile. Despite the physical torture of it, he was enjoying himself too.

When he finally recovered his breath, he said, "Wow. I have no endurance for distance."

"Stating the obvious," she snarked, and gave him a playful little shove.

"Okay. Well, I'll get there. Probably need to start running every day," he said.

"I think the dogs would like that. I'll run with you." He could tell that she was trying to push the pace of their walking. He let her. "Except for Thursdays, of course."

"On the seventh day she rested."

"Yup! With a glass of good wine!" They were both smiling.

He started to jog again, which was more of a survival shuffle, noting that she didn't complain about the relay and how she hated running. Yeah, he was enjoying himself.

▼ ▲ ▼

"Do we have to bring the urn?" Kevin said, feeling a little churlish. He didn't want the damn thing to leave its spot on the counter again until it went back to live with Elise and Jeff on Labor Day.

"Yes," said Mirabelle. She was packing up a bag of snacks, for both people and dogs.

"But it's just two nights . . ."

"Do you really want to have the urn running our schedule? Deciding when we have to leave so that it's not 'left alone in the condo for more than 48 hours?' Let's just bring it." They were heading to a little coastal cabin for the 4th of July. The dogs always freaked out with the noise of the fireworks, so they made arrangements every year to be somewhere remote—where fireworks were not allowed. This would be their first time to visit Cape Lookout State Park.

"Or we could take it over to Tanna's house," he suggested.

"That's going the wrong way. And too last minute!" She looked over at him, reproachful but smiling. "You've learned your lesson. Won't make the same mistake, right? We could leave it in the car the whole time. Plus, it's only an hour and a half drive; we'll avoid sit-down restaurants along the way."

He shrugged. "Yeah, okay. I'll find a beer box."

"I've got Dawn's letter. Let's go."

Not wanting the beer-boxed urn underfoot, Mirabelle put it in a sturdy plastic crate, wedged in and under several spare blankets. Kevin double-checked her work, not wanting anything to happen to it. While he navigated out of the city, she opened the letter from Dawn and looked it over. There were several pages. "It's showing the details of six legs of the relay: half yours, half mine."

"Do we choose? I'll run the three hardest ones."

She scoffed. "You couldn't run more than *one* of these right now!"

"Hey, I'm getting better!"

"You're also old," She teased.

"Not old, just older than you."

"The letter says that I'm leg ten and you're leg eleven. We don't just choose three, we have to run the ones for that spot on the relay team, get it? Each page shows a map of the course and a graph so you can see how the elevation changes, as well as a description of the route and directions for the van to get to the next exchange place. We have to let Dawn know our estimated pace per mile beforehand. There's also a list of food we're supposed to bring: tuna sandwiches, carrot sticks, etcetera."

"Sounds pretty thorough." He changed lanes to go around a slow-but-erratic driver.

"Look closer at your leg-eleven course descriptions later. It would be good to train for hills or distance, or whatever the course says to expect," she said, studying one of the pages.

"Yeah, okay."

▼ ▲ ▼

"What is that smell?" Mirabelle exclaimed as Kevin and the dogs walked in the door. She'd gotten an emergency work call when they arrived, so he had taken the girls outside to look around.

"Dead fish. Bo got to scatter a flock of seagulls to get to it, which made it extra special."

"Oh my good god! Can you wash him off somewhere? Is there a bathtub? Use lots of shampoo!"

"Let's just go for our run now. Maybe a dip in the ocean will help. We can head in the other direction on the beach so the dogs don't get into the fish again."

"Did Sally get into it?" She started pulling her running clothes out of her bag. Kevin was ready to go, in the t-shirt and basketball shorts he'd put on that morning.

"No, just Bo."

"Smart girl," she gave Sally a quick pet. "Ugh, can you please take Bo outside? The reek is too much! I'll be there in a minute."

When she joined him outside, they followed the trail away from the cluster of six cabins among the trees, past the parking lot, and down to the beach. He pointed them in the dead-fishless direction, and they jogged close to water where the sand was not as soft and so Bo could spend a lot of time washing off. Kevin could match Mirabelle's pace now, though he knew she was being easy on him. Although it had only been a week and a half, the short almost-daily jogs were starting to pay off.

"What was the work emergency?" It was mid-afternoon, sunny and just barely breezy.

"One of the riggers didn't show up and the foreman was out sick, so they needed to find the list of other riggers to try to call in a replacement. Gotta get those lights up."

"Oh, the joys of being in charge."

"Not the greatest cell reception here," she commented.

"Good—less of a distraction!"

Their footfalls fell in muted rhythm on the sand, step, step, step. The dogs had their own rhythm, dashing ahead, pausing to discover something, chasing each other, splashing into the water and out. Kevin was starting to tire, especially with the extra effort of running on sand.

"I've always loved the smell of the ocean." Mirabelle breathed in deep through her nose. The waves made a perpetual low roar, constant and heavy, washing in and drawing back.

"You don't seem to hate running," Kevin observed.

"I guess I don't." She seemed surprised to realize this.

"Why do you say that you do?"

She didn't answer right away. He skipped over a rope of seaweed, except he stumbled on it; his legs wouldn't lift as high as he thought.

"I tried track once. The coach was a total perv." She shrugged and glanced at him. "I guess running isn't so bad when you remove the creepy coach from the equation."

"Ah. Makes sense." He wasn't sure if he should be happy for her or sad. "Well, on behalf of all men, I apologize for our terrible behavior." No, that wasn't the right thing to say. "I just mean, sorry that you had to deal with that."

"Geez, don't worry about it," she laughed, strong and steady beside him. "I'm here now, and I'm running. Guess I'm okay."

They ran a few miles in the one direction, enough for Kevin to be spent. So when they turned around, they retraced their footprints back at a walk, enjoying the sea spray and the birds floating on the breeze. The mosquitoes were more bothersome at this slower pace. They urged Bo into the water as much as they could. As they headed up the path from the beach and along the parking lot, Mirabelle hesitated and then abruptly took off sprinting. Unable to keep up, Kevin plodded after her, wondering why she felt the need to show off by beating him to the cabin. Then he realized what had hurried her, and where she was now standing.

In an empty parking spot. The car was gone.

23

Her hair tied up in a pile on the top of her head, Mirabelle seemed manic as she scrubbed the suds into Bo's fur. It was an operation that she'd been at for longer than probably necessary. Kevin kept his distance while he listened to the canned hold-music through his cell phone, but he could see them through the open bathroom door. Sally was in there too, apparently supervising.

The cell connection mostly held, glitching out twice but not entirely dropping. In the process he found the best spot in the room for reception: at the kitchen sink.

He was suddenly connected to an insurance agent. "Good afternoon, this is Anita, how can I help you today?" She sounded very young.

"Hello! Yes, my jeep was stolen."

"Can I have your policy number, please? Or your name and date of birth?" Kevin could hear the click of the keys as the woman typed in the information he gave. "Okay perfect, Mr. Lucky, was that the 2014 Jeep Wrangler?"

"Yes."

"I'm sorry to hear that. And did you make a police report?"

"Yes."

"Okay perfect. I'll need that report number. And what personal property was inside the vehicle?"

"A Frisbee, some dog toys, a phone charger, uh," Kevin pretended he had to think, wanting to delay the unavoidable, even though he'd just gone over the list with the policewoman. "A golf umbrella, uh, sunglasses, some spare blankets. And an urn."

There was a slight pause before Anita said, "Urn?"

"Yes, my mother's urn." Oh, it was painful. He could feel the embarrassment burn on his face as he stared at the view of trees through the little window above the sink. The splashing in the other room sounded akin to wrestling an alligator, but only briefly.

"Oh. I'm so sorry, sir. Wow, that's terrible!" She seemed to be off-script now.

He didn't want to discuss it and steered her back to the pertinent question of next steps. "My wife and I are at a cabin on the coast. Can we get a rental car out here? We need to get back to Portland by Sunday." As the agent referred him to the nearest car rental agency and explained how to include the expense in his claim, he could hear the water turn on in the bathroom, then off again. Done with the insurance call, he followed up with arranging a rental car. He got off the phone and paced to the wide front window of the sparse-but-adequately-furnished cabin, taking a minute to contemplate the situation.

His mother's ashes were gone. Yeah. He was fucked.

"So? What do we do?" Mirabelle asked behind him. As he turned to face her, Bo did a thorough full-body shake and spattered the room. Sally must have sensed Kevin's dread and padded over to nuzzle his knee.

"We get a ride service to take us to pick up a rental in Tillamook. But we better hurry because it's a twenty-minute drive and they close at five."

"Not 'we;' I'm staying here." She was cross.

"Shit, I didn't ask if dogs were allowed in the rental car," he realized.

"Oh, they're allowed! They have to come home with us, don't they?" she snapped. He wanted to remind her that he had wanted to leave the urn at home, but he kept quiet. Fighting wouldn't help the situation. So the inheritance was a lost cause, so what? Maybe their marriage could still be saved.

He walked to the good-reception spot by the sink and requested a ride on his app, only to find nothing available. So he looked up a taxi service and called them.

"There should be enough time, barely," he told her as he pulled a windbreaker on, putting his wallet and phone in his pockets. "I'll pick up some dinner. What do you want?"

She dropped into the couch and crossed her arms. "I don't care."

"Chinese it is," he chuckled, attempting at humor. She wasn't laughing. "No, I'll just see what there is." He checked his watch. The taxi said they'd be there to pick him up in fifteen minutes, now ten. "I told them I'd be at the junction where it forks to the cabins and all the campsites, so I better go."

"Yeah, I heard you tell them."

He paused, and said gently, "Thanks for washing Bo," before going out the door.

That night he returned with clam chowder and fish and chips, and sushi for good measure. Also an expensive bottle of rum and a six-pack of Coke. Her spirits seemed improved. They toasted as though celebrating a death, and lavishly said goodbye to Cleah's inheritance money.

A perfect evening, in the end.

And in the morning, Mirabelle woke Kevin up with a plan.

▼ ▲ ▼

After a leisurely breakfast of a bag of pretzels and leftover chowder, they walked the dogs and then locked them in the cabin. With high spirits and carefree attitudes, they hopped into the rental, a beefy new Crown Victoria, and cruised to town.

They stopped at the first thrift store that they found. Inside, it had a modest collection of ceramic jars. After carefully inspecting the lot, they admitted defeat and got distracted examining the store's VHS collection. Nothing good there, or in the shoe section. Mirabelle did find a nice wide tie for Kevin: orange and brown paisley.

"Are there other second-hand stores in town?" Mirabelle asked the staff person that rang up her purchase. "Or anywhere that sells ceramic jars?" The helpful man told them three possibilities and the treasure hunt resumed.

"What will we fill it with, when we find the right jar?" Kevin asked as they stepped off the curb to their car.

Mirabelle shrugged affably and pulled open the door. "Campfire ash?" They both laughed. That would be perfect; Cleah hated camping.

Kevin drove and Mirabelle navigated to another second-hand store. This one was bigger, with larger items for sale, like furniture and curtains. There was an impressive section of pottery, and they even found a ceramic jar with swirly blue lines reminiscent of Cleah's urn; however, it was too big and had no lid. Kevin insisted on trying on a wetsuit, but it turned out to be a woman's cut and he didn't fill the boobs out properly. He found a blue sweater that she said looked 'smashingly sexy' on him, so definitely a keeper. Mirabelle added an amazing set of salt and pepper shakers to their shopping basket: of a cat and a fishbowl. They played with the sunglasses for a while, such a variety of styles; they each chose one for the other, which was great since he'd lost his with the car. Then she tried on a string of prom dresses, like a catwalk through the history of proms, ultimately rejecting them all.

By now they knew this was a fool's errand, but it was fun to play the fool together.

The next shop they'd been directed to was a hardware store. Not going directly to the ceramic-pot section, they instead roamed every aisle, methodically taking stock of everything the store had to offer. Kevin lingered over the power drills and Mirabelle was particularly impressed at the selection of putty knives. They did eventually find a section of ceramic jars, primarily planting pots, but nothing close to what they sought.

As they left, they heard some early fireworks explode a few streets away.

"Let's get back to the girls," Kevin said, even though there was still one more place the thrift-store guy had recommended. "It would be awful if someone started shooting off fireworks out there."

"Yeah, they would freak out, the poor hunnies."

He reached for her hand as they walked to the rental car, entwining fingers. He gave her hand a squeeze. "Fun day."

She smiled at him. "Yeah. Fun day."

▼ ▲ ▼

That night, as the sun started dropping into the ocean, they wandered back out to the beach, carefully avoiding what was left of the dead fish. There were other people out there too, but everyone kept to themselves and adhered to the state park's no-fireworks policy.

Kevin spread a blanket over the sand and they settled onto it, sitting close together with the dogs draping over their feet. The air was markedly cooler, in the weaker rays just before twilight. He breathed deeply, feeling centered and full; he'd made his peace with losing the urn.

"Gorgeous," Mirabelle remarked.

"Yeah." It was a view he never tired of. Sunset on the water seemed new every time. He inhaled the salty ocean air.

"You know, I was thinking." She leaned closer. "What if we said the jar broke but we saved the ashes? Just find a different urn to put them in. It's the possession of the ashes that matter, right?"

He glanced at her, considering. "Huh. Possession of the ashes—which may not even really be her ashes in the first place."

"Exactly."

"I've been thinking, though, too: there's a problem with this idea of getting a replacement jar. What about the police report and the insurance report saying the urn was in the stolen car?"

"Right, that's a problem . . . we could amend our reports, say we had the urn after all, just misplaced." She stroked Sally's nose. "I don't know. It was just a thought. I mean, it would mean lying."

"A fake urn with fake ashes. Totally unethical," he nodded, his brow crinkled. "But who would it be hurting? Elise and Tanna would probably prefer an imposter to the alternative of no inheritance."

"Ends justifies the means?"

"Yeah, maybe."

"Sure," she said. "Or maybe we should just call it what it is. I'm okay with the whole Will-Requirements thing being over, a forfeit. Your sisters will get over it."

"Really? You're not upset?"

"Kevin, when are you gonna learn? I'm not with you for your money."

He smiled, feeling free and mellow, better than he'd felt since his mother died eight months ago. A personal independence day. The brilliant sky with ribbons of pink clouds fading to orange fading to purple over the sparkling water would have been enough fireworks for anyone. They leaned into each other, would-be partners-in-crime, as the sun slid below the horizon.

▼▲▼

They woke up early, lounged a bit, then took the dogs for a jog on a nearby forest trail. Bo was now pungent with shampoo; only a hint of the fish carcass lingered. It did occur to Kevin that they didn't have to train now, they wouldn't have to run the Hood to Coast. But he found that he wanted to go on the run with Mirabelle and the dogs anyway.

After showering, they munched on bananas and muffins—variety pack since Kevin liked blueberry and Mirabelle preferred poppy seed—while debating about visiting the beach again before they had to leave. They decided to finish packing up first and were nearly done, those fun thrift-store finds from yesterday crowding their suitcases, when the same policewoman who had taken their statements two days before knocked on the cabin door.

"Good morning," Officer Fields smiled. "Your vehicle has been located,"

Kevin stood dumbfounded at first. "Where? How?"

"That's good news." Mirabelle appeared at his side. "Won't you come in?"

The woman took off her police hat and walked through the door. "There's not much to tell. We got a call early this morning reporting an abandoned vehicle on a forest road. It's being processed and dusted right now. Once they're done, you can take possession. I'll take you out there."

"Wow. Okay. Is the car okay?" Kevin asked.

"I don't believe it's damaged. Wanna come with me and take a look?" They were all still standing, the dogs watching Officer Fields as attentively as the humans. She wore a tight yellow braid and a pressed brown uniform and was practically standing at attention.

Mirabelle met Kevin's eye and asked, "Actually, Officer Fields, we need to check out of here pretty soon, so could we quick do that and then follow you out there?"

"Yeah, that's fine. It's not terribly far, although the road is a bit primitive."

The officer went back outside as they scurried around grabbing bags and throwing it all in the trunk of the rental. The caravan first visited the park attendant to drop off the cabin keys.

The last bit of the road was bumpy, but the Crown Vic could handle it. The tall trees towered over what was essentially a one-lane gravel track. When they came upon the jeep, they could see all the doors were open, even the back one, with its spare tire still attached. It was partway off the road but didn't look like it was crashed. Officer Fields pulled up behind the cop car already there, and Kevin parked behind her. Leaving the dogs in the car, they went for a closer look.

"From your report, looks like there is a phone charger and a Frisbee missing," one of the officers on the scene said. Kevin went to the back and peered past the open door. There she was, good old Mom, the urn still sitting in the beer box in the crate, the blankets pulled back and the lid off. He leaned in; yep, she was still in there.

"Is this how it was found?"

"Yes, the doors were all open when we got here and likewise according to the call-in. We think it was a joyride grab. But maybe they got spooked by the surprise passenger back there," Officer Fields said, clasping her hands behind her back.

"Can I put the lid back on? Should I not touch anything?" The open urn was making Kevin anxious, which surprised him.

"Go ahead, we're done here."

He gingerly closed up the urn.

Another officer came over with a clipboard. "I just need your signature, and you can take custody."

Kevin and Mirabelle looked at each other, smiled, and shrugged. Taking the clipboard and pen, Kevin looked over the form, which basically just stated that he had received the car. He signed and dated it as Mirabelle re-secured the crate with the blankets and shut the doors. She grabbed the keys. They waited to make sure the jeep would start, and the four cars paraded back out of the little forest road to the main highway, where they split off.

The rental place was closed, it being Sunday, but they found the after-hours drop box, transferred all their bags back into their own car, and headed home.

"Weirdly, I'm almost disappointed," Mirabelle said as she drove. Kevin was inclined to agree. He didn't say, though. He was feeling contemplative, relieved, and content—perhaps even mournful. They were mostly quiet on the trip back.

And they didn't stop at any restaurants.

24

"So, if you're so happily married, Kev, what are you doing in a bar with me?" The pretty blonde leaned in and stared deep into his eyes from inches away, only their drinks between them. How well he knew those eyes.

Kevin was taken aback by her question. He looked around and realized that most of their classmates had left. "What time is it?" he asked her.

She checked her phone. "1:30."

"I gotta go," he said, then smiled like she was being ridiculous. "And I'm not 'with you,' Jennifer, I'm with the reunion."

"Aw," she pouted. "We were having such fun catching up. Why get all distant now?"

He got up and grabbed his fleece from the back of his chair. "It was nice to see you."

"Still Mister Cool." She leaped onto him with a big hug, planted a quick sloppy kiss on his mouth, then whispered, "I'll see you tomorrow," into his ear. He extracted himself and went out the door without a backward glance.

Shit. What was he thinking?

At the last minute, he had decided to go to his 20th reunion. It was a two-day thing: Friday night for grads only at a local bar, then Saturday would be a dinner that spouses or partners were invited to as well. It had been fun to see old high school buddies again, although he'd gotten there a bit late and the guys were several drinks deep already. Most were generally thicker, but they behaved just the same. A few had excitedly told him that they'd seen the damn newspaper article; he'd quickly changed the subject. Then his old girlfriend had cornered him. She was still unbelievably hot, and her singular attention on him had dropped Kevin into memories of good old times. It felt awesome. He had started to forget himself, become a high-flying eighteen-year-old again. Oh, the ego.

Once he'd climbed into his car, he checked his phone. Damn, a text from Mirabelle about an hour ago saying she was going to bed. His phone had been in his fleece pocket and the bar had been loud. He wondered if she would believe him. Hoping she would be less irritated at being woken up at 1:30 a.m. by a text than not hearing from him at all, he wrote back: *Sorry, I didn't see your text. Loud bar. I'm heading home now.* He was still over a thirty-minute drive away.

After sending the text, he impulsively called Jeff, immediately cringing, as the phone rang in his ear, for calling in the middle of the night. He started to hang up when the call connected.

"Hello?"

"Hey! Jeff, how are you?" He watched the bar's door.

There was a pause. "What time is it?"

Kevin didn't say anything.

"What the hell?" Jeff said in a low voice. "Is everything okay?"

"Yeah," Kevin said quickly. "Yeah, sorry." He exhaled heavily. "I was just at my high school reunion. I saw a lot of old friends." He paused, but Jeff said nothing. "Sorry," he said again. "G'night." He hung up, still watching the bar entrance. Jennifer exited the building, and he scrunched down, trying to be small and still until she'd driven away.

When he climbed into bed, as quietly as he could half an hour later, he stared at Mirabelle's back in the dark. But she didn't stir.

▼ ▲ ▼

The reunion dinner the next night was at a winery on the outskirts of Vancouver. Mirabelle wasn't too impressed with the location. When they drove up to the place, she'd said, "Really? A winery across from a run-down residential neighborhood and next to a rock quarry?" Then she had to suppress her laughter when they were handed their nametags, each with their own names but both with Kevin's senior picture. At least it wasn't a bad photo, albeit with the chin resting on the fist.

Kevin had his reservations about the whole thing, after last night, and would have skipped it if Mirabelle hadn't pushed him. "But I want to go; I'm curious about your past. We can leave early," she'd said during their run that morning. They'd gone six miles, very slowly. That was the longest run Kevin had done, which made him feel a little more prepared for the relay race, now less than six weeks away.

She hadn't commented on his lateness of the night before, only asked him if he'd had fun. He said he did.

One thing's for sure, he was proud to have her on his arm. She was stunning in a short, simple yellow dress and black heels, her long black hair shimmying as she walked. He'd gone very casual, in a green plaid short-sleeve and jeans.

The scene was what one would expect of a high school reunion. Someone had put in a lot of effort to set up several table displays with yearbooks and paraphernalia, even a stripey cheerleader outfit, a marching band uniform, and a red graduation robe and mortarboard was tacked to the wall behind it all. Mirabelle laughed outright when she saw the boxy mascot with its cartoon face: a Papermaker. "What is that? A machine that makes paper?"

"Well the paper mill employed, like, half the town back then."

"Wow. I love it." He could tell she really did; she wasn't laughing at him. She picked up a yearbook and thumbed through. "Do you have your old yearbooks?"

"Yeah, somewhere."

"Can I see them later? At least the last one? I'd love to see what people wrote in it."

"Sure." He wasn't sure he wanted to see what people wrote.

Then the inevitable greetings with the people milling around. "Good to see you!" "What have you been up to?" He found that everybody was great friends now, thrilled to see everyone, even if they hadn't actually spoken to each other during those high school years. Something about a shared past. Greg was there, his lab partner from Chemistry. He saw Bob, the class clown, who hadn't changed a bit, personality-wise. Brian, Paul, and Rick were reminiscing—football buddies who had also been at the bar last night. Kevin introduced Mirabelle to a whirlwind of smiling faces and let them introduce their significant others. The nametags made sense now; he knew who belonged with whom. Not to mention he didn't have to guess which ones were classmates; there were some he had no memory of at all. Comparing the teenage portraits to their thirty-eight-year-old faces was a trip.

Soon Mirabelle suggested to Kevin they find the wine; it was a winery after all. Becky, who had been their senior class president (and took charge then just like she was taking charge now), overheard and pointed them to the table that was set up as a bar, explaining that the first drink was included with the price of the event. After waiting their turn, he chose a merlot and Mirabelle got a cabernet.

"Hey, Kevin, good to see you!" said Cliff, who had been Kevin's locker partner in middle school, but they'd drifted apart in high school. "Say, how's Tanna doing?" Being just one grade ahead of them, it made sense that some of these classmates would remember her.

"She is really good. Works as a nurse. Has two little girls. Doing good."

"Great, that's great. Tell her 'Hi' for me."

"Sure will," he nodded.

He wished he had prepared a tidy little statement summarizing, impressively if possible, the past twenty years. Off the cuff, he came up with "I work for Metro, overseeing all the concessions for the events." That wasn't bad. When pushed, he elaborated: "The Trailblazers, sure, big concerts, all that stuff. Yeah, I started at the bottom rung and climbed to management. My wife, though, she's at the top of the whole thing." Mirabelle, the powerful, hot executive-in-charge, was unnervingly cool. He could see it in the way his classmates looked at her. And she seemed to be enjoying herself, at least she was very convincing.

"Hey! I saw the article about you in The Oregonian a few weeks ago! Classic Kevin!" Cody, another football buddy, laughed and slapped him on the back while holding his wine glass in the other hand—definitely more coordinated than when they were in high school.

"Oh, that was no big thing. Kind of a joke, really," Kevin attempted to kill the topic.

But President Becky, who now lived in Montana, was insuppressibly curious. "What article?"

Only too happy to explain, Cody retold the article's cringy details of forgetting one's mother's ashes in a restaurant, hours from home. A few others intoned that they'd read it too. Kevin smiled and sighed as the group laughed and drank.

"That's nothing," Mirabelle said. "I insisted on leaving the urn in the car while we were at the coast two weeks ago and it got stolen."

Lab-partner Greg gasped. "The urn? The car?"

"Yep," Mirabelle nodded. "The urn. *And* the car. See, sometimes these things just happen! Am I right?" She lifted her wine glass and several loudly joined in a collective toast. He stared at her, his eyebrows high, realizing she was trying to help. She didn't sound too convincing to Kevin; these sounded like things that only happened in Crazyland to crazy people. Who carries an urn around, after all? But no one seemed to care about that, and he went with it, shrugging in agreement and clinking glasses all around, because yeah, sometimes these things just happen. God, he loved her.

"Did you get it back?" Ex-girlfriend Jennifer said, apparently having just arrived. Kevin took a quick gulp of his wine, trying to hide any involuntarily nervous expression.

"Yes. Yes, we did." Mirabelle leveled a look at Jennifer, as though she could read in her face who this woman was in Kevin's past.

"Mirabelle, this is Jennifer. We went to prom together," Kevin said, and the women shook hands like they were beginning a boxing match. He could almost hear the bell ding to start the round.

▼ ▲ ▼

He was flanked between his wife and his ex-girlfriend during dinner, not by his choosing. Jennifer didn't appear to have come with anyone and kept pulling on Kevin's arm with another question or pressing topic she had to discuss with him. He was starting to feel like he'd been dropped into a scene from Fatal Attraction. Trying to diffuse his exploding brain, Kevin struck up a conversation with Dan, baseball buddy, on the other side of Mirabelle. Dan was gay now, which on reflection was no surprise. Kevin was struck, actually, at how many of his classmates were with same-sex partners. What a sheltered and closeted time they'd grown up in.

The meal was chicken Cordon Bleu, too salty; pasta, a little overcooked; and salad, too iceberg. Jennifer kept inserting herself into the conversation, leaning close to Kevin's elbow. His complimentary first glass of wine drained, Kevin excused himself to visit the no-host bar.

"What is her deal?" Mirabelle murmured to him under her breath, having followed him to the table of alcohol. They each bought a glass of red.

"Guess she's crazy now," Kevin tried to be flippant. "I don't know. She seemed normal enough at the bar last night. I think I may have encouraged her by talking to her then. I'm sorry." Oh boy, was he sorry. He hadn't gone to any of his other reunions and was thinking he didn't need to go to any more.

Mirabelle shrugged, looking somewhat amused, which helped to calm his nerves. "I'm done with my dinner. Wanna wander? I could take another look at that yearbook," she said.

They revisited the memorabilia table. Mirabelle picked up his senior yearbook and flipped to the senior photos pages and Kevin pointed out the folks she'd just met, sometimes with a little descriptor like "fastest runner at our school," "he was homecoming king," or "I don't know how that guy graduated; he was always stoned."

He looked up as Jason approached them.

"Hey, man!" They did a cool-guy half-embrace: clasping right hands and clapping each other on the back with the other. "Mirabelle, this is my buddy Jason. We played football together. He's a lawyer now."

She shook his hand.

"Hey! Nice to meet you! This guy definitely needed domesticating. Yeah. And I heard about the urn-left-in-the-restaurant incident. Oh man!" he chuckled and mock punched Kevin in the shoulder as Jennifer joined the group. "That is so funny, man!" Jason went on. "So, you decided to not file a lawsuit contesting the Will?"

Mirabelle's smile disappeared.

▼ ▲ ▼

She had the keys, and he was pretty sure she'd leave without him. He followed her to the parking lot, gravel crunching underfoot, arms open and palms up, trying to explain.

"Just listen, Mirabelle! I figured it sounded harder than just putting up with Cleah's stupid list, and then I honestly forgot about it! I mean a lawsuit was gonna be expensive and a longshot and we had already hosted—"

She whirled to face him. "I'm not mad that we could've tried to override the Will, Kevin!"

"You're not?"

"I just can't believe you didn't tell me!"

"Shit, I'm sorry!"

She stared at him. "You have to let me be part of these decisions. We're partners! You didn't trust me."

He dropped his hands to his side. "You're right. I'm sorry."

"You're a good man, Kevin. I wish you believed that about yourself." She walked toward him holding out the car keys. "Can we go home?"

When he reached for the keys, she pulled him to her and they clung to each other.

25

More jogging. Very slowly this time, because of the ridiculous distance. It was the first Sunday in August—less than four weeks before race day. They had taken two cars, parked one in the Sellwood neighborhood and driven to start their run near Main City Park in Gresham. They were attempting to follow the route they would be running for Hood to Coast, starting with Mirabelle's leg 10 and running through Kevin's leg 11. Nearly eleven miles altogether along the Springwater Corridor Trail. It had been Mirabelle's idea.

"I think a lot of this used to be railway line that got paved over," she said as they paused at a crosswalk. Kevin grunted, leaned over with his hands on his knees. He was winded. Sally seemed to appreciate the brief rest as well and laid down in the path.

"You doing okay?" she asked. "My watch says we're at six-and-a-half miles, so we're on your course now: leg 11." She held Sally's leash and Kevin had Bo's.

"I'm okay," he panted. There was a break in the line of cars, and they were able to cross. He was feeling really spent; this was a crazy-long run for him.

"Hey, have you requested to have the time off from work for the relay yet?" she asked.

Shit. "No. I'll do it tomorrow."

"Don't forget."

It was a cool morning, relative to the 80-plus degree days they'd been having. The trail was nice, for a paved city trail. A lot of it felt really removed from civilization. It primarily followed Johnson Creek, separate from cars, mostly only hitting traffic when it had to cross streets. It was not too crowded, though they did have to negotiate passing others who were using it for walking or biking, often going single file for a minute. The dogs seemed to like it.

For a while, Mirabelle chatted about a surprise retirement of one of the top marketing executives at work and how they were scrambling to get things set up for moving forward. It was nice that she was carrying the conversation; he was working too hard putting one foot in front of the other. Then she fell silent. The sweat on his back made his shirt stick to his skin.

A few cross streets later, she said, "I was thinking about you not including me in your decision about contesting the Will."

O geez, here we go, he thought, not sure he was up for a confrontation in the middle of an eleven-mile run. Not to mention he thought they'd resolved the issue.

"I just mean it was the same as me not including you in my decision about the abortion. I was just thinking . . ." she trailed off.

He had not expected this. He plodded alongside her, pounding pavement. "You mean, your body, so your decision; my mother, so my decision?" he finally said.

"Yeah. And maybe that's fine," she said. A pair of cyclists passed in the other direction. "Unless we decide together to bring all decisions to the partnership of our marriage? At least decisions that involve or affect the other."

"You sure think about things a lot." She made a lot of sense. It seemed so obvious that he wondered how it wasn't an edict of their marriage already. "I like it. Sounds reasonable," he said.

"Me too," she said. "Better to let each other know what we're dealing with and what we're thinking, especially when things don't have a universal, one-size-fits-all right-or-wrong answer."

She was talking about agreeing on expectations. It was a conversation he was glad to have; he didn't like to be guessing, to worry about being wrong. Oh man, his legs were starting to feel like Jello.

Mirabelle abruptly slowed to walking. Although surprised, he was happy to follow her lead. "This is too far for Sally," she said, leaning down to pick the little beagle up. They walked, carrying her.

"How much further to the car?" he asked.

She checked the GPS on her phone. "Still three-and-a-half miles away." They continued walking, contemplating what to do. He could feel his calves already starting to tighten up.

"We can just walk the rest of the way," he said.

"Yeah."

The day was getting warmer. Kevin looked at Sally, limp in Mirabelle's arms. "We should have brought water."

"I'm gonna run to the car. There's a water bottle in there. Then I can come pick you guys up," she said.

"Good idea." He took poor Sally from her and handed her Bo's leash. "Here. Bo can run with you."

"No, I'll just go myself, in case Bo gets tired too. I'll call you when I'm there. We can meet up at an intersection."

"Right." He didn't really want to split up, but she jogged away. He shifted Sally's weight in his arms.

Bo seemed to enjoy this slower pace; she was finding all sorts of interesting things along the path and had more time to inspect other dogs. She had just finished checking out the terrier going the other way with his person when Kevin's phone rang.

He set Sally down and fished it out, impressed at Mirabelle's fast time.

But it wasn't Mirabelle. "Hello?" he asked.

"Kev, hi! Good to hear your voice. How are you?" said a voice from the past. Jennifer?

"Fine." What else do you say when you're completely caught off guard?

"It's me! Jennifer! I hope you don't mind I got your number from the reunion committee. I've just been thinking about you since the reunion and the way you and your wife ran out of there in a big fight. I was just really worried. Are you okay?"

Freaking hellfire. "Sure. Of course." That was two weeks ago, and this was weird.

"Yeah, well, I just can't stop thinking about you, Kevin," she said.

It was uncomfortable, to say the least. "Look, you don't need to. I'm gonna go now."

"Wait! Kev?"

"What?" He could feel his apprehension and irritation growing.

"Seeing you that weekend, I miss you. Do you ever wonder what could have been?"

Starting to lose his cool, he searched for a good response. "Nope. That's the past, Jennifer. Hey, best of luck to you. Okay, 'bye." It was probably pretty rude, but he didn't want to encourage a stalker situation. He cut the connection and shivered, a spasm of revulsion that made Sally and Bo look up at him in concern.

"Maybe I should've told her not to call me again," he said to the dogs. "Damn." He whistled, feeling a sense of gratitude for being with Mirabelle and not any of the women in his past. It was a good feeling. A lucky feeling. Not only that, over the past few weeks he'd been starting to realize he wanted more with Mirabelle, which really surprised him; he wanted a family with her.

Picking Sally up once more, they resumed their walk, but at the next intersection, he found a place to wait and texted Mirabelle their location. Then he blocked Jennifer's phone number, just to be sure.

▼ ▲ ▼

Since it was a surprise, all he would tell Mirabelle was that they'd need to take two days off from work: Tuesday and Wednesday.

He had been planning their anniversary for months, an attempt to impress her. He felt like it would somehow prove his love and his ability to be responsible, to think ahead. He had requested the Friday off for Hood to Coast already and was pretty proud of that. This thinking-ahead thing felt good.

So, Tuesday morning they packed an overnight bag, took the dogs to the overnight kennel, and headed east—only Kevin knew to where. They left the Cleah urn at home since it was only one night. But Kevin had written a note that he left beside it on the counter: *Please do not steal this urn. It has no value other than sentimental.* In case a thief broke in while they were gone. Yeah, he knew he was being paranoid.

First stop: Multnomah Falls. He pulled left off the freeway to the parking lot in between the eastbound and westbound lanes. They circled the lot three times before a space opened up, it was so crowded. They held hands through the tunnel below the freeway and wound their way past the steep-rooved lodge and up along the waterfall, hiking up the path with the hordes of other visitors. On the bridge, they felt the intermittent spray on their faces. Being August, there hadn't been any rain in a couple of months and the water was running a little slow. They followed the trail winding up alongside the cascade of water. At the upper viewing area, a planked platform with a view of the falls and down to the lodge below, he snapped some photos—of just her, of both of them—and turned to go back.

"Whoa, hold on!" she said, resisting. "I'm not done watching the waterfall. She shifted her gaze. "Isn't it beautiful? It just seems endless, drop after millionth drop."

"Yeah, beautiful." Conscious of the time, he steered her back to the car, taking them further east. After a brief stop at the dam to see the giant sturgeon, they continued to Hood River. It was a cute little town, though very touristy. Driving through the downtown streets was annoying, as pedestrians would walk to the crosswalks and then stand there, deciding perhaps, while the cars waited, expecting them to cross.

They found a little bagel place for lunch, then walked around, window shopping. There were several bicycle shops, a sporting goods store, jewelry shops, a yoga studio, a bookstore, coffee shops, a gallery, and even a shop entirely devoted to toys. It all seemed fitting of an outdoor-sports tourist destination. But they both found the lingerie shop on the corner puzzling. A whole shop of fancy underwear in such a little town?

He remembered to keep tabs on the time, just in time to realize it was time to go.

"Oh shit! I mean, hey, let's go find the car," Kevin said, trying to recover his cool after his initial moment of panic. They got to the waterfront with just enough time to change into swimsuits.

"Surprise!" he said, steering her toward the arranged spot. There were a few other people there. "I booked us a windsurfing lesson!"

"Okay," she said, sounding uncertain. But she grinned when they handed her the wetsuit. After some lecture-learning, they tried out a board set up as a simulator. At first, Kevin felt a little silly, pretending to surf on dry land, but Mirabelle went for it, so he got into it as well. In what seemed like no time, they were hauling awkward boards with a sail attached at the middle out to a somewhat protected cove on the river. Kevin was finding muscles he'd never used before. Mirabelle was of course a natural at picking up the technique. They did a lot of laughing and stayed past the end of the lesson to practice until they were tactfully thanked for coming and asked to go. Kevin took a few pictures before they peeled off the wetsuits.

By this point, it was time to check into the vacation rental. It was close to downtown but with a river view; he figured they could wander around later, maybe find a bar after dinner. While Mirabelle showered, Kevin did a quick run to the grocery store to get ingredients for dinner. When he got back, he put the groceries away and whisked her into the car for the next part of his plan: wine tasting at a local winery. He'd chosen this place, from the many he'd looked at online, because of its lodge-like interior and the view it had of the vineyard. The real thing did not disappoint. The tasting room attendant was funny and thorough, and it took a while to get through the flight of eight wines. In the end they bought several bottles.

As they drove back to the rental, the sun was setting, throwing an eerie golden hue over everything. They uncorked a dry white and stood on the porch, taking in the view. While Kevin retrieved the lasagna recipe he'd saved on his phone, a figure darted past. He looked up.

"Was that a bat?" Mirabelle asked. It swooped again.

"Woah! Yeah, must be feeding on the bugs," he said. There were two of them now, flying a blurry figure-eight route. Kevin watched, mesmerized. Until one smacked into his face. He stepped back as it fell to the ground, swirled and flopped a minute, then flew away. Kevin and Mirabelle looked at each other, aghast, and they fled inside.

"That was so weird," she laughed, settling onto the couch—which was black leather, voluminous, and practically swallowed her—while he made dinner. "Don't bats have echolocation that keeps them from running into things?"

"I don't know."

"I didn't think bats could take flight from the ground. The whole thing—so weird."

Kevin shrugged, trying to not feel creeped out. He shook it off and concentrated on finding a baking dish. The kitchen was open to the living room and Mirabelle fussed with the playlist on her phone to amuse him, a range of music from folk to samba to metal. He didn't cook much on a normal basis and to do so in an unfamiliar kitchen was doubly challenging. It was 10:30 p.m. before they were sitting at the table, but at least he'd brought a candle for a romantic touch. She had settled on a bluesy jazz playlist, and he watched her taste his creation with not a little trepidation.

"Well?" he asked.

"Well, the garlic bread is charred and cold. The salad is good, for a bag kit. But this lasagna is either amazing or I'm just famished." Her eyes twinkled through her grin.

He laughed with an oh-well attitude. "Sorry."

"You know, you got a little sunburned." Leaning forward, she brushed his cheek gently.

"Oh shoot," he said, touching his face. It did feel weather-beaten. "How is yours not?"

"I put tons of sunscreen on every day," she said and yawned as a saxophone crooned.

It was late.

"I tried to fit too much into today, didn't I?" Kevin shrugged, realizing that he had been ticking through his planned anniversary activities the whole day. He tried to think back, recapture the moments together. How do you treasure an experience after the fact? But he found that he could remember and savor sharing the cool sights, the effort at learning something new, and a lot of laughing together. Even just hanging out together while he cooked was fun.

"Like an activities director," she laughed. "Maybe we should do something like this every week, so we could spread the good ideas out."

"Deal!" They established date-night Mondays, as it was the day least likely to be interrupted by work events. As they ate dinner, they decided to alternate being the one taking the other out, so next week would be up to Mirabelle to plan.

When they were done eating, he cleared their plates. He came back with a little box and led her to the couch.

"Here." He set the box into her palm.

Inside she found the earrings he had bought for her on Elise's birthday. "I love them!" She seemed surprised that she did.

"Happy anniversary." He reached an arm around her.

She cocked her head, looking at him sideways. "If you were to make me a promise, what would it be?"

He took her hand, playing with her wedding ring gently. "I would promise . . . to be true to you. And to treasure you."

"You are cheesy," she chided, "and I like it." She kissed him then, letting it linger.

"Okay, what about you?" he asked, feeling the closeness of her body.

"I think I would promise to expect the best of you."

Her answer surprised him. He hesitated. "You might need to expect to have patience with me for not thinking of everything or not saying the right thing." She laughed at this, and he went on. "But you can expect that I'll try." *Sometimes you change your behavior for your partner's sake,* he reflected, *and sometimes your partner changes their expectation.*

Mirabelle hopped up abruptly, retrieved their wine glasses, and settled beside him again. "Here's to four years, and forty more." He took the glass she held out to him.

"Fifty." He clinked his glass to hers, "And—here's to maybe starting a family? You would be a great mom." She looked at him, but he couldn't read her gaze. "If you want to, I mean," he amended. "I actually think I would."

"You would, huh? Hmm." She smiled, thoughtful, as old soulful jazz floated around them. The candle flickered on the table, and she snuggled into him. "Thanks for today."

▼ ▲ ▼

"You're *where*?" Mirabelle asked over the phone. Kevin explained again how he'd gone to the gym after work and happened to mention the bat-flying-in-face episode to Tom, his lifting partner. Tom had cut their lift session short and ordered him to go to an emergency room.

"What? That's crazy," she said.

"Well, I'm at the E.R. waiting to be seen. I'm just letting you know. Tom's here, too; he went looking for coffee, I think." He was feeling stupid now, starting to doubt his friend's advice.

They were both silent for a beat.

"Kevin, were your eyes open? Did you get scratched? Wouldn't you have blinked?"

"I don't think I'm scratched, but, yeah, I think my eyes were open. It all happened so fast. I did blink, but maybe not before it hit my eye." Tom appeared with two blue Gatorades, handing one to Kevin.

"I'm coming down there." She hung up before he could object.

▼ ▲ ▼

Mirabelle arrived at the hospital waiting area just before Kevin was called back by a nurse. Tom went home, and she and Kevin followed the nurse, who first took his weight.

"So, a bat, huh?" the nurse asked, motioning him toward the exam table. He appeared more like a surfer dude than a healthcare professional. He took Kevin's vitals and wrote notes on a clipboard while Kevin relayed the story again.

"Do you think I should even be concerned? I'm probably wasting your time," Kevin said.

"Let's let the doctor decide that. I'll be right back," the nurse dude said, and left.

Kevin looked at his phone. "God, it's so late. I'm sorry!" he said.

"Don't worry about it," Mirabelle swiped the air and smiled, staring at him as if she were trying to see signs of rabies. Soon she sat down in a chair.

They waited forever. Kevin was getting hungry and feeling a little sore from windsurfing yesterday. Finally, a doctor breezed in, washed his hands, and pulled on blue surgical gloves. He was very pale and skinny. At his prompting, Kevin told the bat story yet again.

"Show me where it hit you?"

Kevin pointed to his left eye.

"And when was this?" the doctor said, peering closely at his face.

"Yesterday. Last night around sunset," he said as Mirabelle nodded.

"So about 8:30 or so. Less than 24 hours anyway."

"Yeah, I guess."

"Good. The thing about rabies is that if you wait for symptoms to show up, it's probably too late. And of course, the sooner treatment is administered, the better. You do have some scratching here that looks recent."

"Do I?"

"Yes, a bit." The doctor shifted his weight to his heels and put on a serious face. "Look. Without being able to examine the bat, we can't know for sure, but the behavior you're describing is certainly not normal in a healthy bat. I would recommend proceeding with treatment, just to be safe."

Kevin looked at Mirabelle, who raised her eyebrows and nodded.

"Wait, do you mean those daily shots in the stomach?" Kevin didn't know much about the treatment but seemed to remember hearing it was pretty miserable.

"No, no, it's not so bad anymore. We'll give you a big dose of human rabies immune globulin, which will basically kill any bad thing in the body. Then there'll be a series of rabies vaccine shots on a strict schedule. Okay? I'll have them get it ready." He left.

Turning to Mirabelle, Kevin said, "I'm feeling very aware of my mortality right now." She hopped onto the exam table and leaned into him.

After more waiting, they heard wheels rolling toward them and voices outside the door. "This poor guy, he's gonna be so sore!" "Oh my god, I know." The door opened and two wide-smiling nurses rolled a cart in with a tray of several unbelievably humongous needles atop it.

"Jesus, I could hear you out there!" Kevin was feeling faint. Mirabelle was shaking beside him, crying. Then he realized she was just trying not to laugh.

"Okay, we're doing two in each of your buttocks, then one in each thigh. The dosage is based on your weight," the smaller of the two said, handing him an informational sheet. "Then we'll give you the first of the four vaccine shots today in your arm. Prefer left, or right?"

Seven shots! He swallowed and choked out, "Left."

"Left arm," she repeated, picking up a syringe. With a toothy grin, the nurse added, "Okay. Drop your pants and turn over."

▼ ▲ ▼

"How many tuna sandwiches can six people eat? Seriously!" Mirabelle said, seeming genuinely perplexed at the amount of food Dawn had assigned them to bring.

Kevin shrugged. "I can eat a lot." At least that made her laugh. "It is a twelve-person team; maybe we're supposed to give half of the sandwiches to the other van."

"Yeah, about those other six teammates of ours, I'd have thought Dawn would've arranged a meet-and-greet beforehand," said Mirabelle. "I just think that would've made sense. I mean, who are those people?"

"Yeah, I don't know. Dawn's letter says she placed an ad to fill the other van."

"I know what she said." Her tone was surly.

It was the night before the relay, and he was nervous. They had finished eating their plates of spaghetti, carbo-loading, which she had scoffed at, but he had insisted. Now Mirabelle was smearing tuna into two dozen sandwiches while he chopped three pounds of carrots into sticks. The little bottles of chocolate milk and Gatorade were chilling in the fridge, as were the grapes, and two bags of ice were sitting ready in the freezer. An empty blue cooler sat on the floor, next to a bag of energy bars and corn chips, and Dawn's letter of instructions lay on the table between them.

"How far is it again?" Kevin said.

"198 miles. From Mount Hood to the Coast."

"Seems crazy as fuck." He was referring to his mother.

They had tapered their workouts, per Dawn's advice, not having run at all the last couple of days. It added to his antsyness. What were they in for, really?

The Monday date nights had been fun. They'd had two since their anniversary. Mirabelle planned ice skating and dinner for the first one, and the next week Kevin took them to dinner and a movie. They'd been spending more time together training for the relay—a very good thing—and adding date nights gave their relationship another dimension: being together in a dressy, fun, going-out way, too. He didn't know what Mirabelle had planned for this Monday, but being so soon after the relay race, he hoped it didn't include running.

The three additional rabies vaccine shots had not been fun, but at least they weren't as bad as that first set. Although, as terrible as those seven initial massive shots were, he had not felt better in his life. It was like an injection of youth; he had no aches, no tiredness, not even a runny nose. It made for some really good workout runs, productive workdays, amazing sex even. For a while. After a week his superhuman strength reverted to normal-human ability. He'd had his final vaccine shot on Tuesday.

"We can leave here by 10:15 tomorrow morning," he said. "That'll give us plenty of time to drop the girls at the kennel on the way."

"I know," she snapped. "I said I read her letter, too."

"Yeah." She was being so touchy. It made Kevin not want to say anything.

According to Dawn's instructions, they were to meet at Tanna's house at 11 a.m. where they would load the van Dawn was bringing with their cooler, water bottles, sleeping bags, changes of clothes, personal items, extra shoes, and headlamps.

Meanwhile, Van 1 will have started at 8 a.m. from the top of Mount Hood, each of those six runners running a leg. That van was expected to be finished at 12:25 p.m. at the first major van exchange, and then it would be Van 2's turn, except Dawn wanted Van 2 there by noon, so as to have no chance of being late.

"Do we need to bring the urn?" Mirabelle said.

"No way!" Kevin said. "I am *not* bringing the urn along in a van of people jumping in and out. Besides, Dawn said to expect our team to finish the whole race in 27 hours max, so it's nowhere near the 48-hour limit."

"Well, if *Dawn* says so," Mirabelle snapped again, then paused mid-packaging another sandwich. She dropped it on the table and sighed. "Sorry. I don't know why I'm so anxious."

"It's okay. I am, too." He grabbed a carrot stick from the Ziploc and stuck it in his mouth, chewing as he chopped some more. He was deeply regretting not contesting the Requirements in his mother's damn Will, but he certainly wasn't going to say so. He hoped she wouldn't either.

It was too late now anyway.

26

"Finally!" Dawn exclaimed as soon as Kevin and Mirabelle got to Tanna's house, the last to arrive. "We've got to leave right now!"

Confused, he checked his watch; they weren't late. As they scrambled to transfer the gear from their car to Dawn's van, she explained that she had been in contact with the captain of the other van and those runners were finishing way ahead of their projected times, expected to arrive about 40 minutes before they had originally calculated.

"Put these on before we get there!" Dawn tossed matching tie-dye t-shirts to them, just like the one she was wearing. Kevin saw that everyone had one clutched in their hands. "You don't have to wear it while you run, unless you want, but we'll need it for the photo at the beginning and the photo at the end." It said *Cleah's Kids* on the front, apparently their less-than-inspiring team name. Between the tie-dye, her fluorescent pink compression socks, and orange pigtails, Dawn looked like a kid's show sidekick. There would be no missing the van, either, entirely painted up with what looked like either bright tie-dye spots or bursts of fireworks. *Cleah's Kids* was written across the back of the van, like it too was wearing the matching t-shirt.

Six people in a Dodge minivan felt tight, especially with all the gear and the knowledge that they would be packed in there together for 27 hours, give or take. As they drove the 45 minutes to Sandy to begin their part of the race, Dawn did a lot of explaining. About how the relay worked: runners 1 through 6 were in the other van, this was Van 2 which were runners 7 through 12, and the vans would take turns being on the course, leapfrogging each other three times; about the slap bracelet, that was like the baton passed from one runner to the next in the exchange zone; about her iPad, that she'd downloaded a Hood-to-Coast-relay app for them to track the times for each leg as they went along—Van 1 had the iPad right now and they would trade it back and forth, whichever team was currently running the course; about the buddy system she'd devised, so that two people would be responsible for looking after each other with whatever they needed, like water and getting to the exchange area on time and ready to go. Her buddy system was based on which leg each person ran—7 with 10, 8 with 11, 9 with 12—so that the helper wasn't just coming off a leg or needing to prepare for their leg at the same time. She went over some of the rules, like not peeing in woods or yards, no headphones, no alcohol, no littering, or they could be disqualified. There was so much! And even though it was a rushed Reader's-Digest-condensed version, probably due to the altered timeline, she exuded a chipper excitement. Captain Dawn was intense about the organization and over-the-top about the party of it all. Kevin couldn't tell if this was Cleah's doing or if it was just Dawn's personality.

Sitting in the backseat, he pulled the team t-shirt over his other shirt as instructed. "I don't want to do this," he quietly confided to Mirabelle, who just laughed at him. He meant the t-shirt, but he meant the whole relay, too. Neither of them had slept well and it had already been a busy nerve-wracking morning, making sure they had all the stuff they would need and dropping the dogs at the kennel. They'd left the same note beside the urn that asked any would-be prowler to leave it alone.

What seemed like a totally insane van looked like an alien finding its homeland when they pulled into the high-school parking lot, filled with other vans decorated with clever team names and goofy drawings. One had a blow-up doll on a lawn chair tied to the top. Two women crossed the street sporting troll-doll wigs. Dawn parked, and from the back she pulled a stick with a poster-board sign that read *Cleah's Kids, 184* on both sides. She grabbed a passerby from a group clad in Hawaiian shirts to take the group photo, before rushing them toward the tennis courts, where the runners were to switch. It was hard to stay together, threading through the meandering crowd. They passed someone dressed as Elvis, but most people were decked out in athletic spandex with bright color accents for visibility. Kevin imagined this was close to a sporty Woodstock experience.

When they neared where the runner exchanges were happening, Dawn glanced around and thrust the tall sign into Kevin's hands, saying brightly, "Find the Van 1 runners! We'll need to get my iPad from them! They have a sign, too, and the same team t-shirts." She grabbed Mirabelle and Elise and pulled them to the edge of the roped-off exchange-zone chute for runners-on-deck.

▼ ▲ ▼

"You two are buddies," Dawn said cheerfully, dropping four safety pins into Mirabelle's palm. "Remember, that means you have to help each other when it's the other's turn to run, okay? So Mirabelle, help Elise pin her race number on."

Elise was runner 7, so she was up next. Petrified, she watched sweaty runners come in and fresh runners take off. People shook cowbells and cheered for their own. She realized she wouldn't recognize the runner she was waiting for. "How do

I know which one is our team member?" she asked. "I've no idea what she looks like!"

"Just remember the team number: 184," Dawn chirped with enthusiasm, pointing to the race bib Mirabelle had just pinned to her shirt. Elise now noticed that someone was bellowing out numbers through a megaphone, so she listened hard for number 184. There were so many runners—all ages, shapes, and sizes—arriving one after the other, usually only seconds between them. One guy finished his leg wearing a glittery red skirt and was met by another runner in a similar red skirt. Most of the wigs and costumes were on the spectators, though, not those currently running. Their own matching t-shirts seemed tame now. It occurred to Elise that she didn't want to run in the cotton t-shirt; it was too hot! She quickly pulled it off and thrust it at Mirabelle. Her blue tank top would be enough.

"Wait! Your race number!" Mirabelle hurried to re-pin the race bib to her tank top.

All set and needing to move, Elise bounced around nervously, wondering if she should be warming up with a jog. No, she was going to be running over fifteen miles this weekend and didn't want to add any more. Instead, she leaned over and stretched.

"One! Eight! Four!" the caller shouted, and Elise's heart jumped. Dawn started whooping and pushed her into the exchange lane. A short, hairy man sprinted toward her and clapped a slap bracelet onto her wrist. She turned and sprinted in the direction the others had run.

Elise hadn't gone far before she realized she needed to slow down. There was no way she could keep this pace up, not even for a mile. And this leg was five and a half, rated moderately difficult! It was hard to slow to what seemed more her normal plodding pace. She was immediately passed by several runners, but she tried to not care about that. She remembered Dawn's letter, saying they didn't have to win, just had to finish. "Slow and steady," she repeated to herself like a mantra, in rhythm with her footfalls on the shoulder of the paved country road.

A few team vans passed with their windows painted: *Run Now Drink Later* and *HTC pickup lines: The tag on your skort must say 'made in heaven.'* One van had a bevy of clown heads somehow attached to the roof. Crazy! She smiled. Her body felt strong—not fast, but strong. This is what she'd been training for, usually with Jeff, and once a week they'd made the kids run with them, too. She wished Jeff was running with her instead of next. Stupid relay.

There was a runner up ahead but pulling away. She tried to keep the woman in her sights, but she grew steadily smaller. Elise was startled by screaming and honking behind her, and then the tie-dye-decorated van passed by, familiar arms waving out the windows. Her mood and her steps got lighter, then shifted, and she had a sudden urge to flag them down to pick her up.

The van disappeared into the distance. Now she felt entirely alone, with a long way to go.

▼ ▲ ▼

Dawn was in the chute, ready to run her leg, and started jumping and waving her arms, screaming "Jeff! Jeff!" when she spotted him coming. She did this for a while, since he still had a long way to run after he appeared; it felt anticlimactic to Tanna. She was there as Dawn's buddy, though Dawn didn't seem to need any help. Jeff fumbled to slap the bracelet onto her wrist, having not pulled it off his own wrist until he was already there. Tanna, took note so that she would have a smoother transition. Dawn dashed away in a blur of bright colors and

Tanna, holding the iPad they'd gotten from Van 1 at that first van exchange, swiped the digital bar on the screen that told the app that a new runner was on the course.

Breathing heavily and dripping sweat, Jeff pushed his way past the crowd watching the exchanges. Tanna and Kevin followed him, Kevin trying to shove a water bottle into Jeff's hands since he was his assigned buddy.

"Hot," Jeff gasped, finally seeing the water Kevin held in front of him and taking it.

"Yeah. Wasn't there a storm in the forecast for tomorrow?" Kevin asked. Tanna shrugged and Jeff didn't answer.

They walked, letting Jeff cool down and rehydrate. "What time is it?" he said.

"About 1:45. How was it?" Tanna asked, knowing he'd just run six miles.

"Not bad, pretty flat," Jeff panted, finally catching his breath. "Just long. And I kinda sprinted at the end."

Kevin and Tanna exchanged looks, stifling smiles. It had not looked like sprinting to her.

They took their time getting back to the van, knowing they had only about four miles to drive to the next exchange. Dawn had nearly five-and-a-half miles to run and would take close to an hour to get there, so they didn't need to hurry. Jeff climbed onto the bench in back and sprawled out. Tanna handed the iPad to Elise and took the wheel. Mirabelle, who was to run next, sat up front to navigate. Kevin and Elise sat behind them, sharing a bag of chips. They pulled into traffic. There were no runners on the road here, as they were running on the Springwater Trail now, but a long parade of race vans piled up at every intersection.

"Jeez, look at all these vans," said Tanna. She didn't like driving such a big rig, especially in such tricky traffic.

"Aren't there, like, a thousand teams out here?" Elise mused. "Which means twelve thousand runners!"

"Two thousand relay vans," Kevin added.

"Insane." This was the weirdest thing Tanna had ever done.

"You'll take a left at the next light," Mirabelle said. There was lots to keep track of: who's next, figuring out directions, remembering to hydrate, when to eat, who was whose assigned buddy.

"I guess my running time isn't accurate," Elise said, examining the data on the app, "since it didn't get swiped when I started." They hadn't connected with the Van 1 runners for maybe ten minutes after Elise had started running. "It makes me look like I was faster than I was. The runners in our other van are super fast! I think they averaged a pace of about seven-and-a-half minutes per mile."

Tanna snorted. In this van, most of them projected a pace of nine- or ten-minute miles, although Mirabelle's pace was projected to be under eight and a half.

"They sure weren't talkative," Mirabelle said.

"It kinda makes sense," Elise said. "I mean they must just be here for the running, not necessarily for any team stuff. Can you imagine answering an ad to run this relay with a bunch of strangers?"

"I'm okay with runner-nerds," Tanna remarked. "If they weren't here, Mom would probably have expected us to each run six legs, instead of just the three. I'm glad we're a team of twelve."

"Yeah, no kidding," Kevin said.

"Oh, Kevin, by the way. Tanna and I went to cull through stuff and do some cleaning at Mom's house a few weeks ago, but when we got there it was basically cleared out. There was only some furniture, mostly chairs and a few tables."

"Yeah, that was strange," said Tanna. Unnerving, and even a little violating.

"Who did that? I wonder where all her things are," Kevin said. "It only gets weirder."

"I was relieved, actually," Tanna added, about Cleah's house, as she found a place to park in a line of too-small spaces. "Hey, can I see that?" she said, pointing. Mirabelle passed her the handbook full of information and rules, that Dawn had called the race bible. As Elise helped pin a race number to Mirabelle's shirt, Tanna studied the van's route to the next exchange.

▼ ▲ ▼

Kevin's first leg was less than five miles, and he was glad he'd run some of the route earlier in the month. It was harder in the 90s heat of midafternoon, as opposed to the morning cool it had been back then. Even though it was hot, he was feeling fine. It had been surprisingly enjoyable to receive the race bracelet from Mirabelle, her face flushed with sweat, so sexy. Now he came upon a race marker telling him he had only one mile to go. The whole way along, some runners passed him and he passed others. He wasn't particularly fast, but this relay was definitely doable.

A voice called out, "Passing on your left." Kevin looked, as this was the first time anyone had announced their intention. Two runners pushed by him moving fast, one almost directly behind the first, and they were tethered together by a leash at the waist. Kevin realized the second man was being guided. He was simultaneously hugely impressed and quite humbled to be passed by a blind runner.

▼ ▲ ▼

Up ahead, a relay van pulled off the road and its team spilled out. Tanna smiled; they looked like they were having quite a fun party. Her six-and-a-half-mile leg started on the paved-over-railway creek trail and then quickly hit Portland city streets, heading to the Willamette River. The shadeless pavement soaked up the sun's heat and raised the temperature a lot. At least there was a volunteer in a highlighter-yellow safety vest at every turn, keeping her on the right path. And she had Mumford and Sons playing on a little speaker on her wrist that Leif had lent her. He was never far from her thoughts, though still a cautious arm's length from her heart.

Watching all the others in the van finish their legs, Tanna had felt her nervousness grow. She was the last one and was glad to be finally running. Dawn was, of course, a great buddy, making sure Tanna had warmed up a little with movement and stretching before her leg, and had even asked her what kind of drink she wanted waiting for her at the end of it. Tanna couldn't decide between chocolate milk and water, so Dawn said she would bring both. She felt spoiled. It also felt a little nerve-wracking, being Dawn's buddy. She couldn't quite identify why. Perhaps the woman's underlying power of being able to decide whether the three siblings were complying with Cleah's Will Requirements or not.

As she grew closer to the partying team, they started to cheer and clap for her. Sweat-drenched, Tanna was surprised at how the cheering from these strangers, sharing a common course, buoyed her. As she waved back, one of them took her photo. That seemed a little strange, until a runner breezed past her, and she realized they had been cheering for him. She was the roadkill for his picture.

▼ ▲ ▼

Elise was still finishing a tuna sandwich when Jeff parked the van and they all followed Dawn a few blocks to the exchange area under the Hawthorne Bridge. She had thought it was busy at the first major van exchange, but the crowds here eclipsed that. It was overwhelming, yet understandable, she supposed. The exchanges when the slap bracelet was passed to the first runner of the other van meant both vans and all twelve teammates were there, unlike the exchanges between the six runners in the same van. On top of that, there seemed more than just team members here. It was the city, after all; there were spectators and even news reporters milling around.

The long rows of porta potties were astounding, and the lines of people waiting were even more unbelievable. Jeff quickly got in line, with Mirabelle right behind him. Elise and Kevin followed Dawn's lead of searching for the other van's half of their team, Kevin carrying the *Cleah's Kids* sign like a battle flag. With the churning of the crowd, it was an effort to stay together.

"Dawn, how long until Tanna gets here?" Elise asked.

Dawn consulted the iPad. "Should be in two minutes ten!" she exclaimed, still moving toward the exchange. "There they are!" She pointed to the matching *Cleah Kids* sign floating above the crowd not far away.

"Wanda is already in the chute, ready to go," Paul, the apparent captain of Van 1, told them once the groups had reached each other. Elise introduced herself to the runner who had handed off to her earlier. His name was Bill. They pressed forward toward the exchange zone. They could only see where Tanna would appear under the bridge from running along the river; there wasn't much lead time because of the blocked vantage point, so they were watching closely. And suddenly Tanna was there! She'd run just a little quicker than she'd estimated for her pace. Elise felt dismayed at realizing she was the slowest runner on the team. She watched as Tanna handed off smoothly to Wanda, who followed the route up onto the bridge. Dawn swiped the iPad and handed it to Paul.

"Okay, see you at exchange 19!" Dawn called after them as they left quickly; Wanda was a fast runner on a short four-mile leg, and Van 1 needed to move to get there before her.

It took a while to get to Tanna in the crush surrounding the exchange zone, and when they did, they found her hugging two strangers. She blushed as she introduced her friends Denise and Leif. Elise caught Kevin's eye, who nodded. So, this was the boyfriend! He was cute and seemed nice.

But Dawn didn't want to dawdle, even though they had some time now while Van 1 took the course. Denise and Leif said goodbye, and Tanna said she wanted to pee. They found Jeff and Mirabelle still in line at the porta potties, so they collectively decided to find a gas station and use those facilities.

"Okay!" Dawn declared from the driver's seat, with a celebratory air, as they sat down and strapped on seat belts. "We're done with twelve of the thirty-six total legs of this relay! Be sure you're drinking lots of water!"

Elise took a deep breath. One leg done. Two to go.

27

In any city, Tanna knew that 5:30 p.m. on a Friday means commuter traffic. Add to that the Hood to Coast vans all trying to get to the same place, and a forty-five-minute drive can take two hours—and did. Along the way, they passed hundreds of runners on the course, maybe thousands. First on the sidewalk and, when that disappeared, on the shoulder. Tanna figured they must have passed their teammate from the other van at some point, whichever one was running right then, but she didn't care. She was tired and could feel her legs starting to cramp.

Dawn did the calculation aloud as they finally reached the exchange where they would start their next set of legs. "Okay, so Van 1 has just over 34 total miles to run, and readjusting based on how fast they ran their first set means they will probably get there in just under four-and-a-half hours, so we should figure 9-ish." Tanna checked her watch simultaneously with Dawn, who went on, "So we have two hours to eat and rest! And I would really suggest doing both. It's gonna be a late night."

Everyone climbed out of the van, except Dawn, and went straight to the coolers in the back. Tanna grabbed an energy drink, a peanut butter sandwich, and a few grapes. They sat close behind the van in the field-turned-massive-parking-lot and ate for a bit, though Elise ate very little. Because she would be running next, Tanna assumed. Tanna stretched her legs out in front of her; they felt leaden, like blocks of wood. She was just glad to be outside the vehicle.

Soon they could hear soft snoring coming from inside the van. Elise giggled. Painted-up vans drove past, arriving and leaving, people walked by. It was starting to get dark, but they couldn't see the sun actually set, with all the hills and trees surrounding the field. Jeff stood up, announcing he had to find the bathroom, which was probably another row of blue porta potties closer to the exchange area. Kevin got up to join him in the search.

Tanna finished eating and laid back onto the grass, spread eagle. She felt heavy enough to sink into the ground. "God, I'm tired."

Mirabelle and Elise agreed.

"So where are your kids this weekend?" Mirabelle asked.

"My three are at sleepovers. They were pretty excited." Elise laid down on Tanna's left.

"What about you, Tanna?"

"With their dad." She closed her eyes. It would be bedtime for the girls soon, although she knew Joe was terrible about the bedtime routine. She breathed deeply, reminding herself not to care: losing battle. Not the end of the world.

"My sister, Risa, had her first baby in June," Mirabelle said.

"Oh nice!" said Elise. "What's the baby's name?"

"Harper."

"Wait. Sorry, but is that a girl or a boy?" Elise said.

Mirabelle laughed. "Girl. Harper Lilly."

"Pretty name," said Tanna, smiling, her eyes still closed. She folded her hands on her stomach.

"Risa seems tired and happy, and fully in it. It's her whole world now."

"Yeah, that's how it works," Elise said with a chuckle.

It was quiet for a minute, Dawn's cute little snores setting a rhythm. Tanna nearly drifted into weary sleep.

"Can it work, though? Doing both kids and a career?" Mirabelle asked.

Tanna opened her eyes. It was dark now, and stars were starting to emerge. "It can work," she replied. People walked past with flashlights, and the headlights of vans cut through the darkness periodically. But it was relatively quiet.

She could feel Mirabelle lay back, beside her to the right. "Yeah?"

"Sometimes I wish I didn't have to work," Tanna said. "But I love my job. You figure it out. I imagine it would help to have a good co-parent." She closed her eyes again and folded her knees up into the air, putting her heels onto the ground near her butt. "Now that they're in school it's better. You just do it."

Elise said, "Having kids makes you old and keeps you young."

"That sounds like something you would cross-stitch onto a pillow," Tanna chided. "Hmm. It's true though."

"Not to change the subject," said Mirabelle, "but Tanna, how well did you know Kevin's high school girlfriend?"

"Whoa, where did that come from?" Tanna laughed. "Oh, the twentieth reunion! Did you guys go?"

"Yep."

"Painful?"

"Yep. Also interesting," Mirabelle said.

Tanna laughed. "Yeah, I went to mine last year. It's a hate-to-but-want-to type of thing, for sure."

"You probably knew all of those people I met."

"Probably. Yeah, I remember Jennifer. That was a good one to let go of, honestly."

"She didn't like me," Mirabelle said.

"I bet!"

"What was Kevin like in high school?"

Tanna considered. "He was busy. He was social. He annoyed the heck out of me, like a little brother does. Mom's affair happened early in his junior year and that seemed to steal his childhood a little, shut him off. But those were his teenage years, so maybe he was bound to get angsty anyway." She paused. "He was a good kid. Just a little lost."

Elise had stayed quiet through this exchange between Tanna and Mirabelle, because she had been gone at college during those years, Tanna assumed. The three women laid there until the men returned and Dawn climbed out of the van, chastising them gently for laying in the grass, which was apparently against race rules. There were designated areas for sleeping—safety issue. As they pulled themselves to their feet, Dawn presented a pile of gear to Mirabelle.

"Elise needs to put on a reflective vest, a headlamp, and two flashers, front and back. I've got two sets of this stuff, so we don't have to deal with passing it off between runners in the exchange. Oh, and don't forget the race number!"

Mirabelle nodded. "Okay, Buddy," she said to Elise. "Let's get you dressed."

Dawn got the *Cleah's Kids* sign out and clicked on an LED trim that Tanna hadn't realized was there. She handed it to Tanna as she said, "I got a text from the other van and they're pretty much on schedule, so we should get up there."

They ambled toward the exchange area. It felt good to move.

Elise fidgeted. "Do I have time to pee?"

"Oh! If we hurry!"

▼▲▼

Kevin swiped the iPad as Jeff took off on his second leg and Elise came in. She had just finished what sounded like a grueling leg, nearly six miles all uphill. Mirabelle gave her water and a protein bar and walked around with her to help her cool down. She was proving to be a very good buddy, Kevin observed with a fair amount of pride.

Not needing to use the restroom, Mirabelle returned to the van. Elise looked really spent, Kevin noted, standing behind her in line for the porta potties. A blinding flood light was set up to the left.

Elise turned around with her hand on her forehead. "I have this nagging headache. Dawn says I'm dehydrated." She lifted the water bottle she was holding and gave a strained smile. "Working on it."

Kevin nodded and smiled back. "Well, maybe you can sleep a little. You're lucky you're done with this leg."

"Yeah, two down," she sighed, sagging.

The long line moved forward, and Elise turned to take the few steps to close the gap, Kevin likewise behind her. They had already driven to the next exchange. Jeff was out on the course now, but his leg was long and hard, so he was expected to be running for at least an hour. Everyone else was resting back in the van.

Elise turned sideways to Kevin, her arms crossed. She looked tired but also sad.

"Hey, are you okay?" he asked.

She shrugged, staring at his feet. "I'm tired. It's late. You know how all your worries seem worse in the middle of the night."

He waited; she didn't seem finished.

"I just wonder about Jeff. Last fall I was sure he had a secret girlfriend, and then not, and then the last few months he's been weird." She stepped forward again with the slowly advancing line.

Kevin laughed. "Jeff cheating? That's ridiculous!"

Elise's brow crinkled and tears started forming. "But there's been several late-night phone calls. He even left really late one night, and it was past midnight when he got home. I don't know; I'm going crazy."

"When was the last late-night call?"

"I think about a month ago. That I know of."

"Oh god, Elise. Jeff's secret girlfriend is me," Kevin realized.

"What?"

They looked at each other, confusion on her face, comprehension on his.

"*I've* been calling him, Elise. I was going through some things, rough-marriage-patch stuff, and after these family gatherings I just felt like I could talk to Jeff. Wow, I even told him not to tell you because I was embarrassed. I'm so sorry!" The line moved, but Elise didn't seem to notice. Kevin gently guided her forward. It was almost her turn. She abruptly hugged him around the waist, then a toilet became available, and she disappeared inside. A minute later another one was vacated, and it was Kevin's turn.

When he came out, rubbing sanitizer on his hands, she was waiting for him.

"I really like Mirabelle." Elise said, as they walked back to the van together.

▼ ▲ ▼

Dawn was on the course now, wearing neon green knee-high socks and a yellow bandana on her face because of the dust. Jeff was in the backseat, dirty and dust-choked, and exhausted from his steep gravel uphill-and-downhill leg. Perhaps they were all sleeping; it was pretty quiet in the van. Elise was taking a turn driving and had to concentrate hard because her vision was worse at night, and that headache was still there, just lurking at the edges near her eyes. She could see the blinky lights of the runners ahead and tried to pass them slowly on the gravel road, to kick up as little dust with the van as possible. The air was so dusty.

"There's a couple roads coming up, but you want to stay right," Tanna said, reading the race bible with the light from her phone, which made seeing the road even harder for Elise.

"Wait, there's a right turn coming up?" Elise felt on edge. It was dark and curvy and getting close to midnight.

"No, not turn, just stay to the right!"

"All right, don't shout." Elise smiled to herself. Tanna was being impatient with her, but Elise was feeling charitable. Kevin's reassuring words kept ringing in her head. They drove in silence for a while, those left turns barely registering as roads as they passed, keeping to the right.

"I was thinking," Elise said. "If Mom's house hadn't been cleared out, would you have wanted anything?"

"No, I didn't care. I don't need any of it," Tanna said. The road curved to the right and climbed up steeply. They passed several walkers here, poor things. What a terrible road to have to run.

"I think I would've taken the green serving platter," Elise said.

"Was that a family heirloom?"

"I don't think so; I just liked it. She had nice measuring spoons, too."

"Why didn't you take them when we were there at Easter?" Tanna asked.

"We were in a hurry." Elise hadn't even thought about taking anything but the board game that they needed. "I'm not sad, though. The stuff isn't what matters. It's probably better this way, really." They watched the road. The exchange had to be soon. Elise started to fantasize about sleep.

"Quilts. Mom had some nice quilts," Tanna said. "And there was that angel nightlight that I always liked when I was little. I don't even know if she still had it."

"Oh yeah, I remember that. It was usually in your room," said Elise.

"I don't need a nightlight." Looking at the map again with the light on her phone, Tanna said, "Take a left on Apiary. It should be right there."

▼ ▲ ▼

There was wind now, a little gusty. What had started out as mist had turned into rain. It was so dark, so far from ambient city light, the moon hidden behind rainclouds. The light from Kevin's headlamp was swallowed by the darkness, except for a wimpy projected spot that zipped around when he moved his head. It was trippy, as though the world had become void of up or down. He felt disoriented. And he was tired. He didn't know how long he'd been running, but knew his leg had started at 1 a.m. Who the hell goes for a run at 1 a.m.?! After several really fast racers at the beginning, no runner had passed him, and he hadn't passed anyone else in a while on the narrow country road. Only the vans, projecting his giant shadow in front of him which grew smaller until it disappeared when the van passed. Van after van after van. He felt like he was chasing his shadow.

With nothing but time, he thought about how ruined Jeff had seemed after his last leg. It was long and hilly, all on gravel, and he'd been coated in dust when he finished. Kevin had taken care of his buddy, getting him water and anything else; whatever he needed, Kevin was going to make it happen. It had felt good, after all the times Jeff had been there for him, to be the helper.

▼ ▲ ▼

This was supposed to be an easy leg, according to the race bible: less than five miles, pastoral and flat along the Nehalem River. Tanna snickered; the pastoral part didn't matter since she couldn't see any of it anyway, and there was no such thing as an easy leg in this relay, just easier. Everything was relative.

Even wearing a baseball cap, rain dripped into her eyes. She wasn't allowed to play music on this leg, restrictions laid out in the race bible, which she was pretty sour about. The reflective gear was all wet with sweat when she put it on, which she didn't like. And the little set of lights she had borrowed from Dawn that clipped to her shoelaces kept flying off somehow, making her have to go back and pick them up, breaking her rhythm. At least she could find them in the dark, but her irritation was growing. She wasn't sure she liked the shoelace lights anyway; too much bouncing with each step, like a strobe light.

It grew lighter for a minute, just barely, and then a strong-looking runner with a headlamp zipped by, encircled by a blue rope of LED light. Tanna's shoelace lights kicked off yet again, and she scrambled to pick them up, again, and was clipping them back onto her shoes when it occurred to her to give up and just carry them in her hand. She laughed out loud that it had taken so long for her to come to that conclusion.

"Definition of insanity," she said to the black trees standing in darkness as she ran on.

Just get to the end so I can sleep.

▼ ▲ ▼

"Yeah, I've got no cell service either," Dawn said. Kevin realized it was the first time she had sounded less than cheerful. "We should look for them. I've got the iPad; I'll stay here. You all split up and check back in ten minutes."

It was 2:10 in the morning and raining. Tanna was expected to finish her run in less than fifteen minutes and Wanda from the other van would take over, but they hadn't seen anyone from Van 1 yet. There was parking on both sides of the road at this major van exchange; Jeff and Elise headed to the closest field. Kevin searched his brain to remember what these people looked like, as he and Mirabelle crossed the road to look through the huge parking field on the other side. The mist made visibility difficult.

"Do you remember their van?" Kevin asked as they jogged along the first line of parked vans.

"It was grey, a Honda," she said. "Look for the *Cleah's Kids* on the back window."

"Right." This was not ideal. The last thing Kevin wanted to do was more running. But run they did, scanning as they went. "Wish I'd hung on to that headlamp."

Ten minutes later they were back at the exchange area, unsuccessful and rain-soaked. Elise and Jeff hadn't returned yet. Dawn was hysterical.

"Well, they'll show up. Eventually. It doesn't matter," Kevin shrugged, trying to calm her down.

"One eighty-four," the caller yelled out. Tanna ran in, finishing strong and several minutes early. They watched her scan the exchange area, the other runners there waiting. Kevin could see in her face the realization that Wanda was not there, a mix of irritation and exhaustion. It probably also didn't help that she was being periodically blinded by the headlamps of other waiting runners milling around. Dawn swiped the iPad and went over to hand Tanna some water, who couldn't leave the exchange area until her replacement runner showed up.

"Let's go look again. Maybe they've just arrived," Mirabelle said, turning her gaze toward the parking area. "There!"

Kevin looked in the direction she was pointing and saw Jeff and Elise running toward them, with Paul and Wanda. He shouted for them to hurry. As they neared the exchange, Paul was switching on Wanda's flashers and headlamp, both still running.

"Where were you? What happened?" Dawn demanded of Paul once Wanda had gotten the slap bracelet from Tanna and was off on the course.

He was apologetic but defensive. "I thought I'd set my alarm, but I guess I didn't. Sorry."

"Well, you better hurry!" Dawn gestured wildly. "She's got an easy leg; don't screw up another exchange!" She handed him the iPad.

Kevin said, "Let's go, guys. We should get dry and try to get some rest." They followed him back to the parking field.

▼ ▲ ▼

Elise's phone alarm went off beside her ear. She almost didn't hear it over the sound of the rain drumming on the van roof. She turned it off. Never had she been this tired. It was still dark out. How could it be time to run again?

She forced the fog from her head; it didn't entirely clear. She remembered they had driven to the sleeping area near their last big van exchange, where they would wait for Van 1 to run their 31 miles. It was more crowded with all six of them in there, no one out on the course. On the way, slow with relay van traffic, Elise had eaten a tuna sandwich and some carrot sticks, then fallen asleep. When they got there, she'd roused and heard someone say she would have to be ready to run by 5:40 a.m. so she'd set her alarm for 5:15. That meant less than two hours of sleep, holy shit. She had tried to hide the math from herself.

Someone was shaking her. "Elise, time to go." It was Mirabelle whispering. As Elise floated toward consciousness, the rain grew louder and the van shook as a gale hit it from the side. It reeked of armpits and feet. "Come on, buddy. You've got to be out there in fifteen minutes."

Elise shot up and scrambled around, frantic and awkward, changing out of sweats and into running shorts, pulling a reflective vest over her raincoat and tying shoes, while Mirabelle pinned the race number on and then the flashers. "Where's a headlamp?" The well-ordered van was by this point a hodgepodge. She'd secured her hair into a ponytail and was looking for her other shoe when Dawn popped into the van, bringing a soaking in with her.

"Listen, everyone, wake up. I've got news," she said, quite serious for Dawn. "I've just talked with a race official—there's no cell coverage but they have walkie-talkies—and there's a huge storm coming through. Wind gusts are close to sixty miles an hour and there are lots of trees down on the course. The race is at-your-own-risk at this point. They've pulled race support. So, what do you want to do? Finish or quit?"

The van was silent inside as the storm outside howled.

28

There wasn't much time for debate. It was a hurried, bleary predawn discussion, mostly of whether there still was a Will mandate to continue, considering the safety concerns. Questions raised but not answered. In the end, they chose to finish. Unanimously. Elise felt it wasn't a hard choice, really; they had come this far. And although no one said as much, she suspected that for all the effort and hardship and insanity, they were enjoying each other.

It was dark and storming, but warm as Elise ran. Almost immediately she found she was too hot in the rain jacket, but with all the reflective gear strapped over it and the race number pinned to that, she struggled to take it off. Finally, she had to stop and undo things properly. It felt wrong to be standing still. Every person who passed her made her more anxious.

Then the van was there; it had slowed beside her on the narrow paved country road. "Are you okay?" called Jeff from the passenger window as she strapped the reflective vest back on.

"Take this!" she shrieked, shoving the jacket into his hands, relieved she wouldn't have to carry it the nearly four miles in this wind.

"Do you need water?"

Elise had barely started the leg. "No, just go!" she said, resecuring her headlamp, aware of vans being held up behind them.

Turns out running in a windstorm is exhilarating. She couldn't see well in the dark, but the trees around her were rattling their leaves and branches in a loud chorus. She felt very alert, adrenaline pumping through her arms and legs and chest, ready to sprint out of the way of any falling limb. It felt good to move her legs after being in the tight van while her muscles stiffened up. She was being passed a lot; she guessed that the faster teams that had started later were now catching up.

"Good job, runner," she said to each one as they passed. She felt almost joyful, like she shared a bond with each of them, running in this craziness together. Slowly the sky lightened; the storm clouds couldn't stop the dawn. It was all the more glorious for the wind, and the knowledge that she was almost done with her very last leg. She could practically hear the angels singing as the rain dripped from her nose.

The road headed steeply uphill, and she knew she was close—the triumphant movie-music swelling in her head, carrying her smiling to Jeff, who was ready and waiting. She expertly slapped the bracelet onto his wrist and watched him run away.

"Water?" Mirabelle offered her as they moved out of the exchange area.

"Yeah, thanks," she panted. "Where are the toilets?"

Mirabelle led Elise to the line at the blue porta potties, only four of them, but the line wasn't long. When it was her turn, she handed the water back to Mirabelle and went in.

It was inside that she made the discovery and started laughing. Not wanting to linger longer than necessary, she finished and exited, still laughing.

"What's going on with you?" Mirabelle asked.

"Look!" Elise could barely breathe, it was so funny. "Oh my god, this whole time!"

"What?" Mirabelle sounded concerned.

"Look at my shorts!" Elise's stomach hurt with laughter. "They're inside-out! Oh god, and every person who passed me I said, 'good job, runner'. I'm such a weirdo!" They were dark green runner shorts, the kind with underwear lining attached, so inside-out it was like a green diaper with a ruffle.

Mirabelle laughed with her. "At least it's all the same color. Probably no one noticed."

"But the tag!" Elise was mortified but quickly decided it didn't matter. The race was so big, she felt anonymous. They laughed all the way back to the van.

▼ ▲ ▼

Kevin was beyond exhausted. Clearly he had not trained enough. This last leg was his longest one at nearly seven miles and it had changed from paved to gravel on the Lewis and Clark Mainline Trail, which was rutted and ankle-bending, especially when he came upon a walker and had to hop over the ruts to pass. There was no hop left in his legs, only shuffling. And the blustery headwind seemed to want to prevent him from ever finishing.

Step by step, he told himself. There was a blister on his little toe.

At least the rain had eased, somewhat. Elise, Jeff, Dawn, Mirabelle, everyone had finished their legs wet like they'd swam it. But each one had seemed exultant at the end, perhaps for just being done. Oh, how he wished he was done.

Step by step.

There were some figures up ahead, standing there, and as he slowly approached, he could see that they were dressed in camo and armed with bows. Hunters. It seemed so strange, and it took him several minutes to remember that life existed outside of this race.

▼ ▲ ▼

"I'm glad you're here, Dawn. You're a great captain. And buddy! But why are you doing this?" Tanna asked her as they walked in the wind and spitting drizzle toward the exchange area. Jeff was quiet, following them. This was it, the final exchange; when Kevin came in, Tanna would be running leg 36 to the finish line. She was wearing their tie-dye team shirt. "I mean, I know why the rest of us are here, but what do you get out of this?" It had been a question that had been growing in Tanna's mind.

Dawn laughed. "All part of the job." Her orange hair was pulled into two high pigtail buns.

"Really? You showed up at Christmas, you're running in this crazy relay, you even gave yourself the hardest leg in Van 2. It seems above and beyond, just for overtime."

"Oh, it's not the hardest leg," she said quietly.

"Yes, it is. The race bible says it is," said Tanna.

She shrugged as they walked. "You three are lucky to have each other, you know."

Now Tanna shrugged.

"I had a sister. She died. Cancer. We hadn't spoken for two years. I didn't even know she was sick. For a while after, I was really depressed, but one day I woke up angry, maybe a little looney. I decided . . . I sorta developed a philosophy to love life, and to treasure the people *in* my life. Even when they make you mad." Dawn was staring straight ahead, and even from the side Tanna could see that her smile was wide. "When your mom came to Mr. Kantola with this Will idea of hers, I got excited! And worried. Because it was meddling and could go very wrong. But there was something about her trying to connect with you all, I found myself wishing my sister had tried something like that. Really, I was hoping Cleah would find a way to do that while she was still alive." Dawn shrugged. "When she did die just a few months later, I wanted to help in any way that I could, help it go okay, and I told Mr. Kantola so."

"So, you knew Cleah?"

"Not well, no. But I liked her."

Tanna heard what Dawn said but couldn't make sense of it. That someone read her mother in such a different way than she would've ever imagined—her mind was bursting and blank, trying to process. They arrived at the exchange area, and she stood in the chute until Kevin showed up and slapped the bracelet onto her wrist. She turned and ran into the storm.

The sky was a murky grey and there were lots of branches and even a few trees down, but not across the narrow windy road. Tanna ran and ran, ignoring the protests of her thighs; she could understand now why Leif had warned her not to take that first leg too fast. The road tipped downhill here, not as punishing as that first leg, but steep enough to help keep her speed up. So many runners, most like zombies, all running so doggedly. She came to the highway and crossed above on a temporary wooden staircase overpass, obviously built just for this. She was glad to be running, distracted from Dawn's words. She wondered why she felt so indicted by them. Dawn wasn't blaming her, but she felt the heaviness of responsibility. Part of the problem. Had she contributed to her mom being the way she was by expecting her to be?

The nearly five-and-a-half miles brought her onto streets, the coastal town of Seaside, the wind whipping harder. She followed along after runners ahead and knew she was close when sand was stinging her face. And suddenly it was over. There was no fanfare, just a few wind-battered race officials checking her in and sending her away. She was bewildered and lost, and then found by Elise and Mirabelle, Dawn, Kevin, and Jeff; they were all there, cheering for her. Dawn held out a chocolate milk, which Tanna took with a smile. Then Dawn slipped a participation medal around her neck. Tanna realized they each wore one.

"Come see this!" Dawn said, and they fought their way against the wind two blocks west, where a beach party lay in ruins. It was where the race was supposed to end. Tanna was shocked to see the big awnings torn and tossed, a stack of boxes fallen, mustard spilling from them, hot dog buns dumped from another fallen stack. Every blue porta potty, the constant of this race, was overturned. Chaos.

"Perfect backdrop for your photo!" Dawn laughed, motioning them to move closer, with their backs to the beach. "Squish together! And show me your *Cleah's Kids*!" Mirabelle and Jeff unzipped their coats to reveal a bit of tie-dye while Elise shrugged out of her raincoat. Kevin pulled off his sweatshirt, stretched out his arms and yelled, prompting cheers and howls from the rest in the wild weather, until they were laughing. Tanna felt like they were yelling at Cleah and laughing at themselves. Tanna started to shiver. After Dawn took several pictures, they made her take one with her in it: a selfie of faces barely fitting on the screen. Then they all turned toward the destruction again.

But it was too painful to linger, the sand biting, and they hurried to the van parked several blocks away, paint dripping off it with the rain.

▼ ▲ ▼

Before they left town to drive back to the city they found a restaurant, and the six of them piled into a wide corner-booth and ordered some hot food. It was close to noon and Elise realized she was famished. She'd eaten only snacks and sandwiches over the past 24 hours, which seemed much longer than just 24 hours, with everything they'd been through. Dawn said Van 1 didn't stick around after they finished their last legs, having heard that the party at the end was canceled.

After giving their orders to the waitstaff, pancakes and eggs and sandwiches, Dawn raised her water glass. "Here's to a good finish! Only half an hour slower than expected! And no major injuries—cheers!" They hurrahed heartily and clinked glasses all around. Simply finishing did seem like something to celebrate, given the craziness of it all.

"I could use a shower," said Kevin, taking a mock whiff of his armpit.

"A hot shower," Tanna moaned. She had changed into sweats and looked dazed, her blonde bob matted to her head.

"Mom would not have approved of how we look," Elise laughed, glancing around. They were a bedraggled bunch. Elise knew she looked as unpresentable as the rest. She also knew she was too tired to care. Even Mirabelle seemed unconcerned at having no makeup on, although she had such a natural beauty. Elise went on, "Remember some of Mom's comments? 'Are you sure you want to wear that?' 'What's happening with your hair?'"

"Or saying nothing and just trying to 'fix' your hair with that pained look on her face," Tanna said, playing with a napkin.

"She re-combed my hair before I went out the door all the way through ninth grade." Kevin shook his head. "Nice little part on the side. I hated that." Mirabelle reached up and playfully tried to comb a side-part into Kevin's hair with her fingers, who laughed and grabbed her hand; it was endearing.

"I hated to cook until I moved out on my own. Every time I tried, she would just criticize me; everything I did was wrong and made her upset. It was paralyzing," Tanna said.

"The worst for me was the phone critiques. She would listen in on my conversations and then tell me what I said wrong and what I should've said," sighed Elise. "To this day I don't like talking on the phone."

"Oh geez, she probably thought she was helping you. That's so sad," Dawn said.

"It's horrible," said Mirabelle.

Elise said, "Maybe she was so controlling because she felt she had no control in her marriage."

Tanna had a faraway look. "Do you suppose that Mom not telling us about her past and her parents' death was part of her control?"

After a pause, Kevin said, "Who knows."

The food arrived and they dropped the conversation in their concentration on eating. Elise thoroughly enjoyed her stack of blueberry pancakes; it felt well-earned. She was sore and satisfied and oh-so-glad to be done.

29

Zucchini Relish
From the kitchen of: Cleah Lucky

Mix:
4 c. zucchini, shredded
1 small red onion, chopped
½ c. white onion, chopped
1 red bell pepper, chopped
1 carrot, grated
1 garlic clove, minced
3 T. salt

Cover and let sit for 12 hours.
Drain well and place in a large pot.

Add:
½ c. white sugar
1 c. white vinegar
1 tsp. dry mustard
1 tsp. celery seed
½ tsp. pepper
¼ tsp. turmeric
¼ tsp. nutmeg
Bring to a boil and cook for 30 minutes. Cover and chill.

"It seems so strange that we're all gathering together again, just a week later, you know?" Kevin said as Mirabelle drove.

"Are you saying that's a good thing, or that it's too much family time?" she asked.

"Neither. I mean . . . it's just strange."

That Labor Day morning, Mirabelle had announced that she wanted to take the long way to Stevenson, on the Washington side of the river, and drive past Kevin's childhood home on the way. She'd never been there. They didn't have to be at Elise's house until 11:30, so a longer leisurely drive was fine. He preferred that route anyway, for any consideration other than time. It was more scenic and more fun to drive than the four-lane highway that cut a straight path along the Oregon side. Then Kevin's car refused to start. It had felt like a stubborn declaration to him, like it didn't want to go to the Required family gathering, and he wondered if he was projecting his own feelings on the situation.

But no, somewhat to his surprise, he didn't mind that he had to go.

Deciding to deal with the dead jeep later, they had taken Mirabelle's car. With Kevin directing, they pulled up to the old house where Cleah lived alone for so long. He noted that the witch by the front door was now gone.

"Oh, it's cute," Mirabelle said, after they'd gotten out. She zipped her fleece coat up against the unseasonal early-September chill. She stood surveying the modest blue rambler. "Your mom wasn't loaded at all, was she?"

He considered. "There were things she would say, threats to disinherit, snobbish comments about finances, usually disapproving of someone . . . I honestly don't know."

She shrugged. "Perhaps she was frugal."

"I don't have a key, but let's walk around back," said Kevin, leading the way. He checked his phone clock—plenty of time. Once in the backyard, Kevin watched as Mirabelle walked around to each corner, looking at the house from every angle. Finally, she stood at the back door, peering in through the little window.

"So, this is where you grew up."

"Yeah." Kevin looked in beside her. "It's pretty bare in there. Dang, that must've been a ton of work. Mom had lots of knick-knacks," he said. He recalled his sisters saying it had been somewhat cleared out, but seeing it so stripped down and impersonal was jarring even so. "So weird."

She nodded, then looked at him.

"What?" he said.

She grinned. "Just imagining little Kevin playing here in the backyard."

He chuckled. "It was more often little Kevin on his bike in the street. There were some woods a couple of blocks away. It's all been developed now."

Looking through another back window, he peered into the old dining room. There was a table and chairs, but the china hutch was gone and only two pictures left on the wall.

Beside him, Mirabelle said, "It looks staged. Like it's ready to be sold."

"She must really be gone," he said. "Do you think she could've moved?"

She turned to him. "I think she's dead, Kevin. I think you've spent more time on her this year than you had in a long time, and she just seemed more present."

He knew she was right.

They returned to the car and continued on. Eventually, Kevin had to consult Elise's email for the directions to her house. It was easier to find than he thought it would be.

"Come in! Wow, you guys beat Tanna!" Elise said, holding the door open for Kevin and Mirabelle, a lighter in her hand. Caleb stood grinning beside her in a white button-down shirt. Elise didn't seem frantic, Kevin noted, as he gave her a quick peck on the cheek. "Oh, you can put the urn on the mantel. In the living room." She and Mirabelle embraced.

"I'll take it," offered Caleb, his hands outstretched.

Amused at his eagerness, Kevin handed it to him and followed them into the living room. Once Caleb set the urn on the mantelpiece, Elise lit the new red Cleah Candle beside it.

"Did Dawn drop this off?" Kevin asked, pointing to it, looking closely at the familiar swirling indentations.

"Actually, she gave it to me last weekend, when we got to Tanna's house before the race. Along with Mom's ice cream maker. She had it in her van. It sat in my car while we ran."

"Ice cream, huh? Nice," he said. "Is Jeff around?"

"In the kitchen. It's down that hall." As Kevin headed in the direction she'd indicated, he heard Mirabelle and Elise begin to compare post-race soreness. Kevin had been embarrassingly stiff, especially his quads, even having to walk backward down the stairs for a couple of days.

He found Jeff and the twins lancing vegetable chunks onto kebab skewers. The room smelled of baked peaches and cinnamon.

"Hi! Nice shirt, uh, sorry, is it Daphne? Or Beth?" said Kevin. Although white predominated everyone's clothing, as per Cleah's Requirements, one of the girls wore a familiar *Cleah's Kids* tie-dye shirt over her white jeans. It seemed a pretty spunky decision. He approved.

"Daphne," she retorted with a teen-girl stare that said 'not impressed.'

"Daphne. Right. Apologies," he smiled, unfazed. The two looked the same to him. With time he felt sure he'd be able to tell them apart. "Smells great in here, by the way. Can I help?"

"Sure," said Jeff, handing him a bamboo skewer. Several bowls of different vegetables sat across the counter. Kevin pierced a mushroom and slid it down the stick, followed by a chunk of onion and then zucchini and so on. The veggies were tossed with oil, so his fingers got slick. When he'd filled his kebab, he set it on the growing pile on the platter and began another.

"So is school starting tomorrow?" he asked the sisters.

Daphne looked disdainful. "It started last week."

"This is their first year in high school," said Jeff.

"Oh, okay, cool. How's it going so far?" Kevin asked.

"I'm learning to play the flute," Beth offered.

"Yeah, she quit volleyball and joined the band," said Daphne. He couldn't tell if she was just surly or if she didn't like her sister's decision.

"Well, it's good to try different things," said Kevin.

"Mom starts classes next week," said Daphne.

"She was accepted into a master's program in education," Jeff said, seeing the question in Kevin's face.

"Oh wow, that's cool," he said, impressed.

Caleb came skipping in, followed by Elise, Mirabelle, Tanna, Leif, and Tanna's two girls. Kevin glanced at the wall clock: 11:30 a.m. arrival time, as Cleah had decreed. The room had suddenly tripled in occupancy, and the white clothing that Cleah had ordered they all wear was almost laughable, as though they were dressed in costume for a play called Stereotypical Rich People on Summer Holiday.

"Everyone's here," Elise announced. "And this is Tanna's friend, Leif." He smiled and gave a little salute or nod of greeting to each one as Elise went around the room introducing.

"Great. Well, I'll put the food on the grill," said Jeff when she'd finished.

"Okay. I'll get the Appletinis started," said Elise, plucking a green apple from the fridge.

"I'll give you a hand with the grilling," Kevin said, washing up at the sink. He picked up the platter of kebabs.

"Leif, can you bring those tongs," said Jeff, pointing.

"Sure!" Leif grinned at Tanna, picked them up, and followed Jeff out the back door.

Outside, Cleah's ice cream maker hummed as it stirred.

▼ ▲ ▼

"Need help?" asked Tanna, as Elise got out the vodka.

"Yeah. Put us to work," said Mirabelle.

Giving direction always seemed more work than just doing it herself but, thinking of her mother-in-law, Elise also knew it was hard to be the guest not allowed to help while the host rushed about. "Okay, well, someone could get out the martini glasses, I so rarely use them. This cupboard here. And this apple needs slicing, thinly." As the women got on to those two tasks, Elise checked the Appletini recipe saved on her phone.

She had written out the list of the Required Activities again this time but there wasn't a lot, mostly a series of yard games that they would play later. She felt well-prepared.

What did cause her some anxiety was seeing her mother's urn enter her house again. It had been such a weight those months at the beginning, and such a difference when she'd passed it along to Tanna. Elise shivered, remembering how unhinged the urn had made her feel. She didn't want it to do that to her life again.

It wasn't long before the Appletini was mixed and in a pitcher, a green apple garnish in each martini glass, and the counter was crowded with Required menu dishes. Elise was pouring apple juice into the kids' glasses when the men returned with the grilled salmon and vegetable kebabs, temptingly aromatic. As soon as everyone had the right drink in their hands, they toasted, as Required. Just a simple "To Cleah" repeated all around.

In the quiet moment of sipping, Mirabelle said, "Mmm, this is delicious, Elise!"

"Thank you! I know!" she had to agree, and then flushed with bashful pride. "Okay, I'm gonna play the song while you all help yourself to the food. Buffet style." She piped the Required song through a small speaker Bluetoothed with her phone. Other than the dancing of Tanna's little Cassidy and Susan, it seemed to her that no one really paid attention to Connie Francis singing *Who's Sorry Now*—too focused on dishing up lunch. Just as well. When it came to the lyric *Whose heart is achin' for breakin' each vow*, Elise hazarded a glance at Jeff. He seemed to hear her thoughts and looked at her—a trust-me expression that made her feel weak, in a good way. The song ended, and she switched the music to classic oldies turned down low.

People sat where they wanted around the dining room table, expanded as large as it could go with all four leaves added to it. Elise circled it, putting down several piles of paper napkins, before taking a seat between Mirabelle and Beth.

"So Mirabelle, how is baby Harper doing?" she asked between bites.

"She's growing so fast! Here. Risa sent me a picture the other day." She found it on her phone and showed Elise. Beth wanted to see, too, and cooed in delight. "We're flying down to visit in a couple of weeks for her three-month birthday."

"Fun! Babies are so cute at that age; they get smiley. But it's more than smiles, they have such huge and genuine reactions to the world: absolute joy, utter betrayal. No pretense. It's amazing," said Elise. She was taking another messy bite of corn, smothered in mayonnaise and Cotija cheese, seasoned with lime and chili powder, when the doorbell rang.

Hopping up, Caleb yelled "I'll get it!"

Conversation paused and there were some exchanged glances. Elise was still mopping her face and fingers with a napkin when Caleb returned, Dawn's familiar beehive right behind.

"Hello all!" she said brightly, her purple and yellow dress in such stark contrast to everyone's white. "It's so nice to see you again!" Returning the greeting, Elise, Tanna, and Kevin got to their feet. Elise was surprised to find that she wasn't surprised. Of course Dawn was here, she was practically part of the family by now—part of every family function. And with that sweet and positive demeanor, she was easy to have around.

"Dawn, have some lunch with us," Elise invited, wondering what madness she had brought for them this time, but not wanting to ask.

"Oh, thank you! I would love to!"

Jeff got her a plate and found a chair, and they made room for her while she dished up. Comfortable chatter again filled the room as they ate.

Jeff had grilled the salmon and the vegetable kebabs to perfection. The zucchini relish for the salmon was a recipe that Cleah had been especially proud of; Elise remembered not caring much for it growing up, but she found it so tasty now. She was pleased to see people taking second helpings of the sides: broccoli salad, Mexican-style corncobs, seasoned potato wedges, watermelon. Cleah's menu was a hit.

"This is so nice, but I should get to why I'm here," Dawn said, checking her watch. "There's a blood drive being held at the nearby grange hall today. You three have appointments to donate starting at 2:00 this afternoon." Elise gasped, but Dawn smiled. "Oh, you'll be fine, dear. Just drink plenty of water." She got up and went to where she'd set her orange purse down. "And here is your final Trust Requirement," she said, holding up three tiny vials. "This is ash from your mother that's been specially processed to be used in tattoo ink."

"Tattoo?" Tanna repeated.

"Nooo—" It was the only word Elise's mind could form.

"I'm afraid yes. A simple triangle," Dawn went on, her head tilted sympathetically. "It can be any size and anywhere on your body, but it must be done before the one-year anniversary of Cleah's death. No big deal."

Mirabelle suppressed a laugh.

Too much, Elise's mind screamed. *Too much, too much.*

"And can I get a little help with some boxes?"

▼ ▲ ▼

After bringing in three large boxes, Dawn stayed for dessert: peach cobbler and homemade vanilla ice cream. Conversation was sparse. No one discussed Dawn's pronouncements, though it seemed obvious to Tanna that it was on everyone's mind. She felt self-conscious about Leif's impression of a tattoo Requirement.

Once again, Dawn took the photograph, Leif beside her smiling at the group. The family stood together in front of the house, dapper and subdued in their stately white duds—with the exception of the tie-dye shirt on Daphne. Tanna didn't mind the spot of incongruity, but was surprised Elise allowed it; good for her. An arm around each of her daughters, Tanna focused on Leif and his eyes rested on hers. She found herself wishing Leif was next to her, part of the picture.

"Now remember to let us know the plan for the Celebration of Life as soon as possible," said Dawn, as she grabbed them each into a tight squeeze in turn. After reminding them to send any proof if they hadn't already, like pictures or copies of letters, Dawn waved goodbye and left, and it was time for the siblings to go donate blood. The compelled-to-be-civic-minded group climbed into Elise's van. Leif and Mirabelle joined them. Jeff stayed behind with the kids.

From the middle row in the van, Tanna watched Elise as she drove them toward the grange, knowing her fear of needles. But Elise seemed nonchalant.

"Oh my god, you guys, do we really have to get a tattoo?!" Elise cried after turning onto a main road. Tanna smiled to herself. Apparently, she *was* concerned. Must've been waiting to freak out until after the kids weren't around. "I mean it's not like putting on a white dress, it's permanent! She can't require that, can she? It must be illegal or something!"

Tanna glanced at Leif. She really should have clued him in to the bizarre Will-Requirement situation before they came.

"I don't think it's anything to get upset about. Tattoos are no big deal," said Kevin from the back. "Just get a tiny one on your hip or something. No one will even see it."

"You have one, don't you?" said Tanna, remembering the glimpse from Easter.

Kevin pulled his left sleeve up to his shoulder, exposing several black birds in flight. Elise strained to see in the rearview.

"A murder of crows," said Mirabelle.

"That's really beautiful. Why crows?" said Tanna.

Kevin shrugged. "It signifies death and mystery, but also intelligence."

"I like that a crow is not flashy, just steady and protective," Mirabelle added.

"Do you have any others?" Tanna said.

"Did it hurt?" Elise blurted.

Kevin lifted his shirt to reveal a compass rose below his left breast. "It was fine." Mirabelle showed them the little owl on her hip. With blending blues and greens, hers looked like a watercolor, tastefully subtle and stunning.

Elise was not convinced. "But the ash mixed in! I've never heard of that. Is it hygienic?"

"It does seem somewhat invasive," Tanna said. "I don't have anything against tattoos, but the idea of Mom literally under my skin . . ." She grimaced.

"They call them ritual tattoos, or commemorative tattoos. Yeah, it's a real thing. And it is hygienic. You just want to find an artist that does that kind of thing," Leif said. They arrived at the temporary blood draw site, which put an end to the conversation.

As a nurse, Tanna was, of course, used to needles. She didn't regularly give blood but managed it every once in a while. After every time, she would resolve to do it more often, but then life would get busy. This time the person checking her in asked if she wanted to schedule her next donation appointment, and so she did. The man who drew her blood made an almost-mocking comment about wearing white to give blood, and Tanna did wonder what her mother had been thinking.

It was an hour and a half before all five of them were finished, Leif and Mirabelle having to be worked into the schedule. The whole time, *Who's Sorry Now* replayed in Tanna's head, an unwelcome earworm. Elise seemed to have managed her fear of needles well enough, but she did let Kevin drive them home. Tanna took the front passenger seat on purpose, so she could ask him about what she thought she'd overheard.

"Kevin, did you say you had a rabies treatment?" she said. "What happened?"

He kept his eyes on the road. "A bat flew into my face on our fourth anniversary last month. I wasn't bitten; the vaccination was just precautionary."

"Wow! And you say that so matter-of-factly! They still let you donate blood?"

"They said it was fine as long as I wasn't given live virus in the vaccine, which I wasn't. Also, they said the donated blood is tested for all sorts of things and won't be used if they find an issue, and then they let you know, so you can get medical care if needed," he said.

"Makes sense," said Tanna. "I saw a bat outside my kitchen window a few months ago, come to think of it. It was weirdly hovering."

"I had a bat in my house!" Elise interrupted, leaning forward. "On Halloween night. I swear I thought it was Mom's doing, somehow."

Apparently bat sightings went along with urn guardianship.

"The worst part was the bill: seven thousand! And insurance only covered part of it," said Kevin.

"Wow," said Tanna. "Hopefully the inheritance is enough to cover it."

"Ha! No kidding."

"It's a left at the stop sign."

He slowed to a stop and made the turn. Elise sat back again in her seat.

"Hey, did you bring Leif along to keep us from fighting?" Kevin said in a low voice.

Tanna grinned. "No, actually. I just brought him because I like him."

Kevin nodded. "That's cool."

"You know, I don't think we would've argued anyway," she said, reflecting. There didn't seem any danger of a fight. It was a pleasant realization.

When they returned, Elise declared she wasn't feeling up for the yard games yet. So they sat down in the living room to look at the boxes Dawn had brought. Regular cardboard moving boxes, each bore one of their names written in Sharpie, though not in their mother's hand. Leif sat down beside Tanna. They exchanged a smile. He was certainly a great go-with-the-flow guy.

Opening her box, Tanna laughed to find her favorite of her mother's quilts, the one with the log cabin design in earthy russet tones. She saw that each box had a quilt, perfectly suited for the recipient. Elise's was the jelly roll pattern in pastels and Kevin's was zig-zag in primary colors. Dawn had said that these were items Cleah had selected specifically for each of them. Tanna was impressed, and felt seen by her mother, more so than she'd ever thought.

Continuing through the box, Tanna found a mix of personal items, like the jade necklace and a pair of Precious Moments figurines, and of useful things, like garden tools and oven mitts. Carefully wrapped at the bottom was the green platter that Elise had wanted.

"Hey, Elise," Tanna said, holding it up. Elise held up the angel nightlight. They laughed together with the mirth of an inside joke as they traded.

▼ ▲ ▼

Looking at his box of stuff, primarily things that had belonged to his father, Kevin wondered why his parents hadn't split up. There was no way to ask, of course, but he truly wondered what each of them would have said. He looked at Mirabelle, feeling again the weight of responsibility in holding up his part of their marriage commitment. They'd been tested and were still together; more than anything, he felt lucky.

The day had warmed up, which was perfect since they needed to get to Cleah's list of yard games. Apparently mentally recovered from the ordeal of donating blood, Elise split the group of eleven into two teams, she and Jeff alternating in.

They did an egg relay. Each team member took turns running with the raw egg balanced on a spoon around a chair marker in the yard and back, transferring the spoon with its fragile egg to the next runner.

The pass-the-card-with-only-mouth-suction relay was comical and dangerous, with the playing card too often slipping and leaving the participants in an accidental kiss. Reactions to this ranged from anger (Daphne and Caleb) to embarrassment (Mirabelle and Jeff) to clear enjoyment (Tanna and Leif). Kevin suspected Tanna let the card slip on purpose, which was fine with him since she was on the other team. It occurred to him he'd never liked Tanna's boyfriends, or husbands, before, not that he'd put much thought into it at the time. But this guy was no Alex or Joe. Watching them, he felt happy for her.

Then they played several rounds of water balloon volleyball, using a sheet held taut by all the team members to launch a water balloon over a badminton net, like a firefighter's rescue net. The game required group coordination that was mostly lacking, but it did result in lots of shrieking and laughter. It ultimately devolved into a free-for-all water balloon fight, with very wet results, especially for Jeff, who seemed particularly targeted, mostly by his own kids. Kevin found the afternoon yard games to be wholly fun.

The competition shifted to teams of two with a raw egg toss, back-and-forth, with the goal of lasting the longest without breaking or dropping their egg. The pairs were directed to step further apart as the game progressed, so the tosses became more unwieldy. When an egg inevitably broke on someone's white shirt, dress, or trousers, a verbal calling-out of Cleah for dressing them in white ensued. It was funnier each time it happened—or so Kevin thought until Jeff's toss slipped through Kevin's fingers and splatted yellow goo on his white crotch.

They were down to the final two remaining teams—Mirabelle and Daphne against Leif and Tanna—when Caleb cried out in a panic, "Where's Fred?" It took some time for Elise to calm Caleb down and explain to the group that Fred was their Ecuadorian tortoise that had been grazing in the yard.

"He was only seven! He had his whole life ahead of him!" Caleb said.

No one had been keeping an eye on the guy, since tortoises move so glacially. Meanwhile, the tortoise had managed to run away, an achievement that Kevin quietly found hilarious. Their final impromptu game was therefore find-the-tortoise.

This was not a fun game, Kevin soon decided. Fred could be anywhere in this massive, fenceless yard, making no noise in his slow-motion escape and blending into his surroundings completely. Growing bored of the tedious search, Kevin offered to go find drinks for everyone, as an excuse to find a beer for himself. Inside, he took some time to try to rinse the egg from his shorts, with only marginal success. He'd bought them for this lunch event, because who has white shorts? Not very practical. He was unlikely to ever wear them again anyway. He felt only slightly guilty at taking so long to bring out the pitcher of what was left of the Appletini. Elise and Tanna were happy to accept, but the rest deemed the drink too sweet for seconds and, of course, it was not a drink for kids, so he took orders and went back in for apple juice, water, and beer. Anything to not comb through the foliage.

Kevin did have to help with the search party eventually, with no more excuses to not. To kill time as he peered under the abundant bushes, he asked Leif about his experiences running Hood to Coast in prior years. Leif's glowing description of the huge beach party at the end made Kevin wonder if a second attempt would be worth it. The weekend did have its fun moments. Then he remembered the drudgery of the actual running, three legs successively and through the sleepless night, and tossed the thought out of his head.

Elise and Tanna had been quietly consulting in a corner of the yard and came over to where Kevin was searching.

"About the Celebration of Life, we think it should be the 31st. At Cleah's house," said Elise. "She died on the 27th and the 31st is the following Saturday."

Kevin shrugged. "Whatever. That's fine."

"We'll keep it low-key," said Tanna. "You know what's weird? With all the over-the-top, ultra-specific Requirements we've had to do for these family gatherings and all the stuff in between, it's strange that Mom didn't plan out the Celebration herself."

"That's Halloween, you know. We should come in costume," Kevin joked. They all laughed as he went on: "Hey, how are we ever going to find this turtle?"

"Tortoise," Elise corrected.

"Tortoise. Couldn't you have taught it to come when it's called?" He really wanted to go and was getting sassy in his restlessness. "No, but seriously, how bad could it be for the little guy? You live on a cul-de-sac, so not much danger of getting run over. He has plenty of food. Maybe let him have his freedom?"

"Fred wouldn't starve to death," Elise said, "but come winter he would freeze."

"Oh."

In the end, it took over two hours, carefully combing the underbrush in all directions, everyone's patience growing thin, before Beth and Susan discovered Fred burrowed under the lavender bushes on the far side of the garage. Kevin felt it was a perfectly heroic end to the day.

"Okay, that just leaves the Celebration of Life," said Elise to Kevin and Tanna, as they all said their goodbyes.

"And getting that tattoo," said Kevin, mostly to get a rise out of Elise.

"Oh my god, Kevin, goodbye," she snapped.

30

Elise had soaked the egg-stained white clothes in cold water overnight and was up early the next morning to start the wash before getting the kids ready for school. Passing through the living room, she paused, her attention caught by the still-burning Cleah Candle on the mantelpiece, half melted into a pool of red. She was glad she'd thought to put it in a bowl.

She stared at the ceramic urn beside it, fighting the crazy-making stirrings in her chest, resisting its odd ability to plunge her into those paranoid feelings of insufficiency and irrational doubt, like it had last fall. There was as much to be angry at Cleah about, now as then. How dare she require them to ink their bodies with her ash! Elise had worked hard to temper her fear of needles at the blood draw yesterday by focusing on the good it would do for someone in need, and she was surprised to find the experience not that bad, though not good enough to do it again any time soon. But it was hard to mentally prepare for the impending pointless tattoo experience.

Daphne came down the stairs, still in her pajamas. "Beth's hogging the shower."

"You can use mine, honey," said Elise as she followed her into the kitchen.

"Gonna eat breakfast." Daphne got out a box of cereal and milk. Elise put two bowls and two spoons on the table. They dished themselves up and started eating, Daphne reading the cereal box.

"Did you have fun yesterday?" Elise asked.

"Yeah," she muttered, concentrating on the box.

"How are your classes going? Do you have a favorite?"

Daphne shrugged, still reading. "I don't know."

"It's hard to be the youngest at a new school when you just spent a year being the biggest at your old school," Elise said as Caleb burst into the room. Daphne rolled her eyes and sighed.

"I'm the oldest at my school!" Caleb said. "I'm hungry!"

Elise poured him a bowl and patted Daphne on the back. "It'll get better, honey."

"Good morning," Jeff said as he walked in. He gave each of them a peck on the head before putting some bread in the toaster. Daphne put her bowl in the sink and left. The morning continued with its normal flurry until they all climbed into cars, Jeff driving to work in one direction, Elise and the kids in the van heading the other.

First, she dropped Caleb off at the grade school and then drove the girls to the high school. It felt strange for school to be in session but not be substitute teaching. She had removed herself from the sub list since she would be working on her master's. Feeling both nervous and excited about that, she was glad to have a week to prepare in a quiet house while everyone else was at work and school. She had plans to fill the freezer with lasagnas and soup, in anticipation of the demanding schedule.

Walking back into the silent house from the garage, she kicked off her shoes and sat down on the couch. With her phone, she sent the photos from Labor Day to Dawn and called the lawyer's office to inform them of the Celebration plans, a brief conversation, all the while watching the urn. What was this power that Cleah seemed to still have over her? Was it simply that she still had power over the inheritance?

She isn't here, Elise reminded herself, going to check on the laundry.

▼ ▲ ▼

"Close the door quick, honey," Elise said to Caleb as he climbed into the van after school, setting his backpack at his feet. The air was acrid with wildfire smoke, giving her a headache and stinging eyes, also canceling his Kung Fu class. Wildfires, and the accompanying smoke, were becoming a more and more common occurrence each year. They were in no danger from the actual fire, but the poisoned air spread on the whim of the winds.

It was Friday. Daphne had volleyball practice and Beth was going to a friend's house. Caleb seemed pensive.

"What's up, kiddo? How was school?"

He sighed and turned to look out the window. "It's the anniversary of the Twin Towers, when the planes ran into them. Mr. Lopez said the air was terrible in New York that day from the buildings burning and falling down."

"Like the air here is terrible now?"

He nodded. Poor honey.

"Yeah, that was terrible. Really sad," she said. They drove in silence for a while. She wasn't sure what to say, what he needed to hear, such a terrifying event. She wondered what exactly the teacher had said about it. "Hey, want to get an ice cream cone?"

"Yeah," he said, with less excitement than normal for him. She turned the car in the direction of the ice cream shop.

"You know, wildfire smoke isn't quite as bad as smoke from a burning building. There's sometimes bad chemicals in buildings that get released into the air when it's burned."

"And when people are burned up?"

This question caught her off guard. "I think people are made up of pretty natural compounds." She was grasping now, guessing. "I think people are more like a tree than like insulation in a building."

He seemed to consider this. "Mom, I think it's really neat, getting a tattoo made with Grandma's ashes. Natural, like a tree."

"Hmm." She had no other response.

"Mom, what is tattoo ink made of?"

"I don't really know." It had never occurred to her to wonder about that.

"I'll get the tattoo with Grandma's ashes for you, if you want," he offered.

Eyebrows raised, she gave him a grin. "That's very sweet, honey. Thank you. But you're not getting a tattoo. Maybe when you're all grown up."

He was clearly disappointed. "Okay." The sun cast a strange orange hue as it filtered through all the ashy particles in the air. She parked the car, and they got out and ran into the ice cream shop, trying not to breathe in the smoky air. He chose mint chocolate chip, and she chose death by chocolate.

When they sat down with their cones at a little round table, Caleb said, "Are you going to make a list of things for us to do after you die, Mom?"

She looked at him, not liking the question at all. "Would you want me to?"

"Yeah! It's fun, like a scavenger hunt or something, a game that we get to play with you even when you're dead!" He had regained much of his usual enthusiasm. Elise smiled.

"How about we have lots of fun together while we're both alive for now."

He smiled, nodded conspiratorially, and took a big lick of his ice cream.

▼▲▼

The dirty dinner dishes were stacked by the sink and Elise did her best to ignore them, though she could see them from the kitchen table where she sat with her laptop. Jeff was in a late meeting at the Lodge and the kids were who-knows-where in the house, hopefully doing their homework. She was trying to work but everything was distracting her.

Barely three days into the semester, she'd already been assigned a ten-page research paper on educational theory; this professor wasn't messing around. It had been a long day, adding in the commute to the college, an hour each way. Luckily, she only had to do that three days a week, with online classes the other two days. Though she preferred the in-person classes, she appreciated the flexibility the online classes allowed.

She couldn't help but notice that she was the oldest person in all of her classes. She found herself fighting feelings of inadequacy and fear of failure. It had been years since she'd been a student, with assignments and deadlines. Decades! Maybe this was a mistake. In the search line of her web browser she typed 'What is tattoo ink made of?'

"Mom?" Beth stood before her. "I was wondering if I could audition for the school jazz band."

"Oh really! You're liking the flute a lot, huh?" She had noticed that Beth practiced quite a bit and was starting to sound decent, for having just started.

"Yeah," Beth grinned, but sobered again. "Only, jazz band happens during zero period before school, so I would need a ride in early. Unless I can find someone to carpool with."

She looked at her daughter. "I'm sure we could manage that, honey."

Smiling, Beth said, "Okay, thanks," and rushed from the room.

"Good luck!" Elise called after her, amused.

Back to the theory of education.

Daphne sulked in, sighing melodramatically. She opened a cupboard door, then exhaled, closed it, opened another, and so on.

"What are you looking for, honey?" Elise finally asked.

"I don't know. Snacks."

"How about some nuts? Or crackers? They're in the next cupboard over. Or there are bananas on the counter."

She only exhaled in response. Elise could understand having a hard time choosing, but this was getting ridiculous.

"You okay?"

Daphne slumped into a chair at the table. "Why is it that girls lose brain cells when their boobs come in? Is it like a trade-off or something?"

"Oh. Yeah, I guess it seems that way sometimes. Who's losing their brain cells?"

She shrugged, then mumbled, "Beth."

"Ah-ha." Elise closed her laptop and went to get out the chocolate.

"It's the only reason she wants to do band. I hate boys."

Elise unwrapped a bar and broke it into squares. She put a piece in her mouth, waiting for her daughter to elaborate.

"His name is Stan Holbrook and he plays the trombone," Daphne said.

"He's giving Beth some attention?"

"He's so lame."

"You know, your boobs are coming in, too."

"Mom! Don't look at my boobs!"

Elise smiled. "I just mean that you girls are growing up. Change is always hard."

Daphne put two pieces of chocolate in her mouth, and then a third. “It’s just, she spends all her time either with him or talking about him.”

“And you miss her.”

Picking up another square, Daphne cartwheeled the chocolate across the opened paper wrapper. She put her elbow on the table and rested her head in her palm.

Elise went on, “Well, you can’t control anyone else, but you can choose to keep being there for her, reaching out to her. While still giving her some space.” Her own words smacked Elise in the face, and her thoughts settled on her own siblings.

“I’m not hungry,” Daphne stated, still chewing her chocolate as she marched from the room.

▼ ▲ ▼

“I have no idea where to even start.” Elise knew she was being whiny. But she was mentally exhausted after two weeks of her demanding graduate classes.

“Why don’t you ask Kevin if he knows of a good artist,” Jeff suggested. It was a sunny and cool Saturday morning, and they were about to go for a run. “You could do it now.”

“Yeah,” Elise said. Stalling, she pulled her ankle to her butt to stretch her quad.

Jeff watched her. “You only have a month, you know.”

“Yeah, I know,” she snapped. She grabbed her phone from her pocket and dialed his number. As it rang, a smile spread over her face. How well Jeff knew her—making her mad distracted her from remembering that she hated using the phone.

“Hello?” Kevin said.

“Hi. It’s Elise. Hey, do you have a tattoo artist you would recommend? You know, one that does ritual tattoos?”

"I mean, I have just the two tattoos. It's not like I have an artist on retainer. I have a friend I can check with, though." He paused. "Are you doing okay with this?"

"I'm fine. I mean, yes. I'm working on it. I just don't know where to start."

"I'll do some digging. Is a Portland shop okay?"

"Sure. I'm down there a few days a week for classes anyway."

"I heard! Master of Education. That's very cool. Good for you, Sis."

It felt good to have him say that. Elise could tell she was blushing. "Thanks." She smiled at Jeff, meeting his gaze, as she put away her phone.

"You don't want to let them down," he said. "It's the same for them, you know. What you three started out doing for yourselves, you're now doing for each other."

Pacing beside him, she mulled that over, surprised to realize he was right. They jogged one of their regular routes, only four miles, but Elise could tell she was out of shape, having not run as much as when they were preparing for the relay. When they got back, she was breathing hard.

"We should find a fun run. Something to train for," she said as they walked into the house.

"Yeah. Good suggestion. I'm gonna shower."

"Okay."

As he walked up the stairs, her phone chimed, and she saw that Kevin had sent a contact. Staring at the artist's name and number, she felt the anxiety return. She just couldn't get herself to call. Instead, she called Tanna.

"Hi, Elise."

"Hi. How are you?"

"I'm fine. You?"

"Fine." Starting to feel silly about this mundane exchange, Elise took a breath. "I am freaking out a little."

"Oh no, why?"

"The tattoo. I don't know if I can do it." She'd recovered from the run by this time, but her heart was now pounding for a different reason.

There was a pause. "You don't have to do this."

"No, I can do it." Elise thought of what Jeff had said on their run. She didn't want to let her siblings down.

"Would it help if we went together?" Tanna said.

"Yes! You haven't gotten yours already?" She paced around the living room, caught sight of the urn, and paced down the hallway to the kitchen.

"No, haven't figured any of that out yet."

"Kevin sent me the number of a good place in Portland."

"Okay. I can call them if you want. See if we need an appointment or anything."

"Sure," said Elise, in no way feeling as nonchalant as she meant to be. Absolutely yes! Maybe if someone else could take care of all the arranging, and all she had to do was show up…

"I can do it after my classes on Monday, Tuesday, or Thursday. I'll be down there anyway."

"Classes? Are you subbing in Portland now?"

"No, I got accepted into a Master of Education program." She realized she was parched and got out a glass, filling it from the sink.

"Really? So, you're getting out of the sub game?"

"Yeah. With just my degree in Anthropology, subbing is all they'll let me do. And that's only because they really need subs. I can't actually get a teaching job without a certificate or a master's. So I'm going for my master's."

"Wow! Nice! Okay so send me the tattoo-guy's contact info and I'll set something up."

31

"Mommy, I'm cold." Caleb had padded stealthily into the kitchen, where Elise was engrossed in her studies, surprising her. She looked at the clock; it was somehow nearly midnight.

"Oh honey, it's so late," she said, scooting away from the table and pulling him onto her lap. Her little boy was growing so big but would still allow these little snuggles when he was tired. She rubbed his arms to warm him up. "Shall we get you an extra blanket?"

"Yeah." His head was on her shoulder, heavy and solid with a faint little-boy musty smell. She held him, not wanting to let go.

But it was late, a school night. They should both be in bed sleeping.

"Okay, well, let's find you one." They got up and she led him back down the hall. She glanced at the urn as they passed through the living room and remembered the box Dawn had delivered on Labor Day, set in the laundry room to be dealt with later. Holding his hand, she walked them there and picked up her mother's quilt that lay on top. "How's this?"

"Grandma's quilt?" he said sleepily. "Okay." They walked upstairs and he climbed into bed. She spread the quilt over her son. Seeing it laid out like that—blocks of pale blues, greens, and yellows—revived memories of making forts with Tanna between their twin beds when they were little. She had forgotten about that.

"Better?" she asked, brushing his hair back from his face. He nodded and she kissed him goodnight. "Love you," she said as she closed the door.

Although knowing she should go to bed as well, she found herself returning to the box in the laundry room. She peered into it, finding again the crystal candlestick holders, a wooden toy mouse she'd played with as a child, the green serving platter, and other seemingly random items. There was an envelope she hadn't noticed before and she picked it up. It was not sealed. Inside was a handful of assorted photographs, in no apparent order, some with writing on the back, some without. There were black and whites that looked very old. There were some poor-quality square ones in color: herself as a kid in front of a birthday cake, standing in a posed row with her siblings in front of a tree in their backyard, her father standing with her mother beside an old car. She walked into the living room, sifting through.

She paused. It was so late, not the right time. She pushed the photographs back into the envelope and set it on the coffee table.

▼ ▲ ▼

"He plays trombone," Elise whispered as she and Jeff strained to see the band kids in the far corner of the high school bleachers they were all sitting on. Flooded with stadium lights, the football players on the field were getting set for their next down and the cheerleaders were chanting something inspirational at the crowd.

"You don't know him? Don't you know all the students?" Jeff whispered back.

"I think he must be new."

"Can you see Beth from here? The flutes are usually in the front," said Bob loudly, sitting next to Jeff. Some of their oldest friends, he and Dina had a tenth-grader on the football team, so they were experts at the workings of high school football games.

"I don't think so," said Jeff. "We'll just have to walk down there at some point."

The weather was decidedly autumn: overcast and cool. Elise shivered in her down jacket. Daphne sat in front of them, slumping over her phone. She'd refused to wear her coat, but at least she had on a hat and scarf, one that Beth had knit for her a couple of years ago. Caleb was around somewhere, probably wandering with Justin after leaving to get nachos from the concessions stand.

It was nice to be out from under books and away from her computer screen. Her classes demanded so much of her time, which wasn't unexpected, but it was, well, hard to get used to. She had known this going in, of course, and was resigned to another eighteen months of it. It would all be worth it in the end.

"I'm gonna go meet up with Cheryl," Daphne announced, standing up.

"Okay honey, but be back by the end of the game," said Elise. She watched as her daughter sauntered away, sympathetic with the challenge of navigating through teen years.

Elise's phone dinged, a text from Tanna: *Appt is 4:30 on Monday 19th. OK?*

The crowd roared as the home team scored a touchdown. The band began a triumphant refrain.

OK, Elise texted back, after taking a minute to clap and cheer. *Meet you there. Thnx!*

She took a deep breath, feeling gratitude and foreboding simultaneously.

▼ ▲ ▼

Years of habit and routine meant that if the Mom was home, the kids would be needing her. It seemed no amount of telling them she was not to be disturbed got through to them. Jeff was great about helping out, but he didn't always think to avert a problem before it got to her. She had a paper due and needed to focus with no interruptions. So, she'd put a sticky note on her door that read "go ask your father" and locked herself in her bedroom, where she'd set up a card table, in order to get work done.

Her phone chimed and a text appeared, *Mom, can Justin come over?*

Elise huffed and wrote back, *Ask dad.* She had found a great resource article for her paper, but it was long and the way it was written was taking concentration to follow.

Her phone rang, making her jump. Irritated, she went to silence it but saw it was Kevin calling.

"Hello?"

"What the heck, Elise! Why did you make the Celebration a costume party? That's insane!"

She was incensed. "Well it was your idea!"

"What? No, it wasn't!"

"Don't you remember? While we were all out in the yard looking for Fred, you said we should all wear costumes!"

"I was kidding! It's totally inappropriate!"

"What?! Oh my god, I thought you were being . . . whimsical! I figured if you and Tanna thought it was a good idea, then fine. I didn't care and didn't think too much of it." She could feel the panic threatening.

Neither spoke.

"Well, it's too late," Elise said. "The announcement is in the paper, and it tells everyone to come in costume."

"Yeah, that's how I know about it," said Kevin.

"Well . . . shit," she trailed off. "It won't seem disrespectful, will it? I wouldn't want to offend anyone." There was another silence, that Kevin broke with a chuckle. Soon they were both laughing. "Probably no one will even come. It has been a year, after all," she said.

"I can't believe we're having a costume party for our mother's memorial. Well, okay," he said before hanging up. "I'll have to think up a good costume."

Outside her window, Elise could hear geese honking as they migrated south. It sounded like slow-motion mocking laughter. Helplessly mortified, she got back to work.

▼ ▲ ▼

Elise stood staring at the glass storefront lined with close-up images of tattoos on skin. The variety and artistry overwhelmed her.

Tanna showed up beside her. "Hi," she said.

"Hi!" said Elise. "Oh my god, did you hear Kevin and Mirabelle's news?" Seeing Tanna reminded her that Mirabelle had called the night before.

"Yes! You mean about them being pregnant, right?"

"Yes, it's so exciting! I never pictured Kevin with kids," Elise said.

"They sound really happy."

"They do! I like her." Elise remembered the worries Mirabelle voiced in the dark during the Hood to Coast, wondering how to balance career and family.

"It has been cool to get to know her," Tanna said. "So . . . hi! How was class?" She gave Elise a hug.

"Thanks, I needed that."

"Rough day?"

"Oh! No, classes were fine. Great, actually. Just—" Elise turned to the window again. "At least Mom isn't making us get 'MOTHER' tattooed across our shoulder in a flaming heart."

Tanna crossed her arms. "It's just so gross, putting someone's ashes into your skin."

"Actually, I did some research. Tattoo ink is oftentimes made from soot, from animal bone char anyway, as well as gelatin or animal fat as the carrier. It's not so different from human ash," Elise said. She was reasoning with herself, an attempt to stay calm.

"Oh, okay. Interesting," said Tanna.

"And we already carry Cleah's DNA."

"Guess that's true. So, is it just the needles for you, then?"

"Yeah. Only the million pokes of needles that are bothering me." Elise sighed.

"At least it can be small. Mine's going to be small for sure."

"Oh yeah, mine too. Definitely. And I hate to admit it, but a triangle is pretty cool. Three sides, three of us. A triangle is the most stable shape found in nature."

"Yeah, it's not bad. I don't mind having matching tattoos, either. It was the ash in the ink I didn't like. But I guess I never thought about what's in the ink already."

Tanna checked her watch. Elise knew it was time but couldn't seem to walk to the door. She did allow herself to be steered into the store, however. They were greeted by a tiny woman with a massive pile of curly blue hair tied up in a see-through gauzy headscarf. Tanna told the woman their names and re-explained their situation, as she apparently had done when making the appointment. They both handed her their little vials of ash.

"You go first," Elise whispered as the artist mixed their mother's ash into the black ink.

"Ok, ready," she said when she finished, and Tanna stepped forward. The artist asked some questions and finally settled Tanna onto a medical gurney, sitting up and with her left leg bent so her foot could be flat on the table; she had chosen to put the triangle on the top of her big toe. The tattoo gun hummed hypnotically as Elise watched the progress, a line, tight corner. Even just watching, she could feel her face grimace but couldn't get it to stop. Soon the lines were joined, and the little triangle was complete. It was Elise's turn.

"Did it hurt?" Elise asked.

"Yeah, a little. But it's over quick. You can do it," she said, inspecting her toe. The skin looked red and irritated. "I like it! Don't tell Mom."

"Why the toe?"

"Stupid," Tanna smiled. "I wanted it as far away from me as possible."

"Toes can hurt more," said the artist. "It's one of those places that's boney, less padding."

"I want it really small, right here," Elise told the woman, pointing to her butt. To Tanna, she said, "It's my squishiest part. Least likely to hurt."

"Plus, then it's literally, as well as symbolically, behind you," Tanna said with a giggle.

The artist directed her to lay on her stomach. "Oh gosh!" Elise could feel the dread in her chest growing. "Wait, should I be on my elbows or fully lying down?"

"Whichever is most comfortable for you," the artist said, warm and reassuring. "Find the position you can hold; I'll work around you."

Elise laid on her stomach and hugged the table. "I don't know if I can do this."

"You can," soothed Tanna. "Hey! You went back to school; you're a fierce academia warrior woman!"

"Yeah, okay, fierce, yeah, yeah. Keep talking to me!" Elise said as the tattoo gun fired up and started humming.

"Right!" Tanna moved closer to Elise, squatting so they could see each other's faces. "So, a master's in education, huh? You must've been working on that for a while. Did you have to take the GRE?"

"Yeah." She forced herself to keep breathing.

"Yeah, and the whole application process. Did you have to write an essay?"

"Yeah. Oh. holy crap!" Elise grabbed Tanna's hand.

"Wow, Elise, it's a lot of work to get into a master's program. That in itself is an accomplishment. You should be really proud of yourself!"

"Too soon to be proud of myself. It's so much time; it's really hard to not be very available for my kids. And what if I fail?" She inhaled sharply. "Ow! This really hurts!"

"Elise, I know you. You won't fail." Tanna squeezed her hand.

"Thanks." They smiled at each other. "Thanks for being here right now, too." The tattoo artist kept poking Elise's butt cheek with her needle gun, the humming constant. She could feel the threat of tears. "I can't believe I'm doing this! Keep talking!"

"Okay, so let's figure out the food for the Celebration."

▼ ▲ ▼

Elise and Jeff put Caleb to bed after they got back from the homecoming game, the jelly-roll quilt spread over him. The girls were at the homecoming dance and would need to be picked up later. They had dressed up each day for spirit week, trying to help the freshmen win the class spirit competition. Even Daphne had participated in Color Wars Day and Pajama Day.

The freshman didn't win; the seniors did, like they did every year. But their team had won the football game, so the week had ended well for all.

As Elise followed Jeff down the stairs, she scratched her ass. She knew she wasn't supposed to, but the tattoo was itchy and irritated. She gave it a slap and tried to resist more scratching.

"Hey, I signed us all up to run in a fun run like we talked about. It's the Turkey Trot on Thanksgiving," Elise said.

"Okay." He stopped at the bottom of the stairs and turned to face her. "Movie?" he invited, pulling her into his arms.

She shrugged. "Okay. The dance ends at 11:30. Should be about right." A kiss.

"Want something to drink?" he said.

"Open a bottle of wine?" Another kiss.

"Sounds good. Red or white?" He started toward the kitchen.

"How about that chardonnay?" She followed him.

"Sure," he said, finding the bottle and uncorking it. She got out the wine glasses that Tanna had given them for Christmas and led the way back to the living room where the TV was.

"Remember how I was convinced you were cheating on me last fall? And we went to therapy together and I went myself and I realized it was just me being paranoid? I mean, there wasn't any evidence and no reason for me to suspect you. Totally crazy. I still think the urn had a lot do with it, by the way." She knew she was killing the mood, but continued, "Anyway, over the summer I started thinking you were cheating again."

"Really," he cocked his head, looking concerned. "I wasn't. I wouldn't."

"Kevin set me straight. He explained about your little rendezvous and the late-night calls." She looked at him slyly. "I would be jealous but I'm too busy being relieved. And happy. I'm glad you guys get along so well."

Jeff chuckled, shaking his head.

"He said you're a good guy. But then, I already knew that," she said. The mood restored, they sank into the couch, and he poured the wine into their glasses. She noticed the coffee table was covered with photos. "Oh! These are from my mother's box. I wonder who spread them out like this."

They looked them over as they sipped. Elise realized she was in most of them. Perhaps Tanna and Kevin had a different selection of mostly themselves.

"Is it terrible that we're having people come in costume to Mom's reception?"

He shrugged. "I think it'll be fine. It's not a funeral, it's a Celebration. Cleah called it that herself. And it is on Halloween."

She nodded but couldn't get rid of the anxious tug in her gut.

She watched him pick up an old black and white photo of little-girl Cleah holding the hands of her parents in front of a house that Elise didn't recognize. He set it back down. "How about you choose one or two. We could make a large reprint and have it at the Celebration of Life," he suggested.

She leaned forward, scanning the rows of photographs, and picked up one of herself and Kevin and Tanna, so little, dressed as the Three Musketeers for Halloween. Cleah, not in costume, stood behind them, reaching down to keep Kevin upright. She looked young and vital. Beautiful. They were all smiling, even Cleah.

"This one," she said.

32

"The witch is gone," said Jeff. Elise gave him a side-eye look. "No, I mean the Halloween decoration! The stuffed witch that was sitting in the chair! Not your mother!"

She laughed as they arrived at the house. The Adirondack chair was indeed empty.

There was also a 'for sale' sign set prominently in the yard. "It wasn't for sale then, though."

"When were you here?" she asked as the kids piled out of the van.

"Kevin and I hung out here one night, sometime in July, I think."

"Oh yeah. Your secret scandalous rendezvous." She smiled. With her arm wrapped securely around the urn, she shut her door and walked to the back compartment. "Okay kids, help carry, please."

Toting several bags—Cleah's reusable bags she'd gotten at Easter—and a folded-up card table, they were an eclectic procession: Caleb as Batman, Daphne a ninja in black, Beth a minion, Jeff a pirate with an eyepatch, and Elise as D'Artagnan—the fourth Musketeer, complete with thin mustache and sword.

Elise opened the door using the emergency spare key she still had from the neighbor, Mrs. Cushing. Inside, there was a modest collection of nice furniture: Mom's matching couches still in decent shape, a simple floor lamp, a few tasteful pictures on the wall, some that Elise recognized and some she did not. All of the book and curio shelves were gone, even most of the end tables. Although thankful not to have to deal with all the stuff accumulated over the years, the house didn't seem like the home she grew up in. She didn't remember the room ever looking so spacious and classy.

She checked her phone; it was 5:40 p.m. and the Celebration of Life was to start at 6:00. The kids set stuff down and wandered into the house, presumably to explore. She and Jeff went to the kitchen. While she filled a vase with water, he looked through the drawers.

"You were smart to bring paper plates, cups, and napkins," he said, peering at the mostly empty drawers and cabinets. He took the containers of food from the bags and set them on the table. With no mandates from Cleah for the specifics of her Celebration of Life, Elise and Tanna had decided to serve finger foods and make it as simple as possible: sandwich quarters, grapes, and bite-sized brownies.

Caleb sauntered in. "I'm bored."

"Where are your sisters?" asked Elise as she put lilies in the vase.

"They're lying on a big bed in one of the bedrooms. Daphne's got her book and Beth's on her phone."

"Did you bring your notebook?" Jeff said, starting a pot of coffee in the coffee maker they'd brought.

"Yeah." He sighed. "I wish I could've trick-or-treated with Justin tonight."

"Yeah, I know," said Jeff. "And like I told you, we might get back in time and we might not. But celebrating Grandma Cleah's life is pretty special."

"But she died a whole year ago. We could've celebrated anytime."

Holding out the urn, Elise said, "Could you help me with the display, babe?" He took it and followed her to the living room. They set up the card table, covered it with a blue tablecloth, and placed the ceramic urn in the middle.

"Go get the vase of lilies," she told Caleb as she set up the framed photos: the one of them as Musketeers at Halloween and what she assumed to be her mother's high school graduation picture. She still had the newspaper obituary she'd stolen from the library a year ago and set that on the table as well.

"Nice costume," Tanna said from the doorway, dressed as a mime, a vase of carnations in her hands. "Where should we put this? It's from Great-Aunt Audrey."

"Oh, nice! How about on the coffee table. Or the dining room table?"

"Dining room table," Tanna decided. "It can dress up the food." Behind her was Leif in a graduation gown, Susan as Wonder Woman, and Cassidy as one of the Incredibles.

"Sure. Hi, everyone! You all look great," said Elise, picking up the framed photo from that Halloween so long ago. "Check this out." She showed it to Tanna.

"Wow, that's a good one. I don't even remember that. Three Musketeers? Look at Mom, she's so young." Tanna took it from Elise, then looked at her. "Look at you! I see where you got the inspiration for your costume."

Jeff came in from the kitchen and embraced Tanna. "You know, you're awfully chatty for a mime." He shook Leif's hand. "Congratulations, graduate."

Leif laughed. "Tanna says I'm dressed as Elise eighteen months from now."

"Right!"

Caleb returned carrying the lilies. His face seemed to light up when he noticed his cousins. "Hey! You're superheroes, too!"

he said after he set the vase beside the urn, then went over to give Wonder Woman and the Incredible a high five.

The front door opened, and Mirabelle appeared. Elise gasped to see her in a lacy white wedding dress with a hugely pregnant belly.

"Her costume is a shotgun wedding," Kevin explained, seeing the reactions.

Mirabelle patted her stomach. "It's all padding. I'm only two months along. Happy Halloween!" The room erupted in laughter, which brought Daphne and Beth to the living room.

"And what are you supposed to be?" Tanna asked Kevin. "Big Bird?"

"I'm a stork," he grinned, spreading his feathered arms.

"I think someone's pretty happy to be expecting," said Leif, nodding in approval as he grasped Kevin's hand. There were hugs and congratulations all around.

The door opened again and a short, bearded monk walked in holding a satchel. He was a little early; it was still ten minutes before 6. "Hello! I'm Mark Leevy," he said, joining in the hand-shaking and addressing the group. "You must be the Lucky family? The house is listed with me and I'm here to help, in any way I can! Here are my business cards," he said, holding up a handful. "I'll just put a stack on the coffee table." He walked over and set the pile down. Elise realized that this realtor was usurping a memorial reception for an open house. She was too impressed at his gall to be affronted. "And if you'd all put these shoe booties on, that would be excellent! Protect the wood floors and carpets, you know." He produced what looked like a tissue box from his satchel and started handing out blue paper booties, then pulled some over his own shoes. Everyone seemed so surprised that they complied, stretching them over their shoes, until he got to Daphne, who kicked off her shoes and declared she would go sock-footed instead, which seemed perfectly acceptable to the realtor. All the kids followed suit, leaving their shoes in a pile by the door.

▼ ▲ ▼

Kevin was a little surprised at the guests that showed up. Firstly, there were more than he'd anticipated; secondly, most were actually wearing costumes.

He recognized the short energetic woman from the Salvation Army, dressed as a farmer; she'd brought a few others with her, perhaps also from the food kitchen. A group of older women came in together all wearing Gryffindor scarves, a few with Harry Potter glasses as well. They introduced themselves as Cleah's book club. As the evening progressed, Mrs. Cushing was there wearing a witch's hat, and several other neighbors Kevin faintly recognized. There were a few who came alone, particularly men, who shook hands somberly and said little. They tended to have made not much effort in their costumes, like a chef's hat or Groucho Marx glasses, or wore just regular clothes. He wondered if they had been suitors but couldn't bring himself to ask.

Cleah's Celebration of Life proceeded with mourners/celebrators shifting in and out, most not staying very long. The monk-realtor seemed to have appointed himself door monitor, making sure that each person who came put on the booties and received a business card. They all had pleasant and sympathetic things to say about Cleah: what a lovely woman, she was so special and kind, isn't it a tragedy when one so young and full of life is taken. These people certainly didn't know her the way he did.

"They seem so normal," Mirabelle said quietly to Kevin, standing sideways to him since her pregnant dress kept her too far from his ear.

"Well, they are all dressed kind of weird," he teased, surveying the room. Mirabelle giggled. The guests mostly kept to their groups, all wearing the blue shoe booties.

"I just mean it's been such a bizarre year of bizarre Cleah Requirements, I guess I expected crazy mourners to match the crazy larger-than-life woman. But from the groups she'd been part of, I would guess her to be pretty normal. Even mundane." She rested her arm on her fake belly. "I'm gonna use the restroom, then get some water. Want anything?"

"I'll have some coffee, thanks." As she left the room, Kevin went over to the couch where Elise was visiting with Mrs. Cushing.

Mrs. Cushing got up before he could join them. "Well, it was lovely to see you both. I want to get back home before the trick-or-treaters start coming. I hope you'll still visit the old neighborhood. Just come by and we'll have some tea!"

After they bade farewell, Kevin and Elise sat down. The pile of realtor cards was still lying on the coffee table. He picked up a card.

"Maybe you should buy this place, now that you have a kid on the way?" Elise said.

He laughed.

On the other hand, he hadn't thought about needing more space for the baby. They hadn't talked about staying or not staying in the condo. He shrugged and put the card in his pocket.

Mirabelle returned and handed him a coffee in a disposable cup. "Oh hi, Elise. Can I get you something? Buddy?" They both smiled.

"No, I'm fine, thanks. I was just thinking that this was going pretty well and that we're almost done!" She seemed in high spirits, not stressed.

"Hey, we've got some trick-or-treaters here," called out Mr. Leevy, the door-monitor-monk-realtor. "Any chance you have candy to hand out?"

"Of course!" said Elise, who hopped up and went toward the kitchen. She soon returned with a big bowl of candy, as well as the superheroes eager to help. Kevin met Mirabelle's eye and they grinned at each other. Someday they would shepherd their own kid through Halloween traditions. He couldn't wait.

▼ ▲ ▼

It was dark outside and though they were getting plenty of trick-or-treaters, the guests were dwindling. The Celebration was nearly over. The book club from Gryffindor was deep in conversation in the corner of the living room.

"Those book club ladies are a spunky group, aren't they," Tanna said to Leif. "I wonder what they're reading."

He took her hand. "Let's go ask them."

She laughed, marveling at how comfortable it always was with him, so grateful she had let herself be vulnerable. "Okay, let's!"

But before they got there, Dawn and Mr. Kantola showed up. She was dressed as Rosie the Riveter, which suited her quite well. He was not in costume, unless he was a secret agent, and even though he was wearing a classic spy trench coat, Tanna didn't think he was.

She couldn't work out why she was so startled to see the lawyer here. It felt like the teacher had just walked into the room, making the students feel like they were doing something wrong even though they weren't—a sense of being observed, of potential discipline. Tanna suspected she would have felt the same way, initially, if Cleah had walked into the room, before remembering to be shocked that her dead mother had just arrived.

But, of course, her mother was already here. She glanced toward the urn.

"I want to introduce you to these guys," she said to Leif, leading him over to greet them.

Dawn saw her coming and pulled her into a squealing hug.

"This is my boyfriend, Leif," Tanna said when the hug was done. "Mr. Kantola is my mother's lawyer and executor of the Will, and Dawn ran the Hood to Coast with us." She gestured to them as she spoke.

"Hi!" Dawn exclaimed. "Tanna told me how you helped her train. So neat!"

"Pleasure to meet you," said Leif to them both, shaking hands.

"Hello, hello," Mr. Kantola mumbled affably, pulling on his mustache. "Tanna, my dear, I need a word with you and your siblings, if I may."

"Sure." Tanna looked around the living room. Kevin was sitting on the couch with Mirabelle. "There's Kevin. I'll go find Elise."

"In an out-of-the-way place," the lawyer said, patting her on the arm. "Private."

"Okay, well, let's try the kitchen. Elise might be in there already."

"Yes, yes," he said as he ambled toward the card table holding Cleah's urn. "Oh now, this is nice."

Tanna walked over to Kevin. "Mr. Kantola is here. He wants to talk with us in the kitchen."

"Oh! This must be the part where he gives us the inheritance!" he said, getting up. "Hopefully not another Requirement?"

"Can you show him the way? I'll go find Elise," Tanna said, now worried, as she hurried off.

Thankfully the kitchen was empty. Tanna found Elise coming out of the bathroom. Once they were gathered, Mr. Kantola tapped his fingers together and said, "Well now! My, my, my, very nice to see you again. The year went by in a flash, didn't it. But now then, to get to it, please show me your tattoos."

Elise scoffed and Tanna knew why. She felt a little sorry for her as she pulled off the blue shoe booty and then her black clog and finally her sock from her right foot. Tanna drew her knee to her chest and balanced, to show the lawyer the triangle on her toe. Kevin pulled up his left pant leg and exposed a larger triangle on his calf, pointing outward. Mr. Kantola had to bend down to inspect it. Finally, they all turned to Elise, standing there with arms crossed.

"All right," she huffed, hitching up her doublet and tugging down her black leggings to reveal her small tattoo, healing nicely on her backside. Mr. Kantola nodded, and she reassembled her ensemble.

"You have met all of Mrs. Lucky's Will and Trust Requirements. Well done," he said. "Dawn will email instructions for Monday. Bring bank account information for the transfer."

"Uh, Monday is fine," said Elise, "as long as it can be after 4:00 p.m. I have class."

The lawyer smiled and nodded, "Yes, yes, fine," and waved as he turned to go.

"Congratulations!" Dawn the Riveter said, giving them each a quick squeeze before following him out. "I'll send the email right away!"

The three stood alone in the kitchen. "So, I guess we're not quite done," Tanna said. She smiled. "We have matching tattoos! It's funny: seems like something kids would've done in secret, hidden from their parents, except it was Mom that made us do it."

"I like how you have that, Kevin. Not pointing up or down," said Elise, pulling up his pant leg to look again.

"Yeah, thanks. It seemed like a moving-forward look to me." He shrugged.

Suddenly the five kids showed up.

"There you are!" Batman said in Caleb's voice.

"We want to go trick-or-treating," said Ninja Daphne. "Beth and I can be in charge. We'll just go down the street and come back the other side. Is that okay?"

"Please, Mommy?" cried Susan, the little Wonder Woman. "We've been keeping the house safe from evil all night!"

Cassidy adjusted the 'I' pinned to her red stretchy shirt. They all turned pleading eyes to Tanna and Elise, who looked at each other. Amused, Tanna gave her a nod.

"Yes, that'd be okay. But stick together! No stragglers," said Elise. "And just go down a block or two. We'll be done here pretty soon."

"Yes!" the kids cheered.

"Oh, can we use those bags?" Beth the Minion asked, pointing to the pile of reusable shopping bags from Cleah.

"Sure." Elise handed them to her, and the kids rushed out toward the inviting street.

33

Dawn's email instructed them to all gather at the mausoleum at 4:30 p.m. with the ashes. She'd included driving directions that were based on landmarks instead of street names; Elise struggled to find the obscure shop sign or postal box indicated. Driving separately, Jeff had planned to meet her there with the urn so it wouldn't sit in the car all day while she was in class. She wondered how he was doing with the directions.

The mausoleum was a large concrete building beside the river, surrounded by people's homes, which felt odd. She came to the entrance, a smaller structure in front, with Southwestern-style stucco walls and tiled roof, odder still. She wondered how her mother had chosen this place. When her father died, Cleah had him cremated and scattered his ashes. There was no marker for him anywhere.

She checked her phone. Damn—it was low on battery. Five minutes early, she squeezed into the tight parking lot and looked around to see if anyone else was here yet. Deciding to find a place to recharge the phone, Elise went inside.

"Good afternoon," greeted a very plain woman at the reception desk, brown hair pulled tightly into a ponytail. To Elise, she was the antithesis of Dawn. Even the receptionist's clothes seemed without color.

"Hello. I'm Elise Rodgers, with an appointment to inter my mother's ashes, Cleah Lucky. I'm just waiting for the rest of my group."

The woman nodded. "Certainly. I'll take you to place your mother's ashes in the columbarium when the others have arrived."

Elise thanked her and sat down to wait near a wall outlet. Her phone didn't have much time to charge before Tanna came in, dressed comfortably in jeans, as Elise was. They'd scarcely embraced when Mirabelle and Kevin arrived in their smart business clothes, probably directly from work. Finally, Jeff walked in, carrying the urn, only a few minutes late.

"Okay, we're all here," Elise told the receptionist, who smiled and wordlessly moved to the back of the room where she punched a code into a keypad on the wall to open the door.

They followed her.

Inside, the mausoleum was a maze of corridors and rooms, every wall was covered with marble panels, several layers floor to ceiling, with someone's name and dates on each one: birth date, death date. There were family vaults with several names. Though some had a military seal by their name, marking them as veterans, there was mostly no other personal information. The air was cold, perhaps a crypt requirement, and she shivered, struck by the thought of all the bodies inside the walls.

A sign beside a staircase said they were on the fifth floor, so there must have been four floors belowground. The receptionist led them up two sets of stairs to an area of glass-fronted niches, each one a small crypt holding one or more urns, all so different. These nooks allowed for more personalization, some with photos or books inside. One looked like a scene in a dollhouse, with a tiny rocking chair and table and even miniature framed photos attached to the inside wall.

They wound their way in, room leading to room, to where the receptionist unlocked a glass panel just at eye level. Inside was a small bronze plaque that read:

Cleah Margaret Lucky 1948–2014

Jeff set the ceramic urn inside, repositioned the plaque in front of it, then pulled a picture from his pocket—Cleah's high school graduation photo. Elise smiled, touched he would think of it. He settled it a little behind the white urn with its swirly blue lines and stepped back. The receptionist re-secured the glass, and with a little nod, she left.

"Should we say something?" Kevin asked once they were alone. No one spoke for a minute. Elise scanned her mother's silent new neighbors, names and dates, seemingly endless shelving of people's remains. She felt a calmness.

She looked at the urn and said, "Goodbye, Mom. Be at rest."

▼ ▲ ▼

From the mausoleum, they caravanned to the lawyer's office. Tanna checked her watch; it was just before 5:00 and the traffic was terrible; they'd be a little late for their appointment. She was glad Denise had been able to take the girls.

Somehow, they all fit in the elevator. Dawn squealed when the five of them walked in together, her orange beehive shaking. She hugged each one and escorted them to that same back room with the big oak table. Tanna noticed that everyone gravitated toward the same chair they'd sat in a year ago when they were here for the reading of the Will. As soon as they were seated, Mr. Kantola stepped in, documents in arms, and took his seat at the head. Dawn followed him in, messed with her phone, and the now-familiar song started to play.

Who's sorry now? Who's sorry now? Whose heart is achin' for breakin' each vow.

Who's sad and blue, Who's cryin' too, Just like I cried over you.

Right to the end, Just like a friend, I tried to warn you somehow.

You had your way, Now you must pay, I'm glad that you're sorry now.

On its second time through the lyrics, Tanna remembered when she'd heard it for the first time at Christmas. Such a very long time ago. Yet she didn't like to think too hard on it, refused to struggle with whatever message Cleah had intended through that song.

When the music ended, the lawyer handed them each a manila envelope, marked with their individual names, and motioned for them to open them. Inside hers, Tanna found documents of the transferred assets from the Trust: a deed to some acreage property in Central Oregon, several stock certificates, a receipt for a substantial donation to the Boys and Girls Club made in Tanna's name, and a cash payment amount for more than she could earn in ten years. Also, there was a small, sealed envelope with her name on it, written in Cleah's handwriting.

Tanna sat in shock, while Elise gasped, and Kevin had a short coughing fit. It was all more than Tanna had dared to hope. Mr. Kantola folded his hands and said, "Read the note from your mother at your leisure later. As to the matter of the Camas house, when it is sold you will each be issued an additional final check. And that is that! So then, are there any questions?"

"Wow, uh. Did we each receive property? Is it all in Oregon?" said Kevin.

"Yes. There was one piece of land that has been divided and individually transferred to your name. The charitable bequest recipients are all different, but the amounts are the same, as is the cash amounts, which will be wire-transferred into an account you direct."

"What about her other personal items?" Elise asked. "Her pearls for instance?"

"Mrs. Lucky directed specific items be set aside for each of you, which you received in the boxes Dawn delivered on Labor Day. The rest was liquidated, per her instructions, and the cash distribution is included in your wire transfer."

When there were no more questions, there was paperwork to fill out: a banking form for the wire transfer, which Mr. Kantola stood and collected.

"It was a pleasure to serve you," he said, gave a little bow, and then held the door open for them to leave. Dismissed, they returned the documents to the envelopes and went back down the hall in a line. Tanna felt grateful and humbled. She'd never seen her mother as generous in the least. What a complicated woman.

On the way out of the office, Dawn claimed her hugs and handed each of the three siblings a book. "I made these for you," she whispered. On the front was a picture of Cleah's urn.

▼ ▲ ▼

No one spoke as the elevator rumbled down to the main floor. Kevin tried to sort his emotions—somber, pensive, excited, relieved. Shocked. When the metallic doors slid open, he said, "Anyone want to get a drink?"

They all quickly agreed and, once on the street, went into the first place they encountered: Rose City Karaoke Bar. After they sat down and ordered beers, Elise asked the waiter for some fries, onion rings, and mozzarella sticks.

"I've been in class all day; I'm starving," she shrugged. "Plus, we are celebrating!"

"What is this book?" Mirabelle asked, taking Kevin's from him and setting it between them where they could both see. There were no words on the cover, only the large color photo of the urn. She opened it. On the first page was the group selfie Elise had taken on Kevin's birthday, outside of the Burgerville. Kevin laughed at their looks of annoyance, remembering that first awkward lunch. Tanna and Elise opened their books as well, which were identical, and followed along.

There was a picture of Tanna's kids beside the Christmas tree. Then came the group Christmas photo in festive holiday sweaters, Elise and Jeff in hysterics.

"What the hell were you laughing about, anyway?" Kevin said.

"Oh, I don't know. Just at the ridiculousness of all the Requirements. Having the urn in the house. It had been a long few months," Jeff smiled.

"Hey! She's included the recipes for eggnog, pumpkin carrot soup, and British Christmas pudding!" Elise said. "Nice!"

"I'm never making that pudding again," Tanna stated.

The waiter brought their beers and Kevin took a swig. He then turned the page to find the three of them at Tanna's birthday dinner, smiling behind the big ice cream Sunday they had shared. "That was fun," he said.

There was the family Easter photo in their condo, nicely coordinated in blues and greens. Great-Aunt Audrey was in that one, as was Cleah's urn, sitting on Cassidy's lap. Then recipes for Old Fashioneds and sausage egg casserole, and instructions for egg-dyeing using onion skins and cabbage. Also a few candid shots of the kids dyeing eggs that Mirabelle must have taken. Elise cooed over those.

Tanna giggled and Kevin groaned to see his newspaper article on the next page, almost too small to read, immortalizing the horrible ordeal of losing and finding the urn at that restaurant. He quickly turned the page. Elise's birthday photo. He grew quiet, remembering how Mirabelle had moved out and how Sally's running away had brought her back.

The next several pages were full of Hood to Coast Relay pictures, with mostly unflattering candid shots that Dawn must've taken without their realizing, sandwiched between the start and finish group photos in the tie-dye *Cleah's Kids* t-shirts.

"Oh my god, these are excellent," said Tanna, laughing. "Look at the difference between all of us at the start compared to at the finish. It's like we've been tortured!"

"That storm was insane!" Jeff said.

"The race was insane," said Mirabelle.

"Oh hey! By the way, we're doing a fun run on Thanksgiving, it's just a 5k, if anyone wants to join us. In fact, come for dinner too!" Elise said.

"That sounds good," said Tanna. "Not too far."

"Sure," Kevin said, sharing a look with Mirabelle for agreement.

On the next page, the white-clad family Labor Day photo was dotted with Daphne in the tie-dye *Cleah* shirt. Kevin guessed that Elise was thinking about the Red Cross needles or tattoo needles, or both, judging by the strained smile on her face in the picture. Dawn had included Cleah's recipes for zucchini relish and peach cobbler. There was a picture of the spread of food and even one of Kevin donating blood and some hilarious action shots of the wet and messy yard games.

"Elise, did you take all of these pictures?" Tanna asked.

"All but of the food. That must've been Dawn," she said. "For verification."

Tanna nodded. "I'm glad you did. These are great. Aw, look at the kids!"

On the last page of the book was Cleah's obituary with her glamour shot. What wasn't included were their letters to their mother. Kevin appreciated that omission.

"Quite a year," Jeff observed.

"Mom was so out of line," Elise said quietly, shaking her head.

Tanna inhaled. "It's not okay, what she did," she said. "I almost hate to admit it—it totally doesn't justify her actions in any way—but I do like having relationships with you all again."

"Do you think that was what she intended? Or do you think she just wanted to make us suffer and go insane?" said Elise.

They looked at each other and shrugged.

Mirabelle asked, "So. Was it worth it?"

They looked around the table, eyebrows raised and smiles spreading on their faces.

"Well, the money certainly is nice." Tanna finally said. They laughed.

Kevin raised his glass "To Cleah," he said.

"To the year of the urn," said Jeff.

"To the end of the urn's rule!" declared Elise, and they all clinked and drank.

As the food was delivered, Tanna excused herself. Kevin had a mouth full of onion rings when she came back, a sly look on her face and three microphones in her hand. Elise started laughing as *Who's Sorry Now* began to play.

Nodding through her smile, Tanna pulled Elise and Kevin up to the little stage area. They sang through the song together, laughing, hamming it up, hardly needing the lyrics on the screen at all.

. . . You had your way, Now you must pay, I'm glad that you're sorry now.

When the song was over, Kevin put down the mic, followed the women back to their table, and picked up his nearly empty glass. Lifting it, he said, "And may we never hear that damn song again!"

"Hear, hear!" they all agreed.

Sitting back down, Kevin noticed Tanna had retrieved the small white envelope from the manila packet the lawyer had given her and was reading the letter from inside. He found his envelope on which Cleah had written *to Kevin.* Elise likewise dug out hers.

Once he read it, Kevin looked at his sisters and held up his note. They did as well, and he saw that they all said the same thing:

I'm sorry.

Acknowledgments

Thank you to Steve Aita PLLC, Jennifer Marquez MSN RN CDN, Brad Coulon, and Dr. Chris Samuels MD, for expertise in their fields.

And thank you to my dear early readers: Erin Spaeth, Susan Coulon, Sarah Samuels, Jim Matthias, Kathe Yokers, Emily Biggins, Peter Knowles, Kirsty Lindaas, Sean Ingersoll.

Finally, huge gratitude to my publisher and editor, Summer Stewart, and the folks at Unsolicited Press.

About MARI MATTHIAS

Born and raised in the Pacific Northwest, Mari Matthias lives with her spouse in Southern Washington, in the nook of the Columbia and White Salmon rivers, where deer and turkey amble through the yard. She's run in the Hood to Coast relay six times. ***Cleah's Bequest*** is her second novel. Her first, ***The Runestone's Promise***, was released by Unsolicited Press in 2022. Find more at marimatthias.com.

About UNSOLICITED PRESS

Unsolicited Press is based out of Portland, Oregon and focuses on the works of the unsung and underrepresented. As a womxn-owned, all-volunteer small publisher that doesn't worry about profits as much as championing exceptional literature, we have the privilege of partnering with authors skirting the fringes of the lit world. We've worked with emerging and award-winning authors such as Amy Shimshon-Santo, Brook Bhagat, Elisa Carlsen, Tara Stillions Whitehead, and Anne Leigh Parrish.

Learn more at unsolicitedpress.com. Find us on Instagram, X, Facebook, Pinterest, Bsky, Threads, YouTube, and LinkedIn. Unsolicited Press also writes a snarky newsletter on Substack.